"I like being alone."

He raised his head slowly and uncurled his fingers where they had caught hers. "Liar," he whispered gently.

Her hand lay in his palm. She could withdraw it anytime she liked. Instead, she left it right where it was.

Because Alexander Lavoie was right.

Very slowly, he lowered his head, his mouth inches from hers. She could feel his breath whisper against her cheek. She was frozen in place, afraid to move. Afraid not to. He would kiss her. Right here. Right now.

And God help her, but she wanted him to. She wanted him to do a whole lot more.

ACCLAIM FOR KELLY BOWEN

A DUKE TO REMEMBER

"This isn't a Regency comedy of manners. It's way better. This bright, surprising romance sets aside the intricate social rules and focuses on forging trust and love even when it seems like the whole world is against you."

—Best Romance of August selection,
The Amazon Book Review

"Top Pick! 4½ stars! The powerful emotions, action, adventure, and passion are what readers desire, and Bowen delivers, and brings readers her most memorable characters yet. Many will cherish this beautifully rendered tale."

—*RT Book Reviews*

DUKE OF MY HEART

"Wonderful! A charming, clever, and engaging storyteller not to be missed."

—Sarah MacLean, *New York Times* bestselling author

"Top Pick! 4½ stars! Bowen begins her Season for Scandal series with a nonstop murder mystery that sizzles with tension. This suspenseful tale unfolds quickly, and readers will be captivated by the well-drawn characters who move Bowen's inventive plot forward. Readers will savor this unconventional romance."

—*RT Book Reviews*

Between
the
Devil
and the
Duke

Between the *Devil* and the *Duke*

KELLY BOWEN

FOREVER

New York Boston

Copyright © 2017 by Kelly Bowen
Excerpt from *I've Got My Duke to Keep Me Warm* © 2014 by Kelly Bowen
Cover design by Elizabeth Turner
Cover illustration by Judy York
Cover hand-lettering by Jen Mussari

Cover copyright © 2017 by Hachette Book Group, Inc.

Forever
Hachette Book Group
1290 Avenue of the Americas, New York, NY 10104
forever-romance.com
twitter.com/foreverromance

First Edition: January 2017

Forever is an imprint of Grand Central Publishing. The Forever name and logo are trademarks of Hachette Book Group, Inc.

The publisher is not responsible for websites (or their content) that are not owned by the publisher.

The Hachette Speakers Bureau provides a wide range of authors for speaking events. To find out more, go to www.hachettespeakersbureau.com or call (866) 376-6591.

ISBN 978-1-4555-6341-8 (mass market), 978-1-4555-6340-1 (ebook)

Printed in the United States of America

OPM

10 9 8 7 6 5 4 3 2 1

*In loving memory of my grandparents
who always had a deck of cards
at the ready.*

Acknowledgments

Once again, I'm so very grateful to the people in my corner who have helped make my dreams a reality. Thank you to my agent, Stefanie Lieberman, for her guidance and advice, and to my editor, Alex Logan, for her unerring attention to detail. And to the entire team at Forever who work so hard behind the scenes to make each story come alive.

And of course, a huge thank-you to my family for their continued support.

Chapter 1

London, April 1820

Lady Angelique Archer's opponents were all drunk.

She had made sure of it, not because she didn't think she was clever enough to beat them, but because she had learned never to leave anything to chance. And a drunken card player was a foolish card player. They forgot to guard their expressions. They forgot that a small fortune rested on the table in front of them. And they forgot that the last ace had been played three hands ago.

Angelique felt a trickle of icy sweat slide down her spine as she touched the mask that was covering her face. It was starting to itch terribly, but she ignored the discomfort. She would leave after this hand, before she brought undue attention upon herself. Angelique could not afford to have the other patrons of this club start to wonder who she was and how she had managed to win as much as she had. She could not be remembered. Because a fortnight from now, she would need to do this all over again.

There were not many places in London where a lady might indulge in the very unladylike sport of gambling, at least the sort that went beyond pin money and a few hands of whist in a sedate drawing room. But the club known as Lavoie's was one of them. It was exclusive, catering to individuals who possessed titles, wealth, power, or a combination of all three. Men were dressed in immaculately tailored evening wear, the dark colors the perfect foil for the brilliant, rich hues of the silk and satin gowns worn by the women who swirled throughout the club. A king's ransom in jeweled accessories sparkled under the soft, subtle light. And to add to the illusion of mystery and extravagance, each woman wore an elaborate mask, meant to conceal her identity. A chance for a daring lady to enjoy herself in a manner forbidden by propriety and daylight.

Though Angelique didn't consider herself daring. She was simply desperate.

"You'll take another card, milady?" The gentleman who was dealing this hand swayed slightly beside her, and his eyes were fixed firmly on her breasts.

Angelique kept her expression neutral, smothering the sharp retort that sprang to the tip of her tongue. If she had a penny for the number of men who had gawked at her overly generous cleavage since she had turned sixteen, she would be richer than the pope. And she certainly wouldn't need to be sitting at this table enduring the unwelcome attentions of another.

A baron, she recalled, as she eyed the heavily whiskered gentleman who was still staring at her décolletage. But more importantly, a baron in possession of a newly minted fortune thanks to a lucky investment, and Angelique was only too happy to relieve him of a portion of it. She pretended to consider his question. Of course she wasn't taking another card. She had the last two face cards in her hand. If the baron had bothered to take a look at his hand and that of the two players at the table who had already exceeded twenty-one, he would realize that the odds of her possessing those cards were quite high. But the combination of French brandy and English breasts was making him careless.

"I don't know." Angelique pursed her lips and let a hand drift down to the front of her altered bodice, fingering the lace that trimmed the gold silk. Predictably, the baron's eyes widened.

God, she hated this part.

"You have only two cards," the baron reminded her, feeling for his glass of brandy without looking up at her face. "Perhaps I could...entice you to take a risk."

"Hmmm." Angelique put her hands on the table. She needed to make sure that, if this man lost, he did so happily. Because he would lose quite a bit. "An intriguing offer." She allowed her lips to curl into what she hoped was a smile.

"Isn't it?" the baron murmured, taking a healthy swallow of his brandy.

"I'll keep my cards." Angelique feigned helplessness. "For I fear I am not so adventurous as you."

The baron grinned sloppily at her. "I do have a reputation of being rather adventurous. Perhaps I might show you."

Angelique eyed the remaining cards in the deck and the two he had facedown on the table. There were two deuces, a seven, an eight, and a nine left that had yet to be played. It was still possible for him to win with the right combination, depending on what he already had in his hand. She shifted, her stays feeling like they were squeezing the breath from her. "Why don't you then? Show me yours?"

The baron laughed, and the other two players who still sat at the table snickered.

Angelique forced out a giggle even as her stomach twisted.

"Very well, milady." He turned his cards over.

An eight and a seven.

Angelique nearly collapsed in relief. It was impossible for him to beat her. "Fifteen," she murmured.

"Enough to take you?" The baron was leering slightly now, and Angelique suppressed a shudder. The man was old enough to be her father.

"What do you think?" she quipped, trying for the flirtatious tone she had never quite gotten right in her youth.

But the baron seemed to like it just fine. "Not enough." He put his glass aside and turned over another card.

"Seventeen," Angelique counted. The two other men they'd been playing leaned forward with interest.

"I never do things in half measures," the baron declared. He turned over another card.

"Nineteen." One of the other men reached for the bottle of brandy Angelique had brought with her to the table. He refilled his glass almost to the rim. "What are you going to do?" he asked the baron, his eyes sliding to Angelique's cards still lying facedown on the table.

There was a single card remaining in the deck. The nine. If the baron turned it over, he would be well over twenty-one and forfeit his hand. If he stayed, her twenty would beat his nineteen. Either way, Angelique would keep the pantry filled for another week, the worst of the creditors at bay, and most importantly, the remainder of her younger siblings' tuition paid.

The baron looked up at Angelique. "Nineteen, milady. A fine score. I'll stay." He picked up his brandy and swirled the her current opponent, the Baron Daventon, had yet to raise his lecherous gaze north of her neck.

Alex wasn't surprised when the woman laid down a pair of queens and neatly relieved Daventon of all his remaining money. But what did surprise him was the ridiculous sense of satisfaction he felt when she did it. *The baron deserves it*, Alexander thought before catching himself up short and wondering why he should care. Or at least, why he should care beyond the parts that affected Alex's own interests. Like how much more Daventon might yet lose of his newly acquired fortune, and how much of those losses might be funneled directly into Alex's coffers. Or to what extremes the baron might go to recoup his money, if any. If Daventon was a man easily provoked into challenges or threats or any other form of idiocy, Alex preferred to know ahead of time.

Because cleaning up blood in his club was tedious. And expensive. And inconvenient if he was required to entertain the law for an extended period of time.

Alex pulled out his timepiece, noting it was still a little before two in the morning. The woman in the gold dress would be leaving soon, he knew. If her previous visits were any indication, she never stayed more than three hours. Long enough to get what she had come for. Not long enough to be remembered by anyone.

Except him.

As if on cue, the blue-eyed stranger stood, the gold silk that clung to her body shimmering in the light as she subtly deposited her winnings into a matching reticule. The baron did not look pleased, and for the first time since Alex had begun watching, Daventon finally dragged his eyes up to her face. His hand shot out and wrapped around the woman's wrist as she tried to turn.

Alex straightened abruptly, watching as the woman

flinched, though she stood her ground and her expression didn't change. She wasn't wearing gloves, and he could see the discoloration of her skin where Daventon's fingers dug into her flesh. A wash of what felt like possessive anger caught Alex off guard, even as he started forward. Across the room, he caught the eye of one of the leviathans he employed to keep the peace on his gaming floor. The goliath had also noticed the altercation and was already heading toward the subtle disturbance.

Alex waved him off. This was a situation that warranted his personal attention. And it would give him the opportunity to determine once and for all the identity of the clever card player in the gold dress.

⁓

The baron had been shocked into silence as Angelique had laid her cards on the table, though his companions had jeered and laughed loudly. Angelique kept a watchful eye on the stricken man as she deftly gathered her winnings, resisting the urge to stuff the money into her oversize reticule and run like a common thief. Her heart was pounding in her ears, and another bead of cold sweat slid down her back. No matter how many times she did this, it never got easier.

Angelique thought she was clear until the baron's hand shot out to grasp her wrist as she turned from the table.

"Where do you think you're going, my pretty?" he asked, his fingers biting painfully into her skin.

It required a monumental effort on her part not to give in to the desire to yank her hand away from him in revulsion. Above all, she needed to keep her head. She couldn't afford a scene—couldn't afford to bring any attention to herself. So instead of kicking the baron in the shins the way she longed to, she leaned into the man, her hip pressing up against his chest, ignoring the way her skin crawled. "I thought it might be time to seek out a new diversion," she purred. "The night is still young, after all."

The baron's grip loosened slightly, though not enough for her to pull free. "You stole all my money," he said, the words uneven.

"Hardly," she soothed. "I won but a mere card game. If it makes you feel better, remember that it is a drop in the ocean for a wealthy man like yourself." Her experience had taught her that men like this were better handled when their egos were being stroked.

The baron seemed to consider this. "Maybe," he slurred. He wrenched on her arm, pulling her closer to him. "But maybe you should think of another way to make me feel better tonight." The fingers of his free hand reached up and squeezed her left breast.

Angelique struggled for balance, trying to tamp down the futile fury that was starting to claw its way up into her throat. She was not like the other women here in this club. Women who were experienced in the art of seduction, veterans at wielding their feminine wiles as expertly as they wielded their painted fans. Angelique had never excelled at those life lessons. At least, not when it had mattered, anyway.

"I'll trouble you to remove your hands from my person," she said coldly.

"I'll put my hands wherever I wish," Daventon sneered.

"Then are you planning on fondling all the players at the table, my lord?" she asked. "Or only the ones within easy reach? Because the gentlemen beside you might have something to say about that."

There was a chorus of intoxicated snickers and guffaws from across the table. Clearly, there would be no assistance coming from these cretins who seemed only to find her predicament funny.

"I think you're confusing this club with Almack's," the baron replied. "I'll do as I like."

"And I think you're confusing this club with a brothel." It was a monumental effort not to simply drive her elbow into his nose. But aside from the unwanted spectacle it would create, blood was devilishly hard to get out of gold silk.

"But you have my money in your possession." Daventon's breath was foul. "Surely I should get something for it." He increased the pressure on her breast.

Angelique twisted, stopping abruptly as she saw one of the hulking men who patrolled the gaming floors start toward them. She was relieved when he stopped and turned away. The last thing she needed was to draw the notice of—

"Good evening, gentlemen. And my lady."

She froze, her eyes closing briefly in horror. She recognized Alexander Lavoie's voice instantly. She'd studied the owner of this club covertly and heard him speak a number of times, though whenever he'd drawn near, she'd kept her head down and made every effort never to look directly at him. Made every attempt to remain unnoticed at all costs. And it had seemed to work. He spoke often with the men who gambled, conversed with the women who fluttered their fans and their lashes. But he had never looked twice in her direction. Which was exactly how she wished it.

She needed this place, she needed the men who came to gamble at the vingt-et-un table, and she needed the money they brought with them. She could not afford to catch Lavoie's attention or for anything to happen that might somehow jeopardize her access to what had become her family's only source of income. But now, it seemed the worst had happened.

"I believe, Lord Daventon, that you have your hand on

something that does not belong to you," Lavoie continued behind her, sounding bored.

"This does not concern you," Daventon griped.

"I must disagree," Lavoie said mildly. "This is my club, and thus very much concerns me. Because I am feeling generous this evening, I will extend you all the courtesy of reminding you that this woman is a lady, not a whore. I will take grievous exception to those who may think otherwise."

Across the table, the two other men who had been playing abruptly stood and excused themselves, one of them knocking a chair over in his haste. He righted it, his eyes darting toward Lavoie before he vanished.

Angelique remained motionless, her back still to Lavoie and her cheeks burning in mortification. It was just as well that he couldn't see her face.

Her wrist was still caught in Daventon's meaty hand and the baron looked past her, his lip curling slightly. "This *lady* took a great deal of my money," Daventon said. "And she was just thinking of ways to make it up to me." His fingers squeezed her breast again, and Angelique tried to jerk herself away. Her arm felt like it was being pulled from its socket.

"Was she indeed?" Lavoie mocked, his voice dropping.

Angelique wanted the floor to open up beneath her and swallow her whole. She was embarrassed, she was furious, and she was terrified that she was losing any opportunity to extract herself from this situation without everything blowing up in her face.

"Do you know who I am?" Daventon demanded.

Behind her, she could hear Lavoie chuckle, a sound devoid of humor that sent shivers across her skin.

"I do. You are a small man who happened to make a smaller fortune on a drugged and drunken whim. Though I might caution you on spending too much of it. Because your partner, with whom you made that prosperous investment, might one day sober up enough to remember and realize that he was never paid his share. It's a wonder no one has thought to tell him so already, isn't it? Fortuitous for you, though, because I have been advised he has a terrible temper. And a fondness for pistols."

Angelique felt her mouth fall open even as Daventon's grip on her wrist suddenly loosened. She staggered backward, nearly tripping over her skirts. A strong hand steadied her, catching her at her lower back, warmth bleeding through the layers of her clothing. Another shiver chased its way across her skin, this one entirely different from her reaction earlier. This one was laced with heat and the insane urge to press herself farther into the contact.

Unsettled, Angelique shied away, and Lavoie's hand dropped almost instantly. She should have been relieved. Instead she felt almost disappointed.

"I suggest you find further entertainment elsewhere, Daventon," Lavoie said quietly near her ear. "Some other establishment where I won't need to witness your appalling lack of judgment and be forced to think of ways in which I might correct it."

The baron had paled beneath his whiskers, and he was opening and closing his mouth like a landed carp. After a moment, he heaved himself to his feet, his eyes skittering around them as if ascertaining who might have overheard Lavoie's words.

"Get out," Lavoie repeated. "Now."

The baron staggered away from where Angelique stood without a backward glance, headed for the door, and vanished out into the darkness. Angelique stared down at her hands still clutching her heavy reticule and wished she could do the same. Wished that she could just disappear into the night.

But wishes, she had learned, were utterly useless.

"Are you all right, my lady?" She felt Lavoie move, coming to stand directly in front of her, while she tried to collect the shreds of her dignity and figure out just how she might remove herself from his attention.

"Yes, thank you."

"Are you sure?"

There was no help for it. She would need to address him or risk making more of a spectacle by simply fleeing like a scared rabbit caught in a cabbage patch. She lifted her head and met his eyes. And stared.

She had seen him from a distance, of course, but never this close. In the daylight, his eyes would probably be called hazel. In this low light, they were a dark amber, and the intelligence that shimmered in their depths was unmistakable. He was a head taller than she, his body lithe and lean. He had dark hair that fell carelessly over his forehead and around his ears, framing sharp cheekbones and a strong jaw. His complexion was a shade darker than common, and a long, thin scar ran from his upper lip over his right cheek to the top of his ear.

She'd heard the rumors, of course. That he was a retired assassin. A retired spy. Or maybe not so retired at all. He kind of looked like an assassin ought to, she thought disjointedly. Dark. Dangerous. Unyielding. For a wild, reckless moment, Angelique wondered what it would feel like to touch such an untouchable man. Wondered what would happen if she ran her fingers along the edge of that scar. Wondered if his lips were as soft as his face was hard. Wondered—

She recoiled inwardly, appalled at the direction her thoughts were slipping. What in God's name was wrong with her? Alexander Lavoie was not a man to be objectified or trifled with under any circumstances, never mind the debacle that had made her the object of his scrutiny. He had the power to take apart what remained of her life should he wish it.

He seemed to be waiting for her to answer something. Her mind floundered before it came up with the appropriate response. "Ah yes. Yes, thank you. I'm quite fine."

"And I've been remiss. Allow me to introduce myself. Alexander Lavoie at your service."

"A pleasure." If he was expecting her to return the favor of introduction, he was in for a long wait.

"I believe Baron Daventon will offer you no further difficulty. Though you will alert me if that proves not to be the case." He said it like he was inviting her to comment on the weather.

"You were rather, ah, persuasive." It sounded better than *threatening*. Especially since she was having a hard time meeting his eye.

"Persuasive," he repeated with pleasure, as if trying that word out for the first time and discovering that he liked it. "Indeed. Well, I do make it my business to know exactly who is in my club. And I make it my business to know why they are in my club. I find such details infinitely valuable."

Her heart missed a beat, and another ripple of clammy sweat prickled at her skin. Dear God. She didn't even want to consider the very real likelihood that Lavoie knew exactly who she was. And the possibility that he knew about every shovelful of family dirt she'd tried so valiantly to sweep under the rug. She needed to go. Now.

"Thank you again, Mr. Lavoie." She edged away.

He followed her. "Perhaps you will honor me with your company? It troubles me to know that you were put in an...uncomfortable position while in my establishment."

"Um…" *Think*, she ordered herself. Say something that will facilitate your escape without offending him. Her eyes darted in the direction of the door, but no words presented themselves. Why couldn't she think?

"In the future, I will ensure that you will not suffer such unwanted attentions while you are here," he continued smoothly.

The idea that he believed her helpless suddenly loosened her tongue. "While I appreciate your assistance, Mr. Lavoie, please rest assured that I did not require rescue. I can handle myself." She dropped her eyes, instantly regretting her tone. Picking a fight with Alexander Lavoie was not smart or helpful.

"Of that, I have no doubt." Lavoie sounded as though he found her outburst amusing. "If your winnings are any indication, you can handle yourself quite admirably."

Angelique's head snapped up, her gaze colliding with his. There had been an excuse on the tip of her tongue, an explanation that would defuse any suspicion. Except her breath caught and her clever words fled under the impact of his intense gaze.

"Regardless, I must insist you come with me." His eyes hadn't left hers.

Angelique tried to remember how to breathe under the potency of his stare. "I can't. I have to go home." She hated the words the moment they were out. They made her sound like a scared little schoolgirl. And she'd stopped being scared a long time ago.

"And you will." His unnerving eyes flickered over her shoulder and then down to her heavy reticule. "Unfortunately, I think we have drawn more attention to ourselves than either of us would like. And I will not send a lone woman out into the night with a bag full of money. I will arrange an escort home for you to ensure both you and your winnings arrive safely."

Angelique gaped at him, unable to help herself, even as her mind struggled to produce all the appropriate excuses to facilitate a faster escape. "Thank you, Mr. Lavoie, but I am with someone here tonight. I won't be alone." There was still a chance he didn't know who she was. So he certainly couldn't discover where she lived. He couldn't discover anything about her.

"Lying does not become you, my lady." Lavoie's voice was conversational. "Now, we can discuss this here in front of all and sundry or we can find a more private location to work out the...details of our arrangements."

Angelique's stomach dropped toward her toes. Briefly she considered simply bolting.

"You won't be able to run far in that gown, my lady." It was as if he was reading her mind, which was horrifying. His lips twitched, pulling at his scar. "And it's raining now. It would be a much colder walk home than it was on the way here."

For the second time in as many minutes, Angelique gaped at him. How could he have possibly known she'd walked?

"The hem of your gown, my lady. There is mud on it near the back. You would be better to have worn the dark green gown you wore four weeks ago in inclement weather such as this. While the gold is exceedingly flattering with your coloring, the darker fabric would have been better at hiding the mud stains."

Whatever illusions Angelique had that she'd remained invisible were effectively shattered. And had he just... complimented her at the same time he'd called her a liar?

"You saw me." It was a ridiculous thing to say, but Angelique's mind seemed to have stalled.

An enigmatic smile touched his austere face. "Of course I saw you. You've generously purchased a full bottle of

French brandy from one of my serving girls at the beginning of every evening on behalf of your opponents. Expensive, but I expect that the effects of the alcohol on the average gentleman's acumen are well worth the investment. You alternate the green and gold gown, though you've used a different mask on each occasion you've been here. Nothing ostentatious or particularly memorable, which, I suspect, is your aim. Though I might suggest that the clever tailoring of what exists of your bodice is designed to obliterate whatever masculine wits the brandy didn't."

A bubble of something was rising in her throat, and she wasn't sure if it was hysterical laughter or a hysterical sob.

"Your play is what intrigues me the most, however, my lady. Small wagers early on, larger wagers as the hands progress and the deck wanes. Tonight your winnings appear to be greater than your previous evenings combined, which is saying something, indeed. You win far more than can ever be attributed to luck, yet I have seen no evidence that you have ever cheated." He left that last part hanging, and Angelique thought it sounded more like an accusation than a comment.

She was done. Alexander Lavoie would bar her from his club. And Angelique would be out of options. Or at least options that she could bring herself to consider. Another wave of impotent fury rose fast and hard, nearly choking her.

Curse the circumstances that had brought her here. Curse the fates for creating her a woman instead of a man. And curse the one who stood before her, so quick to label her as something less than clever.

"I don't cheat," she whispered, her voice raw.

"I know. Which makes you all the more fascinating."

"Fascinating?" Angelique repeated it stupidly. Was he complimenting her again?

"Yes. Fascinating."

She was still pinned under his intense gaze like a bug on a collector's board. Never had she felt so exposed. And she despised the thrill that coursed through her that a man such as this one should find a woman such as she *fascinating*. "Th-thank you," she stammered, unsettled by how easily he left her unbalanced.

"You're very welcome. But please, just grant me one favor."

"Yes?" Was she agreeing or asking?

"Excellent." Clearly he thought the former. "You will accompany me," Lavoie said, holding out an arm. "So that I can make the necessary arrangements to see you home safely tonight."

Angelique's exhilaration burst like a soap bubble jabbed by a needle. She'd been outmaneuvered by charm and pretty words. Anger rose again, though it was directed at herself now. Lavoie had just manipulated her as easily as . . . well, as easily as she manipulated the men she had sat across from at the card table. Yet somehow he had managed to fold gallantry into his manipulation, which made it unreasonable to refuse his request. Despite herself, she was impressed.

"Would you prefer I walk you home?" he asked into the silence, and now there was an edge to his voice.

Angelique knew when she didn't hold a winning hand. This was one of those times. "That won't be necessary. It would be my pleasure to accompany you." Her words were devoid of conviction, but she slipped her fingers under his arm anyway, still clutching her reticule with her other hand.

Lavoie led them across the club, past the richly papered walls and gleaming furniture and through the milling, laughing crowds. An occasional glance was cast in their direction, but never with anything more than idle curiosity before the patrons quickly returned their attention to their own pursuits of pleasure. Angelique knew that a masked woman on the arm of Alexander Lavoie was a common sight. But she had not, in a million years, ever wanted or intended to be one of them.

She tried to keep her touch light, but she could feel the strength of his body beneath her fingertips. Halfway across the room, he covered her hand gently with his, and the feel of his skin against hers was instantly electrifying. She'd forgone gloves because it was impossible to play cards with them, but she regretted their absence now, if only for the barrier they might have provided against his caress. If only to dull the sensations that were winging across her skin, licking through her veins, and crackling deep within her body. Never had she met a man who set her on edge as much as this one did. And for an entire host of conflicting reasons.

There was a part of her that still clung to her furious humiliation. Made worse because Alexander Lavoie had intervened. She did not appreciate being manipulated. She did not need his help. She certainly did not need him to rescue her from a drunken, grey-haired lecher.

Yet there was another part of her that was thrilled he had. It was the same pathetic part that had reveled in his compliments and had made her pulse race when he had offered his protection and assistance as though she was a princess worthy of such veneration, and not just a vingt-et-un player he might have considered a cheat at one point in time.

They approached a heavy wooden door at the rear of the club and a monster of a man who looked like a cross between an ox and a pugilist stepped aside, opening the door for his employer.

"Have my carriage brought around back, would you please, Jenkins?" Lavoie said.

"Of course, Mr. Lavoie." The ox-man nodded, and as they

stepped inside the room, he closed the door behind them as quickly as he had opened it. The sound of music and conversation abruptly ceased.

"You may take off your mask, my lady," Lavoie said, moving behind a polished desk where large ledgers lay open.

"Why?" Angelique demanded.

"Because there is no one here except you and me. And I've been told such things become devilishly itchy after an extended period of time."

"It's not itchy," she lied, fighting an urge to scratch. Her eyes darted around the room, taking in the somewhat sparse, if masculine, furnishings. Paintings of fast-looking horses hung on the gleaming wood walls. Two leather-covered chairs were placed by the hearth, the low fire chasing shadows across the woven rug on which they sat. A bookcase flanked the wall closest to her, though whatever ledgers or volumes it held were concealed by wooden panels, each with its own keyhole. All things that one might expect to see in an office such as this. All things that told her nothing important about the man who stood across from her.

Lavoie looked up at her briefly before shrugging and fishing a key out of his coat pocket. "Suit yourself." He slid the key into a lock on a drawer of the desk and turned it. In the muffled silence of the room, it made a soft click. "Put your money on the desk, my lady," Lavoie said.

"No." Angelique clutched her reticule more tightly against her.

Lavoie looked up, his strange eyes finding hers. "I'm not going to steal it," he said, and Angelique wasn't entirely sure he wasn't laughing at her.

"What do you want with it?" She knew she sounded like a suspicious fishmonger, but she was past the point of caring. If he was going to prevent her from ever setting foot in his club again, then she would need every farthing until she could find another solution.

"I was going to convert your winnings for you. So that it's not quite so bulky. And obvious." From the desk drawer, he withdrew a flat wooden box and placed it on the center of the desk.

"Oh." She made no move to obey, eyeing the box with distrust. It looked like one of her brother's dueling pistol cases. She was aware he was still watching her.

"I only rape and rob virgins on Mondays and Wednesdays, you know," Lavoie said dryly, leaning a hip against the massive desk. Now she knew he was laughing at her.

"I'm not a—" she started to snap, only to bring herself up short, her face burning again with furious horror. Furious that he should find such amusement at her expense. Horror that he had nearly managed to goad her into blurting out something so inappropriate. Though perhaps it no longer mattered.

Because Lady Angelique Archer was standing in a gaming hell, alone with a probable assassin, clutching a bag of money she had won gambling. And all because a boorish baron had kept squeezing her left breast. The issue of her virtue was moot at this point.

"I'm not an idiot," she tried to recover anyway, raising her chin.

Lavoie looked down briefly before raising his head again. "I never thought you were. I apologize. That remark was crude and uncalled for. I was trying to put you at ease."

Angelique looked away. "It doesn't matter." It really didn't anymore. A happily ever after was no more in the cards for her than a castle in the clouds. *In the cards.* She would have laughed at the pun had she not felt so desolate.

Lavoie opened the box that still lay on his desk. In the candlelight, the gleam of gold caught her eye. He gestured at her reticule.

"Let me help," he said.

Those three words almost undid whatever composure she still clung to. He was the first person to ever say that—to offer help, though he couldn't possibly know just what she wished that meant. Because the truth of the matter was that Lavoie couldn't really help her. She was in this alone.

But he could exchange money.

Angelique stiffened her spine. "If you insist." She dropped her reticule on his desk.

Lavoie gazed at her a moment before reaching for the bag, pulling at the strings and letting her winnings spill out across the surface of the desk. "Would you like something to drink while I count this?" he asked.

"No."

"Something to eat?"

"No."

"Would you like to stand here and watch me count this?"

"Yes." She raised her chin.

"Very well." He began stacking coins in neat rows.

Angelique crossed her arms and watched, her eyes drifting to the ledgers next to the growing stacks of coins. The one closest to her was open and looked like a delivery ledger, documenting everything that had been purchased by the club this past week from brandy to bread. No different, really, than the one she kept for her own household, except that there seemed to be a lot more zeros involved. Her eyes skipped down the neat columns of numbers before frowning slightly as she reached the totals.

"Is there something the matter with my counting?" Lavoie asked, still stacking coins.

"Of course not." Did the bloody man have eyes on the sides of his head?

"Are you sure? Because you look like you just swallowed a lemon."

Angelique's frown deepened. He was laughing at her again. "There is nothing wrong with your current counting, Mr. Lavoie," she replied coolly. "But your weekly accounting is another matter altogether." In the next second, she bit her lip, cursing her loose tongue. What the hell was wrong with her tonight? No matter what Lavoie said to her, no matter how much fun he might poke at her, she would be prudent to simply nod and smile. And keep her mouth shut.

Lavoie stopped counting her winnings and raised his head. "I beg your pardon?"

"It's nothing. I spoke out of turn."

"Clearly you don't think it's nothing." He was staring at her in that relentless way of his, making her feel exposed all over again.

Angelique cleared her throat and looked down at the ledger. "Since you must know, your weekly cost total for all purchases is incorrect."

Lavoie raised one sleek brow. "I find that unlikely."

"Why would that be?"

"Because I do the weekly accounting. And I am not in the habit of making errors."

"Of course. Forget I said anything." Angelique looked away, reminding herself that none of this was any of her business.

She could still feel his eyes on her. "And no one can do sums that quickly. Reading upside down at that."

"Like I said, forget I mentioned it."

But Alexander Lavoie didn't seem to wish to forget

anything. He abandoned her stacks of coins and pulled the ledger closer to him.

Angelique felt her stomach sink in dismay. "Perhaps you might just finish counting the coins, and I'll be on my way—"

"Not yet." He was running his finger down the totals column, his forehead creased in concentration. He got to the bottom, and now he was frowning too. "You were right."

There was no victory in that revelation.

"How?" he asked. "How did you do that?"

"Lucky guess. Now, if I might just collect—"

"Bloody hell," he breathed. "I've heard of people like you." Lavoie straightened, pinning her immobile again with those strange eyes of his.

"Really, I have no idea what you're talking about." She backed away from his desk, as if she could hide behind the empty space between them.

"Two hundred and eighty-six multiplied by three hundred and fifty-four."

One hundred and one thousand, two hundred forty-four.

"You just did that in your head, didn't you?" He was still watching her.

"No," she lied.

"Divided by eight."

Twelve thousand, six hundred fifty-five. And a half.

"You can't help yourself." Those amber eyes were seeing far too much. "You know exactly what the answer is."

"No," she lied.

"You...*see* numbers. Is that accurate?"

Angelique shook her head. She had managed to conceal her unnatural aptitude for numbers from an early age, though her mother had become at least somewhat aware that she had far more success understanding complex conjugates than the steps to a cotillion. Especially after she'd caught

Angelique filching her brother's mathematics schoolbooks from his room the Christmas that she'd turned eighteen. If Angelique ever wanted to secure an advantageous marriage, she needed to focus on lessons befitting a young lady, her mother had counseled firmly as she'd plucked the books out of Angelique's hands. And geometry was not one of them.

Besides, her mother had whispered, gentlemen—at least the sort that a lady would desire to marry—did not like women whose abilities outstripped their own when it came to masculine pursuits. So Angelique had obeyed, hiding her abnormal tendencies while trying her very best to be what her parents, and society as a whole, had expected.

For all the good that had done her.

"My lady?" Lavoie snapped her out of her musings.

"I'd like to go now," Angelique said.

"Mmmm."

She edged closer to the desk again, her eyes darting to the money still on the surface. She could not leave without her money.

"You count the cards." Lavoie was tapping his finger absently on the open page of the ledger. "You remember what's already been played. And you use that to determine the odds of the next hand. Tell me, do you use a points system? Or can you actually remember each individual card?"

"Again, I have no idea what you speak of," Angelique insisted, though her voice sounded reedy in her ears. Numbers simply stacked and catalogued themselves in her memory.

Lavoie leaned forward. "You remember every card, don't you?"

"I don't know—"

"My lady, it's a yes or no question. Do yourself and your considerable intelligence a favor and just answer it."

Angelique blinked. "Yes."

"Thank you." He'd stopped drumming his fingers on the ledger and had gone quite still. "I haven't had the vingt-et-un tables very long," Lavoie said presently. "I didn't want the hassle of hiring competent dealers, and to be honest, I didn't expect the game to become as popular as it has. I've left it up to the players to deal in rotation, as you know. But that doesn't make the club much money. In fact, the only money that game brings in is what I make on the liquor and anything else my patrons choose to purchase while they play."

"Why are you telling me this?"

"Because I've never seen a vingt-et-un player with your capabilities before. It makes me glad that it was Daventon's money you took and not mine."

"Capabilities?"

"Yes. Which makes you even more fascinating." He paused. "I don't suppose you'd be interested in a job?"

"A job?" She was aware she was repeating him like a half-wit, but she couldn't seem to wrap her head around the last minute of conversation.

Capabilities.

Fascinating.

Job.

Good Lord.

"Yes." Lavoie leaned forward slightly.

"Ladies don't have jobs." Angelique tried to put some conviction into that statement, knowing it was what she was supposed to say. Such knowledge had been drilled into her since she was old enough to walk. Ladies grew up and married well and became wives who lived out their lives in genteel comfort. They did not partake in industry. Or gambling.

At least they didn't until they did not marry at all, much less well, and their parents died, their family fortune went missing, and their newly titled brother couldn't stay sober long enough to look for it. Then ladies did what they had to do to hold their families together.

She glanced up at him, but her sharp reply, like everything else, had only seemed to amuse him.

"A strange thing to say for a lady who already treats my vingt-et-un table as her personal place of business." Lavoie's lip had curled, his scar making it look more like a smirk than a smile.

She looked away, despising the truth in his assessment. "I do no such thing. Ladies don't have jobs," she repeated, though it was a pitiable attempt at her defense.

"Ladies don't have jobs that people know about," he countered.

"What? What does that mean?" Angelique's eyes snapped back to his.

Lavoie moved out from behind his desk and leaned back against the front of it. He crossed his booted feet casually, never taking his eyes off her. "It means, my lady, that once you stop pretending to be aghast, and you understand that I offer the potential to earn more money in a single night than you will earn in three at the card tables, you might wish to reconsider. I wish you to deal a high-stakes vingt-et-un table that can accommodate at least six players who will be playing against the house and not each other. Who will be playing against *you*."

Angelique was at a loss for words.

"I don't need to have your answer now," he said, tipping his head. "You know where to find me. I will pay you for your time, of course, and you will also receive a percentage of whatever you—my club—wins. I promise that your identity will remain concealed. And unlike the men you have had to endure thus far at the tables, I promise that I won't touch your breasts. And anyone else in my club who might attempt to do so in the future will answer to me."

She felt her face heat all over again, even as another hail of unwanted thrills crackled through her like a summer storm.

"Tell me you'll think about it," Lavoie prompted.

"Very well." The shock was wearing off, and Angelique was trying her best to collect her scattered thoughts. She'd be an idiot to deny him outright. She didn't trust him entirely, but her current situation didn't leave her many choices. And she couldn't deny that his offer, like the man himself, was more than a little... intriguing. Exciting. *Fascinating.*

Lavoie pushed himself off the desk, coming to stand directly in front of her. His eyes skimmed over her hair, her mask, her gown, as if he was evaluating—admiring—what he saw. "With a mind such as yours, I think you would be brilliant," he murmured. "I think that you and I would make splendid partners."

The breath was snatched clean from her lungs. Being complimented by Alexander Lavoie was a little like how she imagined being run down by a team of carriage horses might leave one feeling. Breathless. Dazed. Boneless.

He reached up a hand and touched the edge of her mask, his amber eyes following his fingers. And then, without warning, his fingers dropped to her skin, and his touch trailed along the bare skin at the top of her shoulder until it met gold silk. She shivered, and gooseflesh rose.

I promise that I won't touch your breasts.

But for one wild moment, Angelique wondered if he might not consider kissing her.

Lavoie's hand dropped. "I'd get you a better mask," he said. "Something that will cover more of your face. And a different gown. Something..." His eyes drifted over her figure. "Without mud stains." He turned back to the desk and began withdrawing gold coins from the flat box.

Angelique gasped, trying to fill her lungs with much needed air, attempting to regain a sense of balance. Belatedly, she realized Lavoie had filled her reticule with gold and was now drawing the string closed and tying it neatly.

"Your evening's earnings, my lady," he said as he turned and held the reticule out to her.

"Thank you," she mumbled as she took it, careful not to touch him. She frowned. She knew how much she had made this evening. She knew how much each of the gold coins was worth. The conversion was simple, and something wasn't adding up. "It's too heavy," she said, testing the weight in her hand. "You've given me too much, and I will not be beholden to you for your charity."

"Think of it as an advance," Lavoie said smoothly.

"I haven't agreed to work for you."

"Then you can return it with your refusal tomorrow."

Angelique narrowed her eyes. "You aren't afraid I won't steal it? Never come back?"

"You're not a thief, my lady. I know who you are. And I know where to find you."

It was like being doused with a barrel of icy water. That fact had been forgotten under the intoxicating influence of his silvered tongue and heated touch. Now it sat like a heavy weight on her chest, and Angelique recognized that what remained of her honor and good name, and that of her family, was at the mercy of this man and his whims, simply because he knew what no one else did.

He knew who she was.

Chapter 2

Alex still had no idea who she was.

Which was mind-boggling. He prided himself on being able to ferret information out of people without them even realizing that he had done so. He was skilled in making them reveal things about themselves using a carefully honed system of assumption and insinuation, perceived expectations, and vague references that could be interpreted as intimate knowledge. He employed flattery, educated guesses, or when required, flat-out lies. And never had he failed so miserably as he had with the woman in the gold dress. Nothing had worked.

From the very start, it was clear that the woman in gold had no intention of ever taking off her mask or admitting her identity. She was skittish, but not weak. Beneath that cynical, suspicious exterior was a will of steel. That had become inherently obvious. It had also become obvious that the money she had won tonight was of immense importance. She didn't just want it, she *needed* it. But for what, Alex couldn't even begin to guess.

It certainly didn't appear that she spent any of it on herself. She wore no necklace, no earbobs, not even a jeweled hairpin. Closer inspection of her gown revealed slight discolorations along the seams, suggesting it had been altered and not made just for her. She had also walked to his club, which meant that she likely did not have access to a carriage, nor had she chosen to spend the money on a hack. Alex was beginning to wonder if perhaps she might simply be a very accomplished actress and not a lady at all.

Yet short of ripping off her mask and hoping he recognized her, he was at a total loss. His usual tricks had failed. Perhaps the revelation that the woman with glorious curves and beautiful blue eyes possessed a mind of such brilliance had put him off his game. Which was saying something. He was used to being surrounded by very clever women.

His sister, Elise, was one of them, and a very accomplished card player on top of that. But even she could not do what this woman could. Alex very much doubted there were many souls in the entire country of England who could. And the fact that she had landed in the middle of his club was not an opportunity that could be passed up. Alex would not let her go so easily. Lady or not.

And if she were a he, and wore trousers instead of stays, would you be as zealous? a little voice taunted in his head. *Is it business you want her for, or something else entirely?*

Alex scowled. He had been physically attracted to this woman from the beginning, that he would admit freely. And her intelligence made her devastatingly more desirable. And then there was her incomplete declaration. *I'm not a virgin.* Interesting, that, because she didn't appear to possess the practiced skill set of a woman used to handling men's advances, be they a husband's or a lover's.

All these observations were things that might be used to

advance his effort to uncover her identity. Calculated and filed objectively, with the subject kept at a distance, like he had done hundreds of times before.

Except he had gone and made the idiotic mistake of touching her, covering her hand with his own as he had led her through the club, and it was like lightning had sizzled through him, leaving him not a little disoriented. And then later, even when he knew it was unwise, he had given in to his baser urges and ran his fingers across the impossibly smooth, impossibly soft skin at her shoulder. Wishing he could slide that gold silk from her body and explore the rest. First with his fingers. Then with his tongue. And after that, with his—

"Mr. Lavoie? Are you all right?"

Alex jerked, realizing he was still standing in the middle of his office. And the woman in question was staring at him through her mask, apprehension touching her eyes. He shifted, pulling discreetly at the fall of his trousers to conceal his semi-aroused state. He didn't need to embarrass himself further.

"Quite fine." He moved to the wall nearest the bookcase, thankful to have a purpose besides fantasizing about his mystery woman. He turned and gestured for her to join him. "I'll see you to my carriage."

The woman eyed him. "The door is that way." She jerked her head in the opposite direction.

Alex released a latch in the heavy wood panel of the wall. The camouflaged door swung open. "This exit is somewhat more discreet. It leads into an alley that runs between my club and the building beside it. My carriage will be waiting at the top of the passage on the street."

"Oh." Slowly she made her way toward him, still clutching her reticule in both hands as if she feared he would snatch it away. He held the door, allowing her to precede him into the night. Darkness and chilled spring air enveloped them as the club door swung closed. The occasional rain-drop splattered down around them.

At the top of the alley, Alex could make out his driver waiting with the carriage, the horses' breath hanging in small clouds of fog under the gaslights.

"Did you not have a shawl?" Alex asked as he watched the woman shiver. She had to be freezing with all that exposed skin at her shoulders and back.

"It was warmer when I left home," she said stiffly.

"Here," he said, shrugging out of his coat. "Wear this." He draped it over her shoulders from behind before she had the chance to protest.

She stopped abruptly. "I can't."

"You already are." Alex pushed by her and continued up to the top of the alley, leaving her no choice but to follow.

His driver, his cap pulled low over his forehead, saw him coming and nodded in greeting. "Good evening, Mr. Lavoie." His grey eyes flicked over Alex's shoulder to Angelique as he reached the street. "Just the one passenger?" he asked.

"Just the one, Matthews," Alex confirmed. Matthews had worked for Alex since he had opened this club. A veteran of the Peninsular War and a fine hand with horses and firearms, he had proven invaluable over the years. Alex doubted that there was much left that Matthews had not seen or heard, though he got paid admirably well to forget. Like the French brandy, discreet transportation was a service Alex offered. For a price, of course.

"Where to, Mr. Lavoie?" Matthews asked.

"The lady will give you her direction," Alex said easily, hearing the woman come up behind him. It was his best chance at discovering her identity. If he knew where she lived, he could determine her name. He took a step back to face the masked woman. "See that she gets safely in her door, Matthews," Lavoie instructed without taking his eyes off her. He couldn't risk her telling his driver to drop her in the middle of a random street or square.

"Understood, Mr. Lavoie."

Alex saw her brows draw together. She glanced at the carriage and the driver and then made a move to divest herself of his coat.

"Please keep it, my lady. You may leave it in the carriage or return it to me tomorrow night when you bring me my answer."

Her lips thinned. "Mr. Lavoie, I—"

The deafening report of a pistol split the air, startling the horses. At the same time, something whined near his ear and smacked into the masonry just behind him. Alex leapt in front of the woman, pulling her down into a crouch near the front of the carriage. The sound of the shot echoed around them, bouncing off the buildings and pavement. A burst of maniacal laughter sounded then.

"Stand and deliver!" someone roared.

The horses, also veterans of the wars and used to artillery fire, did what they'd been trained to do. Which was nothing. Which gave Matthews the ability to reach down beside him and pull out his own set of pistols from beside him on the driver's seat. Alex heard the sound of the guns being cocked.

Alex edged forward, looking past the horses for the gunman. In the gaslight, he saw the villain about fifteen paces away. There were two other men standing just behind him, and he had no idea if they were friends or foes. A gang of criminals would make this more difficult. And messy. He would be required to resort to blades after Matthews's shot was spent. But unlike the thief, Alex's driver would spend his shot wisely and with much better aim. And truth be told, Alex always favored blades over firearms anyway.

The gunman was standing in the middle of the street, his pistol dangling from one hand and the other clutching something else that glinted dully. And he was...laughing.

"Bloody 'ell, but I should have been a highwayman," the stranger cackled. "I've always wanted to say that. Stand an' deliver!" He lifted his other hand, and Alex realized that it was a flask he held. He tipped it back, taking a healthy swallow, and wiped his mouth with the sleeve of his expensive coat, staggering. He turned slightly to the two men standing behind him. "Whaddya think, chaps? How'd I do?"

Alex groaned. The man was utterly soused. He was also, given the quality of his coat and the gleam of his boots, not a ragged and desperate criminal but a gentleman with an excess of bad judgment and an idiotic sense of humor.

"Shall I shoot him, Mr. Lavoie?" Matthews inquired politely, the muzzles of his guns trained firmly on the man in the street.

"No!" It was the woman who answered, her voice raw with horror and desperation. "Don't shoot him!" She stumbled past Alex, pulling off her mask, and came to stand directly in front of the would-be highwayman, effectively blocking any shot Matthews or he might have had. "What are you doing, Gerald?" she cried.

In a blinding flash of recognition, Alex realized instantly who the drunken fool on the street was. Gerald Archer, the young Marquess of Hutton. Alex had had the misfortune to meet him more than once since the death of his father and his ascension to the title not quite a year ago. Hutton was the perfect storm of arrogance and immaturity, and it would seem he was in fine form tonight. Alex's eyes went to the two men who were still standing behind the marquess. He recognized these men as well. George Fitzherbert, Viscount Seaton, and Vincent Cullen, Baron Burleigh.

"I jus' about keeled over when I saw you jus' now, Ang. I'm saving you from whatever scoundrel you're with," Hutton giggled, lifting his pistol to wave it in front of the woman's face. "'S what a good brother does, no?" He looked back to his friends for confirmation. They were raising their own flasks in a toast but Alex was too busy staring at the woman in the gold dress.

Too busy staring at Angelique Archer.

For she could be no other. He'd never actually met the Marquess of Hutton's sister, though the surfeit of rumors and the sheer number of conversations that had ebbed and flowed around the topic of Lady Angelique in his club in years prior made him feel like he'd known her forever. Or at least, the contradictory character of Lady Angelique that had been crafted by the wagging tongues of the ton.

As the only daughter of the old Marquess of Hutton, she had been rumored to have a staggering dowry attached to her, a sum that put her in the class of some of the American heiresses newly arrived to England's shores. Which, combined with her family's lofty title, should have put her at the top of London's most eligible bachelorette list. Yet in the single season in which she had participated, no man had offered for her. Or at least, no man had offered for her publicly. Alex had heard all sorts of speculation about the reasons behind her failure to find a suitable husband. Or even an unsuitable husband, for that matter.

She was frigid. She had once been someone's mistress. She was a half-wit. She had terrible bluestocking tendencies. She was barren. She had an illicit love-child. The only thing that the gossipmongers had agreed on was that she was strange, cold, detached, and utterly unsociable. She had been unanimously dubbed the Marble Maiden.

Alexander had listened, as he always did, but paid little heed to such stories, for without confirmation, such absurdities held scant value to him. And then the ton had moved on to a more interesting object of interest and Angelique Archer had been forgotten. She had also vanished from society, Alex knew, long before the death of her father had made her younger brother the new marquess.

So why had she suddenly appeared in the middle of the most notorious gaming hell in London now? Good Lord, but this woman became more fascinating by the minute.

"How much have you had to drink tonight?" Lady Angelique snapped, knocking her brother's pistol aside where it still wavered in front of her nose. It fell to the street with a clatter.

In the gaslight, Seaton snickered. "Better answer her, Hutton," he jeered. Women found the viscount attractive, Alex knew, but a clever haircut and fancy clothes could not overcome his callous pomposity.

Angelique looked up, as if realizing her brother was not alone for the first time, and recoiled like she'd been struck. Her face drained of color. "I should have known you'd be here, Seaton," she said.

"Did you really? Because I certainly never expected to find you in a dark alley outside a gaming hell in the wee hours of the morning." His eyes slid down the front of her dress and lodged exactly where Alex expected them to. "My, but that's quite the gown. Almost didn't recognize you." Seaton didn't appear nearly as drunk as his friend.

The young marquess swayed before turning to scowl at his friend. "Tha's my sister, Seaton," he slurred. He drew himself as straight as he was able. "An' for the record, I don' think I've had enough t'drink a'tall."

"I believe the young lord should be taken home before he kills someone." Alex strode forward into the light, his patience with Hutton's childish behavior and the entire episode at an end.

"I don't need your help, Mr. Lavoie." Lady Angelique seemed to have found her voice again, though it sounded a little ragged.

"I'm aware. That doesn't mean you aren't getting it." He brushed by her. "Your brother nearly shot me, and came very close to shooting you. I take exception to such reckless idiocy."

"You!" Hutton pointed his flask at Alex and grabbed Angelique by the arm. "You need t' stay away from my sister. You an' your wicked innen…intentions—"

"You don't need to get involved. This is a family matter, Mr. Lavoie." Lady Angelique managed to pull herself free of Hutton's grip.

"Not when it occurs on the street outside my club," Alex disagreed. "Then it becomes very much my business. And very much my problem. Though I've been told I'm quite good at problem solving."

"Perhaps we should just go?" The suggestion came from the slighter man, Burleigh, who was starting to look nervous. The man was almost a thinner, weedier version of Hutton, with the same blond hair and narrow jaw, but he lacked the air of self-importance that Hutton wielded like a battering ram. "We don't want any trouble," he added, pulling anxiously at a gaudy cravat pin at his throat.

Perhaps one of these fools had some common sense after all. "Sounds like good advice to me," Alex said.

"I'm not leavin'!" Hutton slurred. "I—I—I'm callin' you out!"

"Please don't." Alex turned so he was addressing

Burleigh and Seaton. "I think, gentlemen, that it would be wise to take your friend home before he does something we'll all regret. That coat he is wearing looks new. And expensive. I'd hate to ruin it. Do you know how hard it is to get blood out of superfine? And it'll be worth far less second-hand if it has holes made from bullets or blades. Or both."

"I'm not goin' anywhere till you take your slimy hands off my sister," Hutton all but shouted. "Seaton and Burleigh, you'll be my seconds."

"You know my mother does not approve of duels," Burleigh said. "She would not like it if I got involved in one."

Seaton sneered openly at that. "Then perhaps, Burleigh, you should run along home like a good little boy and let the men handle this."

"No one's runnin' anywhere!" Hutton declared. "We'll settle this like gen'lemen!"

"Think carefully, my lord, before you agree to your young friend's demand," Alex said quietly. "For I am not a gentleman. And bodies bloat terribly at this time of year after a day or two in the Thames."

Burleigh made a sound of distress and cleared his throat. "He means nothing by it, of course. He's off his head with drink." He jostled Seaton. "Don't you agree?"

Seaton's face was set in hard, unpleasant lines. He took another swig from his flask. "Maybe."

"Let's just go and forget this misunderstanding ever happened." Burleigh was looking between the three men.

Seaton slid his flask inside his coat and stepped in front of Alex, so close that Alex's eyes nearly watered at the potency of his alcohol-laced breath. "You don't scare me," he sneered.

"Mmmm." Alex was unmoved.

"Not only am I the heir to a dukedom, I'm a regular at

Jackson's, you know," Seaton continued, his chest inflating with every word even as he curled his hands into fists. "I've brought greater men than you to their knees. And I'll take great pleasure in— *eeerp*."

Alex had drawn his knife, the one his brother had given him on his twelfth birthday and one of the things that was always concealed on his person. Currently, the point of the wide blade was jammed into the soft tissue of Seaton's lower belly, the fabric of the man's trousers slowly giving way beneath the tip, stitch by stitch. He knew very well his actions were concealed from Lady Angelique.

"I believe, my lord, you were about to say that you'll take great pleasure in seeing your friend home." Alex twisted the knife slightly. "The rules here are not nearly as civilized as the rules you're accustomed to on Bond Street."

Seaton's face had paled but now it flushed a dark red.

"Go now, my lord, before another errant shot causes me to startle and slip. I'll see to his lordship."

Hutton yelled something unintelligible and stumbled toward them, but Burleigh managed to catch the sleeve of his coat. The marquess lost his balance and landed on his backside on the pavement. His flask dinged loudly as it bounced, and a stream of expletives followed as Hutton rolled over and crawled forward on all fours in an attempt to retrieve it.

Seaton stepped back, yanking on the lapels of his coat as if he was trying to straighten his damaged pride. "Hutton is all yours," he spat, and Alex wasn't entirely sure if he was speaking to Lady Angelique or himself.

Seaton was stalking away and Burleigh was trying to help the marquess off his knees, but Hutton only swatted at his hands. "Don' need yer help," he grunted. He finally closed filthy fingers around his flask.

Burleigh looked up in helplessness.

"Go." It was Angelique who spoke, and she sounded subdued. "I'll see to my brother."

"But my lady—"

"Go," she repeated.

Burleigh's eyes slid to Alex's, as if seeking confirmation. Or permission. Alex could feel his lip curl. Unobtrusively, he slid his knife back into the sheath inside his coat and shrugged. "You heard the lady."

Burleigh glanced at Hutton, who was now trying to get to his feet. He looked like he wanted to say something but then simply sighed heavily and turned, his slender form melting into the darkness beyond the pool of gaslight.

The marquess had finally gained his feet once again and stood swaying, disheveled and filthy. "I'm callin' you out, you—you…" He gave up on the last part of his sentence.

He looked behind him again for support, a faint flicker of confusion crossing his face as if he was surprised to find himself alone.

"You're not calling anyone out," Alex told him. "You're going home. There you will sober up. Find a pot of coffee. And perhaps some decency and respect. And when you've done all that, you may offer your apologies to your sister."

"What did y' say?" Hutton lurched toward Alex angrily.

Angelique made a sound of distress. "Gerald—"

"Sure you don't want me to shoot him, Mr. Lavoie?" Matthews inquired from his perch. "He's bleatin' awful loud."

"Children often do." Alex sighed.

"What d'you call me?" Hutton demanded. He dropped his flask again and drew up his fists. "You'll answer f'that. C'mon, chaps, let's take him!" he called, seemingly forgetting he was alone.

"Gerald, stop this," Angelique ordered. "You're making a fool of yourself."

"Mr. Lavoie?" Matthews prompted, adjusting his weapons hopefully.

"Don't shoot him," Alex told his driver with another sigh.

Hutton wobbled forward and swung at Alex's head. Alex ducked.

"Coward!" Hutton bellowed, taking another wild jab in Alex's direction.

Alex neatly sidestepped. "You have my apologies in advance, my lady," he said, dodging as Hutton threw another punch that connected with nothing and sent the man pitching forward.

"For what?" she asked as her brother righted himself and prepared for another assault.

"For this." Alex's punch caught Hutton squarely in the temple, sending jarring shocks through his hand and up into his arm. The marquess went down like a sack of stones. Alex winced and flexed his hand. Hell. He'd need to find some ice for his knuckles before dawn.

"Did you kill him?" Angelique asked in a small voice, staring down at the unmoving pile that was her brother.

"Of course I didn't kill him," Alex replied, catching her stricken look. "I only kill peers of the realm on Tuesdays and Thursdays. Really, you're quite fortunate all around that it's a Saturday."

She blinked at him before flushing, her high color obvious under the gaslights. Which was better than the pale, stark pallor that had been there before.

"Should have shot the pup, title or no," Matthews opined from his perch, sounding disgruntled. "Just a flesh wound, mind you. Give him something more permanent than a headache to remind himself to mind his manners the next time he gets into his father's liquor cabinet."

"Perhaps next time," Alex muttered.

Beside him, Angelique was still standing, staring down at her brother. The drunken marquess was now snoring loudly, his flask lying on the ground next to him, leaking liquor into the shoulder of his coat. The man's face already bore evidence of too much drink over a prolonged period—a flaccid puffiness of his jowls and around his eyes, punctuated by a reddened nose. If the man didn't kill himself with liquor, then the whores and the narcotics or whatever else that often went with the drink would finish him off. Alex had seen it too many times.

He grimaced slightly but concealed the better part of his disgust. "Again, my apologies for such measures," he said, watching Lady Angelique carefully while he waited for his driver.

It was the first time he'd had the chance to really study her without her mask. The light from the street revealed high cheekbones that cast deeply shadowed contours along her jaw. Wide blue eyes ringed with dark lashes were framed by a straight nose and arched brows. A beautiful constellation of freckles was scattered over the bridge of her nose and cheeks, hidden until now.

She would never be called pretty—her features were too strong, her bone structure too austere for such an insubstantial phrase. Alex cast about for a better word that also accommodated her quiet reserve and extraordinary intelligence. *Striking* would suit. *Arresting* was better.

"It is I who must apologize on behalf of my brother, Mr. Lavoie." Lady Angelique's generous mouth was drawn into a tight, unhappy line. "He is not usually so—"

"Your brother's behavior was no one's fault but his own, as was the behavior of his acquaintances," Alex said. "And like them, he is the only one who can answer for it."

"But still—"

"But nothing. Your brother is a marquess. He has responsibilities, both to himself and to his family. I believe you have younger siblings as well?" Alex vaguely recalled that there was a set of twins somewhere in the family.

"Yes," Angelique said quietly. "Gregory and Phillip. They're twelve. Attending Harrow."

"Ah. A good thing they are away, then."

"Yes." She sounded subdued. "A good thing."

"Is there somewhere you would like to take your brother?" Alex rather thought a week locked in a potting shed or perhaps a prison hulk would be beneficial to the marquess. If they were in York, the small colony where Alexander had grown up, he would have happily dumped him in the middle of the Canadian wilderness and left the sot to find his own way back.

"Home." Now she just sounded infinitely sad. "I'll take him home. Get him cleaned up."

Alex felt a stab of pity for this woman, though he was careful not to show it. He was quite sure the last thing she would want was pity. One could not choose one's family, and it couldn't be easy dealing with such an imbecile of a brother. A brother she still obviously cared for, whatever his failings.

The Marquess of Hutton had no idea just how lucky he was.

"Come, Matthews," Alex said briskly as his driver joined them. "Let's get his lordship into the carriage so that we can see him home in one piece."

Chapter 3

When Alexander Lavoie had asked Baron Daventon to remove his hand from her left breast, Angelique had thought that the night couldn't get much worse.

She had been so very, very wrong.

Because now Alexander Lavoie, with the help of his flinty-eyed, hatchet-faced driver, was arranging her insensible brother on the plush squabs of Lavoie's carriage, judiciously avoiding the drool leaking from the corner of Gerald's mouth, along with the mud and horse droppings smeared over the back of Gerald's coat.

Though he did take a moment to spread a large piece of burlap over his carriage upholstery before he heaved her brother inside.

She wondered if she shouldn't just take her winnings directly to the London docks and purchase a fare to the Americas. Or Africa. Or India. Or any place the very first ship was departing for tomorrow morning. The idea of simply leaving everything behind was wildly tempting. But she couldn't walk out on responsibilities. She couldn't leave the twins. And she couldn't leave Gerald. When things got difficult, Angelique Archer did not run. Ever.

So instead, she just held the horses while Lavoie and his driver wrestled with their snoring, drooling burden. She rested her head against the solid bulk of the nearest animal's neck. She'd sold her mare and the three geldings her family had kept as saddle horses as well as their carriage horses long ago. Breathing in the earthy, familiar equine scent, she was surprised how much she missed them. How much she longed for the simple, uncomplicated joy that could be found at a brisk gallop—

"They'll not wander anywhere, milady." The address jolted her out of her miserable musings. It was the driver, the one Lavoie had called Matthews, faintly out of breath from his exertions. "But I thank ye all the same."

Angelique blinked. The kind, even tone of his voice was at odds with the harsh fierceness of his face. "Of course," she mumbled, releasing the horse.

"Where to, milady?" he asked.

To the edge of the earth, she wanted to say. She wasn't particularly picky about which edge, as long as it was a long drop down.

"Bedford Square."

"Very good." Matthews nodded and climbed up, taking a moment to stow the firearms still resting on the seat. A mean and miserable part of her, a part that she was afraid to examine too closely, wondered if she shouldn't have just let him shoot her brother. A flesh wound, like he'd said, something that might make her brother understand the seriousness of his actions tonight. Something that might keep him from going any farther down the dark and destructive path he was on.

"My lady." This time it was Lavoie who addressed her.

He was standing at the door of his carriage. "Please allow me to assist you into the carriage. It's a bit of a step."

Angelique swallowed with some difficulty and nodded. She moved toward Lavoie and accepted the hand he offered. The urge to curl her fingers around his was instant. Beneath her palm, she could feel steady warmth and strength and she wanted that for herself, if only for a minute. Instead, she gathered her skirts and stepped up into the interior of the carriage, releasing Lavoie's hand and taking a seat opposite her brother.

She was trying to imagine what she would do with Gerald once they got home. She'd put him in the hall to sleep off his stupor, she decided. It would be better anyway, to be lying on polished marble in the event he cast up his accounts. Last week, Gerald had ruined the only remaining rug in the study.

Angelique gathered whatever shreds of pride remained and prepared herself to offer some sort of thanks to Lavoie before he could close the carriage door. "Mr. Lavoie, I must apologize again and offer you my sincere thanks—"

She stopped abruptly as Lavoie ducked into the carriage and pulled the door closed behind him with a loud snap. He lowered himself to the seat beside her and banged the flat of his hand on the roof twice. The carriage lurched forward.

"What are you doing?" Angelique asked, shrinking away from the hard heat of him that was now pressed up against her. His thigh. His hip. His shoulder. She squirmed, intensely aware of every inch of his body against every inch of hers.

"I'm sitting in my carriage." Lavoie turned away from her slightly and fumbled with the small window near his shoulder. The tiny sliver of space that she'd managed to put between them disappeared as his thigh pressed more firmly against her own.

She tried to move farther away, but short of crossing the interior and sitting on the slumped form of her brother sprawled opposite, there was nowhere she could go. "I can assure you, Mr. Lavoie, I can handle my brother. There is no need to accompany us."

She felt rather than saw Lavoie flex his right hand. "Mmmm."

"I don't want to take you away from your business."

He ignored her.

She tried one more time. "Mr. Lavoie, please, it is not necessary for you to—"

"Perhaps not. But I will accompany you all the same." In the next second, a hinge squeaked and a welcome draught of cool night air washed through the inside of the carriage. "Better." Lavoie drew a deep breath. "If I am to get foxed, I would prefer to do it on good whiskey than the fumes emanating from your brother's person." He stretched his booted feet out as far as they could go in the cramped space and nudged the toe of Gerald's muddied boot with his own. Her brother snorted softly but didn't move. "How long has he been like this?"

"Like what?" Angelique asked flatly. She knew exactly what he meant, but she didn't want to talk about this. Certainly not with Alexander Lavoie.

Beside her, Lavoie shifted, and Angelique could feel him watching her. "My lady." It was gentle and chiding, and Angelique's teeth clenched. His pity was far worse than his high-handedness.

"My brother just doesn't know his limits," she forced out.

She heard Lavoie chuckle, though it was decidedly without humor. "You defend him." There was no inflection in that statement, and Angelique couldn't tell if it was said in accusation or admiration.

"He's my brother." She tried to keep her voice steady. "One doesn't get to abandon them. Even when they make unwise decisions. But I don't suppose you can understand that, can you?"

She felt him stiffen beside her before his body seemed to relax again. "You might be surprised."

Angelique didn't think that likely. "He's young."

"Yet there are men his age who—" Lavoie stopped. "He won't live to be old if he drinks himself to death," was all he murmured.

"Thank you, Doctor. I wasn't aware." Angelique looked sightlessly out the window.

"What is the money for?" Lavoie asked abruptly. "The money you won at my club tonight. And the nights previous."

"What does it matter?" Angelique didn't turn.

"It doesn't. So long as your brother isn't pouring it down his throat."

Angelique spun back to Lavoie, not trusting herself to speak for a moment. "You think I'd give him money to do this?" she managed when she found her voice. "You think I find any of this funny? Less than awful?"

He considered her. "No."

"Then why would you presume such a thing?" She was furious.

"I'm not presuming anything. I'm trying to understand. If you are in some sort of difficulty, my lady, please let me help you."

There he went, offering help again. For a terrifying moment, Angelique nearly gave in to the impulse to tell this stranger everything. Tell him about the solicitors who came to their home with grave faces and dire warnings and no plausible explanations about what her father had been doing when he'd secretly started selling off the Hutton holdings, piece by piece, five years ago. Or where that fortune in cash might be now, and her inability to discover even the smallest clue. She could tell him about her brother's disinclination to help, or even care, so long as his next pint was paid for and his next whore was willing.

But she wouldn't.

No one knew. And she would keep it that way. The silver lining in all of this was that Gerald, while he might carelessly and irresponsibly spend what little he managed to cobble together, couldn't lose the family fortune. Because it appeared it was already lost.

And as much as Alexander Lavoie might be sincere in his offer of assistance, there was nothing a gaming hell owner would ever be able to do. Lavoie couldn't tell her where the family fortune might have gone. He could not tell her how to get it back. He couldn't make her brother into someone he wasn't.

Angelique could still feel his eyes on her in the darkened interior, pale washes of gaslight occasionally stabbing through the dark. "You can't help me," she told him.

"Mmmm."

She wasn't sure if he was agreeing or arguing.

Across the seat from them, her brother twitched and snorted loudly before falling back into his stupor.

Lavoie made a small noise in the back of his throat. "Perhaps then I might be able to help your brother in the event he finds himself in need of assistance in the future. Something as simple as a...ride home on an evening when he might require it. Would that be all right with you, my lady?"

"Why would you do that for him?"

Lavoie uncrossed his feet. "I wouldn't do it for him. I'd do it for you."

Angelique felt a curious warmth curl into her chest.

"Even if you decline my offer of employment, my regard

for you will not be diminished. I'd like to think that I might remain a friend." He spread the fingers of one hand over his knee.

The warmth in her chest started to spread outward.

"Tell me what you know about his lordship's friends. Burleigh and Seaton."

The warmth fled, and her stomach turned, the way it always did when George Fitzherbert, Viscount Seaton, was mentioned. Like it had when she'd realized he'd been standing on the street behind her brother. But then George had disappeared, and her brother had tried to assault a presumed assassin, and she'd been distracted enough to forget about him. But now that same assassin had asked her a question she had no desire to answer. She'd rather talk about her brother's drinking. God, she'd rather talk about Baron Daventon's hand on her breast.

"My lady?" Lavoie prompted. "Burleigh and Seaton?"

"I don't know them," she mumbled. Which wasn't a lie, exactly. Her father and the old Baron Burleigh had been incredibly close and the friendship between their sons was a product of that, even though Vincent was a few years older. And as for Seaton, she had thought she'd known him better than anyone. Until she discovered she hadn't known him at all.

"You're lying again, my lady."

Angelique started before a welcome rush of anger went through her. Of all the autocratic arrogance. She turned back to face Lavoie, trying to see his expression in the shadows. "Yes. I am." It came out harshly.

"Why?" He didn't seem at all concerned with her vitriol.

"Because it's none of your damned business." She could almost hear her mother gasp in shock at the use of such language. But damn, it felt good. She really ought to use the word damn more often. Dammit.

Lavoie watched her for a moment longer before shrugging and settling himself back against the squabs, studying her. A heavy silence descended.

"That's it?" Angelique asked presently.

"I beg your pardon?"

"You're not going to continue to interrogate me further?"

He made a sound low in his throat. "No, my lady, I'm not going to *interrogate* you further."

"You're laughing at me."

"A little."

"Why?" she snapped, feeling a little foolish. "Is interrogation only something you do on Fridays?"

He chuckled, and the rich sound sent shivers across her skin. "Sundays, if you must know. But if I were to interrogate you further, it wouldn't be in a moving carriage."

"What, you'd take me to your dungeon that I'm sure you have beneath your club?" Angelique said, her voice heavy with sarcasm. "Tie my wrists and ankles across a rack and pull me apart until you got what you wanted?"

"Not exactly what I was thinking." The laughter had fled, replaced with something else entirely. "And I wouldn't tie you up to get what I wanted. Unless, of course, you insisted on it. Then I would do anything."

There was suddenly not enough air in the carriage. She should be horrified. Scandalized. Instead, she suddenly felt hot all over, her pulse pounding in her ears. And that same pulse seemed to be echoing somewhere deep within her belly, sending out strange currents that made her achy everywhere. Her breasts suddenly felt heavy and tight, and a restless rhythm was throbbing at the juncture of her legs.

The carriage lurched, tipping Angelique toward Lavoie. She instinctively put a hand out to steady herself, only to find it braced on one of his thighs, the muscle rock hard

"I'm sure, thank you." She didn't want anyone to see the rest of the house. The hall was bad enough—the rest of the house had been stripped long ago of anything that might fetch a price.

The driver shrugged. "Very well. I'll be outside when yer ready, Mr. Lavoie." Matthews headed back out in the direction of his carriage, leaving Angelique standing alone with Lavoie.

She watched him warily, at a complete loss as to what to say to a supposed assassin who had escorted her home from a gaming hell, offered her a job, and now stood opposite her in the middle of a darkened hall. "Mr. Lavoie—"

"I don't like the idea of you all alone in this house," Lavoie said abruptly, startling her.

"I'm not alone," Angelique told him. "I have...servants." Well, one, anyway. "And Gerald is here for me, of course."

"Of course." His lip curled slightly even as his gaze flickered in the direction of her insensible brother at their feet. "If it hasn't escaped your notice, your brother has yet to regain his faculties. And I have yet to see any evidence of a servant."

A new wave of exhaustion nearly made her sway. "He'll be fine. I'll be fine. Everything will be fine, Mr. Lavoie."

"Mmmm." He made that sound deep in his throat that she was starting to hate.

"I thank you for everything you have done for me tonight, Mr. Lavoie. Truly, I am very grateful. But I don't need you further. I can take care of everything from here—"

"You shouldn't have to." In the struggling candlelight, his eyes were a deep gold. He closed the distance between them with a single step. "You shouldn't have to..." he trailed off, a strange expression on his face.

"To what?" The words caught in her throat. He was so

close to her that she could feel the warmth of him, smell a faint scent of tobacco and whiskey and something darker.

"Be alone." He found her hand at her side and brought it up and kissed the back of her knuckles. Her mouth went dry, and that sense of yearning roared back to life, coursing through her, setting her blood on fire.

"I like being alone," she said, realizing that her voice was trembling as much as her body.

He raised his head slowly and uncurled his fingers where they had caught hers. "Liar," he whispered gently.

Her hand lay in his palm. She could withdraw it anytime she liked. Instead, she left it right where it was.

Because Alexander Lavoie was right.

He closed his fingers back over her hand, drawing her toward him. Their hands lowered, and his fingers intertwined with hers, keeping her captive against him. With his free hand, he reached up and found the edge of her face, tracing the line of her jaw down to the curve of her neck. With a flick of his wrist, he sent his coat sliding from her shoulders. She shivered once and then again as his fingers curled around the nape of her neck, though she felt anything but cold.

Very slowly, he lowered his head, his mouth inches from hers. She could feel his breath whisper against her cheek. She was frozen in place, afraid to move. Afraid not to. He would kiss her. Right here. Right now.

And God help her, but she wanted him to. She wanted him to do a whole lot more.

He moved then, angling his head and brushing his lips against her cheek, an impossibly brief, gentle contact that made her close her eyes. And then he was gone, cool night air invading the space between them, chilling her heated body. Her eyes popped open, and she barely managed to swallow the sound of disappointed dismay that rose.

Lavoie disentangled his hand from hers where it was trapped between them and bent, and in the next second, Angelique felt the soft warmth of his coat as he pulled it up and back over her shoulders. She couldn't have put together a coherent sentence at just that moment if her life depended on it.

He stepped back, the shadows across his face deepening as he moved farther away from the feeble light. "I'm afraid I can't linger, as much as I'd like to. But please tell me you'll consider my offer?" His tone was more suited to a conversation about the weather than one about what had just happened.

And what had just happened?

Nothing, she told herself. Nothing had happened. But that *nothing* had left her completely disoriented, her body on fire, and her wits scattered. *Nothing* had left her with a fierce battle of conflicting emotions warring within her—dismay, excitement, loss, wonder. She didn't know what to embrace first. Or last. Or at all.

"My lady?"

What had he asked? That she consider his offer? What offer? Her lust-muddled mind fought through the haze and finally cleared enough for her to realize that he was referring to his earlier offer of employment.

His question was a meteoric plummet back to reality. While she'd been imagining Alexander Lavoie kissing her, she had completely forgotten about her brother who snored not two feet away. She had forgotten that her family teetered on the edge of ruin. She had forgotten her responsibilities. She had forgotten everything.

The excitement and wonder faded away, leaving nothing behind but guilt and unhappiness.

She was not a woman returned from a ball to her castle in

the clouds with her prince and true love. She was a woman returned from a gaming hell to an empty house with a possible assassin and an insensible wastrel of a brother. She pressed a hand to lips that were still tingling in futile anticipation, regret coming hard and fast.

She couldn't work for Alexander Lavoie. Ever.

Not only had the miserable realities of her life been laid before him this night, bared for him to examine and evaluate at his leisure, but she had exposed herself. Bared the vulnerability she had tried so hard to keep buried under layers of duty and detachment. She had wanted him to kiss her with an intensity that shook her. She did not doubt for a second that he knew it.

"I'm sorry, but I cannot work for you," she said, staring at her feet.

"Ah." He was silent for a moment. "I've made you feel uncomfortable again."

"I beg your pardon?"

"I do not mix business and pleasure. Messy bedfellows, those, if you'll pardon the pun." He paused. "Please rest assured that, should you do me the honor of agreeing to my proposal, our relationship will remain purely professional at all times."

Angelique blinked, trying to put a coherent thought together. "That's not what…that is to say—"

"Come to the club tomorrow. Bring me your answer then, once you've had more time to consider it." He didn't give her time to answer but simply spun on his heel and headed toward the door. He paused, his body outlined in the frame. "I do hope you say yes, Lady Angelique. I think you and I could be very good together."

Chapter 4

The offices of Chegarre & Associates were located in the chaotic Covent Square, a stone's throw from the Drury theater and the hulking shadow of St Paul's Church. The old townhome where the offices resided had once been grand, and the square along with it. Now, the rowdy piazzas and boisterous marketplaces boasted a populace of a different sort than it had once attracted a century prior. Entertainers of every variety—both artistic and intimate—were found in droves here. Traffic bustled at all hours of the day and night as people peddled their wares and services. There was nothing that could not be had so long as one had the knowledge of where to find it and the coin with which to procure it.

The unending traffic suited the partners of Chegarre & Associates immensely. Flanked by a teeming tenement on one side and an upscale brothel on the other, the strange hours that were often kept by its members were never noticed, much less remarked upon.

Alexander Lavoie had been a partner in the firm for over

six years, and there was very little that he believed might yet be left to surprise him. Extortion, kidnappings, illicit affairs, elopements, inconvenient deaths—just a few of the things Alex had been presented with by desperate people who were even more desperate to make it all go away. People frantic to cover up a whole host of horrible choices, bad judgments, sinful greed, and utter idiocy. And the partners at Chegarre & Associates were extremely skilled at making scandal disappear.

All for an exorbitant fee, of course.

It was in these offices that Alex found himself as the sun slowly rose into morning proper, staring into the whiskey that sat in the bottom of his glass, brooding. At least, he thought that his current state might be called brooding, though he had little experience with it. He was more of a man of action. Assimilate, calculate, act.

Though last night he would have been better to avoid the last part of that. Assimilate, calculate, and then keep his damn hands to himself.

He had known touching Angelique Archer was a bad idea. Yet that hadn't stopped him from almost kissing her. Which would have been the worst idea ever. She wasn't a courtesan who had come to his club to propose a few hours or even a few months of mutual pleasure. She was a lady. And the most tempting, sensual woman he had ever come across in his life. And the bloody impossible thing about it was that she seemed to be oblivious to the fact.

He'd been deliberately crude in his comments more than once, and in hindsight, he wondered if he'd been making a subconscious effort to put a barrier between them. A reminder that she would be better to keep her distance. A reminder that they came from different worlds. Except her reaction to his vulgar remarks had not been what he'd expected.

I wouldn't tie you up to get what I wanted. Unless, of course, you insisted on it.

He'd heard her breath catch, saw her eyes go hot. And that was dangerous. Bloody hell, but if her reeking, drooling excuse of a brother hadn't been lying at their feet, he might have—

"You are aware that this is my office, are you not?"

Alex raised his eyes from his whiskey, careful not to drop the heavy ledger he was balancing in his other hand. "And a good morning to you too, Duchess."

Ivory Moore shot him a faintly accusing look from the doorway, her brown eyes narrowed. "Some people knock when presented with a locked door."

"It was early. And you weren't in your office. Knew you wouldn't mind."

Ivory closed the door firmly behind her and wandered into the room, moving past Alex to consider the sideboard with its collection of decanters that sat against the far wall. She picked up the depleted whiskey bottle and, after a heartbeat, poured herself a measure in an empty glass. "Did you kill someone?" she asked, setting the whiskey down.

"Why ever would you ask that?"

"You're drinking your breakfast. Never a good sign."

"Cook didn't have kippers ready. And no, I didn't kill anyone. Though I might have considered it."

Ivory turned around, taking a contemplative sip. The morning light streaming in through the window gave her chestnut hair a golden sheen and made her flawless complexion glow. She nodded at the ledger. "Who are you looking for?"

The ledger Alex held was one of hundreds, and it contained the secrets, scandals, and detailed personal information of the most prominent and influential families in England. The collection of ledgers had been started by Ivory's first husband, the very powerful and very clever Duke of Knightley. The old duke had had a reputation as a master meddler, a fixer of unfixable problems, and upon his death, Ivory had not only maintained his diligent information collection but had used that to found the very successful firm of Chegarre & Associates and continue his work.

"The Marquess of Hutton," Alex replied, returning his attention to the notes in front of him.

"The late marquess or the new one?" Ivory wrinkled her nose slightly.

"Both, I think."

"May I ask why?"

Alex hesitated. Why indeed? "I had the good fortune to meet Lady Angelique Archer last night."

A single sable brow rose. "Ah. The infamous Marble Maiden." Ivory frowned. "Where?"

"In my club."

"In your *club*?" It was repeated with disbelief.

"Indeed." Alex ran a finger down the dates noted in the margin. "It says here her father sold his Wooliston estate two years ago."

Ivory pushed herself off the sideboard, her plain woolen skirts swishing quietly as she approached the desk that sat solidly in the center of the room. "Yes. Which wouldn't bear interest except, if you read further, you'll see that the late Marquess of Hutton sold nearly all of the Hutton land holdings." She stopped at his shoulder. "Why was the Marble Maiden in your club?"

"She was playing vingt-et-un," Alex replied, distracted. His eyes skimmed lower over more entries of Hutton properties that had been sold. "Good Lord. I thought grand lords entailed everything so that this couldn't happen."

Ivory shrugged. "If those properties were entailed, it was all cut off at some point in time. Those were all free-hold."

Alex shook his head. "There can't be much left. How could the late marquess sell this much without creating a stir? Surely this would provoke all sorts of speculation."

"The bulk of the holdings were in the very north along the Scottish border, or in the west along the Welsh border. No big houses or grand castles, but mostly farm or grazing land. Also a fair bit of land with working coal mines. That land was the last to be sold because those mines contributed significantly to the Hutton income. But it was all sold to different people at different times with well-spaced intervals for the most part."

"Yet you know about it."

"My husband bought a string of his mines before we were married. He mentioned that Hutton had demanded utter discretion regarding the transaction. I found that interesting, so I chose to . . . investigate further, and discovered what you see there on that page. I wasn't sure if that information was of any importance, but it seemed odd enough to make note of."

"Alderidge bought a coal mine? What, he was bored with being a pirate?"

Ivory made a face at him. "I believe the word you're looking for is *captain*. And my husband believes in diversification when it comes to investment."

"Ah yes. I'm sure they teach that at pirate school. Never bury all your treasure on the same island."

"You did not come here to talk about my husband," she said with a hint of impatience. "You came here for information regarding the Archers. And perhaps to discover the reason why the Marble Maiden was dabbling at your vingt-et-un table?"

"She wasn't dabbling."

"But you just said—"

"She was dominating my vingt-et-un table. I'd like to hire her." Alex scanned the rest of the page. "Tell me about the new marquess. The son. There is almost nothing on him in here."

"That's because he is a nothing. I am made to understand his intelligence is below average, as is his political acumen and anything else not related to whoring and drinking. And even then, I am told that drinking is the only thing he does with any proficiency." She set her glass down on the edge of her desk.

Alex felt his lip curl in distaste. "You may keep any details of Hutton's carnal competence to yourself in the future, Duchess."

"You asked. Wait, what did you mean, exactly, when you said she was dominating your vingt-et-un table? And hire her to do what? Or are those the sort of details you might wish to keep to yourself?" she asked innocently.

Alex shot her a quelling look, though the idea of Angelique Archer reclining across the green baize of his gaming tables made his groin tighten. "The lady divested Baron Daventon and others of a significant amount of cash. I want to hire her to deal."

"Deal?"

"So my patrons play against the house and not themselves. There is more money to be made that way if one knows what one is doing. And Lady Angelique most assuredly does." He slid the ledger back on the shelf. "Tell me why the late marquess was selling the Hutton holdings like a Petticoat Lane fence."

"I honestly have no idea."

"It says here the marchioness died five years ago. Do you remember of what?"

"An illness of some sort. But her husband was killed by a highwayman—"

"Near Bath. Yes, I recall reading about it."

Ivory gazed at him with those shrewd eyes of hers. "Is there something else you'd like to share, Alex? Something that you discovered about the Marble Maiden that prompted this little visit? Aside, of course, from the fact that she's a card sharp?"

She is beyond brilliant. And beautiful. And alone. And I want her. For far more than dealing cards. Alex swirled the dregs of his whiskey before downing them in a gulp. When he faced Ivory Moore, his face was arranged neutrally. "She is not what she pretends to be."

"That's a rather cryptic statement, even from you, Alex."

"The town house in which she and her brother live is empty. It echoes the way houses do when devoid of furnishings and whatnot. Nothing on the walls. Nothing on the floors. No servants. No fires lit in the hearths."

"I see." Ivory ran a finger around the rim of her glass. "And exactly when were you in her house?"

"Last night."

"Did she know you were there?"

Alex threw her a disgusted look. "I wasn't housebreaking."

"Of course not. You save those skills for my office." Her lips twitched.

Alex leaned back and set his empty glass next to Ivory's. "Her brother had too much to drink. She needed assistance getting him home, and I was in a position to help her. I suspect that the Hutton family carriage has been sold right along with the art and the silverware. And every coal mine and sheep pasture." He paused. "You see where I'm going with this, Duchess?"

"It suggests that the current marquess and his family

are living in somewhat…diminished circumstances, though they've managed to maintain an admirable façade."

Alex moved to the end of the ornate Chippendale bookcase that sat alongside the recessed shelves of ledgers. He leaned his shoulder into the bookcase and rolled it neatly sideways, concealing the existence of the shelves and their contents. "The façade will have been paid for with the silverware," he mused. "But I want to know what happened to the fortune old Hutton systematically and secretly amassed."

"Why do you care? The marquess could have invested in something else. Maybe he felt moved to give his fortune to the poor. Or to the church. You know as well as I do that what a peer chooses to do with his money is really no concern of ours. Until they hire us to make it our concern, of course."

Ivory was right. What the old Marquess of Hutton had done with his money and his estate was none of his business. And if the new marquess wanted to drink away whatever remained of it, then that wasn't really his business either. Lady Angelique had not asked him for help nor had she confided anything to him. In fact, she'd likely be horrified to know just how much he knew. But he couldn't simply walk away from her.

Especially after he'd almost kissed her.

"I—" He never got a chance to reply before there was a brisk knock on the door, and he was almost relieved. He strode over and pulled the door open, finding a young boy of approximately nine years wearing neat livery. "Good morning, Roderick," Alex greeted.

"Oh, good morning, Mr. Alex. I didn't know you were here," the boy exclaimed, his eyes wide.

Alex swung the door open. "You saw me come in, Roderick. You were hiding in that hall alcove."

The boy's face fell. "How could you possibly know that?" he grumbled as he brushed by Alex. "I made sure you couldn't see me."

"True. But your surprised reaction to my presence would be more appropriate had a trained gorilla opened the door. Your acting was terrible. I thought you were working on that."

"I am. I've been practicing with Miz Elise."

"Then perhaps my sister has not emphasized that, if you truly want people to believe you, less is more. Too much accentuation always draws attention."

"Huh." Roderick ran a scrawny hand through his dark hair.

"Is there something you need, Roderick?" Ivory asked, coming to join Alex by the door.

"Yes." The boy straightened his bony shoulders as though preparing himself to announce a monarch. "The Harris brothers are here to see you, Duchess."

"See? Now that I believed," Alex said. "That was well done, Roddy."

The boy scowled. "I'm not making that up."

"There are a gang of thieves wishing an audience with the Duchess at—" He reached for his timepiece, but found his pocket empty. He sighed and held out a hand. "My watch, Roderick."

The boy offered him a cheeky grin but reached into his own pocket and retrieved the simple piece. "You should chain it. Not much of a challenge, Mr. Alex."

"I'll keep that in mind. And when your acting ability matches your ability to pick pockets, I'll hire you myself. In the meantime"—Alex consulted the face of his timepiece—"is half of seven in the morning not a tad early to be meeting with thieves?"

"They're not thieves anymore," Roderick clarified. "They are gentlemen since they got rich and retired."

"Right. That explains everything then." He turned to Ivory. "Were you expecting them?"

"No." She shrugged. "But I'll be glad to see them. Send them in, please, Roddy."

"Very good." The boy brightened and disappeared.

"Are they returning something they stole?" Alex asked dryly.

"No." Ivory frowned. "Why?"

"You sounded awfully pleased at their presence."

"I'm pleased that they are here. Their retirement has left a hole for me to fill, and I confess, I haven't been able to do it very effectively. There are not as many men as you would think whose skill with weapons is matched only with an incredible knowledge of the London streets."

The sound of booted feet approaching the doorway made them both turn. There were three brothers, all of differing heights, but all had the same dark hair, the same dark eyes, and the same hard look that long years of soldiering had carved into their faces. The last time Alex had seen them, they were dressed to blend in with the working masses at the London docks, but this morning they looked like . . . gentlemen. They were dressed well, if plainly, each sporting hair that was a lot shorter than he remembered and clean-shaven faces. They looked like a thousand other men who might be found walking London's streets. Alex might have passed by them without recognizing them.

The tallest one doffed his hat and offered some sort of awkward bow toward Ivory. "'Morning, Duchess," he said almost bashfully, clearly the spokesperson for the trio.

"Good morning, Mr. Harris." Ivory's face creased into a smile, and her greeting encompassed all of them. "You remember my colleague, Mr. Lavoie?"

Three sets of eyes turned in his direction, followed by an assortment of murmured greetings.

"I must say, this is a surprise. What can I do for you?"

The men's attention returned to Ivory, and the tallest stepped forward. "Ah yes." His eyes darted around the room. "We were just wonderin' if..." He trailed off. "We don't mean any disrespect from this, ye understand," he tried again. "'Specially since you've been so good to us an' all, what with that last job."

"Your payment was well-earned," Ivory commented.

"It's just that..."

Beside him, the shortest of the three brothers made an impatient noise. "Me brother wants to know if ye might have any more work for us. We like eatin' regular like and wearin' warm clothes, but the truth o' the matter is, we're bored." Tall Harris looked relieved at his brother's bluntness.

"Ah. I see."

"We'd not need to go t' stealin'," Tall Harris said. "But maybe ye've got something you need fetched. Retrieved. From a difficult place, like?"

"I have to confess, I am delighted to hear that your services are once again available," Ivory said. "Unfortunately, I don't have anything that needs to be...fetched at the moment."

Three faces fell in the same manner that Roddy's had.

"Well, ye'll let us know if something changes?" Tall Harris asked.

"Of course."

The brothers turned to leave.

"I know you're good at fetching. How are you at following?" Alex's words stopped them in their tracks. He ignored the questioning glance Ivory shot in his direction.

"The best," Tall Harris replied. "You want the bloke to know about it or no?"

"I have no interest in intimidation. Yet," Alex replied,

continuing to ignore Ivory's raised brows. "There are two people I wish followed. Discreetly. *Very* discreetly. Make note of where they go. Who they speak to. What they do. If they spend any money, and what they spend it on. Anything else of interest that you witness. Report back to me tomorrow evening, early, before my club opens." The idea had been impulsive, but the more he thought about it, the more he liked it.

"Understood, Mr. Lavoie."

Behind Tall Harris, Ivory had crossed her arms.

"If you care to wait just outside, I'll be there shortly to provide details and finalize our arrangement," Alex said smoothly. "I just need a moment with the Duchess."

"Of course." The Harrises were all grinning broadly as they shuffled out.

"Well, that was fortunate timing," Alex said as the door shut behind them.

"You're going to pay to have the Marble Maiden followed?" Ivory said, a little incredulously.

Alex frowned. "Yes, I am going to have Lady Angelique followed. More importantly, I'm going to have her wastrel of a brother followed."

"Why?"

Alex cleared his throat. "Like I said, I want to hire Lady Angelique. And therefore, I need to know everything about her, and about her immediate family. I despise it when skeletons pop out of closets and make messes all over my floors." There, that sounded coolly professional and logical. "Further, I'd consider it a favor, Duchess, if you might do whatever it is you do and see what you can discover about the Archer family that hasn't yet made it into those ledgers of yours."

Ivory unfolded her arms across her chest and regarded him. "Very well. I'll see what I can find out."

"Thank you." If anyone could bleed information from a stone when it came to London society, Ivory Moore could. He strode to the door.

"Where are you going?" Ivory asked, recrossing her arms.

"I've a few errands to attend to. Then home." Alex squinted slightly at the morning sunlight streaming into the room. "It's way past my bedtime."

⁓

It was the late morning sunlight streaming through the windows that woke Angelique. She'd never closed the curtains properly when she'd finally stumbled into bed sometime before dawn, collapsing in an exhausted stupor. Though as tired as she was, sleep had been a long time coming. Because after everything that had transpired last night, it was Alexander Lavoie's words that thrummed through her mind, just as sure as they thrummed through her body.

I think you and I would be very good together.

She had wanted to experience just how good, if only for a moment. Because Angelique was beginning to suspect that her education in the pursuit of pleasure had been horribly ... inadequate. Last night had been a debacle, but for a few stolen moments Alexander Lavoie had made her feel wanted. Admired. Desired. And just the thought of Alexander Lavoie's touch on her skin and his mouth so close to hers had her squirming anew, that restless, throbbing ache beginning to drum a steady beat at her very core. Her hand drifted over her breasts, her belly, and that very sensitive spot beneath the thin layer of her chemise. She closed her eyes, her hips arching. What would it be like to have his lips on hers? What would it feel like to have his hands on her like this? His heat against her bare skin, his fingers delving lower and lower—her eyes flew open, and she snatched her hand back from where it had strayed. What was she doing?

She lay on her back in a mess of twisted sheets and stared up at the ceiling, feeling her cheeks burn and watching dust motes dance in the sunbeams. Around her, the house was silent as a tomb, and for once, she was glad for it. This was why she couldn't ever work for Alexander Lavoie. She was reasonably sure she could get over the idea of a lady working in a gambling hell, dealing vingt-et-un and divesting gentlemen of small fortunes. She could come to terms with the possibility that she might be recognized. She could accept that she was no longer a lady, but an employee, no different than any Drury Lane actress. She could get over all that.

But she could not get over Alexander Lavoie.

She wasn't even sure if she'd ever be able to gamble in his establishment again with any degree of focus or concentration. He was a gentleman and then something far more dangerous all at once. And she found she liked them both far too much.

She sat up, forcing her mind away from selfish desires. She had a great deal to accomplish today. First was to make arrangements for payment to the school for the twins' tuition. Harrow was not a tavern where the proprietor might be put off for a while longer with a sunny smile and earnest promises. The directors had been letting their displeasure at her delinquency be known, though she had managed to stall them with a long list of excuses citing the transition of funds from her late father to the current Marquess of Hutton. But she was on borrowed time, and they all knew it. Best to get the matter of the boys' tuition settled immediately.

Whatever was left over would be earmarked for household expenses. The collier needed to be paid. The pantries needed to be replenished. And Angelique would also need to have a long, serious conversation with Gerald about his actions last night. She wasn't sure it would do much good, but she had to try.

Because it had to stop.

Angelique swung her legs around and sat on the edge of the bed and glanced toward the window. Good Lord, but it must almost be midday. When she had finally found sleep, it seemed that she had slept the sleep of the dead. Next to the window, her gold gown lay crumpled in a pile of silk on the floor. Angelique frowned. She hadn't left it on the floor. She'd left her gown draped over the chair under the window, the skirts hiding her reticule—

No, no, no, no. Angelique lurched from the bed, stumbling over to where the gown lay. She snatched it from the floor, already knowing it was too late, but needing to look anyway. She shook the fabric before tossing it on the bed, dropping to her hands and knees in front of the chair. But it was for nothing.

Her reticule was gone. The money was gone.

For a moment, she thought she might be sick. She drew in shuddering breaths, fighting the urge to retch. And then in the next instant, a fury like she had never known before rose up, leaving black spots dancing at the edge of her vision. Without considering what she was doing, she shoved herself to her feet and bolted to the door, running down the hall. She wrenched open the door to Gerald's rooms to find his clothes from last night in a heap on the floor, a towel flung over the end of the bed, and a half-full basin of soapy water on the washstand, his shaving tools scattered on the surface next to it. But of her brother there was no sign. Angelique bolted from the room and pounded down the staircase.

The hall was deserted, only the blanket that she had covered Gerald with last night draped over the small table in the middle of the hall. A door creaked open from behind her, and Angelique whirled, finding Tildy standing behind her, a small pitcher of water clutched in her gnarled fingers. The woman uttered a startled squeak of surprise as she looked up.

"Where is Gerald?" Angelique demanded hoarsely.

"I—I don't know." The woman was blinking rapidly. "His lordship left, milady."

"Left? When?"

"'Bout an hour ago." The water pitcher trembled in Tildy's hands.

Angelique focused on taking deep, calming breaths. "Did he say where he was going?" Perhaps it was possible to find him. Intercept him before he did something stupid like spend the money that would keep his young brothers in school.

"S—said he was looking to find a new coat. Something about his last one being ruined? And then off to a club?" Faded blue eyes watched Angelique from under a fringe of grey hair with apprehension. "He was in finer spirits than he's been in a long time," the housekeeper offered hopefully.

Oh God. Gerald had taken the money right from her room, and she'd slept through it. She wanted to rail at Tildy, demand to know why the housekeeper hadn't woken her, demand to know why the woman had let Gerald leave the house. But none of this was Tildy's fault. The poor woman hadn't even known about the money, and she couldn't have stopped Gerald from leaving even if she had wanted to. This was Angelique's fault and her fault alone. She should have done a better job hiding the money. She should have put it under her mattress, under her pillow. She should have traveled directly to Harrow from Lavoie's and put the damn money in the directors' hands herself. She wrapped her arms around her waist. How had Gerald even known she'd had it?

And the money wasn't even all hers. The thought made

her blood run cold. Some of that money was Lavoie's—
an advance that she had planned to return to him when she
declined his offer of employment. She swallowed with difficulty, sweat prickling at her scalp.

"Do you know what direction he might have gone?" Angelique asked the housekeeper who was still standing frozen
in front of her.

"No, milady. Is everything all right, milady?"

"No," Angelique managed. "Everything is not all right. It
hasn't been all right for a long time."

Without another word, Angelique spun and hurried back
up the stairs. Standing in the middle of a hall served no purpose. She needed to go and find Gerald before it was too
late. If she was lucky, he'd still be at the tailor, or possibly
the draper, selecting fabric. If she was lucky, she'd catch up
to him and get whatever remained of that money back.

Chapter 5

Angelique hadn't been lucky.

She hadn't managed to find Gerald, though she had spent the entire day trying. Out of desperation, she'd even gone to the homes of Burleigh and Seaton, only to be told that the men were not in, nor were they aware when the young masters might be expected. Angelique hadn't bothered leaving a message for either. No doubt that wherever Gerald was, Seaton and Burleigh were too.

Angelique had no idea what time it was when she finally made it home, but it was well after midnight, her feet blistered and sore, almost faint with hunger, and more discouraged and hopeless than she had ever felt in her life. She crossed the empty hall and started up the stairs. She made it to the third before her legs finally gave out and she sank down, too weary and too heartsick to move. She leaned against the wall, her head swimming.

Angelique must assume that the gold that had been in that reticule was gone. To hope otherwise was not realistic, nor was it helpful. So what she needed to do was examine the current options available to her. The first option was to sell this townhome. It was one of the few things left that had yet to be sold. But she couldn't do that by herself. Only Gerald could sell this house. And even if he did agree to it, finding a buyer would take time. Time she and the twins did not have.

The second option was to withdraw the twins from school and head north. She might be able to find a job as a governess on one of the big estates, though a position that would also welcome two young boys might be difficult to find.

There was no family to reach out to. Her grandparents were long since dead and buried, and both her father and mother had been only children. Whatever remained of her mother's extended family resided somewhere in America, and her father had been the last of the Archer line until Gerald was born. The idea of giving up her independence and throwing herself on the charity of some very distant cousin who would feel compelled to take her in was not appealing. It was the last resort, and if all else failed, she might yet do it for the good of the twins. But not until she ran out of options. And there was still one left.

Accept Alexander Lavoie's offer.

To be honest, she wasn't sure if she had any choice. Lavoie had given her an advance in good faith. And while Angelique might not have much, she had honor. And pride. She would pay him back, if not in coin, then in service. And perhaps, if he could forgive this, and if her performance at the vingt-et-un table was good enough, he might be persuaded to offer her another advance. Enough to at least stay the directors at Harrow.

Angelique wrapped her arms around her knees and drew them up, resting her forehead on them and closing her eyes.

She could do this. She would do this. This...loss, while a setback, was not the end of the world. There was always a way forward. She had gotten through worse.

The sound of the door slamming shut startled her, and the muscles in her neck protested as her head jerked up. Good God, had she dozed off at the foot of the stairs? The sound of booted feet striding unevenly across the empty hall echoed around her, accompanied by an off-key humming.

Gerald was home. At least he was still walking on his own. Angelique waited for the rage she had felt earlier to rise up, to power the confrontation she knew was coming, but she found she had nothing left. There was a great yawning emptiness inside of her, with only remnants of sadness and resignation clinging to the edges.

"Oy!" Gerald had reached the stairs and nearly stepped on her. "Ang, is that you?" There was a fumbling noise, a low curse, and then a candle flared to life. Her brother pushed the stub he held in his hand toward her. "It *is* you. Whatever are you doing sitting on the stairs in the dark?"

"Where were you?" she asked dully. There was a sickly sweet odor that clung to his clothes. His blue eyes were bloodshot, and his blond hair was as rumpled as his clothing. A bruise had purpled the side of his temple, a reminder of last night.

"Here and there." He grinned and peered at her. "I'm glad I found you. I have something for you." He fumbled in his pocket and pulled out a small blue velvet bag drawn closed with a narrow ribbon.

"What is this?" she asked, accepting it as he thrust it into her hands.

"A present," he said. "An apology."

Angelique pulled at the string and tipped the contents of the bag into the palm of her hand. A pair of earbobs gleamed dully in the weak light, mother of pearl edged in gold. She stared at them, unmoving, her heart sinking even further.

"I understand that some of my actions might have been injudicious last evening. I was not at my finest, I admit."

"Injudicious." Angelique repeated it, not quite believing what she was hearing.

"Yes. But Ang, can you blame me? You simply cannot be anywhere near Lavoie's. And worse, by yourself. Do you know what kind of club that is? And what your presence there looks like? And to be consorting with a man like that—"

"A man like what?" A spark of anger flared.

Gerald blinked at her. "Lavoie. He's a devil, Ang, with a reputation. A dangerous reputation that you cannot be tainted with. But don't worry. Seaton and Burleigh have promised that they won't say anything."

"Oh, they have, have they? How very magnanimous of them."

For the first time, Gerald looked as though he realized that something was off. "Ang? Is something wrong?"

Everything was wrong. Angelique dropped her head. "Where did you get the money for these?" She held out the earbobs.

Gerald faltered. "Ah yes. About that. I came up to see if you might have a few coins for a sausage pie. I was hungry, and there was nothing to eat in the kitchen. I didn't want to wake you—you looked so tired." He was yanking at the knot in his cravat. "I didn't think you would mind."

"There isn't anything left, is there?"

His hand fell away from his cravat. Gerald shook his head. "No."

It was what she already knew but it still felt like she'd been slapped.

"I don't have it but it's not like…" he trailed off. "Jesus, Ang, are you crying?" He looked stricken.

Angelique put a hand to her face to find that she was. Tears were escaping unchecked, sliding down her cheeks and dripping from her chin. God, she hated crying. Tears only ever made her skin blotchy, her eyes puffy, and solved nothing. She was quite sure Gerald had never seen her cry. "You're a fool," she said. "That money was important."

"You think I don't know that?" Gerald bristled. "I'm not a complete idiot."

Angelique swiped angrily at her eyes. "No? Do you even know how you got home last night?"

"Yes," Gerald said defensively. "Well, sort of. But I know I was trying to protect you."

"Protect me? You almost shot me!"

"What?" Gerald frowned. "No, that's not possible."

"You had a gun, and you were pretending to be a highwayman."

Her brother was shaking his head. "Burleigh and Seaton said nothing of that. They only said my actions were honorable, given the circumstances in which we found you."

She pressed her fingers to her temples. "Of course they would say that." She looked up. "Where did the gun come from, Gerald?"

He still looked confused. "I don't know. Burleigh always carries one under his coat. He's always afraid he'll get set upon by footpads or the like."

Angelique rubbed her face with her hands. There was no point in reliving the events of last night. It was the events of this morning that were critical. "Where did the money go?" That was what was important.

"I had to get a new coat. And food, of course. But the rest I invested with Seaton."

"I beg your pardon?" Angelique's head came up at that. Perhaps not all was lost. Perhaps it would be possible to retrieve what was left.

"Seaton and his father have invested in a shipping company. They offered me a chance to buy in. Ang, it was an opportunity I could not pass up—the cargos these ships bring in are worth a king's ransom. The payment went to the company this afternoon, and those who were smart enough to invest early will become rich."

"Rich?" Angelique repeated, the hope she had felt withering. "Wasn't that what Seaton told you last time you gave him money to invest?"

"There were storms that sunk those ships," Gerald protested. "Who could have predicted that sort of bad luck?"

"You're sure that the ships actually existed?"

Gerald stared at her. "Just what are you implying?"

Angelique stared back. "What kind of shipping company is it?"

"Nothing you would have heard of."

"Try me." Perhaps she could petition the company directly.

"It doesn't matter."

"It doesn't matter or it doesn't exist?"

Her brother recoiled. "You can't possibly think Seaton would lie to me?"

"You don't really want to know what I think your friends are capable of," she muttered bitterly.

Gerald scowled. "Seaton has gone out of his way to introduce me to the right people with the right connections. Taken me to all the right places. And Burleigh has always been there for me. He was still grieving the death of his father when Mother became ill, but he was a great support through it all. And he's helped me with money all the times I find myself short, even though he's hardly rich."

Angelique closed her eyes, a sound of frustration escaping.

"I don't know what your problem is, Ang."

Her eyes flew open. "My problem is that the money you stole from my room was for the twins' tuition. Among other things."

"How was I supposed to know that?" he said defensively.

"Because you're not a boy anymore. You're supposed to be a man. You're supposed to be the damn marquess!" she cried. "Yet the only person you can think of is you. The only needs you care about are your own."

"That's not true. I invested that money for us. To help *us*. You're not being fair."

"Nothing is fair, Gerald. This isn't a game."

"I know that. I'm trying. But it's hard."

"Hard?" she repeated. "I reckon telling Phillip and Gregory why they were expelled from school will be harder."

"Expelled? The school can't do that!" Gerald sputtered.

"They can and they will." Angelique wiped her face with her hands.

"They won't say no to a marquess. I'll talk to them."

"You already have."

"What?"

"I've written many letters on your behalf, citing delays with funds, paperwork, the general confusion following the death of our father. They've been patient. Until now."

His face had gone red. "Can't you send them something? A partial payment? I'll come up with the rest later."

"There is nothing to send, Gerald." Angelique hauled herself to her feet.

He caught her arm. "Don't be mad. Please. I care. I do. I'll get the money."

"How?"

"I don't know. Maybe Burleigh can lend me what we need."

"Burleigh doesn't have that kind of money. You know that as well as I."

Gerald looked unhappy. "Then I'll talk to the solicitors again. They must have missed something."

Angelique made a rude noise. "They haven't missed anything. But we can sell this house. And the boys don't have to attend Harrow."

A shadow of appalled indignation crossed her brother's face. "No. Every male in this family has attended Harrow for generations. I will not take them out. Father would never consider it if he were alive, and nor will I. And where would we live while we were in London if not here? Some hovel in St Giles? I have some pride, Ang, and you should too."

"I can't afford pride at the moment, Gerald. And neither can you." Angelique pulled on her sleeve still caught in his fingers. "Just let me go. Just leave me alone."

Her brother released her. "Look, I'm sorry, Ang, I am. I'll make it up to you. I promise."

"Your promises don't hold much value anymore," she replied tiredly.

"I can remedy that."

"I don't think you can."

"I'll prove you wrong." His jaw was set in a manner that hadn't changed since he was four.

Angelique turned and began climbing the stairs, concentrating on putting one foot in front of the other. The earbobs were still in her hand, the edges cutting into her flesh. She'd sell them in the morning. But she didn't bother replying.

She'd stopped believing in fairy tales a long time ago.

Chapter 6

She looked a little like something out of a fairy tale.

No, not a fairy tale, Alex thought, for a fairy tale seemed inadequate. She was dressed in her gold gown, the bare skin at her shoulders and plunging décolletage just as breathtaking as he remembered. Her hair was pinned up again, though the wind or time had released strands to frame her face and trail over her bare shoulders. She was vibrant, this woman, in a way that was completely at odds with the watery, willowy beauty that seemed so popular in current society. She could be Frejya or Aphrodite. A goddess meant to be worshipped. A woman of provocative sensuality made only that much more irresistible by her brilliance hidden within.

And she had come back to him.

Alex rose from behind his desk immediately. "Thank you, Jenkins," he said to the enormous man who had escorted Lady Angelique to his office. "Please close the door on your way out."

Jenkins nodded and disappeared as discreetly as he had arrived.

Angelique was left standing just inside the door. Her eyes, shadowed by the decorated mask she wore, surveyed his office before coming to rest unerringly on him. He felt the impact of her gaze spark along every nerve ending in his body. She straightened her shoulders and started forward.

Alex watched her approach, his brows drawing together slightly. She was holding herself stiffly, like a soldier preparing to throw herself into the breach. What he could see of her face was devoid of color, and her hands were clenched at her sides.

Given what the Harris brothers had told him the evening prior, Alex had a very good idea why. Of Gerald Archer, there had been a long list of places he had gone and things he had done with what had appeared to be a wealth of gold coin. Lady Angelique, on the other hand, had flown from the house late in the morning, appearing quite agitated, and spent the day wandering the streets of London, frantically asking after her brother.

Alex was assuming the young marquess had taken her money without her knowledge or acquiescence. Yet Alex wasn't sure what he should do about it, if anything. The honorable part of him would like to skewer the man for the distress he'd caused his sister. The other, darker part of him was pleased that Hutton's selfish, idiotic actions may have just forced this extraordinary woman back to his door.

"Good evening, my lady," he said, coming to meet her as she approached his desk. He caught a faint whiff of her scent—not flowery, as one might expect from a genteel lady, but something more exotic. Stronger.

"Good evening, Mr. Lavoie."

"You're stunning."

That seemed to startle her. She glanced up at him, her eyes wide beneath a swath of brilliant teal feathers that decorated the brow of her mask. "Um, thank you."

He clasped his hands behind his back, as if to remind himself that this was business. Not pleasure. "I'm glad you've returned. I hope you've had some time to consider my earlier offer?"

"Yes." She was worrying her upper lip with her teeth, and Alex had to look away. The force of his desire to kiss her was disturbing.

He waited for her to continue, but she seemed to have run out of words. At her sides, she'd unclenched her hands, but her fingers were now twisting the silk of her skirts.

"Yes, you've considered and have come to let me down gently? Or yes, you've considered and we might now begin what I believe will be a prosperous partnership?" he asked carefully.

Her fingers stilled. "I've come to accept your offer, Mr. Lavoie."

He'd been expecting it, but that didn't stop the fierce thrill of satisfaction that gripped him. "You have no idea how pleased I am to hear that."

"Might I start now? Tonight?"

Alex schooled his expression to reflect nothing but mild interest. There was an edge of something in her voice that she was trying to hide. The same something that was still evident in her rigid bearing. Desperation. Determination. Both. "You're very...enthusiastic."

"I see no value in procrastination. Once the theaters let out, your gaming floor will fill, as it does every night. Why wait?"

"A sound argument, indeed, my lady," he said finally. In the muted light of his office, her eyes were the color of a stormy sea, though it was hard to read them. "Take off your mask." He needed to see her face before this conversation could continue. Too much of her expression was hidden.

She hesitated but then did as he asked. Her eyes met his without flinching.

"Why did you agree to do this? Work for me?" he asked.

"Because you asked."

"You could have said no."

"No, I couldn't." It was barely a whisper, but he heard it echo loudly through the tattered remains of her pride.

Alex unclasped his hands and reached for one of hers, finding her skin cold against the heat of his palm. "You walked here again," he commented quietly.

"It was a lovely evening." Angelique pulled her hand away from his.

"Mmmm." They both knew she was lying. The air still held the bite of early spring and was far from lovely. "From now on, you will have the full use of my carriage."

"That is not—"

"Please don't argue. You will not win."

She fell silent. "Then I thank you," she said after a moment.

"You're welcome."

"There is another matter I wished to discuss with you, Mr. Lavoie, regarding my employment." She lifted her chin.

"Indeed. How much do you need?" he asked.

She jerked like she'd been struck. "I beg your pardon?"

"How much money do you need?"

Her throat worked, but nothing came out. For a moment, Alex wondered if he'd been wrong, until he heard her breath catch and saw her shoulders slump almost imperceptibly.

"I am happy to advance you whatever sum you require," he said, striving for a casual tone, as though this type of situation was something he experienced every day.

"Why would you do that?" she rasped.

"Because you asked." He turned her own answer back on her.

She seemed to be struggling to find words. "But I didn't—"

"And because I can. Because I meant what I said earlier. I can help. With whatever you need." He meant every word of that, and the fervor that accompanied that declaration unsettled him. He'd long since abandoned his white horse and shining armor in favor of shrewd business and profitable commerce. Unless, of course, he was being paid to ride into battle.

She closed her eyes briefly. "My younger brothers attend Harrow. With the death of my father, some funds have been...still are...um, unavailable. Their tuition is past due. I do not wish to withdraw them."

"Of course not." Unavailable? That was one way to put it. "I will make arrangements with the school directly and see it done."

She looked up at him in startled shock. "That is not necessary," she said. "I can—"

"I'll see it done," Alex repeated. Alexander Lavoie was one of the wealthiest men in London, though there were few that were aware of that fact. He could easily pay the tuition of every student currently attending Harrow. Hell, he could probably buy the damn school should he take a notion to do so.

"Then I thank you." She was still looking at him uncertainly.

"Will you be requiring a personal advance as well on the week's wages?"

She looked down. "If you can spare it." It was barely audible.

"It is of no issue to me, my lady, when you choose to get paid," he said carelessly.

"I'll repay you with interest, of course." Lady Angelique met his eye again.

"Very good." He wasn't going to further assault her pride by arguing. "You'll have your money at the end of the night."

"Just like that?"

"Would you prefer it now?"

"No. I...er...no." She cleared her throat. "Thank you."

"No need to thank me," he said. "I am more than happy to accommodate such. Your abilities will benefit us both many times over." Alex reached across his desk and retrieved the crystal decanter of whiskey. He poured himself a measure, if only to give his hands something to do besides touching her again. "If there is anything you require assistance with in the future, please do not hesitate to ask. A good partnership requires a certain amount of trust between individuals, would you not agree?"

"Yes." It didn't sound convincing.

"Is there anything else I should know? Whatever you tell me in this office will remain in the strictest of confidence, of course."

"No." Clearly, she was not going to confide in him. Yet.

"Mmmm. Is there anything you would like to know? About this club? Anything you'd like to ask me?"

She opened her mouth and then closed it again, as if she had reconsidered whatever she was going to say. Her shoulders once again straightened, and her tone, when she spoke, was brisk. "Have you given any thought to the formula you would like me to run?"

Alex nearly lost his grip on the decanter. "I beg your pardon?"

"At least a few of your patrons will need to achieve

moderate success, and the occasional player will need to achieve considerable success at the vingt-et-un table if you hope to attract those individuals whose pocketbooks match their greed and belief that the next hand will change their fortune. I will require instruction as to how you wish me to deal in order to maximize both profits and popularity." She withdrew a small square of paper from a hidden pocket somewhere in the folds of her skirts and held it out to him. "I've run some scenarios, allowing for a margin of error that I will not be able to avoid. It's all basic accounting worked into a matrix of probabilities, but I thought you might want to review it."

Alex very carefully replaced the heavy crystal on the surface of his desk, struggling to draw a breath. This was not good at all. Forget his alarming charge into the fray on a white horse, he was rather afraid he had just fallen in love.

"You've put thought into this," he said evenly, accepting the paper from her outstretched hand.

"Of course. I take pride in my capabilities, Mr. Lavoie. And I do not wish to be in your debt any longer than necessary."

He unfolded the paper and examined the neat lines of numbers and the slanted, bold handwriting. In an instant, he saw that she had provided estimations for earnings using a variety of strategies, depending on predetermined rules.

"You'll see that all probabilities are calculated for cases using either one or two decks. Of course, removing various cards from the game will also affect the outcomes, as will capping the dealer at a particular score during each game." She paused. "I wasn't sure what you had in mind."

He had nothing in mind, because his brain had ceased to function. He found himself staring at her, his heart pounding and desire shredding whatever remaining wits he had.

"Have I overstepped?" She was biting her lip again, though she met his eyes steadily.

"No." It came out hoarsely. "God, no." Bloody hell, he needed to pull himself together. He put the sheet on his desk next to the decanter. "You have impressed me immeasurably, Lady Angelique."

He was rewarded with a smile, one that actually reached her eyes, and the first one he had seen all night. "Good," was all she said.

Alex cleared his throat and took a judicious step back. Angelique Archer debating gaming strategies would be hard to resist. Angelique Archer smiling at him while she did so would reduce him to an ignoble puddle. He may not have his wits, but he too still had some pride.

"Before we get to that"—he jerked his chin in the direction of her equations—"there is another detail to be dealt with regarding your employment here. Less important, but necessary all the same." He sent a pointed look at the faint mud stains on the hem of her dress. "The matter of your attire."

Her smile faltered. "I don't have anything—"

"I am aware." He left her where she stood and retrieved a long, flat box from the back of his office. He returned to place the unwieldy package across the top of his desk.

"What is that?" she asked warily.

"A gown."

"For me?"

"Yes. I've discovered the color doesn't complement my complexion. And the skirts show too much of my ankle. The ladies might riot."

She frowned. "Very funny."

"If you recall, we discussed the matter of your gown the last time we met in my office."

"We didn't discuss anything. You made…comments."

"Mmmm." He smiled faintly. "Well, in this case, I was simply being—"

"Presumptuous?" Her eyes narrowed slightly as she glanced down at the box.

"See now, I was going to say *prepared*. I do hate to point out the obvious, but here we find ourselves."

He saw a muscle tighten along the side of her jaw.

"Come, my lady. Open it. Take a look. See if it meets your approval."

He watched as Angelique opened the box and peeled back the layer of fine paper. Her hand stilled, and he heard the soft exhalation of her breath. She reached into the box, touching the smooth satin silk with her fingertips almost reverently. It was the color of tropical seas, a sparkling, incandescent turquoise. He had imagined what her skin would look like against that exotic color, the perfect foil for her radiance. He had envisioned the way the bodice would sweep low across the tops of her breasts, the delicate gold and white embroidery along the bodice subtle, yet striking. He had pictured the way the satin would caress each and every curve before flowing over from her waist. What he hadn't imagined was the way her eyes softened or the way she had pressed a hand against her lips.

He moved closer, never taking his eyes off her. The expression on her face made every penny he had spent on the gown worth it. The fabric had been imported, and it had been expensive, made more so by the herculean demands he had made on the army of seamstresses he'd tasked with having the gown ready. He would have paid it ten times over.

She turned to him and he could see the conflicted emotion on her face.

"The gown is exquisite, Mr. Lavoie. But it's too much. I can't possibly accept—"

"You can and you will." He was careful to keep his tone businesslike. "The patrons of my club expect glamour, extravagance, opulence." *And you deserve that and more.* "This is another argument you won't win, my lady. If you wish to work your probabilities behind my vingt-et-un table, you will do so dressed in a manner befitting this establishment." He congratulated himself on the detached, slightly mercenary way that had come out. It was better than confessing he had wanted to gift her with something beautiful. And it was far better than admitting he wanted to see her dressed more magnificently than any other woman.

Her eyes strayed back to the box. She reached for the gown and drew it from its wrappings, the satin slipping soundlessly across the desk and to the floor. She held it up to her chest, smoothing a hand down the front. "I've never seen anything like it. It's incredible."

"Try it on."

She faltered. "Now?"

"I see no value in procrastination," he said, turning her words on her again. "If the gown requires alterations, it will need to be attended to promptly, though I am reasonably confident in the fit. I am a fair judge of women's measurements."

Her nostrils flared, and her lips thinned.

"Ah. You've heard about my harem," he said with no little sarcasm.

She blushed furiously, but her chin rose a notch. "Yes. And it sounds positively exhausting."

A laugh escaped, surprising him. "Doesn't it?"

"Please be assured that I am not often inclined to believe everything I hear."

"Unfortunate. A reputation, such as the one I have as a lover, is a tricky thing to maintain. Sensible people such as yourself are a detriment to good gossip."

Her lips twitched before she seemed to catch herself. "It is not any of my business, Mr. Lavoie, whatever means you use to entertain yourself."

Alex picked up his glass, studying the pattern of the cut crystal. "On the contrary, my lady. Women use me. I am a dangerous distraction from their reality. I am the scandalous, wicked adventure that they crave in their ordinary, boring lives. And on the rare occasions when it suits me, I let them use me, because I derive pleasure from it too." He raised his eyes to hers to find a dark blond eyebrow arched in his direction.

"And this makes you happy?"

His fingers tightened on his glass. What an absurd question. "It has never made me unhappy."

She watched him for a long moment, and he found himself resisting the urge to squirm like a boy. Which was even more absurd. "Despite my reputation, my lady, rest assured my skill in measurements comes not from my harem, but from my sister. Who always seems to require a wide range of…garments, but is often not around for fitting." Just why the hell was he explaining himself? Since when did he need to justify himself to anyone?

"Your sister."

"Yes."

"Does she live here? In London?"

"Mostly."

"Does she work at your club?"

"She has, on occasion."

"What does she think of your reputation?"

Alex chuckled. "Perhaps, if you ever meet her, you should ask."

Angelique's head tipped. "You also have a reputation as an assassin," she said.

"Mmmm. It's a wonder I have time to eat breakfast with all I do."

"Are you? An assassin?"

"Would it matter?"

"That's not an answer."

"Do you need someone killed?"

She blinked. "Not at the moment."

"Just as well. I am fully engaged until mid-October."

Angelique was still watching him, though she had a thoughtful expression on her face now. "You find this all amusing." There was no criticism in her words, just a faint note of wonder.

"Generally, yes. Though mostly, I find it useful. Reputations—public opinion—can be manipulated to achieve one's objectives with startling efficiency."

"Not always," she muttered. Her expression had darkened.

"Ah. You're referring to your past reputation."

"I beg your pardon?" Her forehead creased.

"The Marble Maiden."

Angelique stared at him.

"That was what they called you during your season, didn't they? The marriage mart mamas, the drunken gentlemen, the territorial debutantes."

"How do you know that?" she whispered.

"I know a lot of things, my lady."

She had paled, her earlier color draining. "What does it matter what they thought of me? What they called me?"

"It doesn't."

"Is this you being cruel then?"

"No, this is me being real, my lady. And honest. I want

to know if your past will impede your ability to do your job here."

"I'm not— That makes no sense."

"Aloof. Unapproachable. Cold. That is what—and who—they thought you were. Is that accurate?"

"Yes," she said tightly, though she didn't look away.

"Yet the woman currently standing before me is anything but."

"Is that supposed to be a compliment?"

"Do you want it to be?"

"Does it matter?"

"It's all that matters, my lady."

Her eyes slid away from his, her fingers tracing the embroidery on the edge of the turquoise satin. "At the time of my season, I thought that my future had already—" She stopped abruptly.

"You thought your future had already been what?"

She shook her head. "It's irrelevant now."

Alex rather thought whatever she had been about to say was very relevant. He tried a different tack. "Tell me why they called you the Marble Maiden. What did you present to the world and its observers to cultivate such?"

Angelique's head snapped up. "Nothing."

"I think that is exactly right. But I need you to explain *nothing*."

Her eyes held his. "You're serious."

"Not often. But in this case, yes." He braced himself on the edge of the desk with his arms and studied her. "In my business, opinion and illusion are often one and the same. The illusions I provide here make me a wealthy man. And if you are to work for me, you will need to become a master at it." He'd made her uncomfortable, he knew. More than uncomfortable. Embarrassed. Self-conscious. But she'd stood her ground. Hadn't burst into tears or stormed out. In fact, there was a spark of interest in those intelligent blue eyes. He felt something in his chest squeeze.

"Tell me what *nothing* means," Alex prompted again, aiming for a clinical timbre. "I must insist you tell me as objectively and as honestly as possible."

"Very well." She paused for a long moment. "I wasn't good at the things a lady is supposed to be good at."

"Like what?"

"Dancing. So I didn't dance."

"Ever?"

"Maybe once or twice at the beginning."

"Why?"

"Because I am a terrible dancer. I can't remember even the most basic of steps."

"And did you tell this to your dance partners?"

"Of course not. I was too busy trying not to cripple them." She was looking at him like he'd lost his mind. "Who can't perform a simple waltz?"

"Me. I've never learned."

"I can't imagine assassins need to waltz often," she muttered, though a smile threatened.

"Yes, death by dancing is a horrible way to go." He saw her lips curl. "And I will not require you to waltz behind my vingt-et-un table. So that is immaterial. What else?"

"I could not make charming small talk. I had a hard time pretending to enjoy conversation that held no interest for me. I did try at first, but the redundant, constant comparisons of material things and the spiteful gossip grew wearisome. I...stopped participating after a while."

"Understandable. And also immaterial. I will suggest—no, in fact, *insist*—that you limit any comments and conversation to the cards and the hand being played while you are dealing. I trust you will be both interested and willing to participate in that?"

"Yes. Of course." She was gazing at him in that thoughtful way again.

"So you didn't dance. You didn't gossip. Anything else that you feel distanced you from the masses?"

She looked down at the extravagant gown she still held in her arms. "This may sound shallow and superficial, but my appearance didn't help either, I think. My mother spent a fortune on my gowns for that season. Pretty, pale dresses designed to, ah, disguise the appearance of my..." Angelique extracted a hand from the turquoise satin and made a gesture toward her straining bodice. "In her words, my somewhat unfashionable figure."

"Unfashionable?" Alex felt his jaw drop. Her figure was devastating, with curves that made men stupid. He would know.

"My mother wanted me to look my best. She wanted me to look like a proper, elegant lady. I needed to, she said, if I was to attract the right sort of man. The sort that would treat me like one."

Alex was still trying to understand how anyone could have thought that this woman was anything less than perfection.

Angelique shrugged slightly. "But as such, my gowns were shapeless. Formless. I looked like a wide, pale, ruffled pillar."

"You dressed to please your mother?" It came out a little harsher than he'd intended, but he was angry on her behalf.

"Of course I did. She was dying. Dressing as she wished me to made her happy."

Alex felt his stomach drop. "I'm sorry."

"It was a long time ago. I'm not looking for sympathy.

In her defense, she truly only wanted what was best for me. And in my defense, I was young at the time, and my mother's opinion was very important. I trusted and believed her judgment of my appearance and did my best to hide my flaws." She said it with the objectivity he had asked for, which was good.

Because he had lost all of his.

The urge to put his hands all over those stupefying curves and demonstrate exactly how *fashionable* and *flawless* they really were had his fingers curling so hard around the edge of his desk, he thought he might crack the rosewood. He wondered if any other man had touched her the way he longed to. Or if he would be the first to peel her clothes from her body and pleasure her until she couldn't remember her name. If he would be the first one to feel her come apart beneath him, around him, above him. He wanted to hear her whisper his name, over and over, because once would never be enough—

"Is that sufficient, Mr. Lavoie?" she asked.

Alex jerked. "I'm sorry?"

"My explanation behind my past and unfortunate... illusion."

"Mmmm." He tore his mind from the dark, debauched places it was sliding and reached for the glass of whiskey he'd abandoned on the corner of his desk. He gulped the remains, though the fiery liquid did nothing to clear his head. It only seemed to heat his blood further.

Bloody hell, he was in trouble. "Thank you for your honesty," he managed.

"You're welcome." She had a thoughtful expression on her face again. "But you should know that I am no longer that insecure girl," Lady Angelique continued. "I've learned a great deal in the years since that season.

My past failures will not affect the way in which I conduct myself here."

"I agree."

"You do?"

"You've already proven what you can do with a gold gown and a bottle of my best French brandy."

"Is that supposed to be a compliment?" The question echoed again.

He tipped his head. "Do you want it to be?"

This time, a ghost of a smile touched her lips. "Yes."

"Good. Then consider it such."

"It was never my intention to be different," she said suddenly.

Alex felt his hackles rise at that. He didn't want any other version of this woman than the one who stood before him now. "Different is good."

"Not when one is trying to secure a husband."

"And is that what you wanted? A husband?"

"Isn't that what all well-bred ladies are supposed to want? A husband. A grand house. Pretty gowns. All the things required to make one happy."

"That's not an answer."

She sighed. "I thought that's what I wanted at the time."

"And now?"

She made a low sound in her throat. "No. But there are times I still wonder if a husband might have been . . . helpful."

Alex scoffed. "I must assume you are referring to the current . . . unavailability of your family's funds. You believe a husband would solve whatever dilemma you face?"

"Perhaps," she hedged, suddenly wary. It would seem that, while she was able to discuss her lack of skill on a ballroom dance floor with candor, the topic of her family's mysterious lack of finances was still off-limits.

"I disagree. I say that you have proven that you are more than capable of helping yourself. If you require further assistance, I am not without some small resources, and I come with the added benefit that I will not require you to marry me." He ignored the strange thrill that skittered through him. He wasn't the marrying type, but the idea of such a partnership with this woman and everything that went with it suddenly made the idea a lot more appealing than he'd like.

She stared at him, her eyes wide and her hands frozen on the gown she still held. Her lips had parted slightly, and only the rapid rise and fall of her chest betrayed that she'd heard him.

Aye, he'd never wish to marry her, nor she him, but that didn't mean that they couldn't—

He retreated from that precipice as fast as he could, fleeing to the safe footing of business. "Most of my clientele, at least the ones who will part with large sums, are men. Your beauty will catch their attention. The mystery that will surround you will hold it. You will be enigmatic, but not remote. Unaffected, but not unaware. Men will vie for the privilege of playing at the table you control and compete for the opportunity to lose money to you."

"They will?" She was eyeing him skeptically now.

"You don't believe me?"

"No."

"Why?"

"Because I'm not that woman. I'll admit to intelligence. And I certainly possess...physical assets that men find distracting. But I'm not beautiful, mysterious, or enigmatic." She said it with the same objectivity she'd used before.

"You're wrong." He set his glass aside and approached her, taking the dress from her hands and holding it up to the soft light. A tropical sea shimmered from his fingers to the floor. "This gown was made for you, Lady Angelique. But if you wish, you may leave it here. Leave it and go now, and we will part as friends. You will be welcome to play here as often as you like, but it will not be as a partner." He took a half step closer. "Or you could take a chance. Wear it. Stay. See just how much you might accomplish. Become whatever you wish. Become whoever you wish." He held the gown out to her. "It's up to you."

There was a second door at the back of his offices that Angelique hadn't seen the first night she'd been here. It too was concealed, opened by a hidden latch under the lip of the wainscoting, and it swung open soundlessly when Alexander released it. His private rooms, he explained, with the indifference she would expect had he shown her to his kitchens. She was free to use them to change in privacy. She would not be disturbed. He would be right outside the door if she needed anything.

What she needed was her wits.

She had completely lost her mind, she thought as she stood in the center of what appeared to be Alexander Lavoie's bedroom. Barring Gerald's sty of a room, she'd never been in a man's bedroom before. No doubt she was far from the first woman that had seen the inside of Alexander Lavoie's personal rooms, but still, she felt a little like a voyeur. She should ignore the electrifying thrills that were running up her spine and through her body. She should simply change right here, quickly, and be done with it.

Instead, she laid the gown she held in her hands over a wide chair just inside the door and stepped farther into the room.

This room, like the interior of his office, was not ornate, with the exception of the wide four-post bed that sat in the middle. It was carved from a dark wood that gleamed in the low light and made the lush coverlet the color of dark rubies seem all the more exotic. Embroidered pillows shot through with gold and scarlet were propped up against the headboard, and a throw of the same pattern was draped over the foot. She reached a hand out to touch the plush softness. It was a vast departure from the plain bed that sat in her room, covered with dull grey sheets. But then again, her bed was made for sleeping.

This bed was made for something else entirely.

Her fingers drifted to the decorative silk sashes tied around the bedposts.

I wouldn't tie you up to get what I wanted. Unless, of course, you insisted on it. Then I would do anything.

He had said that to her once, to set her off balance. A sudden vision of Alexander Lavoie reclining naked against the decadent fabrics made her knees wobbly. A vision of her joining him, having him at her mercy, touching him the way she had already imagined he might touch her, made her belly clench and dampness gather between her legs.

She snatched her hand away from the bed. Alexander Lavoie was the owner of a gaming hell, and while he likely wasn't an assassin, she did not fool herself into thinking he was not a dangerous man. A dangerous man with a wry sense of humor. And an unexpected sense of honor. And an undeniable sense of gallantry.

And a man who had hired her to deal cards. Not warm his bed.

She turned away and crept farther into the room, the sounds of her feet muffled by the heavy woven rugs that covered the wooden floor. A washstand sat on the far side of the room, dwarfed by a massive wardrobe and flanked by a long cheval mirror. A shaving kit sat on the edge of the washstand, a towel tossed carelessly over the chair beside it. The air was warm, redolent with the faint scent of lantern oil and the richer tones of sandalwood and lemon.

A second door in the corner of the room gave her a glimpse of a copper hip tub, the edges gleaming invitingly in the muted light. She padded forward.

"My lady?" Lavoie's voice was muffled through the door, and she jumped guiltily. "Do you need assistance yet?"

Yet? Angelique most certainly did not need assistance undressing or dressing from Alexander Lavoie. "No, I'm almost done," she lied, hurrying back closer to the bed, pulling at the laces to her gold silk gown. What was she doing, creeping and nosing about his rooms like a common thief? A common thief with a depraved imagination at that. Lavoie had been nothing but kind to her. Brutally honest and direct, but she found that incredibly liberating. He did not seem to want her to be anything she wasn't. He was, after all, the only man who had ever called her fascinating. And clever.

She knew she could do the job. She knew very well that she would make Alexander Lavoie a pile of money at the card tables. What she didn't know was if she could be beautiful, mysterious, and enigmatic while doing it. Up until now, all her efforts had gone into being plain, unnoticed, and forgettable. But given all he had done for her thus far, he certainly deserved her to make an effort.

And thus she found herself stripped down to her shift, stays, stockings, and a single petticoat in the middle of the bedroom of the owner of the most notorious gambling hell in London.

The gold gown pooled at her feet. When she had reworked this gown from one of her mother's old ones she had found in the attics, she had made certain to make it possible for her to don it without help. Everything did up the front or the side, easy for her to secure.

But when she reached for the turquoise gown, she found that it was a completely different story. It was a dress unlike anything she had ever seen. The bodice, instead of being gathered high and allowed to flow over her body, clung to her torso, following the curve of her breasts, her ribs, and cinched in to her waist. It was joined to the skirts at her hip, a profusion of delicate gold and white embroidery swirling at her waist and down toward her feet like trailing vines. The sleeves were capped at her shoulder, draping over her upper arm, the same gold and white embroidery gracing the hem of each. It was lavish and unique, risqué and unexpected. But if the entire thing were to stay up, it would require her to tighten the gold ribbon that threaded through the dozens of tiny eye-holes that ran down the back.

She hadn't noticed the construction when she'd taken the gown out of the box, probably because she'd been distracted first by the extravagance and then by the man who had given it to her.

Do you need assistance yet? She closed her eyes. No doubt Lavoie was finding great amusement at that on the other side of the door.

But she'd come this far. She reminded herself that she was doing this for the greater good, and the luxury of propriety and privacy had been forfeited the moment she'd accepted a job and all the monetary benefits that went with it. The moment she'd stepped into a gaming hell, really.

She pulled the gown on and adjusted the bodice against her breasts, plastering the satin to her front as best she could with one hand. With the other hand, she shoved open the door, girding herself to be as coolly professional with him as he had been with her tonight.

Except he was sitting on the edge of his desk, one hand idly swirling a glass of whiskey, the other holding a letter of some sort. He'd taken off his coat and rolled up the sleeves of his shirt and suddenly he didn't look quite so formal. Not quite so imposing. Instead he looked infinitely...touchable. Making him look like every wanton thing she had ever heard whispered in a ballroom, every breathless moan she had heard from concealed alcoves. Everything she had once imagined she might want for herself.

He raised his head and settled his gaze on her, his body unmoving. Her free hand went to the top of the bodice, as if that might provide another small piece of armor to protect herself against the way he was looking at her. His eyes were hot and hard, and it was all she could do not to bolt back into his bedroom.

"It laces up the back." She'd meant it to be brisk—she would have settled for accusatory—but instead, it came out far more tremulous than she had intended.

He seemed to shake himself mentally, and his eyes cooled, making it easier for her to breathe. "Of course it does," he said, sliding off the desk. "It's meant to be extravagant and extraordinary, not pedestrian and practical." He set his letter and his glass aside and crooked a finger at her. "Come here. I'll do your laces for you."

Angelique clutched the gown to her chest, desire coursing through her. Those words, accompanied by his gesture, were the most provocative and arousing things she had ever heard. The impropriety of this was beyond measure, yet all she could think of was how reckless she felt. How free. She moved forward, watching as his eyes shifted again. Watching as he swallowed, watching the way his hands curled around the edge of his desk where he leaned. He wasn't unaffected either.

She stopped just in front of him.

He pushed himself away from his desk. "Turn around," he told her. His voice was rougher than it had been a minute ago.

She slowly turned, presenting him with her back, a shiver chasing its way down her spine. It wasn't as though she was naked. Her stays were securely fastened over her shift, and the gown was pulled up to her shoulders, even if it gaped open to her waist at the back. It wasn't the first time she'd been dressed by another. Before everything, she'd shared a lady's maid with her mother when she was old enough, and dressing had always been a chore, something to be endured in deference to whatever fashion demanded.

This was not a chore. This was something completely different. This was an intimacy and a surrender of control that was more breathtaking and dangerous than anything she had ever experienced.

She felt his hands first at the side of her neck, his fingers gathering the rebellious strands of hair that had escaped the knot at the back of her head and sweeping them to the side. He brushed the bare skin at her shoulder blades with his knuckles, sending ripples of gooseflesh across her skin. She could feel his heat at her back, the warmth of his breath as he bent his head to his task. He'd drawn the top of her bodice tight, her breasts pushed up high and hard against the embroidered edge. Her nipples pebbled and sent bolts of pleasure through her body each time the fabric rubbed.

"Tell me if it's too tight," he said in a low voice at her ear.

She only nodded because words had escaped her—breath had escaped her—though it had nothing to do with the constriction of the gown. His hands moved lower, down the center of her back, clever fingers that were making her desperate. Desperate for him to put his hands on her properly.

Span her ribs, cup her breasts, trace the edge of her hips, touch everything, everywhere, that was begging to be touched. He was at the base of her spine now, securing the laces, the bodice smooth over her body.

"Are you done?" she managed.

"Not quite." His hands left her back and then they were in her hair, his fingers deftly plucking pins until the weight of her tresses tumbled down her back. She might have protested except the feel of his fingers combing gently through the waves was making her light-headed.

He stepped away. "Now I'm done," he said.

"Yes." She needed to say something, and that was the only syllable she could think of at the moment.

"How does it feel?"

Angelique closed her eyes. It felt like she was going to come out of her skin. "Fine," she whispered with effort. She opened her eyes and glanced down, her hands smoothing the satin over the flat of her stomach to where it flowed over her hips. He had been right. He was very good at measurements.

"Turn around."

Very slowly, she turned, her heart hammering in her chest, her spine straight, her chin up. She met Lavoie's eyes and held them for what seemed like an endless minute. He stepped back, his eyes dropping to skim over her bodice, her hips, to the floor, before coming back to hers. Other men had done just this, and in those cases, such scrutiny had made her feel objectified, as if her value was being assessed by the curve of her flesh, the same way a filly might be when led out into the auction ring at Tattersalls. This was different.

Everything with this man was different.

"Is it suitable?" she asked, and her voice was hoarse. "Are you pleased with the effect?"

"Why don't you see for yourself?" He nodded in the direction of the open door that led to his bedroom. "Take a look in the mirror."

Angelique nodded and slipped back into Lavoie's bedroom. Almost cautiously, she approached the long mirror next to the washstand.

There was a woman staring back at her who looked vaguely familiar. This woman had honeyed blond hair that tumbled over her bare shoulders, making her look a little wicked, as if she had just risen from bed. Or the arms of a lover. This woman wore a gown that clung to her every curve, making her breasts seem impossibly lush and her waist impossibly small. This woman held her head high and looked the way a certain young girl had always dreamed she might look if she wasn't trying to hide her body behind yards of white muslin.

"What do you think?"

She started, not having heard Lavoie come up behind her. "The gown is incredible."

"It is, and you look exquisite. But how do you feel in it?"

"Beautiful." The word popped out without her thinking. And she did. She felt powerful and confident and...truly beautiful. Her eyes met his in the mirror.

"Good." His gaze was intense. "Now we just have mysterious and enigmatic to conquer." He lifted his hands and brought them over her shoulders. "Close your eyes."

Angelique did, feeling the length of him pressed up against her back. It was all she could do not to press herself against that heat, and the sensation of something cool and firm against her face was a welcome distraction. "The gown has a few accessories," he whispered in her ear.

Like you?

The thought made her heart stutter. She concentrated on taking steady breaths. What had happened to her in the last minutes? What had happened to the woman who had hidden her mind the same way she had hidden her body until circumstance had forced her to reveal both?

She had met Alexander Lavoie. That was what had happened.

His fingers were at the back of her head, securing the ribbon on her mask.

"Can I open my eyes?" she asked.

"Patience, my lady." His voice was like velvet, and then his touch was gone for a second before it returned.

There was a gentle pressure at her throat, the sensation of something cool settling against her skin, offset by the heat of his fingers at her nape. It was a necklace of some sort, she knew, and the idea that it would be a piece that was on par with the extravagance of the gown stirred up all sorts of strange emotions that she couldn't seem to sort out. "Mr. Lavoie..." She started to raise her hand to her throat, afraid to open her eyes.

"Alex," he whispered.

"I beg your pardon?" Her hand froze halfway to her neck.

"When you are not dealing on the gaming floor and are in the privacy of my...office, you will call me Alex."

Alex. Not even Alexander. It rolled through her mind like sin, like something that she imagined would be whispered in the darkness surrounded by red silk sheets. Something that might slip from her lips as he teased and—

"Open your eyes."

Angelique sucked in a breath, taking a moment to compose herself. She should be doing everything possible to distance herself from the temptation that was this man. She had thought she had obtained adequate experience with men and the relations that existed between them. Two seconds in the presence of this one and she knew she had been very, very wrong.

She forcibly reminded herself that Alexander Lavoie was not courting her. He was not showering gifts upon her like some lovelorn swain, hoping his generosity might earn him a few fumbling moments behind a potted palm. These were not gifts from an admirer meant to steal her heart. What she wore was nothing more than a uniform. No different, really, than fine livery. The clothes had a purpose. The mask had a purpose. The jewelry had a purpose. Alexander Lavoie had a purpose in having her here and it had everything to do with business.

He had been very direct when he had specified just what type of image he wished her to achieve on his club's behalf—an image that would benefit them both, of course.

She opened her eyes.

The mask was simple, a gilded gold that matched the embroidery on the gown, with no decorations or adornments other than a tiny diamond at the corner of each eyehole that tipped up toward her temple. It covered the entirety of her upper face, settling lightly over the bridge of her nose and then gracefully sweeping down to the lower edge of her jaw. But she barely noticed the mask.

Instead her eyes were drawn to the necklace at her throat. The chain was not a chain at all, but a string of small diamonds resting against the skin just above her collarbones. From the center, another single strand of diamonds dripped, each stone getting larger as they descended. Her eyes followed them down to where they ended, a breath away from the deep valley between her breasts. It was a design unlike anything she had ever seen—starkly sleek and lacking flamboyant ornamentation.

She brought her hand the rest of the way up to touch the brilliant stones at her throat. They were warm now from her body, and they slid over her skin like a whisper. She trailed her hand down to the end of the strand, to the tops of her breasts, knowing that the design of the necklace, like the dress, had been nothing less than deliberate.

She considered herself in the mirror again. Of the awkward debutante there was no sign. Of the desperate woman in the second-hand gold gown armed with only her wits and a bottle of French brandy, there was no trace.

The woman staring back was a queen. A courtesan. A lady. A lover. All of those, all at once.

"It's spectacular," she said, pleased with how steady that had come out. Livery, she chanted in her head. Livery, livery, livery. Made out of satin and diamonds. "I've not seen anything like it. Draws the eye down rather...dramatically, does it not? Better than a bottle of brandy, I'll give you that." She waited for a witty, cutting rejoinder, but none came.

Behind her, Lavoie remained silent.

Her eyes skipped up to his in the mirror again, where he still stood near her shoulder. He had a strange expression on his face.

"Is there something about my appearance that displeases you, Mr. Lavoie?" she asked, using his proper name deliberately, trying to put another sliver of distance between herself and the vortex that was this man.

"No. Yes." He was still staring at her in the mirror, and Angelique wasn't sure he had even heard her. He skimmed her upper arm with his fingertips, pulling her heavy hair back away from her shoulder, letting the cool air kiss the side of her neck.

She shivered.

"You are irresistible." He bent his head, replacing the cool air at her neck with his lips.

A searing heat tore through her, making her limbs liquid. Dampness gathered between her legs, and a throbbing ache that matched the pounding of her heart radiated through her body. Her breaths came in shallow gasps.

"I want to taste you," he murmured quietly. His mouth was now at the sensitive skin just below her ear, and his breath was hot, his tongue teasing where his lips had left off. "All of you."

Her eyes closed briefly, every nerve ending in her body attuned to this man's touch. She knew what she should say. She knew that all she had to do was ask, and he would withdraw. Except she found herself wanting more. Wanting him. She looked at herself in the mirror, this woman she didn't recognize. She watched as her head tipped to the side, watched as Lavoie's dark head bent, his lips trailing fire along her skin. Watched her hand come up to stroke his dark hair. She'd never felt as reckless as she did at that moment. Had never felt as powerful.

He lifted his head, and his smoky eyes met hers in the mirror. "I don't mix business with pleasure," he whispered harshly, as if he was reminding himself of his earlier pledge.

She should agree and step away, she knew. End whatever insanity was threatening to overwhelm her.

"I haven't started working quite yet," was what came out of her mouth.

He went completely still behind her and then he reached up and pulled at the ties to the gold mask. He set the mask aside on the edge of the washstand and gazed at her for a long moment in the mirror.

"Turn around," he finally said, and his voice was rough.

For the second time that evening, she obeyed that command.

His fingers smoothed her hair away from her face, tracing the edge of her cheekbone, the curve of her jaw. His touch traveled down the column of her neck to the diamond necklace. "They suit you, these diamonds," he whispered. "Different. Brilliant."

Angelique didn't know what to say. She had spent a great deal of her life trying not to be different. And it had made her miserable. Now in the presence of a man who seemed to consider such desirable, the effect was intoxicating.

He fingered the strand that dropped toward her breasts, and Angelique felt her nipples harden further.

"I've wanted to do this from the first moment I saw you." He dropped the strand of diamonds and raised his fingers to her mouth, running the pads of his fingers over her upper lip and then her lower lip, a feather-light touch. It was torture of a sort she had never before experienced.

"Alex." His name slipped out, somewhere between a question and a demand.

His fingers went still against her lips, and then they were gone, his expression dark and hot. She dragged in a breath, the scent of whiskey and starch, sandalwood and something undeniably male enveloping her.

He lowered his head, his lips a breath away from hers.

Angelique closed her eyes.

His lips suddenly brushed hers, once, twice, a fleeting, teasing touch. She felt the scrape of the stubble on his jaw, felt the heat of his mouth as he found her lips, first the bottom one, then the top. He withdrew ever so slightly, waiting, one hand sliding along the side of her neck to her throat, his other hand skimming over the curve of her waist, coming to rest against her hip. He bent his head lower, ever so gently replacing his fingers at her throat with his lips, pressing a scorching kiss at that sensitive spot where she could feel her pulse hammering against her skin. Her head tipped back, and her entire body was consumed with a yearning that was almost debilitating in its power.

He lifted his head, his cheek brushing hers, his lips once again poised a breath away. This time it was she who closed the distance, catching his mouth with hers. He made a muffled sound before he increased the pressure of his kiss. He caught her lower lip in his teeth, pulling gently, releasing it only to graze his tongue along its edge. She whimpered softly, wanting more.

His hand at her waist slid around her lower back, pulling her against him, and through the fabric of their clothes, she could feel the hardness of his body against the softness of hers. Her inner muscles squeezed, the throbbing that had started earlier becoming a wicked, excruciating pulse that hammered at the very core of her being. Her own hands came up, sliding over his chest and around his neck, fearful that, if she didn't hold on to something, she would fly away into a thousand pieces.

His lips covered hers again, though this time they were no longer teasing but demanding. His tongue slipped inside her mouth, and all she could taste was whiskey and heat. She slid her own tongue against his and felt his hand tighten instantly on her back, pressing her harder against his body. She could feel his erection now, trapped between their bodies, his arousal making her own even more potent. His mouth increased its demands, his lips crushing hers.

This is what it felt like to be ravished, she thought dimly, tangling her fingers into the silky softness of his hair. Gloriously and thoroughly ravished, and she wanted it to go on forever. Wanted him to release that coil of want that was twisting within her, wanted him to make love to her body the way he was doing to her mouth. She didn't want him to stop.

Except he did.

He pulled his lips from hers, resting his forehead against her own, his breathing rapid and harsh. "Jesus Christ," she thought she heard him mumble.

Her breasts were aching, she was wet and throbbing, and her skin was sensitive to every whisper of breath that touched it. And only now did she hear the knocking that was coming from his office door in the other room.

"Mr. Lavoie?" The query was muffled.

Angelique's hands slid from his neck, and she straightened. Dear God, what would have happened had they not been interrupted? Her eyes strayed to the massive bed and all of its luxurious coverings. She knew exactly what would have happened. She would have let Alexander Lavoie take her to bed and finish what they had started.

She suspected it would have been different. Something truly memorable. Because with the most subtle of touches, he had already obliterated whatever she had thought she knew about sex. But it could never happen, no matter how much her body regretted that.

Because Alexander Lavoie was a businessman first and foremost. Provided Angelique didn't scuttle this business arrangement before it ever set sail, this man could provide the help she needed. Steady employment and the income that would come with it. Angelique needed his club more than she needed him, and she would be wise to remember that. She could do nothing to jeopardize this arrangement.

"My apologies, Mr. Lavoie," she said through gritted teeth. "That will not happen again. It was very unprofessional of me."

"Of you?" He was still standing before her, though his hands had fallen away and were now tightly clasped behind him.

"I got caught up in the moment, I'm afraid," she told him. "I suspect diamonds will do that to a girl, even if they are only part of her uniform."

He was looking at her, his eyes shuttered. "Diamonds."

"Yes," she lied. "It was all a bit much, really."

"Mr. Lavoie?" There was a sharper, firmer knock on the office door, and the muffled voice came again. "There's a man here to see you. Says it's urgent."

Lavoie made some sort of indecipherable noise and turned from her, stalking out of his bedroom and into his office. She heard the door open, and the sound of low voices.

Angelique exhaled a breath she hadn't realized she was holding. She stared at the mirror, trying to reconcile the reflection of the woman in the turquoise gown with the girl who had come here dressed in gold. Except she couldn't. What was more, she didn't want to. While there would never be a repeat of what had transpired here tonight, something deep within her had irrevocably changed, and she could not bring herself to regret it.

She let her gaze roam, noting her half-lidded eyes, the flush still in her cheeks, and her slightly swollen lips. She wasn't skilled or experienced when it came to pleasure. But she wasn't so naïve that she did not recognize desire when she saw it. When she had stood in front of that mirror, with a man who had never treated her as anything less than his equal, a man to whom she'd revealed more of her true self than she'd ever done with any other, she had witnessed just how much he had wanted her.

And whether he knew it or not, Alexander Lavoie had gifted Angelique with a knowledge that she hadn't possessed when she'd first come here tonight. She finally understood beauty and the power that came with it. And she finally understood that it had nothing to do with how she looked.

With a bittersweet smile, Angelique reached for the golden mask on the washstand and tied it back over her face. Whoever was out in the office area was still there.

And despite her newfound knowledge, Angelique had no intention of emerging from Lavoie's bedroom looking like a well-pleasured member of his harem.

She squared her shoulders and glided into the office with as much casual nonchalance as she could muster. There was a tall man speaking to Lavoie just inside the door, and it was plain from his lack of evening wear that he hadn't come to gamble. His clothes were of fine quality, giving him the appearance of a gentleman, but the heavy sword that hung from his waist was completely incongruous. It looked military in appearance, the scabbard scarred and battered, the hilt polished to a dull sheen from use. He held his hat in his hands, and his voice was low, his face grim. Lavoie's face didn't look that much better, though he was firing a rapid series of questions at the man now.

Lavoie seemed suddenly to become aware of her presence and abruptly stopped. Both men turned toward her.

Angelique faltered, feeling like she had just been caught eavesdropping. "I'm sorry to interrupt. I can wait in the other room."

"No. Stay." Lavoie's lips pressed into a thin line, and he shook his head. "Mr. Harris and I are done here." The tall man nodded at Lavoie and made some sort of awkward bow to Angelique before he slipped from the room, placing his hat firmly back on his head.

"Is everything all right?" Angelique asked, not really expecting an answer. Not sure if she wanted an answer. Surely the business of running a gaming hell had its unsavory moments.

"Yes." Lavoie strode over to his desk and found her sheet of probabilities. "But time is getting away from us. Like you said, the club will soon fill, and it will do us no favors if we are not adequately prepared with some sort of plan in place."

His tone, like his expression, was cool. There was no trace of the man who had kissed her senseless in his bedroom.

She supposed she was relieved.

"Let's talk strategy," he said, gesturing to the chair in front of his desk as he walked around to seat himself behind, putting a solid barrier between them. "I suspect there will be a bit of a trial-and-error period, but I am confident you will handle that with little difficulty. And like you said, we will need to establish winners to draw more players. We will need to devise a system."

Angelique slid into the offered chair and folded her hands neatly in her lap. She could be as cool as Lavoie. She would tuck the memory of his kiss deep inside, wrapped carefully in the wonder of the discovery that had come with it. She would keep both hidden under a smooth veneer of professionalism because, no matter what, she could not afford to lose this job.

"My lady?"

His address snapped her back into reality. "I beg your pardon?"

"I asked if you would prefer to deal with two decks or one?"

She cleared her throat and forcibly reminded herself why she was here. And what she needed to do.

"Two, Mr. Lavoie. Most certainly two."

Chapter 7

Alex sat at his desk, brooding.

He didn't like it one bit, because men who spent time brooding instead of taking decisive action lost great opportunities. But when it came to Angelique Archer, he'd discovered he'd completely lost his way.

For the fifth night in a row since Angelique had donned that turquoise-blue gown, Alex had forced himself to circulate through his club, paying clever compliments to the ladies and making small talk with the gentlemen. It was what he did every night, and he'd always done it with a subtle flair that entertained his guests and amused him. But now it had become a chore.

His eyes had continually strayed to his vingt-et-un table and the woman who sat behind it, cool and composed as a monarch presiding over a court of her favored subjects. He'd set the table up for six players, but the crowd that the table had drawn was at least four times that. The novelty, combined with the beautiful and mysterious dealer, had proven irresistible. He had bloody peers waiting for a chance to play at the table like anxious schoolboys, for God's sake.

There had been something different about Lady Angelique since the very first moment she had sat down behind that table, something he hadn't seen in her the times she had gambled here before. She'd worn a small smile on her face that he'd not witnessed before on any of the occasions that he'd watched her play, as if she were privy to some private amusement. Her every movement had been smooth and almost sensual, as if she had suddenly become aware of the power of her physical appearance and was now wielding it with the same confidence she wielded her mind. Her voice never rose above a soft murmur as she dealt, the soft cadence of her speech silky and almost suggestive. The men who sat at that table were mesmerized. They couldn't seem to get enough.

Alex wasn't sure what had wrought the change. Perhaps it was because she was no longer trying to remain invisible. Perhaps it was a brief respite from the desperation she had carried with her on those earlier visits.

Or perhaps he was just losing his mind.

He'd certainly lost it when he'd kissed her. Just the thought of the way she'd looked at him in the mirror, her fingers tangled in his hair, her head tipped back, and her eyes hazy with desire had him hard all over again. He'd never brought a woman into his private rooms for any reason. He always kept his sporadic relations with women on neutral ground. He'd seen too many times what happened when sex turned into love turned into jealousy turned into hate. And he had no desire to ever expose himself to that. He would give freely of his body, but not more. Not his privacy, not his thoughts, not his affection.

He was at an absolute loss as to why Angelique was different. Why he had allowed her in. Why he had done anything he'd done in the last five days.

All he knew was that he could no longer look into his cheval mirror without all the blood rushing straight to his groin.

He stood up from behind his desk abruptly, closing the ledger with an irritated thump. There was a reason he never mixed business with pleasure, and this was nothing if not the perfect example. It was distracting. Which meant it was dangerous. He needed his wits sharp, and kissing Angelique Archer was not the way to ensure they remained so.

Lady Angelique, thank God, had let his faux pas slide and had been nothing but the consummate professional. They'd made a bloody fortune that first night and every night since. *She'd* made a bloody fortune. It had shocked even him, the ease with which she controlled and manipulated that damn table. Granted, many of the players were relatively inexperienced, but that couldn't account for it all.

She'd arrived punctually every night in his carriage, already dressed for the gaming floor. Her attire should have been a relief, but Alex was instead struck with an irrational sense of regret. He'd found an unholy satisfaction in dressing her once. But dressing Angelique was a task that was no longer his, and Alex now found himself insanely jealous of an old woman called Tildy.

Another reason why one did not mix business with pleasure.

.He'd had a second gown made for Angelique—a masterpiece of indigo and silver—and it, even more than the turquoise gown, made her look like a Grecian goddess. And as much as he told himself he was pleased with the effect, he found himself resenting the way every man in his club looked at her. Like they were imagining just what it might be like to peel that damn gown away from her glorious body, stitch by silver stitch.

Alex ignored the fact that he was no better. Because when he wasn't fantasizing about dressing Angelique, he was fantasizing about undressing her.

His eyes caught a flash of glitter on the corner of his desk. As usual, she'd left the necklace and the diamond-studded mask behind in his care at the end of the night, unwilling to wear them home. She did not wish the risk of them getting stolen, she had said. *By her brother* was the part that had remained unsaid. He picked up the chain of diamonds and let it slide through his fingers, remembering how they had dripped over her skin and between her incredible breasts. What he would give to see her wearing these. And nothing else.

A new surge of arousal made him groan. He had to stop this or he was never going to be able to walk straight.

He glanced in the direction of his bedroom, the door firmly closed. Normally he would retire to his rooms now. Sleep for the morning and into the early afternoon before rising and attending to whatever business matters were required. But he was far too keyed up to find sleep now. And if he slid between the cool sheets of his bed in this state, he had no doubt his mind would continue to be consumed by Angelique Archer and that he'd be forced to find release by his own hand. He told himself he wasn't that desperate.

Yet.

"Good Lord, Alex. Did you rob the palace?"

Alex froze, his fingers tightening on the diamonds. "Duchess," he said, turning around slowly, "I didn't hear you knock."

"That's because I didn't." Ivory Moore was standing just inside the hidden door that led out into the alley.

"That door was locked."

"Was it?" She looked inordinately pleased with herself as she smoothed her plain brown skirts.

"You've been practicing."

"I've learned from the best." She swept across the room to peer over Alex's shoulder. "That is absolutely stunning." She reached for the necklace and drew it from his hands with an appreciative murmur. "Are you planning on wooing an empress?" She glanced up at him. "Or have you fallen in love?"

"When hell freezes over on both counts, Duchess." Alex retrieved the diamonds and placed them, along with the gold mask, in the top drawer of his desk, closing it firmly. "To what do I owe the pleasure of your company?"

Ivory's eyes lingered on the desk drawer. "I come bearing information."

"I like the sound of that. Don't keep me in suspense." He crossed his arms.

She glanced up at him. "What do you know about the Viscount Seaton? Son of the Duke of Rossburn."

Alex frowned. "Have you been talking to Tall Harris?"

A crease formed between her brows. "No. And it's Jed."

"Pardon?"

"The tall Harris brother. His name is Jedediah. Then there's Theodore, and Frederick is the shortest."

Alex blinked and swallowed a bark of laughter. "Jed, Ted, and Fred?"

"Who are all probably better than you with a blade," Ivory admonished with a warning frown. "Don't be juvenile."

"I doubt they're better, but I take your point, Duchess."

"Good to hear." She paused. "What does Mr. Harris have to do with Seaton?"

"They are doing a little surveillance work for me, if you recall. Young Gerald has spent a great deal of time with Seaton as of late. In rather insalubrious parts of London, near the docks."

"For what purpose?"

"Tall— Jed Harris is unsure at the moment. It could be for the thrill of it, or possibly for the cheap gin. Or maybe something else entirely. I've requested that they keep watching. Both Hutton and Seaton."

"Why?"

"Because Hutton seems to lack any sort of intelligence or judgment, and I'm not convinced Seaton isn't taking advantage of that. And it may be in my best interests to do something about it in the near future." Alex drummed his fingers on his thigh. "Your turn."

Ivory leaned against the edge of Alex's desk. "There are old rumors that tie Seaton to the Archers. Not to the new marquess, but to your new vingt-et-un dealer."

Alex's fingers stopped before he forced them to resume. In his mind, he saw Angelique's visceral response to Seaton's presence on the night her brother had made his idiotic appearance as a highwayman. At the time, he'd attributed it to the situation. Now he wondered if it was something more. "That's a rather ambiguous statement, Duchess. Please expand."

Ivory tipped her head and watched him steadily. "During Lady Angelique's single season, it was rumored that the Duke of Rossburn and the Marquess of Hutton were flirting with the idea of merging the families by way of marriage."

"Rumored?"

"The couple, together with their families, was seen together on occasion. Theaters, museums, Rotten Row, the usual public show grounds. Nothing was ever declared or confirmed, but a few individuals drew the obvious conclusions."

At the time of my season, I'd thought that my future was already—

Angelique never finished her answer when he had first

asked her why she'd held herself aloof. Had she believed herself to be betrothed? Had she believed that her future had already been agreed upon? A marriage pact all but consummated?

Or perhaps it had been.

Alex made an effort to relax his jaw that he didn't remember clenching. "And was this rumored union driven by a mutual affection shared by the young lord and lady, or by usual parental selections based on pedigree and wealth?"

Ivory shot him a curious look. "It wasn't clear. Does it matter?"

"Maybe," Alex replied, feigning carelessness he wasn't quite feeling. "You know me. I always like to know what motivates people. How I might manipulate that to my advantage."

"You want to know if your lady was in love." Ivory blinked at him. "Good God. You're smitten with her."

"I'm certainly smitten with the amount of money the lady made me recently," Alex drawled, careful not to sound too defensive. "But I am not interested in Lady Angelique's emotional state save for what impact it might have on her ability to make me more. I want to know if Seaton was a problem in the past, or if he may become a problem again. I want to know exactly how those families may have been or might yet still be intertwined and if it is something I will need to worry about so long as the lady remains in my employ."

"Of course." There was a knowing smirk playing about Ivory's mouth. "Tell me, did your lady like the diamonds?"

"She is not my lady, she is my employee. An asset to this club. And the diamonds are part of her costume. Same as the mask. In fact, Lady Angelique will be the first person to tell you so." It sounded stiff.

"Her costume?"

"Yes."

"Costume implies feathers and bits of pretty paint. Not a fortune in diamonds."

"Do you have a point here, Duchess?"

"Have you kissed her?"

"I'm going to pretend I didn't hear that. You know as well as I do that I do not mix business with pleasure." Alex crossed a booted foot over his leg, his movements casual. Dammit, this woman knew him too well.

"You did," Ivory breathed. "You aren't smitten, you're completely besotted."

"We're done discussing this." He paused. "Tell me what became of this *rumored* union between the Hutton and Ross-burn titles."

Ivory was still watching him.

Alex stared silently back.

"Oh, very well." She straightened and trailed her fingers along the spine of one of the accounting ledgers sitting on his desk. "Nothing became of it. The Marchioness of Hutton fell ill, and it is accepted that Angelique Archer withdrew from society to care for her mother in her last months of life. Lady Angelique did not return to society after her mother's death."

"And Seaton abandoned his lady in her hour of need?"

Ivory shrugged. "That is something you will have to ask the lady directly if you wish to know. Or Seaton himself."

"Mmmm." Angelique had never mentioned Seaton. Not after that first disastrous night, not in her description of her failed season.

At the time, I thought a husband was what I wanted.

Seaton?

Had the man kissed her? Touched her?

There was a rather foreign and unpleasant sensation roiling through him at the thought of Angelique kissing another man, and it took a moment for him to identify it. Possessive jealousy.

He quashed it ruthlessly. What Seaton did or did not do in the past with Lady Angelique did not signify. It was the present that concerned Alex, and what, exactly, Seaton's role in it might be. And whatever his relationship with Lady Angelique, it was his relationship with the dissolute and current Marquess of Hutton that had his instincts on edge.

"What about the missing fortune?" he asked, trying to distract himself.

"Society, as far as I can determine, still believes the Hutton title to be synonymous with money. However, it wasn't long after his wife fell ill that the old marquess started selling the Hutton holdings. That seems to have marked the start of their slide into financial misfortune, while interestingly enough, the Rossburn family has since flourished."

"Flourished?"

"Five years ago there were rumors about money troubles within the Rossburn duchy, but since then, Rossburn has assembled a stable full of racehorses, built a staggering collection of Renaissance paintings, purchased a grand townhome in Mayfair, and bought a castle somewhere near Swindon. The duke and his duchess are known now for hosting lavish balls, garden parties, and other entertainments—the type of events that Prinny attends."

"Coincidence?"

Ivory shrugged. "Coincidences in our business are about as common as leprechauns. You know that."

"Mmmm."

"That being said, I could find nothing that proved or disproved that it was, in fact, a coincidence. Alderidge offered to investigate further, but I declined. Once a duke starts asking questions, no matter how carefully, someone sits up and takes notice. My husband and his position are helpful in some cases and a complete liability in others."

"I appreciate that, Duchess. As much as he holds my regard, I don't need a ducal pirate mucking about in my affairs." He paused. "Where is your dear Davy Jones at the moment?"

"Alderidge is at the docks."

"A kraken attack one of his ships?"

Ivory heaved a theatrical sigh, though she was smiling. "Goodbye, Alex." She crossed the room to the hidden door.

"Leaving so soon?"

"There's nothing further I can tell you." She pressed the latch, and the door swung open silently, the shadows of the alley visible just beyond. "If you really want answers, you should be talking with your lady instead of kissing her."

Alex would have argued except Ivory was already gone, the door closing as silently as it had opened.

He stalked across the room and back, feeling restless and dissatisfied. First impressions had left him with little regard and even less respect for George Fitzherbert, but there were many men like him who Alex did not trouble himself with.

But those men were not linked to Angelique Archer, a little voice whispered in his head.

Alex paced back to the long bookshelves that lined the far wall. He was aware he was teetering on the edge of behaving like a jealous swain, and that revelation was not sitting well. He needed to focus on the facts. Ivory was probably right. The procurement of answers did not need to be so convoluted. He would ask Lady Angelique. Before she stepped out onto his gaming floor once more, he would try and discover exactly what he might be dealing with. What sort of skeletons might not only fall out of closets onto his floor but bite him in the arse afterward.

There was a sharp rap on the alley door and Alex whirled, reaching for the latch.

"Forget something, Duchess?" he began, only to realize it wasn't Ivory but Jed Harris who stood in the doorway, his hat once again in his hands and his face once again grim. "Mr. Harris."

"'Mornin', Mr. Lavoie," Jed replied.

"You must be here for payment." No doubt young Hutton was finally passed out somewhere by now. Hopefully in the vicinity of his home and not in a pile of offal in a rookery somewhere. Alex peered past Jed's lanky frame into the murky morning light of the alley. "Your brothers with you?"

Jed shook his head. "No." He dropped a hand and rested it on the hilt of his sword. "Theodore is still watching the viscount's house. But Fred is at the Tower."

"The Tower." Alex frowned slightly in incomprehension. "Why?"

"The Marquess of Hutton is currently at the Tower."

Alex rolled his eyes. "Tell me he didn't lock himself in one of the lion cages and pass out." That was something Alex had no trouble imagining Hutton would do. No doubt he would have thought it funny. At least until he got mauled.

"No. Not the lion cages."

"Oh God. Martin's cage then?"

"Who?" Jed looked perplexed.

"The grizzly bear. It's called Martin. Did Martin eat Hutton?"

"No. His lordship is not at the menagerie. Nor did he, ah, get eaten by anything."

Alex leaned on the door. "Then I don't understand. Why is he at the Tower?"

"Because, Mr. Lavoie," Jed explained, "the Marquess of Hutton has been arrested."

Chapter 8

The Marquess of Hutton has been arrested." It was Vincent Cullen, Baron Burleigh, who delivered the news, standing in the middle of Angelique's hall, his hat in his hands, his owlish eyes even rounder than usual in his narrow face.

Behind him stood his mother, Lady Burleigh, dressed suitably for social calls, and the sight of her was almost as much of a shock as Burleigh's declaration. Angelique hadn't seen her even once since her mother's death, though the women had been close. She'd aged dramatically in the intervening years. Her features were sharper, her eyes harder. Her grey hair was pulled back from her face, and she was staring intently at Angelique as if waiting to evaluate her reaction to Vincent's news.

Angelique ignored the immediate dread that twisted through her. She should know better. She couldn't imagine what would have possessed Burleigh to bring his mother along, but this was obviously some sort of prank. Not that long ago, her brother was pretending to be a highwayman. Today it seemed he was pretending to be something worse. And she didn't find it funny.

"Of course he has," Angelique said flatly. "Caught spying for the French, was he?"

Burleigh blinked at her. "N-no." His voice dropped to a whisper. "He's been arrested for murder."

Angelique scowled at the thin, weedy man but tempered her response in deference to his mother. "I'm afraid I don't have time for this, Lord Burleigh," she said shortly. "When you see my brother, tell him he needs to come home. There are matters that I need to discuss with him."

"But he's in the Tower," Burleigh blurted. He pulled at the turquoise pin at his throat as though his cravat had been knotted too tight.

"The Tower?" Angelique looked hard at the man's face and noted it was paler than normal. Icy points of sweat suddenly pricked at her scalp.

Lady Burleigh chose this moment to step forward. She placed a cold, papery hand on Angelique's sleeve. "It's true, dear. They took him there after they found him. After they arrested him."

Angelique pulled away. She was trying to understand why this woman would lie to her. "I don't understand. If this is supposed to be a joke—"

"It isn't. I swear." Burleigh was shifting anxiously, looking between his mother and Angelique. "It's the truth."

A wave of nausea threatened. "Tell me," she croaked.

"Hutton was found in the Earl of Trevane's house in the small hours of the morning. It seems that..." Burleigh trailed off.

"It seems that what? Speak up." It was rude, but her patience was losing a rapid battle with fear.

"They're saying that he was trying to rob the house. And it seems a maid caught him in the act."

Angelique felt her mouth go dry. "And?" she croaked.

"And he killed her. Slit her throat." Lady Burleigh said it without emotion.

Angelique felt as if she were suddenly in the middle of a dream, drowning in a sea of disorientation. Her surroundings seemed to waver before righting themselves. "That's impossible," she heard herself say. "My brother would never..."

I'll fix it, Ang, I promise. I'll get the money.

The edges of her vision blurred as she struggled for breath. "Oh God."

Burleigh's hand was suddenly on her arm, and for once, Angelique was glad for the touch. It brought her back to the present. "My lady—"

"It's impossible," Angelique repeated. *Impossible, impossible, impossible.*

Burleigh patted her awkwardly on the shoulder. "I'm so very sorry—"

"Tell me what happened," she gasped, a bead of clammy sweat sliding down her spine. "Don't leave anything out."

"I don't know, exactly. We were supposed to meet up with him—"

"We?"

"Seaton and myself. We were on our way to, ah..." His eyes slid to his mother before returning to Angelique. "To one of Seaton's clubs, but your brother said he had something he, um, needed to see to before."

"In Trevane's house?" Angelique choked.

Burleigh ran a nervous hand through his thinning hair. "Your brother was very secretive, my lady, but it seemed like a harmless adventure, you understand. He made it sound like he was sweet on one of the maids and she on him and that they..." he trailed off again. "That they had an assignation."

Angelique put a hand out and found the edge of the small hall table as if that spindly piece of furniture might anchor her. "And then what happened?"

Burleigh pulled a kerchief from his pocket and dabbed at his pale forehead. "I-I don't know. Your brother...um...well, he wasn't going to be long. But it was raining and I wasn't keen on waiting in the bushes outside the earl's house. So I went ahead to a nearby coffeehouse to wait. But Seaton stayed."

Out of the corner of her eye, she saw Lady Burleigh shake her head, her lips pressed into a disapproving line. "Seaton never did have much sense," she murmured.

"Yes, well, the next thing I know, Seaton shows up at the coffeehouse and drags me out, telling me Hutton's been arrested. This has shocked me as much as it has you, my lady."

"How— Why..." She tried to gather her thoughts.

The baron leaned closer. "The earl himself found him with the body, my lady. Covered in blood." He cleared his throat nervously. "I imagine the authorities will be coming soon to notify you. Question you."

Angelique concentrated on taking deep breaths. The last thing she needed right now was questions. "Who else knows?" she asked.

"By the end of the day, everyone will," Burleigh whispered, his dark eyes darting about the room as though he were searching for a different answer. "He's a *marquess*."

"I need to see him," Angelique said bleakly. She had to speak to Gerald. He couldn't have done this. Gerald was not a killer. Yet...given enough alcohol, given enough narcotics, given enough desperation, and suddenly the impossible seemed terrifyingly possible. She pressed a hand to her mouth, fighting to keep her composure.

Lady Burleigh was shaking her head. "They're not letting anyone see him. No visitors of any sort."

"They?"

"The warders."

"How do you know that?"

"We already tried. Before we came here." She reached for Angelique's other hand, squeezing it.

Burleigh sighed. "I'm so sorry, my lady. I'm only a baron, and to be honest, not even a very important one. I don't have the kind of power your brother needs right now."

Angelique swallowed with difficulty.

"I'm sorry that I am the one to bring you such terrible news. But I thought it would be better you hear it from me. Gerald has been my closest friend since we were children. I would do anything to help him. You must know that."

Angelique nodded numbly. "What do I do?" She didn't really expect an answer.

"Seaton is asking the same thing of his father right now, my lady. If anyone has the power to help, it will be the Duke of Rossburn. He has many influential connections. You should go and see him straightaway."

"Yes," Angelique said mechanically, pulling her hand from his. "I should do that. Straightaway."

Burleigh worried the brim of his hat with his fingers. "Do you want us to go with you?"

"No." The last thing she wanted was to spend another minute in the presence of a man who was complicit in this, however indirectly. Or his mother, for that matter.

"We can stay—"

"No." She wanted to be left alone. She needed to be left alone to think.

"Right. Of course," Burleigh said, the anxious expression back on his face. "Then I'll go."

"Do that."

He hesitated. "Again, my lady, I'm so sorry to be the bearer of such distressing news."

Angelique nodded numbly and turned to find Lady Burleigh standing directly in front of her.

"You have his eyes," the woman said, once again staring at Angelique.

"What?" It was enough to jar her from her distress.

"You have his eyes," Lady Burleigh repeated slowly. "I never saw it before, but I can see it clearly now."

"My father's?" God, what the hell did this have to do with anything?

"Mother," Vincent warned.

"Yes. You'll have his strength too," she said abruptly, as if shaking herself out of a trance.

Angelique supposed that the woman was trying to offer her comfort, but she didn't feel strong. The sudden urge to scream or hit something was overwhelming. She just wanted Burleigh and his mother gone.

Vincent was jamming his hat on his head, ushering his mother to the door. "Please know that your well-being is very important to us. If there is anything I can do, please, just—"

"I think you've done enough," Angelique replied. "Thank you," she forced herself to add.

He swallowed hard and nodded once, holding the door open for Lady Burleigh. They left silently, and Angelique closed the door behind them.

Angelique rested her forehead on the smooth wood, closing her eyes, listening to the empty silence around her, broken only by the sound of her heart pounding in her ears. She willed herself to wake up now. To open her eyes and realize that this had been a nightmare. A bad dream that had left her shaking and gasping and weak.

She opened her eyes to find herself staring at the grainy pattern of a polished oak door.

She turned, leaning heavily against the door, and found herself sliding down its length until she came to sit on the cold marble floor. But she didn't scream or hit something. The shock was starting to fade, leaving her mind racing. And one thing was clear.

Burleigh was right. She needed help. She needed someone who knew her family, knew Gerald. Someone in the peerage who would have the power to demand real answers and speak on her brother's behalf. Someone who would keep this matter private for as long as possible, if not out of regard for her family then certainly out of regard for his own son's proximity to the entire mess.

The Duke of Rossburn. George's father.

As much as she might wish otherwise, there was no other option.

You could go to Alex.

It slipped unbidden into her mind. And just as quickly, she shied away from the idea. Telling Lavoie now about this debacle wouldn't fix a thing. For there was absolutely nothing a gaming hell owner could do for a marquess incarcerated in the Tower of London. Except, of course, dismiss the sister of an accused murderer from his employ. As much as Alexander Lavoie had been kind to her, even he would have limits.

She didn't doubt that Alex would hear of it eventually, but if there was even the smallest chance of keeping Alex ignorant of her brother's predicament, at least until she was seated behind that vingt-et-un table for one more night, she'd take it. She was going to need money, more than ever now. And Lavoie's was the only source she had.

She pushed herself away from the door and staggered to her feet, dry-eyed, though her stomach was in knots. She could do this. She had done a lot of things she'd never imagined that she could do and this would be only one more.

⁓

An hour later, Angelique found herself in the drawing room of the Duke of Rossburn's opulent town house, deposited there by a glacial butler and instructed to wait while he went to see if His Grace was available.

Angelique clasped her hands in front of her, her fingers icy even in her gloves. Of course it was the drawing room she'd been shown into. Had she known, she might have insisted that she'd wait outside. She avoided looking at the wide settee that dominated the center of the room and instead stood in front of the window, staring sightlessly out at the watery sunlight that cast a strange light on the green space in the center of the square. Somewhere a dog barked and the sounds of shod hooves on stone drifted through the window. Everyday life continued on as normal. Even when hers was falling apart.

"To what do I owe the pleasure of this visit, Lady Angelique?" Seaton's smooth voice came from the door, and Angelique closed her eyes, feeling her stomach drop and another layer of nausea rise.

She turned from the window to face him, reminding herself that she was the one here seeking assistance and trying to choose her words with care lest she say anything that she might regret. Seaton stood just inside the room, dressed impeccably, as he always was. His dark brown hair was cut stylishly, his boots were polished to a brilliant luster, and his posture spoke of a man supremely confident in his place in the world. He was watching her expectantly, and if she didn't know better, she would have thought that he wasn't yet aware of Gerald's arrest.

She met his eyes squarely. "I'm here to see your father."

His expectant smile disappeared. "Burleigh came to see you." He sounded displeased.

"Yes, he did. Along with his mother."

Seaton's handsome face twisted into a condescending sneer. "His mother? Of course he would have told her too. Still in leading strings. Should have kept his mouth shut."

Anger ignited low in her belly, and Angelique welcomed it. It was better than the despair and terror that rose in alternating waves and threatened to suffocate her. "You would rather I had remained in ignorance that my brother is currently locked in the Tower? Been oblivious until I read it in the newssheets this afternoon? Or until they decided to hang him?"

Seaton winced at her words and stepped into the room, closing the door behind him. "I did not see the point in upsetting you unnecessarily."

"Upsetting me?"

"I'm sure this unfortunate misunderstanding can be rectified quickly and quietly. Hutton is, after all, a marquess."

"Who stands accused of murder," Angelique snapped. "Burleigh said you were there. Were you with him? Inside that house?"

"Keep your voice down, my lady," Seaton said sharply. He crossed the room, skirting the settee. He reached her side. "Please, sit."

"I'll stand." Bad news was bad news whether or not one was planted on one's backside. A soft pillow did nothing to lessen the impact. She should know. She had been weathering a constant storm of bad news for a long time now.

Seaton slid his hand around her arm and tugged her in the direction of the settee. Angelique pulled away and took two steps back.

A faint shadow of annoyance crossed his face. "Contrary, as always."

"You never answered my question."

He glanced back in the direction of the door. "Of course I wasn't with him. Hutton told me to wait outside the house. Said he wouldn't be long. And I did. At least until the officers showed up."

"And then you just left him?"

"*He* left *me* hiding in the bloody bushes," Seaton snapped. "It's a wonder I wasn't found and accused of being an accomplice. If I had known what he was going to do—"

Angelique recoiled. "You think he did it?"

"He was led out of that house covered in blood, my lady."

"Did he say anything? To any of the officers?"

"Not that I heard."

Angelique's anger suddenly drained as fast as it had risen, leaving her feeling gutted. She turned back toward the window, fighting to keep her composure.

Seaton was suddenly behind her. "Have you been to see him?" he asked, and his voice was softer.

"No," she whispered. "The warders are denying anyone access."

"Just as well. It is not a place for a lady."

"It is not a place for my brother," Angelique hissed. "Gerald is not a murderer."

"When the time comes, a jury of his peers will determine that," Seaton soothed. "He will not be mistreated."

"I need your father to speak on his behalf," she said, forcing herself to hold her ground. "He's known Gerald since you were in school together."

"He will do what he can, I'm sure." His hands were on her shoulders now. "As will I."

She shrugged, trying to dislodge his hands, but they remained where they were, his fingers squeezing into the muscles of her shoulders. "Don't."

"You're different."

"I'm not different. I'm upset."

"No. You've changed. You're different. Beautiful." His hands slid along her upper arms. "Let me make you feel better."

She jerked from his grasp. "Please don't touch me."

"Why?" he asked. "You liked my touch just fine before. Right here in this room, you were more than willing. Do you not recall just how good I made you feel?"

Angelique looked away, revulsion and self-disgust rising even through her misery.

"I can make you feel like that again," he murmured, sidling closer. "Make you forget your troubles. I'm going to be a duke. I can take care of you—"

The drawing room door suddenly swung open, and the Duke of Rossburn entered, leaning heavily on a walking stick. He stopped abruptly when he saw Angelique and his son, and his expression hardened unpleasantly.

"Leave us," he ordered Seaton.

Out of the corner of her eye, Angelique saw Seaton stiffen. "I think it is important that I stay, Father. There is—"

"I said, leave us."

His son turned, his face set into angry, resentful lines, and without another word or glance at Angelique, stalked from the room.

"You are here on behalf of your brother, I assume?" The white-haired duke gazed at Angelique through small, grey eyes. "My son has told me what has happened."

"Yes. I was hoping you might be able to help secure his release."

"Unfortunately, there is little I can do for your brother

at this juncture," he said. "Young Hutton has gotten himself into a mess that even I cannot fix."

"But surely there is someone you can talk to? Because he can't possibly have done what he is accused of doing." She heard the naked desperation in her voice but didn't care.

"I'm sorry. It is an unfortunate situation, one that the uneducated public will undoubtedly try to use as an excuse to further their own political agendas or fire up a new riot. They are so temperamental these days." He peered down his nose at Angelique. "I feel obliged to suggest that you leave the city, my lady. For your own safety, at least until justice has been served."

"Leave? But Gerald would never—"

"Sometimes young men go astray," the duke said, his voice dropping an octave into a patronizing tone. "An evil fever grips them that cannot be explained. No amount of good breeding can overcome such. And as much as I would like these circumstances to be rooted in falsehood, I cannot rationally argue with facts. Nor, unfortunately, can any valued member of our society."

"So you won't help?" She said it dully, the prospect of defeat a terrifying reality.

The duke sighed heavily. "I have a responsibility to this family. Your brother's unfortunate choices have destroyed one life, and I will not allow them to destroy that of my son's. His future—this family's future—must be protected. We cannot and will not be viewed as guilty simply by association. As far as I am concerned, neither my son nor I know anything about this unfortunate occurrence. I cannot help you." He looked back in the direction of the drawing room door, where the butler now stood, holding Angelique's cloak. "I trust you understand, my lady."

"But Lord Seaton said—"

"My son agrees with me," Rossburn said grimly. "He will fall into line in this matter, as he has done in the past with all matters that affect the interests and security of this family." He flexed his fingers around the head of his walking stick. "I trust you will not feel the need to seek either myself or my son out in the future."

Angelique stared at the duke, a man whom she believed her father had once counted as a friend, and saw the way the winds were blowing. The message was clear. The ton would scramble to distance themselves from a marquess labeled as a murderer. There would be no help coming from any quarter. Most certainly not from this one.

"My butler will see you out." The duke turned away.

Within minutes, she found herself outside on the street, the struggling sun doing its best to penetrate a hazy blanket of clouds and coal smoke. She stood shivering in the meager warmth, feeling battered and bruised. She was on her own now, more alone than she had ever been in her life. But she was not a quitter. She would not give up.

Pulling her cloak more tightly around her, Angelique thought about the money she'd brought home from Lavoie's. She'd thought to use it for living expenses, and if she was smart and thrifty, it would have sustained the household for months. Except now her brother languished in the Tower of London for a crime Angelique couldn't believe he'd committed. At the very least, she had to know what really happened. The money might just be enough to get her the answers she needed. Because she couldn't do nothing and live with herself.

Her eyes drifted east to where she knew St Paul's Church sat, hunkered at the corner of Covent Square, and the business she knew sat in its shadow. She wasn't defeated just yet.

There was still one more option.

Chapter 9

*C*hegarre & Associates.

It was written on a small plaque near the door, and it might have been a firm of bankers or barristers for all the clue the name gave to its true purpose. Which didn't mean it wasn't known. No, anyone who was anyone knew of Chegarre & Associates, though to a soul, every one of them would deny that knowledge. This was the place where scandals came to die before they ever had a chance at living. This was the place where one might find solutions when convention and perception and even the law were not on one's side.

Angelique had heard Gerald speak of it once, mention some sort of trouble one of his friends had gotten into with a young lady in Chelmsford. The trouble had seemingly evaporated the moment Chegarre & Associates had become involved.

She had no idea what the firm might be able to do for her brother. But she had to try.

Angelique glanced around, but no one was taking any

notice of her. There were people coming and going in constant streams from the tenements, and next door, a group of men spilled out onto the street, their fingers wrapped firmly around the necks of liquor bottles and their voices raised in laughter.

She lifted her hand and grasped the heavy brass knocker, rapping it sharply three times against the solid, if worn, wooden door.

It was opened almost immediately, and Angelique found herself staring down into the face of a young boy, no more than nine or ten years of age, dressed in some sort of livery. "Good afternoon, my lady," he said cheerfully. "Can I help you?"

Oh God, I hope so, Angelique thought. "I'd like to speak with Mr. Chegarre," she said.

"Ah." The boy swung the door open a little wider. "May I ask who is calling?"

"Lady Angelique Archer," she said. Was there a point to lying? The boy stared at her for a second too long and then pulled the door all the way open. "Please come in," he said. "Follow me."

Angelique stepped inside, and the heavy door shut behind her. Almost instantly, the raucous sound of the street vanished, muted by the silence of a house that smelled of baking and furniture polish. Angelique stared as she followed the pint-size butler, unable to help herself. She wasn't sure what she had been expecting, but the restored splendor of this house was not it. Everywhere, wood gleamed and crystal sparkled. She was led into a drawing room, decorated in pale blue, barely noticing when the young boy departed. She found herself surrounded by understated luxury. The furnishings were rosewood, mahogany, and ebony. The carpet under her feet was an Aubusson, and Angelique knew exactly how much it was worth, even second-hand, having sold all twelve of her family's Aubussons in the last year. A tall Edward East clock sat along the wall, keeping time. She wandered closer, examining the brass relief of the tympanum of the clock. It depicted the goddess Diana, looking fierce and fearless with her bow in her hand and her hounds at her heels.

If only Angelique could be that fearless.

"My lady, good afternoon." Angelique turned to find a woman standing in the drawing room.

Diana's sister, was Angelique's first thought, for the woman had the presence of a warrior and a face that betrayed nothing except cool confidence. Her next thought was somewhat murkier—more a vague sense of déjà vu, as if she should know this woman. As if she had met her before. It was elusive, that sense of recognition, dancing along the edge of her consciousness.

"I'm sorry if I've kept you waiting long."

Angelique shook her head. "No need to apologize."

The woman walked into the room, her plain brown skirts at odds with features that would have set her apart in any royal ballroom. "My name is Miss Moore," she said. "And I understand that you require assistance." Her voice was rich and throaty.

"Do you work with Mr. Chegarre?" Angelique asked, unsure what Miss Moore's role here was.

Miss Moore gazed at her impassively with steady, dark eyes. "Yes. Very closely."

"Then you can help me?"

Miss Moore was studying her intently. "It depends on exactly what it is you need us to do."

Angelique took a shaky breath. "Right. Thank you. That is, I . . . you see . . . um . . ."

"Why don't you start at the beginning?" Miss Moore suggested gently.

The beginning. Angelique had no idea where the true beginning was. So she started at the end. The part that had brought her here. "My brother, the Marquess of Hutton, was arrested. For murder."

"Ah." There was not a flicker of surprise.

"He's been locked in the Tower," Angelique pressed on, wondering if Miss Moore had heard her correctly.

"I see."

"Do you?"

"Of course. They would not hold a peer at Newgate, even one accused of murder."

Angelique stared at Miss Moore. The woman had heard her just fine. And it would seem that Miss Moore was unshockable. She supposed that was a good thing.

"My brother couldn't have done it," Angelique forged on. "What they're saying he did."

"Which is what, exactly?"

"Thieving." She swallowed. "And then killing a woman who allegedly caught him in the act."

Miss Moore's expression didn't change. "Why do you believe he didn't do it?" she asked curiously.

"Because he's not a killer. He's a silly boy who refuses to grow up. But he would never kill anyone!" Angelique cried. She had to believe that.

"Perhaps." Miss Moore, on the other hand, didn't have to believe anything. "What do you want from us, Lady Angelique?" she asked.

"What do you mean?"

"There are a number of options that lay before us. Do you wish us to covertly extract your brother from prison? Arrange for him to sail anonymously to India or perhaps the Americas? Set up a new life under an alias for him?"

"You could do that?" Angelique felt her face go slack.

"The Tower poses a good deal more of a challenge than either Newgate or Ludgate, but yes, we could do that." Miss Moore paused. "Though you should know that he could never return to England. And it is likely that you would never see him again."

Angelique sank down on the pretty brocaded sofa, suddenly too weary to remain on her feet. The small part of her embraced the idea of simply sending Gerald safely away. Send him to some far corner of the earth where Angelique would no longer be required to look after him. No longer be required to clean up his messes.

But she couldn't. He was her brother. He was her family. And their family name mattered, if not for her then for her two younger brothers.

"I want to clear my brother's name," she whispered.

"More difficult, of course, but a noble sentiment," Miss Moore said. "Should you choose to pursue that avenue, know that along with that will come the truth. Is that what you want?"

"What kind of question is that?" Angelique stared at her.

"A fair one. The truth is not often palatable. The truth in your brother's case may not be what you wish it to be. You must be prepared for that."

Angelique squeezed her eyes shut briefly.

"We can arrange for your brother to disappear without asking hard questions," Miss Moore said, not unkindly. "Without asking anything at all, really. Without requiring the truth."

"You think he did it?"

"I don't get paid to form opinions, my lady. It doesn't matter what I think. It only matters what you want."

"I want the truth." Angelique needed the truth. She needed that information so that she might devise a new set of options. No matter how painful or how awful they might be. She would endure this as she had endured everything else.

"Very good." There was something that looked like approval in Miss Moore's eyes.

"So you'll help me?"

"Of course we will, my lady. Whatever is required. We can start immediately."

It was just as well Angelique was sitting down because the relief that crashed through her left her limp and shaking. "Thank you." For the first time since Burleigh showed up at her door, she felt like she wasn't alone. She felt like there was some hope.

"Of course. Now, there are a few things we need to—"

"I can't pay you everything now," Angelique blurted, knowing that details like this needed to be dealt with up front. She gazed at her hands clasped tightly in her lap. "But I have a deposit with me, and I'll pay you weekly for as long as it takes." She knew the services of Chegarre & Associates were obscenely expensive.

"That's been taken care of," Miss Moore told her.

"What?" Angelique's head lifted in confusion. "By whom?"

"By me." Alexander Lavoie was leaning on the doorframe, an empty glass balanced in his hand.

Angelique shot to her feet even as her heart stuttered to a stop and then resumed at twice its normal pace. He was dressed in black evening clothes, as if he had just stepped out from his club. But what his presence meant was beyond her comprehension. "What are you doing here, Mr. Lavoie?"

"At the moment, drinking an inferior whiskey." He shot a faintly accusing look in the direction of Miss Moore.

"But how did you know I was...Did you follow me?" she asked, her tired mind trying to assimilate the possibilities.

"I did not follow you."

It was the way he said it that made the hair on the back of her neck stand up. "But you had someone follow me? Why?"

Lavoie shrugged. "London can be a treacherous place, don't you agree?"

Disbelief warred with resentment, and she welcomed it as the distraction it was. "I'm perfectly capable of looking after myself."

"I know."

Her mouth snapped shut, the argument stalled before it had even begun. "I didn't ask for your help."

"I know that also. But you have it regardless."

She sat back down with a thump. For the first time, Angelique considered the ramifications of Lavoie's presence. And not only his presence, but his obvious familiarity with his surroundings. His informal and easy comportment with Miss Moore. "You know why I'm here."

"I do. But before you ask, you need to know that what your brother has or has not done changes nothing between us, my lady."

Angelique's eyes slid to Miss Moore, who was listening to this exchange in silence.

Lavoie followed her gaze. "Miss Moore knows, my lady. The manner of our relationship."

Angelique felt herself flush. An image of Alex in a cheval mirror, his head bent, his mouth on her neck, clouded her vision. She gritted her teeth, forcing it from her mind. "The manner of our relationship?" she repeated coolly.

"That you are a valued employee in my club."

"Of course." Angelique met his amber gaze. "Just like you are a valued employee in this firm."

She'd caught him off guard.

Stupid that she should do so because he should know better than to underestimate her quick mind.

Across the room, Ivory made a low sound in her throat. "Good Lord, I can see why you're smitt—"

"Have a care, Duchess."

Ivory's shrewd eyes went to Angelique and then back to him, considering. She came toward him and slipped past him into the hall. "I'll be in my study if you need anything," she murmured as she closed the door firmly behind her.

Alex put his empty glass on a small table and turned to face Angelique. She was watching him, her eyes narrowed.

"Yes," he said, meeting her gaze. "I am part of this firm. And as such, I am in a position to help."

"Yes, you keep saying that."

"What?"

"That you want to help. Even before...this. Why?"

"Because I can."

"You're going to have to do better than that, Mr. Lavoie." Angelique was still watching him, her eyes unwavering.

She was right. He was going to have to do better than a flippant answer if he wanted her trust. If he wanted her faith. And he wanted both of those. In fact, he was uncomfortably aware he wanted more than those two things.

Except he couldn't really answer her honestly. What was he going to say? That he was thoroughly smitten with her? That he couldn't bear the thought of her disappearing from his world when he had only so recently discovered her? That he wanted as many minutes with this woman as he could get, and he didn't really care how he got them?

He sounded like a lovesick fool. And Alexander Lavoie was neither a fool nor lovesick.

So he considered his answer carefully. "I would do the same for any one of my employees. And I have, many times, in the past, when they've come to me for help. But you've seemed determined to resist my help, even when it was not in your best interests."

"I think I am the better judge of my best interests, don't you?"

"Mmmm."

"I don't require rescue, Mr. Lavoie."

"Yes, and you keep saying *that*." Alex echoed her words. "Requiring help from time to time does not make you helpless. It makes you human. And right now, help is within my power to give."

He saw Angelique's lips compress.

"We are..." He searched for a word that would encapsulate their relationship. "Partners." It escaped before he could reconsider.

"Partners." She made an indecipherable noise and turned away from him, going to stand in front of the hearth.

"Yes, partners," he said with more conviction this time. "And I am not in the habit of abandoning a partner when circumstances become difficult."

She held out her hands to the warmth. "So would you have told me? If this had never happened?"

"Told you what?"

"That you are far more than a gaming hell owner?"

"What is it that you think I am?"

"Your ability to answer a question with a question is astounding, Mr. Lavoie."

"Is that a compliment?"

"No." Angelique stared down at the flames. "How much do you know?" She sounded almost resigned.

"I am well aware of the circumstances surrounding your brother's arrest." Alex hesitated before deciding to save them both a great deal of time. "I've had him followed as well, but at a distance."

"Of course you did." Angelique pressed her fingers to her temples, still staring into the glowing coals.

"I regret that I lacked sufficient insight to have my men intervene to prevent whatever it was that may have happened in that house."

Angelique's hands dropped. "It's not your fault." She paused for a long minute, the clock ticking away the seconds into the silence. "I was asking how much you knew about my family."

His first instinct was to deny any sort of knowledge. Which would accomplish nothing except muddy the waters and continue to forge distrust. "I know that your father sold most of the lands belonging to the Hutton estate before he died. And I suspect that that money is not just unavailable, but missing entirely." He let the last take on the cadence of a question.

Her shoulders sagged fractionally. "Yes."

"I know that you have been doing whatever necessary to keep your household running. One cannot eat a Rembrandt, no matter how beautifully it was painted."

Her head turned, and she met his eyes. "Yes." He was pleased to see that there was no apology in her expression. "But I didn't realize our current financial predicament was common knowledge."

"It's not. London society is oblivious. You've hidden it well."

She made a sound that was not quite a laugh. "And here I thought the excuses I told Gerald to use about redecorating and renovating the townhome would be wearing thin by now."

"In my experience, people only see what they expect to see. Simple explanations are usually the easiest to accept."

"Tell me, Mr. Lavoie, did you know all of this when you hired me?" The question was innocent enough, but he could hear the layers of bitter suspicion in each word.

Alex considered her. "Are you asking if I hired you out of pity? Or if it amused me to be complicit in your charade? Or if I thought I might leverage your situation somehow?"

She held his gaze, unflinching.

"I did not even know who you were, my lady, until you flung yourself between your brother and my driver's pistols."

"Oh." For the first time, the weary, cynical expression on her face vanished.

"I hired you because of your mind, Lady Angelique. Because you can do something very few people can, and I admire that. Because..." he trailed off. Because he was thoroughly smitten. He smothered all the strange emotions that seemed to accompany such an admission. Because emotion never helped solve anything.

Alex took a step closer to her. "Tell me about the Viscount Seaton."

"What does Seaton have to do with anything?" The wary suspicion was back.

"The titles of Rossburn and Hutton have a history."

"I suppose," she told him. "Our fathers were on cordial terms, and my brother and Seaton are friends. But what does that have to do with—"

"I also know that, not so many years ago, it was rumored that they might be bound by marriage."

Alex watched her stiffen. "It was never made official."

"But it was discussed."

She looked back at the fire. "My father was agreeable to the idea," Angelique said. "And Seaton's father was pleased that my dowry would further feather the Rossburn nest."

"And what did you think?" Alex tried to keep his tone neutral, though he suddenly found his fingers clenched into his palms.

She shrugged, though she did not look at him. "I was...not opposed to it. Lord Seaton was handsome. He was charming. And there was the added benefit that our families were friends."

"But?"

She shrugged again. "But nothing. It didn't happen. My mother became ill. His father changed his mind about the marriage. Nothing formal was ever announced."

It was about the same time that his wife became ill that the old marquess started selling off the Hutton holdings, Ivory had said.

"Why?"

"Why what?"

"Why did Rossburn change his mind?" Alex wasn't sure what he was chasing here, but his instincts were goading him on. Or at least that was what he was telling himself.

Angelique turned and gave him a hard look. "I have no idea, Mr. Lavoie. I was nineteen years old, and assertiveness was not my strong suit at the time. While I was watching my mother waste away in pain, I didn't think to petition the Duke of Rossburn for a list of reasons why I was no longer suitable for his son."

Alex studied her rigid posture. He believed her but wasn't sure she was telling him everything. "What about George Fitzherbert himself?" he pressed. "Did he wish to marry you?"

"I thought he did. I was wrong."

"You sound sure."

"I am." She wrapped her arms around herself.

"Do you still wish to marry him?" He cursed that question as soon as it was out of his mouth, but he was unable to help himself. He was well aware he sounded like a jealous suitor.

Her jaw tightened, and her eyes hardened further. "No. And I can't see what this has to do with Gerald. Why are we discussing this, Mr. Lavoie?"

Because the irrational part of me wants to know if you were ever in love with Seaton. If you still are. "Because Seaton was there when your brother allegedly entered that house," he said. He didn't add, *and slit a maid's throat.* "Which makes him of interest to me."

"I am well aware of that, Mr. Lavoie. But they were friends long before there was ever a possibility that I might become Seaton's wife."

"Yet the Duke of Rossburn will offer no assistance to you on Lord Hutton's behalf. Past relationships will not matter in his haste to distance himself and his family from the taint of this scandal," Alex mused.

Her eyes narrowed. "How did you know— Of course. I forgot. You had me followed."

"And you wouldn't be here otherwise." He tried to say it gently.

Angelique bit her lip. "Gerald didn't do it," she said, her voice suddenly small, as if all the fight had drained away. "He couldn't have killed someone."

Alex felt a muscle in his jaw flex, and he folded his arms over his chest. What he wanted to do was to take her in his arms and hold her. Kiss away her troubles and tell her that everything would be all right. Except he couldn't do that. Regardless of his unforgiveable slip that very first night, she was not his lover. She was his employee. An asset to his club. One did not mix business and pleasure.

He needed to remember that. And he would start by ignoring just how fiercely protective he was feeling at the moment. Feelings caused lapses in judgment. Feelings made smart men do stupid things. God knew he had seen the evidence of such in his tenure here.

"I can help you if you let me," was all he said.

She held his gaze, conflict swirling in her eyes. "Yes."

"Thank you." He let out a breath he hadn't realized he was holding. Something that felt like an intense mix of gratification and anticipation swept through him, and he ignored that too.

"This all might be my fault," she said next.

"Now that is the first truly idiotic thing I've heard you say. None of this is your fault any more than it is mine." He forced himself to focus on the problem at hand.

"I was furious with Gerald for taking money that wasn't his. Money that was meant for the twins' tuition. I said some horrible things. Gerald promised that he would fix it. He promised he would replace that money." She sounded miserable.

"So you think he decided to break into the Earl of Trevane's house and steal a necklace?"

Angelique shook her head. "I don't know. That's what scares me. I just don't know."

"Has he ever done something like that before?"

"I don't think so. But I can't know for sure, can I?"

Alex felt his brows furrow. Angelique had a point. Perhaps his reduced circumstances had finally driven the young Marquess of Hutton to do desperate things. Desperate, stupid, dangerous things.

Though Alex wasn't convinced that Gerald Archer possessed the cunning to come up with something like that all on his own.

"Do you know what Seaton was doing with your brother the night he was arrested?" Alex asked.

"What, besides hiding in the Earl of Trevane's bushes and waiting for his first opportunity to flee and save himself?" Angelique's voice was brittle.

"Well, that, but more importantly, what they were doing earlier that day. In Pillory Lane."

Her eyes went wide with confusion. "Why were they there?"

"I was hoping, my lady, you might tell me. They remained at a place called the Silver Cock for a number of hours. Has he ever mentioned it to you?"

"No. I've never heard of it. But then I haven't seen him this last week. Tildy told me he hasn't come home much." She paused. "Was Burleigh there too?"

Alex frowned. Jed Harris hadn't mentioned anything about Burleigh being present. "No. Why do you ask?"

"Because Burleigh told me he was with my brother and Seaton when Gerald decided to go to Trevane's house. Said he didn't fancy waiting in the rain so he waited at a coffeehouse instead." He could tell she was making an effort to keep her voice steady.

"Mmmm."

"What is this Silver Cock?"

"An establishment that serves gin and not much else and is most often frequented by smugglers, sailors, thieves, pickpockets, and whores."

"Well, if you wanted to know why my brother was there, you have your answer. The very first and last parts, that is."

He winced. "My lady—"

"Don't apologize. I am not blind or stupid. Pretending anything other than reality has never served me well. And in this case, it would seem that the Silver Cock and all its charms weren't enough. Unfortunately." Her voice cracked.

Alex cursed inwardly. He rather agreed with her, but if he was to be thorough, he wanted to hear from Hutton himself exactly what sort of business he and Seaton had found in Smithfield.

"Do you think your brother would speak to me?" he asked abruptly.

She stared at him. "Now? In the Tower?"

"Yes. Would Hutton tell me the truth if I asked?" he repeated. "Be honest."

"Um. No." Angelique's eyes slid away. "I don't think he would."

"Mmmm." It wasn't a surprise. "He doesn't like me."

"He doesn't know you," she tried, sounding uncomfortable.

"My lady, my feelings are not as fragile as that." Though the fact that she cared about such things sent a curious warmth curling through him. The craving to kiss her returned, and he jammed his hands in his pockets to make sure he didn't do anything so foolish. These unwanted, unfamiliar feelings were going to be the death of him.

Angelique looked up at him then, her eyes filled with something he couldn't quite identify. Something he was afraid to identify. "Alex—"

"Then you will need to come with me." He interrupted her, afraid that if she kept looking at him like that, he would prove himself the rogue her brother no doubt believed him to be.

She blinked, and he was able to breathe again. "To the Tower?"

"Yes."

"But they are not letting anyone see him—"

Alex stepped back, to distance himself from the temptation that still stood before him and to concentrate on what needed to be done next. "Leave those details to me."

Chapter 10

Angelique could smell the stench from the sluggish Tower moat long before they arrived.

It was a rancid odor that got worse as they drew nearer, eclipsing even the stew of the Thames. She stayed motionless in the small skiff that Alex rowed, maneuvering their way through the mass of watercraft that swirled and thronged the waterway. Up ahead on her left, rising up from the river, the Tower loomed, its stony walls staring back at her, blank and unforgiving. It was hard for her to keep her eyes fixed ahead and not stare up at the great edifices that rose behind the walls, in the hopes of catching sight of her brother.

Which was ridiculous, she knew. It wasn't like Gerald would be strolling the parapets. She couldn't even begin to imagine where he might be within the maze of buildings that were stacked within the Tower's walls. Another wave of hopelessness rose. Even if they could somehow get past the guards and the warders, how would they ever find him?

She took a steadying breath, trying to stave off the anxious worry that once again threatened to overwhelm her. She focused her attention on Alex instead, studying his radically altered appearance. Gone were the tailored and expensive evening clothes. In their place was a soldier's uniform—a blue jacket with dull buttons that ran up the facing and a pair of worn but neat trousers that had faded to grey. The black collar of the jacket came up high against the sides of his face, and the brim of the black military hat he wore cast most of his face in shadow. His knife was jammed into a sheath and belted to his waist, and a pouch was slung across his body,

When she had first seen him in uniform, it had surprised her. Not because the clothing looked strange on him, but because, somehow, it didn't. She recalled the easy way he handled both firearms and blades. Both reasonable things, perhaps, for a gaming hell owner, but the mastery and ease with which he was guiding this tiny skiff made her pause. It was obvious he had spent time on the water. For the first time, Angelique realized she knew absolutely nothing about his past. And it hadn't mattered. Until now. Now there was a part of her that wanted to know. Needed to know.

"You were a soldier," she said suddenly.

She saw his hands tighten on the oars, the rhythm hitching before it resumed. "Mmmm. A little late to verify my skill set beyond a hand of loo now, isn't it?"

Angelique leaned forward, refusing to accept another one of his non-answers. "Were you a rifleman?"

His face tightened almost imperceptibly before he schooled his features into an unreadable slate once again. "Isn't this where you ask me if I really was a spy?"

"See, now a good spy would never answer that. A waste of a question." She paused. "You were a rifleman."

"You sound very sure of yourself." He glanced behind him at the river, adjusting their course.

"You answer questions you don't want to answer with questions, Mr. Lavoie. It's how I know I'm right."

His eyes snapped back to hers. "I don't do that."

She held his gaze steadily. "You do."

She could see a muscle working along the edge of his jaw, his mouth set into hard lines.

"Militia," he said after a long minute. "I was militia. Third York Regiment with Major William Allen under General Sheaffe."

Angelique frowned. "Was that from Yorkshire?"

"Canada."

Angelique felt her jaw slacken. "You fought in the colonies?"

"I grew up in the colonies." The strokes of the oars slowed. "York was our home. At the time, defending it seemed like the honorable thing to do."

Angelique was having a hard time imagining what sort of circumstances might bring a militiaman from the vast wilds to a gaming hell in London. "Why did you leave?"

Alex's entire body stiffened, and he looked away. "Because war leaves nothing behind save ruins."

"What about your family?"

He dug the oars into the water. "Why is my distant past so fascinating all of a sudden?"

Another question. Angelique fell silent, recognizing that this conversation had come to an end. Whatever lay in that part of the story was not something he seemed inclined to share. At least now. Perhaps he might eventually trust her enough to share the rest of that story. Or perhaps not.

"Thank you," she said.

"For what?" He remained focused on the river.

"For your answers. All four of them."

She saw his posture relax as he understood that she had

given him the space to retreat. "You counted them?" he asked dryly.

"I like counting things. I'm good at it."

He turned back to her, a hint of a smile playing around his mouth, his eyes almost gold in light reflecting off the surface of the water. He held her gaze for a moment before he looked away again, concentrating on moving the little boat past the river traffic. Angelique shifted on the hard bench, the welcome distraction of their conversation fading in the face of the reality that was looming just ahead. She watched as they drifted past Tower Hill and the stairs that ran up the bank, angling toward the entrance that cast deep shadows over the greasy surface of the water.

"What are you doing?" she asked.

Alex looked up at her before hauling on the oars again. "I would have thought that was obvious."

Angelique eyed the tunnel that was drawing closer with every steady pull of the oars. "We're going through the Traitor's Gate?" She despised the hesitant way that came out.

"Mmmm."

The boat slid into shadow. Angelique shifted in her seat again, the unfamiliar clothes she wore scratching at her skin. The din of the river traffic was suddenly and eerily muffled, replaced by the dripping and lapping of water that echoed around them. Out of the weak sunlight, the temperature dropped, and she shivered. She eyed the sludge that had gathered along the edges of the stone near the water's edge, lines visible that marked the rise and fall of the tide. Here, the stench was almost enough to make her eyes water, and all around her, a dark, slimy coating covered every surface, making the color of the stone almost impossible to see.

"Why couldn't we go in by Tower Hill?" she asked.

"I don't have friends at that entrance." Alex glanced up.

Angelique stared at him a moment before her gaze followed his. Above their heads, on the platform that overlooked the passage, a red-coated guard raised his hand briefly to the brim of his hat and tipped his head. Alex nodded and pulled on the oars again and the skiff slipped into the pool directly in front of two large gates.

Within seconds, one of the gates swung open, groaning on its hinges and sending sluggish ripples of water to slap softly against the hull. Alex deftly maneuvered their boat through the narrow opening and rested as the craft came to a stop just in front of a wide set of stone stairs. Behind her, the gate banged shut. She felt a shiver go through her that had nothing to do with the cool damp.

"Also, I'm quite sure that your brother would have been brought into the Tower this way. The fewer witnesses, the better."

There was something that Angelique found deeply unsettling about the idea of Gerald being brought in through the Traitor's Gate. As if it somehow condemned him to guilt.

The sounds of footsteps from above jerked her from her dark thoughts.

"Mr. Lavoie. It's been a long time." The guard from the platform was coming down the stairs, glancing quickly behind him.

"Been busy." Alex stepped from the little boat and held it still while Angelique clambered out. "Watch the stairs," he said. "They're slippery."

Angelique's booted foot had already sunk into a soft muck that coated the stair, and she carefully climbed up farther where the footing was less perilous.

"What do you want?" The guard had come to a stop in front of them. He was older, with an obvious air of authority about him. A captain or some such thing, Angelique surmised. He was also short, but standing a foot above them, it put him on equal eye level with Alex.

"Always to the point," Alex murmured. "That is what I like most about you, Hervey. Where are your colleagues?"

The thickset guard made a gesture of impatience. "Sent 'em to look for something they'll never find when I saw you coming. They won't look forever, though, so talk fast."

"There was a man brought here last night. A prisoner. I'd like a word."

The guard raised bushy brows, and his lips curled into a smile that didn't quite reach his eyes. "Sent you to save him, did they?"

Alex shrugged. "Sent me to talk to him first. We'll see about saving him later."

The guard looked unimpressed. "He's denied visitors."

"At whose request?" Alex inquired pleasantly.

"Chief warder."

"Unusual, that, isn't it? No visitors?"

Hervey snorted. "Unusual they brought him to the Tower in the first place."

"It is, isn't it?" Alex mused. "Why do you think he was brought here?"

It was the guard's turn to shrug. "I don't get paid to think. But the toff's a murderer."

Angelique could feel every muscle in her body tense, but Alex only chuckled. "Heard that rumor too."

Hervey squinted at Alex. "You're sayin' he's not?"

"I'm saying it would be helpful for me to speak with him. I'm not here to help him escape."

The guard looked unimpressed. "I've heard that before," he muttered. He crossed his arms, and his eyes flickered to Angelique. "Who's this?"

"A concerned citizen," Alex replied.

It took every ounce of willpower not to look away from the guard's probing look. The bulky, bland men's clothes and coat she wore hid any trace of femininity. Alex had also produced a pair of spectacles and a battered cap that completely covered her tightly braided hair, and the end result had been startlingly thorough. A soldier on Tower grounds with a woman would draw attention, Alex had told her. A soldier in the company of a clerk would be less noticeable.

"I don't work with people I don't know," Hervey said.

Angelique reached into her coat and pulled out the small bag Alex had given her. She held it toward the guard, and he took it from her fingers.

"Diamonds," she said, pitching her voice low, a little surprised at how steady it came out. "I found them and was hoping that a member of His Majesty's service might know what to do with them. Mr. Lavoie thought you would be able to...help."

Hervey pulled open the string and upended the bag. Two stones fell out, glittering against the rough texture of his palm. The guard grunted and eyed her again. "Perhaps I might make an exception."

"I knew you'd see reason," Alex said, and this time his voice had a slight edge.

Hervey grunted again, and the diamonds disappeared into his jacket pocket. "You're lucky you pay well, Lavoie."

"Luck has nothing to do with it, Hervey," Alex replied, moving to pull the skiff into the shadow of the stairs where it couldn't be seen. "And as much as I admire your entrepreneurship, I do expect to get my money's worth."

⁓

The Marquess of Hutton had been imprisoned in the White Tower.

That revelation had taken Alex aback, until he stopped to consider it. The White Tower contained nothing but stores of gunpowder and records. No civilian traffic went in and out, and the only entrance to the ancient keep was guarded. Perfect if one wished to restrict and control access to a prisoner. It also made it easy for Hervey to use his rank to send his men elsewhere on another fruitless mission, deftly clearing the way for a soldier and a clerk to slip inside.

Once they were in, Hervey had joined them, leading them through mazes of barrels stacked in rooms that had once been banqueting halls and council chambers for the most powerful men and women in the country. They followed him up a spiral staircase and stopped in the northeast corner of the upper floor, in front of a door that was almost black with age. Light from the tall, recessed windows spilled across the stone passage, creating long, repetitive patterns at their feet.

"Gave him a room in the old king's chambers," Hervey said with a slight sneer. "He's even got a real bed in there. Can't say we didn't provide him with the best."

"Indeed." Alex eyed the medieval-looking door, bolted and padlocked from the outside. A rectangular metal plate had been added to the upper portion of the door at a more recent time, fixed on one side with heavy hinges. On the other, another padlock secured it. Hervey had produced a key and inserted it into the lock, the sound of it turning inordinately loud in the silence around them.

"Got a visitor, your lordship," Hervey announced as he swung the plate to the side, revealing a long eyehole crisscrossed with an iron grate that would allow a clear view of the room and its occupants but prevent anything from being passed through.

"You're not going to open the door?" Alex asked.

"You said you wanted to speak with him. So speak. Be so

kind as to lock up when you're done, or the next time you come knocking, I might not remember you, diamonds or not."

Alex gazed at him impassively. He was quite sure that he'd be able to pick the locks within minutes if he so desired. He tucked that bit of information away for future consideration.

"You have ten minutes, Lavoie. Ten minutes and then my men on the south side entrance will resume their posts. Though you may not have that long until the warders of the keep do their rounds. The presence of our illustrious guest here today has them a little more diligent than you'll like. And I have no control over those men."

Alex gazed at the guard. "Diligent?"

"They're like mice today, everywhere in the keep corridors, making sure their titled cat stays safely locked away." He paused. "Don't get caught, Lavoie. You find yourself in chains, I can't help you."

"Understood."

"Pleasure doing business, as always," Hervey said, and, without another word, melted into the shadows down the passage, his footsteps fading.

Alex turned back to the door, only to find Angelique already had her face pressed up to the spy-hole. "Gerald?" she said uncertainly.

"*Ang?*" It sounded muffled coming from the other side of the door, but then Alex saw Hutton's face appear. Or rather, he saw the man's eyes appear, and they were bloodshot and shadowed and miserable. "Is that you?"

"Yes." She pulled off her spectacles and shoved them in her coat pocket.

Alex moved a little farther away, pressing himself into the shadows. It was likely Hutton would say more to his sister if he believed her alone.

"What—when—how the hell did you get in here?"

Angelique was shaking her head impatiently, her entire body visibly tense, even under her bulky clothes. "Are you all right?" Her voice was strained.

Alex could see Hutton's eyes narrow. "You shouldn't be here."

"Where else would I be?" she asked. "You've been arrested, Gerald. For murder."

Hutton's eyes darted away but he remained silent, as if refusing to acknowledge that.

Angelique's hands were pressed to the surface of the door so hard the ends of her fingertips were white. "Did you do it? Did you kill her?"

Her brother's reddened eyes flew back to hers. "No! I didn't kill anyone. You believe me, don't you, Ang?"

Alex shook his head. Of course Hutton would say that. Whether it was true or not was more difficult to tell.

"But you were there." Angelique's voice was rising. "A woman died, and you were there. They caught *you*. Covered in blood!"

Hutton's face disappeared briefly before it reappeared in the eyehole. "I tried to help her! But she was already dead. I was set up."

"Set up." Angelique repeated it flatly.

"Yes."

"Why would someone do that?"

"I don't know!"

"Gerald, if they find you guilty, they're going to hang you," she said, her words ragged.

"They can't find me guilty. And they certainly can't hang me," he replied stubbornly. "I'm a marquess. I am above the law."

Angelique's head dropped, and she rested her head on the door. "Not for this, Gerald."

"Your sister is right." Alex stepped out of the shadows. It appeared that Hutton was not going to voluntarily confess anything on his own, and time was not on their side.

Hutton's eyes bulged in horrified recognition. "What is he doing here, Ang?" he demanded.

"He's trying to help me. Help you." Angelique raised her head from the door.

"You need to stay the hell away from my sister," Hutton said.

Alex ignored him. "You have bigger problems, my lord, the least of which is my relationship with Lady Angelique."

"I have powerful friends that will make sure—"

"Shut up and listen, Gerald," Angelique snapped, and Alex saw Hutton's face go slack with shock.

Alex took advantage. "If you are to come out of this with your neck still intact, my lord, I would suggest you start telling some truths. I cannot help a man who will not help himself."

Hutton was blinking rapidly. "I am a marquess, Mr. Lavoie. I can't be—"

"Disgraced? Hanged? Made an example out of? I'm certain that is what Earl Ferrers told himself after he shot his steward and before he found himself dancing at the end of a silk rope. There are laws, my lord, and your title will not be enough to protect you. And while the ton will gorge themselves on the scandal that this will create, they won't be able to distance themselves from you fast enough. You're on your own."

The young marquess suddenly looked uncertain. "I don't believe that. The Duke of Rossburn—"

"Told me to leave London after he made it clear he would not be coming to our aid." Angelique's words were dull.

Hutton paled. "I did this for you, you know. And Phillip

and Gregory. I was trying to help. It was the perfect solution. No one was supposed to get hurt."

"*Thieving* was the perfect solution?" Angelique demanded.

"Where else was the money supposed to come from, Ang?" Hutton sounded angry now. "My friends? Burleigh's only a baron, not a banker—he doesn't have that sort of blunt. Seaton does, but his father controls the purse strings." He stopped. "The Earl of Trevane spends more on his mistress in a month than we spend in an entire year. A man with enough money to commission a necklace fit for a queen and then hang it around the neck of a—" He clamped his lips together. "He wouldn't have missed it."

"Mmmm." Alex drummed his fingers on his leg. This was getting them nowhere. Time to change his approach. "Let me tell you what I think happened. You needed money. A young maid who you may or may not have had a sordid relationship with gave you information. Told you that Trevane had the necklace, told you where he kept it, and probably even let you into the house. No doubt you promised to give her a cut of the profits when you fenced it. But then you changed your mind. Got greedy, perhaps, or just didn't want to take the chance she would talk."

"No! That's not what happened at all! I already told you I didn't kill her. I'd never seen that woman before last night." His eyes were wild.

Alex studied Hutton, reasonably sure now that this, at least, was the truth. "Then if you didn't kill her, who did?"

"I don't know. But someone set me up!"

"Yes, you keep saying that."

"It's true," Hutton wheezed.

Alex wasn't convinced. The more plausible explanation was that someone else had broken into that house to steal a necklace that was worth a king's ransom.

Alex frowned. "Tell me how you knew about the necklace."

Hutton stared at him with glassy eyes. "There was a note."

"From whom?"

The marquess rubbed at his face with his fingers. "I don't know. It was delivered to my house by a street urchin. All it said was that the Earl of Trevane had just that evening picked up a diamond necklace he'd commissioned. That he could be counted on to keep such things in the drawer of his desk in his study. That it could be had by whomever was bold enough to take it."

Alex wondered, for a moment, just how Angelique was related to this man. How this naïve, idiotic boy shared any sort of blood with the woman standing beside him. "Do you still have it? The note?"

"Maybe. It might still be in my room."

"Who knew you needed money?" Angelique asked his next question for him.

"No one. Just...Burleigh and Seaton." His hands dropped from his face. "But Seaton said he'd ask around. He's got...contacts that he thought might help."

"Contacts?" Alex let that hang for a second. "Like the kind you find in a tavern in Pillory Lane?"

Hutton made a pathetic sound. "Maybe?"

"And you thought to trust such?" Alex was incredulous.

Hutton hung his head. "I didn't kill anyone. You have to believe me."

"These contacts that Seaton had—did you ever speak with any of them?"

Hutton shrugged helplessly. "Sort of."

"Sort of? Who were they?"

"They said they were men who worked at the customs houses."

"Did they have names?"

"I don't remember," the marquess mumbled. "Seaton kept buying me gin."

Alex felt his teeth grind. This man probably deserved everything that was coming to him, if only for his colossal lack of judgment and stupidity. Except the woman standing beside him didn't. Angelique deserved none of this.

"It's not too late to extract him," he said, turning to Angelique and holding her gaze. "I'll need probably the better part of a week to get things in order, but—"

"Extraction? What the hell does that mean?" Gerald demanded.

"It means exactly what it sounds like," Angelique replied, not looking away from him.

"You mean to help me escape?"

"Yes. Out of England."

"But that will make me look guilty!"

"You already look guilty, Gerald," Angelique said.

"But I'm innocent! They have to believe me. They will believe me! I won't flee. I am a marquess, and—"

From somewhere in the bowels of the keep, a door slammed. Their time was up.

"We need to go," Alex said, reaching for the metal plate.

"I'm sorry, Ang," Hutton said miserably. "I never meant for any of this to happen—"

Muffled voices from somewhere down below filtered up the stairwell. "My lady," Alex warned, "we're out of time."

Angelique bit her lip, her complexion stark under her cap. She turned away from the door.

Alex stepped forward. "Regardless of your feelings toward me, my lord, if you have any regard for your sister, we were never here, do you understand?"

Hutton nodded.

"Good." Alex closed the metal plate and slid the lock back into place, wincing as metal scraped. With dismay, he realized that the voices were coming closer, the sound of booted feet echoing as they mounted the same spiral staircase that he and Angelique had used to reach Gerald's cell. Alex had no interest in finding out who might be approaching. They would have to find a different way down. "This way," he whispered, and Angelique nodded her understanding.

With quick, silent steps, he guided them farther down the hall and away from the stairs. Up ahead, the passage led to a viewing gallery above the chapel of St. John, the large windows on this floor and the one below him flooding this part of the keep with light.

"Hurry," he urged Angelique. They would need to skirt the gallery to reach the other staircase in the southwest corner of the keep, but with the abundance of light, they would be exposed should a warder happen to look in their direction.

He kept Angelique in front of him, torn between the need to appear as though they belonged should they be spotted and the urge to run. They reached the gallery, and the cavernous space of the chapel opened up. Here the air was thick with the now-familiar scent of charcoal but also with dust and the mustiness of old paper.

"What is all that?" Angelique whispered, looking down.

Below them, where pews or benches might have once existed, were boxes and trunks and leaning towers that resembled crude bookcases. They rose up in tall stacks, creating narrow alleys and casting deep shadows. In the center of the chapel, a massive, scarred table rested like an island amid a sea of flotsam, a handful of chairs pulled up haphazardly around it. Ledgers and loose documents littered the surface, some piled in perilous-looking towers and others abandoned on their own.

"Chancery records," Alex replied tersely. "Most of them centuries old, and not important to anyone anymore." They were hurrying along the south side now, and he kept his attention focused straight ahead, his body tense. But there was no shout that came, no demand to halt and identify themselves, and they reached the staircase in the southwest corner without mishap.

"Go," he whispered to Angelique, her bulky clothes giving her gait an uneven rhythm as she hurried down the stairs. As they drew closer to the second floor, the sound of more voices and more booted feet echoed up from below them. Alex cursed inwardly and caught Angelique's sleeve, pulling her out of the stairwell. Here, the acrid odor of charcoal was strong. His eyes scanned the massive room that opened up before them, shafts of light spilling across the expanse that had once been the grandest banqueting hall in all of England. Now the space was lined with barrels of gunpowder and crates full of powder cartridges and powder horns. It was all stacked neatly in rows extending from the outer walls, creating a single passage down the center of the great hall. They couldn't stay here—there was no place to hide. They'd be seen in an instant.

"Come." Alex headed back in the direction of the chapel. It would be far easier to find a hiding place in among the stone columns and the towering stacks of records and let whoever was coming pass.

They reached the tall chapel doors, the rap of boot heels and conversation beating like an ominous drum behind them. Alex grasped the handle, pulling hard on the heavy door. It groaned on creaky hinges, and the voices in the passage behind them abruptly stopped. Angelique slipped inside, and he followed, glancing up. Here, they were still out of sight from anyone standing in the upper gallery and hidden from view to anyone in the passage. He put a finger to his lips, and she nodded, both of them frozen against the heavy door, listening intently.

He could hear the rapid rise and fall of Angelique's breath, her body pressed against his. It didn't matter that the bulky layers of her clothing hid her curves. Just the feel of her against him had his body responding in a manner more suitable for a randy, green adolescent than a seasoned soldier. And one that was doing his best not to get caught sneaking around the Tower of London at that. He gritted his teeth. Where the hell was his head?

Somewhere south of your waist, a snide inner voice replied.

He felt her put a hand on his arm, and a shudder rocked through him.

God, he was so far over his head with this woman that he didn't know if there was any hope of surfacing with any sort of self-respect or dignity. All he knew was that he wanted her. Dressed as a clerk in a chapel. Dressed as a goddess in his club. Most importantly, not dressed at all.

"Did they see us?" she whispered near his ear.

Alex closed his eyes briefly, trying to focus on her words and not the feel of her breath against his skin. At least one of them was still thinking rationally. He glanced down at her. She was so close that he could see the flecks of pewter in her irises, could count each freckle across the bridge of her nose. She licked her lips nervously, and he stared, remembering just how intoxicating those lips had tasted. Wondering what would happen if he tasted them again. Right now.

He forced himself to concentrate. "I don't know if they saw us." The hinges of the door had been loud. He listened, but it was hard to hear anything from behind the heavy, carved door. Maybe the men behind them hadn't heard. Maybe they'd been too caught up in their conversation to—

"Who's there?" The demand came from the other side of the door, and this time there was the unmistakable sound of steel being drawn. "Show yourself."

"Hide," he hissed to Angelique, and gave her a shove toward the shadows created by the towers of decaying records. She stumbled away from him, and he turned back to the door.

Shit, he swore. This was what he had hoped to avoid. He blew out a breath. He would have to be careful. With a prisoner on the floor above, he couldn't give whatever guards or warders that were on the other side of that door any reason to suspect that he was even aware of that. Give them a logical explanation that would have them moving on as quickly as possible.

Alex pushed open the door, and it swung outward, its hinges shrieking in protest. The edge thumped against the far stone wall, and the noise echoed up around him. Alex took a step forward and suddenly found himself with two sword blades pressed up against his neck.

Two warders stood in front of him, their expressions ones of distrust and suspicion. Their red coats were like spots of dark blood against the dull stone of their surroundings, giving them a slightly sinister air, though that was somewhat offset by the fact that they were painfully young. Which, in Alex's experience, would make them either easier to manipulate or unyielding in their convictions. He sincerely hoped the former.

"Steady. There's no need to saw my head off. I'm standing right here." Alex held up his arms, trying to appear as benign as possible.

The warders examined his appearance before they glanced at each other, frowning. "Identify yourself," one of them commanded. The shorter one withdrew his sword a fraction of an inch.

"Jonathon Lavoie of the Third York Regiment," he told them, as if they should already be aware of this. "I'm here on orders from General Sheaffe."

The warders looked at him blankly.

Alex allowed a frown to pull at his mouth. "Is there a problem?"

"What are you doing in here?"

"What else? Looking for records that I'm likely never to find. The place is a bloody dumping ground." He was hoping that that would be enough to pacify them and send them on their way. At the very least, lower their damn swords from his throat before someone sneezed and he lost his head.

"We weren't advised of this."

Alex shrugged. Carefully. "I'm just following orders. Same as you."

"Isn't Lavoie a French name?" the taller of the two warders asked.

"Suppose so. It's the one I was born with."

"How do we know you're not a spy for the Frogs?"

Alex forced a laugh. "Because a spy would be doing something far more glamorous than looking through a bunch of moldering Chancery papers for a general who wants to know if his grandfather owned property in London."

The warders exchanged another look.

Leave, urged Alex in his head. *Just leave—*

"You need to come with us," the smaller warder said, adjusting his grip on his sword. "Or show us your orders. Anyone given permission to use the records room here will have written permission."

Alex felt an unpleasant apprehension slither through him. This was not good at all. Especially with Angelique hidden somewhere in the chapel behind him. If they hauled him away, it would leave her exposed and vulnerable here. He wasn't sure that she would be able to slip out on her own without anyone catching her.

He eyed the two men and their weapons. He carried nothing except his hunting knife. Which, given the way the young soldiers were nervously looking at each other, would be enough. But the last thing he wanted to do was to get in a fight. It would be messy and inevitably draw all sorts of unwanted attention and put the warders on full alert. Gerald would likely be moved. Probably to the dungeon. More warders would be dispatched. It would make an extraction at a later date nearly impossible.

Additionally, he found himself troubled at the thought of killing either one of these boys. They didn't deserve to die today simply because Alex had been too slow in his retreat.

"What the hell are you doing now, Lavoie?" The hoarse voice came from behind Alex, laced with impatience, and his heart missed a beat. The warders' eyes snapped to a space just beyond him, and very slowly, Alex turned his head.

Angelique had put her spectacles back on and her cap was pulled low over her eyes. In her arms, she carried a massive stack of papers that climbed just past her chin. Some of the edges curled with age, and with every movement, clouds of dust dislodged from the stack and swirled around her head. She coughed and wiped at her face. A streak of grime covered her cheek, and more was smeared across the sleeve of her coat.

"It's about time you found some help," she continued rudely, pushing in front of Alex and forcing the gaping warders to take a step back, their blades dropping away from Alex's throat. She glared at them. "If you're going to relieve him of his head, be so kind as to do it once we're finished. There is another fifty years of records here that need to be sorted. This was only supposed to take an hour, but we'll be here all damn day at this rate."

"Who are you?" the shorter warder demanded.

"General Sheaffe's personal clerk." Angelique somehow made it sound like she had just announced herself as the Prince of Wales. "Didn't Lavoie here tell you anything?"

"Well, yes, but we don't have—"

"I don't really care what you don't have," she snapped, hefting her load of papers. "But I most certainly need your assistance. You look like a smart man. Are you?"

The warder's mouth slackened. "Er, yes?"

"Can you read? Write?"

"Yes, but—"

"Thank God. Lavoie here is good at lifting and such, but not much else. God knows why the general felt the need to send me a nursemaid who's barely literate," she muttered vilely. "He's useless when it comes to property law."

"I'd rather dig latrines," Alex retorted, just loud enough for the warders to hear.

"That will no doubt be arranged once the general hears of your recalcitrance," she said imperiously, turning back to the warders. "But no matter. I have the two of you here now. Stop waving your damn sticks around and let's get started."

The shorter warder drew himself up to his full, if limited, height. "We need to see your orders," he said. "You can't be here without them."

Angelique glared at him and then at Alex from behind the stack of documents in her arms. "Did you not inform them why we were here?"

"I tried." Alex shrugged mutinously and sent an apologetic look toward the warders. "They need to see the paperwork."

The warder cleared his throat. "Otherwise we are

required to escort you to the Wakefield Tower until such time as we can verify—"

"For the love of all that is holy. Saints save me from you military sorts and all your damn rules and orders." She extracted a hand from under the stack and jammed it into her coat pocket. The tower of papers in her arms leaned precariously. "I've got the orders from the general right here," she grumbled, yanking a slip of paper from her pocket somewhat awkwardly. "Just let me— Bloody hell!" The stack of papers that had been listing suddenly slid sideways, and Angelique threw out her hands to catch them. She was instantly enveloped in a blizzard of loose documents, the chaos made even thicker by the choking cloud of dust that erupted around them.

Alex buried his nose in his sleeve, coughing, and he could hear the two warders curse even as they stumbled back, sneezing violently. It took a few long minutes for the dust to subside, and when it did, Angelique was standing over a massive mess of paper scattered in a wide arc around her, her hands on her hips, looking utterly furious. Her eyes bored into the men standing in front of her, brimming with accusation. "Now look at this mess," she grumbled. "You want your orders, you're going to have to help me find them."

The men were staring at her in dismay but made no move toward her.

Alex dropped to his knees and picked up the nearest document. Scanned the first few lines. It appeared to be a document detailing the guardianship of an infant born in 1674. He made a show of squinting at the heading. "Test-test-a-men—" He stopped, bringing the paper closer to his face. "Testamen-ta—"

"Testamentary," Angelique snapped behind him, and heaved a tortured sigh. She leaned over and yanked the paper from his hand. "It's not relevant. We're looking for a deed, a record of tax, or a document of entail of *property*, Lavoie," she growled. "And now we're looking for the general's orders too." She looked up at the two warders. "General Sheaffe will hear about this, no question, and he's not going to be happy with the delay. He is not a patient man at the best of times."

Alex scooped up another armful of papers and shook them out, as if preparing himself to read. Another choking cloud of dust rose. The warders retreated back from the door another step. The taller one was looking at Alex with an almost sympathetic expression.

"Perhaps we'll just come back a bit later," the taller one suggested, looking at his partner. "When you've sorted this out a bit and found the orders."

The other warder sheathed his sword. "Yes. I think that would be best."

Angelique made a noise of exasperated dismissal. "Do whatever you need to do." She bent over Alex's shoulder. "No, not there," she said irritably. "Pleadings in *this* pile. Depositions here. Anything older than 1720 in *that* pile. Think you can manage to keep that straight?"

"Yes," said Alex, and listened to the sound of the warders retreating.

Chapter 11

They'd slipped silently out of the keep and across the bailey, unnoticed, and joined the flow of people near the western side of the Tower who had come to see either the menagerie or had come on other business. No one took any interest in a soldier and a clerk leaving the premises, but it was a monumental effort to keep her eyes ahead and not keep looking over her shoulder. Just like it was a monumental effort to keep walking at a normal, if brisk, pace and not flee as if the hounds of hell were on her heels.

They blended in with the streams of pedestrians and made their way west along Lower Thames Street, past the customs houses that lined the river and angled toward London Bridge. Just east of the bridge, they turned up Pudding Lane, where the familiar bulk of Matthews lounged against Alex's carriage on the side of the road, an old-fashioned pipe in his hand. He saw them coming and straightened, the slight crease of his forehead at their dusty appearance the only commentary he made before opening the door.

"To Bedford Square, Matthews," Alex instructed, the first thing he'd said since they'd left the White Tower. "We'll take her ladyship home first."

"Very good, Mr. Lavoie," Matthews replied, jamming his pipe in his mouth and handing Angelique up into the waiting carriage.

Angelique ducked into the welcome dimness of the interior and thumped back on the squabs. She closed her eyes, the fear and anxiety that had nearly choked her on their flight from the White Tower draining with a sudden violence. It left her shaky and gasping.

"Angelique?" She heard the sound of the carriage door snap shut. "Are you all right?" It was the first thing he'd said to her since they'd fled the chapel.

She opened her eyes to find Alex on the opposite seat, watching her with concern.

Was she all right? She had no idea. Choking fear had been replaced by giddy relief, and the intensity of it was scattering all coherent thought and making her feel almost drunk. "I haven't swooned if that was what you were afraid of," she told him.

"That wasn't what I was afraid of." He pulled the strap from his pouch across his body and over his head and placed it on the floor.

"Right." An illogical giggle suddenly threatened to escape. "If I was going to swoon, I would have done that earlier. At the off-with-your-head part."

The carriage lurched into motion, and Angelique put out a hand to steady herself, the sleeve of her bulky coat catching on the seat. The bubble of laughter died as quickly as it had risen, and she suddenly needed out of the coat, out of the weighty constriction, away from the scent of gunpowder and dust that still clung to it. She yanked at the buttons, pulling on the sleeves.

Alex reached forward, helping her pull the heavy wool from her body. She shoved the coat aside as if that could distance herself from the last hour. "I thought I would give us away," she whispered. She held out her hand in front of her, surprised that it shook only slightly.

"I didn't." Alex caught it and enfolded it in his, the warmth of his palm reassuring and stirring all at once. He was on the edge of his seat, watching her, his eyes searching hers in the murky light. He'd taken off his hat, and his dark hair fell alongside his face. "You were extraordinary."

"I was terrified."

His fingers tightened on hers.

She sucked in a harsh breath. "They were—"

"Angelique."

"What if—"

"Shhh." He had left his seat and was kneeling on the carriage floor in front of her. With his free hand, he reached up and removed her spectacles, then her cap. His hand trailed down the side of her jaw.

"Alex." Her emotions were still high, and a strange recklessness was coursing through her. His nearness wasn't giving her time to think. He wasn't giving her the time or the space to consider what might have happened. What did happen. Or what would happen next.

And she didn't want to think, not about any of it. But she needed something, and she was at a loss to identify what that was. "Please," she whispered, not sure what she was asking. But it didn't seem to matter because he seemed to understand.

"Yes," he whispered, and then he was kissing her.

This wasn't anything like their first kiss. This was a searing, possessive kiss, meant not to tease but to claim. Time seemed to stop, and she allowed herself to be consumed by him, to sink into his heat and his strength. She kissed

him back with the same fierce abandon, her ragged emotions
finding escape. He released her hand and pushed himself
forward, wedging his body between her legs. She wrapped
her arms around his neck and felt his hands go to her back,
sliding over her buttocks, and then he was hauling them
backward and on to his seat so that she was on her knees
now, straddling his lap.

He was cradling her to him, his mouth hard against hers,
his kiss almost desperate in its tempo. She ran her hands
down his chest, feeling the ridges of muscle that lay beneath
her palms and hating the layers of wool and linen that sepa-
rated his skin from hers. His own hands slid over her lower
back and up her ribs, and they fisted in the bottom of her
shirt, yanking it from the waistband of her trousers. And
then they were sliding beneath, his skin on hers, in the way
she had fantasized about too many times. They roamed over
her back and along the length of her spine, coming to frame
her ribs just below her breasts, his thumbs running along the
edge of the binding across her chest. She arched against him
instinctively, wanting more. Her nipples were hard against
their restraints, aching to be touched, and she made a muffled sound of frustration. She'd been here once before with
this man, and this time, *almost* wasn't going to be enough.

Alex was still kissing her, though his urgency had abated
a little. His lips claimed while his tongue dueled, and his
hands went to the back of her bindings. She could feel his
fingers working on the knot, gently and carefully. And then
she felt the bindings give, and his fingers pulled the fabric
down and away, and the slide of it over her sensitive nipples
had her gasping. Sparks of pleasure shot through her, and her
kiss became more demanding, trying to communicate what
she wanted when she had no words for it.

But Alex seemed to understand again because his hands

came up to cup her breasts, his thumbs dragging over each nipple in deliberate movements. Her fingers curled into the front of his jacket, anchoring herself against the pleasure that was pulsing through her, directly from his hands to the very center of her. Her thighs clenched hard around his hips, and she instinctively bore down on the hard ridge of his erection straining against his trousers. She heard him make a low noise in his throat, almost a growl, and then his hands were gone from her skin. She almost cried out in disappointment, but he was shoving the hem of her shirt up to her neck, and now it was his mouth on her breasts, his tongue setting fire to her skin and making her dizzy with want.

Her head tipped back, and her eyes closed, the pleasure throbbing and centering deep within her. There was a dampness at the juncture of her thighs, her unfamiliar trousers rubbing at the sensitive skin along the insides of her legs. She rocked her hips, settling more intimately against him and sending molten heat racing through her veins.

His teeth caught the edge of her nipple as she pressed forward, a groan escaping from both of them. His hands were sliding down her bare back to the flare of her hips, and he slid them just beneath her waistband, guiding the cadence of her movements. He thrust up as her hips rolled down, and he hissed, his fingers urging her tightly against him. She gasped, grinding against the sensation, sparks of searing pleasure rocketing through her.

His lips found the curve of her neck, and her head fell forward, her forehead resting on his shoulder, closing her eyes. She let go of his jacket and twined her hands around his neck, letting her fingers tangle in the thickness of his hair. His mouth was traveling along her jaw now and she turned her head, finding his lips with hers. He plundered her mouth, and his tongue thrust with the same tempo as his hips.

He pushed her down harder against him, and blinding spots of light danced behind her eyelids. It was building, this need that was inside her, coiling and ratcheting tighter and tighter, until all she could focus on was the strength of him between her legs. This was what she wanted. Him against her. Every sensation, every movement, every breath, and every beat of his heart against hers.

"Let go, Angel," he whispered against her mouth. She heard herself whimper, right before one of his hands slid from her pelvis and delved between them, his finger stroking her throbbing, sensitive bud and tipping her over the edge.

Nothing could have ever prepared her for the intensity of it. It ripped through her, catching her unaware and unready, every muscle within her suddenly spasming and pulsing uncontrollably. Her head dropped, her face under the edge of his jaw, her eyes squeezed shut as she rode a riptide of ecstasy. Her legs tightened around him, her fingers curled against his scalp, her hips jerked, and every muscle in her body tightened as she fell tumbling, over and over, in blinding waves of pleasure.

She came to rest against him, spent and breathing hard. The languid rapture that had saturated her entire body made her understand how men and women might forfeit everything for such. The euphoria hadn't even worn off and already she wanted more of him, and she did not fool herself into thinking he would become anything less than an addiction. Nor did she underestimate the danger of that.

She was not in love with this man. What Alexander Lavoie had given her was nothing more than a physical release, and she could not deny that she had wanted it. Welcomed it. Enjoyed every second of it. But that was all it was.

Gradually the sounds of the streets started to filter through to her consciousness, and awareness of her surroundings returned. She lifted herself off him, sliding off his lap, and when she would have returned to the seat opposite him, he pulled her back beside him. His hand found hers and didn't let go, even when she tried to pull away. She abandoned her impulse to retreat and settled back against the squabs beside him.

She could feel his thumb gently tracing patterns over the back of her hand. "Feel better?" he asked after a long silence.

She knew he was teasing her, trying to assuage any discomfiture on her part, but his question sent her stomach dropping to her toes.

Women use me. I am a dangerous distraction from their reality. And on occasion, when it pleases me, I let them, because I derive pleasure from it too.

In her mind, she could hear his voice in her head. Is that what she had just done? Used him and his body to distract her from her miserable reality? As a means to forget, as a means to feel better, if only for a moment?

She wanted to believe that she was above that. But when she had reached for him, she hadn't been thinking about Alex. She'd been thinking about herself. What she craved. What she needed. And then she'd stopped thinking about anything at all.

Something that felt like shame crawled through her chest.

"Thank you," she whispered. "For..." She couldn't bring herself to say it. She wasn't even sure what she wanted to say.

"I've made you uncomfortable again, haven't I?" The teasing has gone from his tone.

Uncomfortable? God, no. She'd achieved that all on her own. He had only made her feel...a perfect, overwhelming, ecstasy. Given her exactly what she had needed, as if it had always been inevitable that this man should come to know her body the way he knew everything else about her.

"No. You haven't made me uncomfortable at all." Her face was still on fire because, despite everything, she wanted desperately for him to do it again. "Thank you for what you did for me today." It was the best she could do without making an utter fool of herself.

His hand tightened on hers.

"And for what you did for my brother." It needed to be said.

"Mmmm."

"There is no one I would rather have by my side at this moment." That too needed to be said. Not because he had stepped forward when no one else would. Not because of what he had done and continued to do for her—he'd given her diamonds to bribe a Tower guard for God's sake—but because, from the moment she had met this man, he seemed to understand her better than she understood herself.

Alex said nothing, only reached toward her with his free hand and gently straightened the neck of her shirt that was still gaping haphazardly. He pulled the edge of her discarded binding from where it had crumpled into her lap and balled it up, shoving it into the pocket of her forgotten coat.

"Gerald didn't kill anyone," she said abruptly, unwilling to dwell any longer on whatever had happened between them.

"No, I don't believe he did."

Hearing Alex's agreement lit a small flame of hope. Whatever foolish, unlawful things Gerald might have done, he wasn't a killer.

"But will the courts believe him?"

She heard Alex sigh. "I don't know."

And there was the crux of it. If he was found to be a murderer, regardless of what he had or hadn't done, he would be hanged. Perhaps she should have asked Miss Moore to set

Gerald on a ship to India at the outset. Gerald still thought his damn title would save him. It wouldn't. And it would be too late by the time he realized it.

"Do you believe that someone set him up?" she asked dully.

"In my experience, things are rarely so convoluted," Alex said gently. "More likely, it was an unfortunate coincidence. The real thief and killer beat your brother to the necklace and was already gone by the time he got there. Your brother found himself in the wrong place at the wrong time."

"Maybe the killer got the same note as my brother," she mumbled.

"Mmmm," Alex said, and he sounded somewhat preoccupied. "Maybe he did."

Angelique closed her eyes, her thoughts chasing each other around in circles. She should ask Alex what would happen next. Ask him where they would go from here to help Gerald. Except she found herself resisting. She was as tired of thinking about Gerald as she was of thinking about herself.

She opened her eyes. "Who is Jonathon?"

He stiffened beside her. "Jonathon?"

"The name you gave the guards. The name that is carved into the leather of your pouch strap. Who is he?"

"What makes you think Jonathon was anyone?"

"The fact that you just answered the way you did."

Alex looked away from her, and the carriage rolled on, the rattle of the wheels muffled beneath them. Angelique let the silence stretch. She was getting better at this.

"He was my brother," Alex said suddenly. Her heart sank. There was something in his voice that made her regret her impulsive question. Alex's fingers were clenched almost painfully around hers, but Angelique wasn't sure that he was aware he was still holding her hand. "He was killed at York when the Americans attacked."

She remained motionless, aware that Alex had retreated from her. Retreated far beyond anywhere she could see. She didn't offer him banal platitudes or trite regrets. Just let him go where he needed to and come back when he was ready.

After a minute, he suddenly pulled his hand from hers, as if he was surprised to find it there. "I couldn't save him. The war..." He didn't finish whatever he'd been going to say.

She'd never been in uniform, never had to face guns like he had. But she had been battling her own version of a war for a long time, and the death and despair it left in its wake was no different. God knew she despised having to revisit her own losses.

"War leaves only survivors," was all that she said.

⁓

Alex had understood her need for oblivion and release before she did. And God help him, but he hadn't been able to stop himself from taking full and complete advantage of that. From taking full advantage of her.

He'd fooled himself into thinking that, by giving in to his need and desire, he'd be able to settle himself. Focus. Get her out of his system. But it had only made it worse. Touching her, exploring her, feeling her come apart in his arms had been an erotic torture unlike anything he had ever suffered. He wanted to sink himself deep within her, wanted to draw out each taste and touch until she screamed his name.

She wasn't an innocent, but it was obvious that she did not possess much experience. Her movements had been unschooled at first, but she'd readily and skillfully accepted his guidance. Her body had responded instantly and honestly to his every touch and every kiss, liquid fire that tested his control. It made him fantasize about all the wicked ways that he might harness her raw passion, all the ways he might show her that what had happened today, on a cramped carriage seat, was nothing compared to what he might teach her when he had the gift of time and space.

He was an idiot.

He reminded himself once more that Angelique Archer was his employee. An asset to his club. A fascinating, sexier-than-hell asset, but an asset all the same. And it would only benefit him to protect such a . . . partnership.

To think that he was doing any of this out of anything other than good business was inconceivable. To think that she had accepted his help out of anything other than necessity was foolish.

There is no one I'd rather have at my side at this moment.

In truth, there was no one else that was even in the running. He fully recognized that she had been backed into a very difficult corner, initially when he'd found her gambling at his club and most certainly when her brother had been arrested. Her reliance on him was more of a default than a choice. Yet there was an intolerable part of him that wanted to believe that he was more than a welcome white knight of convenience to her.

It was probably that part that had let spill his brother's name.

He didn't talk about Jonathon. Ever. The fact that he had done so with Angelique was unsettling. There was too much regret that still came with those memories. Even if it might make Angelique realize that he understood what blind loyalty to a brother meant better than anyone else.

The carriage began to turn and then abruptly stopped. From outside, Alex could hear a hum, as if a swarm of angry bees had descended ahead of them. Above their heads, through the grate, Alex could hear Matthews's muted voice as he soothed the horses. Alex banged on the roof of the carriage. "What's going on, Matthews?"

"We've got company," his driver replied. "Or rather, her ladyship does."

What? Alex pulled the curtain aside. In the square, a crowd had gathered, milling in front of the Hutton town house. There were knots of angry-looking people interspersed with others who looked merely curious. Based on their clothing, the bulk of the mob was from the working class, but they were intermingled with nattily dressed men who were doing their best to stir the crowd. Small sheets of printed paper were being sold and distributed at a rapid pace, no doubt filled with the gory details of last night's events, either made up or embellished by some entrepreneurial soul with a printer and a good imagination.

The neighboring homes had sent out servants—burly footmen from the looks of it—to push the crowd back and keep them from encroaching on their own property. Someone had propped a large, flat sign in front of the Hutton door. Across the weathered wood someone had splashed the words *Hang Hutton* and *Murderer* across it in scarlet paint.

"Drive past," Alex ordered, but Matthews had already corrected the carriage, and it was traveling back on the street past the square. No one spared them a glance. He became aware Angelique was at his side, pressed against him. Her breath was coming in shallow gasps, and he could feel every muscle in her body coiled tensely against him.

Alex had no idea what to say to her. No idea how anything he said could make any of this any less awful than it was.

"Oh God," she suddenly whispered. "Tildy."

"Your housekeeper?"

"What if—what if they get into the house? What if they hurt—"

"It's unlikely she will come to any harm," Alex said, hoping that he was speaking the truth. But mobs could be unpredictable. "I'll send Matthews and Jenkins back to fetch her. Is there anyone else in the house?"

"No. Just her." Her face was white, making the freckles across her nose and cheeks stand out. "But how will they—"

"Don't worry about my men. They are very good at what they do."

The carriage gained speed as the square fell behind them. "Where are we going?"

"The last place anyone would ever look for a lady."

Chapter 12

Alex sat at his desk and stared at the closed door to his dressing room, lost in thought.

He was worried about Angelique. Despite her assurances that she was fine, she had been pale and drawn when they had returned, wandering listlessly about his office, her mind a million miles away. Well, not a million, but more like the distance from here to the Tower. Or maybe Bedford Square.

He'd had a bath drawn for her despite her protests, more to create a soothing diversion than anything else. He'd also washed and changed, making him feel refreshed and, for the moment, reassured that he was still in control of his world and his place in it. He'd been out in his club, ensuring that his employees had already started the process of preparing for the evening's entertainment, and the routine of that too had settled him. He could now address the pressing problem of the Marquess of Hutton with a clearer head.

He was wondering if he shouldn't start the process of extracting Hutton and finding him passage on a ship destined for some far corner of the earth, regardless of the idiot's protestations. The marquess didn't seem to understand just how much trouble he was really in. He seemed to think that his title was like a magic spell protecting him from the law. And while it might protect from some things and put him beyond reach of punishment from others, murder was not one of them.

I was set up.

Alex made a face. It was unlikely. But Alex couldn't ignore the sliver of doubt that was nagging at his gut. And he would be not only remiss but foolish to ignore it. At the very least, it deserved to be acknowledged and examined. He sighed, reaching for a piece of paper and his quill. Assuming, just for the moment, that Hutton was telling the truth and that someone had set him up for a crime he didn't commit, that left a whole host of questions that he did not have answers for.

His quill scratched over the paper, and he stared down at the single word he'd written, the most obvious question of all.

Why?

In Alex's experience, people's actions were most often driven by greed. Money was power, and everyone had their price, whether they wished to admit it or not. In Gerald Archer's case, one might guess that someone may have set the man up now if only to extort him later. Except the pieces didn't really fit. One did not publicly frame a man for murder when one wished to privately leverage him.

In addition to the mysterious note Hutton claimed to have received, Alex had told Matthews to look for any mail that had been delivered to the Hutton home in the event that there was some sort of demand, but he wasn't hopeful. Alex tapped the edge of his quill on the ink pot. If not money, then what? Sex, coupled with jealousy and rage, usually explained whatever money didn't. But Hutton did not have a lover, or at least the sort that one didn't pay by the visit, and there was no talk or evidence of betrothals or any other assignations. He dismissed that idea for the time being.

Alex scowled. He couldn't shake the thought that he was missing something here. Something important. He picked up his quill again, going back to his original idea. *Money*, he wrote. More specifically, the Hutton fortune that had seemingly disappeared into thin air. Now *that* had all the hallmarks of extortion done right. Secrecy. Magnitude.

Alex wished fervently that the old marquess was still alive to question. Or even the marchioness. Except they were both very conveniently dead. One of apparent disease, and the other of a highway robbery gone wrong. And now their son had been disgraced and sat in the Tower of London, faced with the very real possibility that he would be hanged for a crime that he didn't commit.

Alex sat up. Perhaps he was missing something because he wasn't looking at the big picture.

What if someone was not only trying to destroy Gerald Archer? What if someone was trying to destroy the entire Hutton family?

Or perhaps he was just being overly dramatic and overthinking all of this. He ran a hand through his hair in irritation.

"Alex?"

He jerked, ink splattering on the paper before him. His eyes flew to the door of his bedroom and the figure that was standing in it.

Angelique was bundled in one of his robes, her feet bare, her wet hair combed back from her face and left to dry down her back. He could smell the scent of his lemon soap laced with sandalwood, and while that should have been simply familiar, his scent on her was, instead, painfully arousing. Every ounce of blood he possessed surged to his groin, and he smothered a moan.

It had seemed like a good idea at the time, bringing her here, where he knew she would be safe. But now he realized he should have taken her to the offices of Chegarre & Associates in Covent Square. Or maybe to a bloody inn a hundred miles from the outskirts of London. Because having Angelique here, in his space, wearing his scent and his clothes, was testing his sanity.

Her cheeks were no longer pale but flushed with color, and Alex wasn't sure if that was a result of the bath or her discomfort with her current state of dishabille. He tried not to let his eyes linger on the turn of her ankle or the gentle curve of her calves where they disappeared under the burgundy silk of the robe.

He tried not to remember the lines of her thigh, how they had felt clenched on either side of his waist. Or the flare of her hips, and the way he had caged them, bringing their bodies together. He tried not to recall just how smooth her skin had been as he had explored the valley of her spine and the ridges of her ribs and then the delicious fullness of her breasts. If he let himself dwell on how she had arched against him, her nipples hard and tight, her mouth hot and needy, he was no longer confident that he would be able to act with any sort of honor.

The edge of his bed was visible beyond her, and he averted his eyes. Though, really, it was irrelevant. Should he give in to his baser urges, he would take her wherever was at hand. The floor. The wall. The desk. The chair he was sitting in. Probably all of them. Twice.

"Are you all right?" he asked gruffly, shifting slightly in a vain attempt to escape the discomfort of his arousal.

"Yes." She stayed where she was, which was a relief.

He set his quill to the side, trying to get his body under control. "I asked Matthews to fetch your clothes from Bedford Square when he retrieved Tildy, but he isn't back yet. He'll take your housekeeper to our offices first and see her settled. I'm sorry for your current attire. Or lack of it, as it may be."

She shook her head, stepping into the room. "Please, Alex, don't apologize. I cannot ever repay you for what you've already done."

The robe gaped slightly at her neck, and he swallowed, his mouth suddenly dry. Jesus, he was in trouble. He'd never in all his life been so affected by a woman.

"What is that?" She gestured at the document in front of him.

"Thoughts." He shifted again, trying to concentrate on her words and not his libido. "No," he corrected himself, "not thoughts. Questions."

"About what?" She stepped farther into the room and chose one of the chairs on the far side near the hearth, tucking her feet up underneath her. Now all he could see was her neck and head, her entire body hidden from view by the voluminous robe. That should have helped. It didn't.

"A lot of things. Your family, mostly. About how your brother may have found himself where he is. In order to understand what is happening now, I need to better understand what happened in the past." He welcomed the distraction. The return to the real problem at hand.

He saw her take a deep breath. "Ask what you must. I'll try my best to answer your questions."

He held her eyes. "You might not like some of them."

"There have been a great many things that I haven't liked in my life in these last years, Alex. I won't shrivel up now."

"I know that. I just..." He just what? Wanted to spare her the grief?

"Ask me your questions, Alex."

"Tell me about your father." He needed to start somewhere. This seemed as good a place as any.

"He was an only child. Inherited his title when he was twenty-two. Married my mother when he was fifty-one."

"Mmmm." He had come across those details in Chegarre's ledgers, but it still surprised him that the old marquess had waited so long to take a bride, especially being that, at the time of his succession, he was the last of his line. Alex's experience had taught him that such men were usually anxious to secure the longevity of their title. As it was, the marquess had been twice the age of his bride. The age discrepancy wasn't unusual, but the fact that she was his first bride was.

"It was a love match," Angelique said from her chair, as if she could read his mind. Her voice sounded more than a little wistful. "When we were younger, my father was fond of telling us that the day he met my mother was the best day of his life. That she had been the most sought-after woman of her season, and that he couldn't believe she had chosen him."

"Mmmm." Romantic, Alex supposed, if not sensible.

"He loved my mother more than life itself," Angelique continued. "There is nothing he would deny her. Nothing he wouldn't do for her."

Like sell off vast Hutton holdings? The question slid into his consciousness with a whisper. He'd uncovered nothing in the old marquess's past that would explain his actions. But he had not considered the marchioness. And love drove people to do strange things.

"What was your mother like?" Alex asked carefully.

"What do you mean?" Angelique frowned.

"Did she have... any vices?" Alex almost winced, but he kept his tone even.

Angelique stared at him. "Vices?"

"Gambling? Addictions? Spending habits that were... unsustainable?" All things he'd seen that certainly weren't exclusive to the male gender.

"No." Her hands had curled over the arms of her chair. "That wasn't her at all. She preferred the company of her family over the company of the ton. Her pride and joy was her family, and there wasn't a day that went by that she didn't tell us how happy we made her. That she had dreamed of being a mother from the time she was just a little girl and the realization of that dream had made her the luckiest woman in the world. As children, we spent more time with my mother than we did with our nurses."

Alex drummed his fingers absently on his knee. The former Marchioness of Hutton sounded like a bloody saint, not a woman who would be a likely candidate for debilitating scandal.

"My father was never the same after she died," Angelique said quietly. "He had been her greatest protector, but he couldn't protect her from death. He became a hollow husk of himself when she was gone. Distanced himself from everything and everyone, including us."

"Did he speak to anyone after she died? Confide in anyone?"

"About what?"

Alex shrugged. "Anything." *Sheep pastures. Coal mines. Missing money.*

Angelique shook her head. "My father only had one friend he counted as a true confidant. Lord Burleigh's father.

He was like the younger brother my own father never had. But he himself died of a sudden apoplexy not even a year before my mother died." She paused. "I can't think of anyone else my father would have opened up to."

Well, that wasn't helpful either. "Did your father take a mistress?" Alex asked. "Someone who might have made him...less lonely?"

Color rose in her face, but she didn't look away. "Not that I am aware of."

Alex made another note. Given what Angelique had told him about the nature of her parents' relationship, it wasn't surprising that the old marquess wouldn't have taken a mistress after his wife's death. But it was certainly something to be investigated further. Information often surfaced in the most unlikely of places.

"Tell me what you know about your father's death." The account he'd read said simply that the marquess had been the victim of a highway robbery gone wrong.

She took her hands off the arms of the chair and clasped them in her lap. Her expression was stark. "He was on the road to Bath when he was accosted. His carriage was run off the road and destroyed. He was found a short distance away, robbed and shot, along with his driver. They never caught the highwaymen responsible."

Alex hid a frown. To run a carriage off the road and then take the time to extract the occupants and shoot them somewhere else seemed extreme. Not unheard of, but most highwaymen he knew were about timing. And finesse. Minimize the damage, maximize the take. He made another note.

"I'm sorry, Angelique. For your loss and for bringing this up again."

She nodded silently.

"Did your father have any enemies?" he asked.

She was quiet for so long that he thought perhaps she hadn't heard him. "You think someone had him killed?" she asked suddenly.

Alex flinched. The thought had been creeping around in the back of his mind, and he'd had no intention to vocalize it at this point. Certainly not before he could prove anything.

"I don't know," he replied honestly.

Her eyes were unreadable, though her face was pale. "No," she said eventually. "At least, I was never aware of any enemies my father may have had. He was very well-regarded."

"What about your mother?"

Angelique shook her head helplessly. "No."

"What about your brother? A wager gone wrong? An investment gone sour? Anything?"

She shook her head again. "I don't…I don't think so. I do know he just invested in some sort of shipping company with Seaton and his father. He'd done so once before, but the cargo was lost to storms and Gerald lost his money. Our money."

He watched her face. "You don't believe that?"

"I don't trust Seaton."

That made two of them. "What kind of shipping company?"

Angelique shrugged. "Imports of some sort. He wouldn't tell me. Or he couldn't."

"Mmmm." Alex made another note. That might be more relevant.

A knock on his office door broke the silence. Alex stood and strode to the door. Matthews waited on the other side, hefting a trunk in his sizable arms. "The housekeeper is settled," he said without preamble, setting the trunk inside the office with a thump. "Her ladyship's clothes." Matthews reached into his coat and withdrew a thin packet of paper. "Her mail. And the note I believed you wanted from his lordship's room. Took me damn near a half hour to find it. The man is not overly...neat." He handed Alex the entire stack.

"Thank you, Matthews. And well done."

His driver nodded. "May I safely assume that her ladyship will remain here this evening?"

"Yes." Alex wasn't letting her go anywhere. Not without him.

"Very good, Mr. Lavoie." Matthews nodded with approval and then disappeared. Alex closed the door and returned to his desk. Angelique was already unfolding herself from her chair. He set the small pile of mail that Matthews had retrieved on the corner of his desk, keeping the note Matthews had discovered in Hutton's rooms separate.

"Go through your correspondence," he said quietly as she reached his desk. "Tell me if there is anything there that is unusual or unexpected." He didn't expect her to find anything, but it was worth checking.

She nodded, her fingers quickly sorting through the missives. She set aside a handful and opened two more before adding them to the pile. "Bills," she said. "Two social invitations for my brother. Clearly delivered yesterday," she muttered. She opened another, and he didn't miss the way her face hardened.

"Who's that from?"

She shook her head as if she wasn't going to answer but then seemed to change her mind. "A request from Lord Seaton framed in flowery compliments. He wishes to call on me and offers the reminder that a beautiful lady such as myself needs a protector. And that he would be honored to have the privilege of seeing to my every need. In my brother's absence, of course."

Alex forced himself not to react, though there was a childish part of him that wished to rip that letter from her fingers and throw it into the hearth. George Fitzherbert didn't deserve her. He didn't even deserve the right to suggest it.

"Perhaps he is still in love with you." It was an effort to keep his voice even.

"He was never in love with me," she sneered, and crumpled the letter in her fist, letting it fall to the desk. "Seaton is in love with Seaton."

Satisfaction set in hard, and Alex realized he was no longer just acting like a jealous swain, he had become one. And he didn't care.

Angelique reached for the last letter and unfolded it, her eyes scanning the text. "And a letter from Lady Burleigh offering whatever assistance she and her son can provide at what she calls this 'very difficult time.'" Angelique looked puzzled.

"Is that odd?"

"I haven't seen her since my mother died. Yet she came with Lord Burleigh to break the news of my brother's arrest. And now is offering her support." She sighed. "I can't imagine what she thinks she can do, but I suppose that I should be grateful." She put the letter down.

"Mmmm." No extortion notes, no threats, no demands. Nothing of any interest.

The note that Matthews had retrieved from Hutton's rooms, however, was a different story. It was folded in a neat square, the Bedford address printed clearly under the marquess's name. He unfolded it and laid it out on top of the letter so that Angelique could read it as well.

The writing on the inside matched the writing on the outside, a heavy, sloppy script that said exactly what Hutton had described. That the Earl of Trevane had, in his possession, a diamond necklace of substantial value, hidden from his wife in the bottom drawer of his study desk. A large number of the words were misspelled, and Alex frowned.

"Whoever wrote this was educated," Angelique said before he could.

"But not smart enough to muddle the syntax as well as the spelling."

"Rather odd, don't you think?"

"Very." Alex picked the paper up, turning it over and examining the broken seal for any clues. But the sealing wax was ordinary, as was the paper—a middling grade that could be had at a hundred different shops. He turned it back over and examined the address, holding it up to the light. A faint, circular indentation on the surface of the paper was just visible, evidence that a coin had been pressed into the missive.

"Why do you suddenly look so pleased?" Angelique demanded.

"I know where this came from."

Her eyes widened. "What? Where?"

"A place called the Lion's Paw."

"What is that?"

"A tavern."

"I don't understand."

"There is a depository in that tavern," Alex explained. "Messages can be dropped into a lockbox anonymously from the alley that runs behind the building. They need to have the address written on the front and be wrapped with two shillings. The proprietor keeps one, and the other goes to the boy who delivers the message."

Angelique was staring at him. "That is the most..." she seemed to be flailing for a word, "absurd thing I've ever heard. Who would ever need to send an anonymous message?"

"Besides the person who sent a note to your brother trying to appear as something that he isn't?"

Angelique's jaw flexed. "But how does this help us?"

Alex refolded the paper and tucked it into his pocket. "Because sometimes, my lady, it pays to have friends in absurd places."

As they entered the Lion's Paw, Angelique was enveloped by the delicious aroma of cooking meat, rich ale, and wood smoke. The floor was neatly swept, the walls whitewashed and clean, and the long tables and benches filled with patrons devouring meals.

A pretty, young redhead drifted by, her arms laden with empty tankards. She couldn't be much more than thirteen, but she held the promise of an extraordinary beauty. Her face creased into a smile the moment she spied Alex. "Mr. Lavoie." A dimple appeared in her lovely cheek. "Here for supper?"

Alex smiled back at her and shook his head.

"An ale, perhaps?"

"Not today, but thank you. Is Gil around?"

"In back, I think. I'm going there anyway so I'll check for you. Wait here." The girl disappeared, but in minutes she returned, the empty tankards replaced with a tray of full ones.

"Gil's in back. Told her you were here." The girl tipped her head toward the rear of the tavern.

"Thank you."

"Of course." The serving girl's eyes slid to Angelique, curiosity evident in their green depths.

Alex made no effort to introduce them, and the girl didn't seem to expect it. Instead she simply shifted the tray in her arms and continued on through the press of bodies.

"Follow me," Alex said, and Angelique fell into step behind him as they wove their way through the crowd. Near the rear of the tavern, a group of raggedly dressed boys sat around a table, some of them eating bowls of stew and crusts of thick bread, others simply sitting and seemingly waiting for something. As if on cue, a bell rang above the rear entrance, and one of the boys jumped up.

"My turn," he said, as if daring anyone to contradict him.

He vanished from view into the rear. Within seconds, he reappeared, shoving something into his pocket and pulling his cap down low over his ears. He made a beeline for the front door of the tavern and was swallowed by the darkening street.

Angelique looked up at Alex, puzzled, but he was already ducking under the low lintel of the entrance where the boy had just exited.

"Alexander Lavoie." The voice was rich and musical and unmistakably female. "My daughter said you were here. To what do I owe the honor of your delectable presence?" It was also unmistakably sarcastic.

"Gil." Alex stepped forward, and Angelique could now see the owner of the voice. She was petite with thick red hair that matched the pretty serving girl's. Her complexion was creamy, her eyes a startling shade of jade, and the apron she wore over her gown could not hide her voluptuous figure.

It also didn't hide the two pistols she wore at her hips.

Alex caught the woman's hand and bent over it, kissing her knuckles with all the courtly flair one might have once found in the halls of Versailles. The woman smiled faintly, though her eyes slid past Alex to rest upon Angelique. There was none of the idle curiosity that her daughter had displayed. Instead there was unapologetic assessment. Her shrewd gaze traveled from the toe of Angelique's serviceable boots, up past her equally serviceable dress and cloak, until it stopped at her face. Angelique met her eyes steadily.

"She's not really your type, is she, Lavoie?" the woman said.

Angelique blinked.

"I didn't realize I had a type," Alex replied, sounding amused.

"You most certainly have a type, Lavoie, and that type wouldn't ever be caught standing in this tavern." She paused, her full lips compressing. "Don't tell me she's here to ask for a job. Because I've got nothing right now, not even for you. Those boys out there eat too much."

Alex chuckled. "Gilda, this is Angelique. My vingt-et-un dealer. And you couldn't afford to hire her." He turned to Angelique. "Angelique, this is Gilda. The proprietor of this fine establishment."

"A pleasure," Angelique said, more out of habit than truth. The woman's scrutiny was not a little unnerving.

Gil was examining Angelique again. "Your vingt-et-un dealer, Lavoie?"

"Yes." It was Angelique who answered as she met Gil's gaze again. "His vingt-et-un dealer."

Gil snorted under her breath. "And I am but a humble brewer." She moved to an enormous hearth where a heavy black cauldron bubbled and reached for the long-handled wooden spoon that rested on the top. She gave the contents a stir and then wiped her hands on her apron. "The Duchess was here this morning and mentioned you were in love, Lavoie. I didn't actually believe it until now."

Angelique's heart stopped before starting again at an unnatural pace.

"You know me better than that, Gil." Alex chuckled again, though this time it sounded a little off. "And you certainly know better than to believe everything the Duchess says."

"Of course." Gil's lips were curling into a smirk.

Angelique focused on keeping her breathing even. There was a small corner of her heart that was swelling with something that was far too dangerous to identify. A small, irrational part of her that wanted, if only for a moment, to believe that this man was capable of loving a woman like her. She knew better, of course. Alexander Lavoie was one of the best men she had ever met—would likely ever meet—but he did not belong to her. She doubted he would ever belong to anyone.

"You must be very clever," Gil said to Angelique. There was a challenge of some sort in her words, though Angelique couldn't begin to fathom what it was.

"With numbers," she answered simply.

"And cards," Alex added. "You should see what she can do at my gaming tables with a bottle of French brandy and a proper gown." His tone still sounded odd.

"I'll take your word for it." Gil's smirk widened.

Alex scowled. "You might learn something."

Abruptly, Gil turned from Angelique. "Why is she here?"

"*She* is standing right here," Angelique said evenly. "And is capable of answering questions all by herself like a big girl."

A gleam of approval touched Gil's eyes. She shot Alex a sly look. "Like I said, Lavoie, not your type at all."

Alex's expression darkened further.

Gil looked back at Angelique. "Very well, why are you here?"

"Because I have a stake in what Mr. Lavoie is… investigating."

"Ah. I was wondering how long it would take to get to this part." She paused. "What do you want?"

Alex tsked from behind her. "You make this all sound so mercenary."

The redhead lifted a single elegant eyebrow.

Alex lifted the flap of the bulky pouch strapped across his chest—the same one he'd worn over his military uniform earlier. Angelique hadn't paid much attention to it on the way here, so preoccupied was she with the bizarre note that had been recovered from her brother's possessions. But she stared now as he extracted three powder horns. There had been a crate of those horns just outside the chapel in the Tower. She remembered because she had huddled behind it, watching the retreating forms of the warders.

"Perhaps I simply wanted to bring you a gift." He held one out, and Gil took it, examining the exterior.

"You steal a warship recently?" she asked, upending it to open the top. "This is naval issue."

"Ah, I had forgotten you have recently begun dabbling in the commercial sea-trade business."

"Dabbling is profitable," she murmured. "Where did you get this?"

"You ask too many questions when presented with a gift, Gil."

She was examining the contents. "This is good powder."

"The best in all of England." He gestured at the pistols at her hips. "For when you need it the most."

"Hmph." Gil made a face and recapped the horn. "What's this going to cost me, Lavoie?"

"Information."

"Be more specific. And remember there are only three horns here, Lavoie. Not a barrel."

"And I have only a single question, so I think you are getting the better end of this deal."

Gilda put a hand on a curvy hip and waited.

"The Marquess of Hutton. One of your boys delivered a message to Bedford Square recently." He gestured to a heavy iron box mounted to the wall by the back door. The top was hinged, but a padlock kept it securely fastened. The key, no doubt, was safely hidden somewhere beneath Gil's apron. And her pistols.

Gil stared at him for a moment before she threw her head back and laughed. "Yes," she finally said. "They most certainly did."

Angelique sucked in a breath. Alex had told her as much, but for the first time, they actually had a confirmation of something and not another puzzle.

"Is there any way to determine who it was from?" Angelique asked.

Gilda scoffed. "Of course not. That defeats the entire purpose of this system. No one is going to pay to send an anonymous message if they can't do so anonymously."

Angelique shifted. "And you deliver a lot of these anonymous messages?"

"You'd be surprised how many individuals do not wish to have their missives traced back to them through servants or postmen or any other inconvenient witnesses," Gilda drawled. "Between the peers and politicians, the lovers and the criminals, it's a wonder I can keep track of it all."

"Yet you remember that there was something amusing about the message sent to the Marquess of Hutton." This time it was Alex who sounded mildly annoyed.

"Since I like you, Lavoie," Gilda purred, reaching for the other two horns of gunpowder, "and since I like your taste in . . . gifts, I will share a little something with you." She tucked the powder horns into a cupboard far away from the hearth. "The messages I've had delivered to Bedford Square addressed to the Marquess of Hutton in the past years have paid for half of this bloody tavern."

Angelique stared at the woman, feeling her stomach lurch. *Years?* Long before her brother inherited the title. What sort of anonymous messages would her father have received?

"How many years?" Angelique asked suddenly, and out of the corner of her eye, she saw Alex nod slightly. "How long did the marquess receive these messages?"

Gilda shrugged. "Don't know. Maybe four, five years?" She paused and slanted a look at Alex. "This is more than one question, Lavoie."

"And you have been well compensated."

"True." She considered him. "I might have something further you would be interested in," she said.

Alex uncrossed his arms. "What?"

"This will cost you more than three horns of His Majesty's best gunpowder," Gil said silkily.

"Once I know what it is, I'll be the judge of that. Keep in mind I do not have a clipper full of goods to barter."

"Fair enough." Gilda retraced her steps back to the cupboard where she had stored the powder and wrestled out another bulky iron box, similar to the one that was mounted on the wall. This box too was locked. She produced a key from somewhere beneath her apron and, within seconds, was rummaging through the contents.

Angelique was trying to assess the implications of the newfound knowledge that her father had been receiving anonymous messages for years. From whom? And for what purpose?

It took Gil but a minute to find what she was looking for. "Sometimes," she said, closing the box, "my boys are unable to deliver a message. Usually because the recipient has either died, been arrested, or fled the country. The boys don't get their shilling unless it's delivered so they are quite resourceful. But in the Marquess of Hutton's case, he was out of London when this was sent. And I am made to understand he died on that trip."

She held out a folded square of paper, a little yellowed around the edges, the wax seal starting to crumble. *The Marquess of Hutton, Bedford Square* was written across it in dark ink.

Angelique took it from her, hating that her fingers were trembling slightly. This was the last message to have been sent to her father. It hadn't reached him before he'd left for Bath. Before he'd been shot by a highwayman on a lonely stretch of road.

The urge to rip it open was like a physical pain. But she wouldn't read it here. Not in this tavern, not in front of this woman. She had no idea what she might find. What secrets her father had kept from her. But deep down, she knew, whatever it was, it wasn't going to be good.

"Did you read it?" Alex was asking Gil.

"Of course I didn't read it. One can't be forced to reveal things one does not know, and I'd like to keep it that way. I'm convinced it will help me live longer." She was stowing the box back into its hiding place.

"Yet you kept this."

"Only a fool would discard something that might be worth something to someone later on." She straightened, her lips curved into a smile that didn't quite reach her eyes.

"What do you want for it?" Angelique asked. Stupid, really, that she should be asking, because she had nothing to her name that this woman would want. But this belonged to her. This one clue that might offer answers that had been elusive for too long. And she'd be damned if she walked out of this tavern without it.

"Just how clever with numbers are you?" Gil cocked her head thoughtfully.

"Very." There was no need to dissemble.

"If I gave you a shipping manifest and the subsequent receipts submitted to me from the customs houses, how long would it take you to determine if they matched and if the percentage of tax withheld was correct?"

"Depends on how large a cargo."

Gil pursed her lips. She bent and, from the same cupboard, pulled out a battered ledger. She opened it and snatched at the slips of paper that had been stuffed between the pages before they could fall to the floor. She passed Angelique one, a long, neat itemized list of cargo that had come in on a ship called the *Phoenix*. "This is the ship's manifest. And this is what the customs house gave me." She handed Angelique a second sheet. This sheet was not nearly so neat, with columns of numbers and percentages noted beside them and the calculations written at the end in messy confusion.

Angelique quickly compared the manifest numbers, for bales of cotton and their corresponding weight, to the number written on the custom house sheet, noting a number of anomalies. She scanned the sums and the calculations, again finding errors. Nothing one might notice at first glance. But small things like this would add up. Especially over time.

"How long would that take you?" Gil asked.

"I'm done."

She saw the woman's mouth fall open slightly. "That's impossible."

"If you asked me to look at this because you suspect that the custom house is cheating you, it appears you are correct. There are anomalies in the calculations." Something that was obvious to Angelique and would have become obvious to Alex, once he'd taken time to examine them. But probably not as obvious to an individual who was not as skilled at math.

Color flooded into Gil's fair cheeks.

"Who is currently doing your books?" Angelique asked.

"Me," Gil muttered. She looked uncomfortable and embarrassed.

Alex cleared his throat. "If you suspected something, why didn't you ask me to—"

"I don't need your help. You are a busy man." It sounded defensive.

And Angelique, more than anyone, understood just how hard it was to ask for help. How hard it was to admit that someone had taken advantage of you. How helpless you felt.

"I'm going to kill them." Gil's embarrassment had turned into anger. "Serves me right for doing business on what's supposed to be the civilized side of the law."

"There is no civilized side," Angelique murmured. "Just thieves who use it better than others to hide their crimes."

Gil looked at Angelique with startled interest.

"Alternatively, I would suggest that a visit to the custom house to demand compensation with interest would be far more rewarding." Angelique held out her hand for the ledger. "Give that to me."

"Why?"

"So I can determine just how much they owe you. Believe me, I have some experience with individuals taking what is not theirs."

Gil blinked at her and then wordlessly passed her the ledger.

Angelique flipped through the receipts, careful not to frown at the ink-spattered ledger pages that had been Gil's attempt at arithmetic.

"Give me twenty minutes, and I'll have you a total." She glanced at the pistols at the woman's waist before raising her eyes. "How you go about collecting that total, I'll leave up to you."

Gil held Angelique's eyes for a heartbeat before she transferred her gaze to Alex. "Not your type at all, Lavoie," she said with a laugh.

Alex was frowning at her. "Angelique, perhaps—"

"Go have that ale, Mr. Lavoie, and let me work. It is what is owed to this woman." She put the ledger on top of a counter, pushing a handful of bowls out of the way.

Gil laughed again and pulled Alex in the direction of the public room. "I can see why you're in love, Lavoie."

Chapter 13

The note sat in the center of Alexander Lavoie's desk like a bomb that she was afraid might explode at the slightest provocation. She was terrified of what she might find. Terrified that she would find nothing. Part of her was ashamed that she hadn't had the courage to open it on the way back to Alex's club. Another part of her whispered that she didn't ever really have to open it at all. Never had she felt so conflicted.

But there was one thing she knew for sure, and that was ignorance was not bliss.

Ever.

Alex had very subtly disappeared into his rooms, closing the door firmly behind him. To change for the evening, he'd said, but she knew that he had wanted to give her the time and space to read this on her own. She wasn't sure that was what she wanted until she actually reached for the note and was glad that there were no eyes to judge just how much her hand was shaking.

"Stop being such a chicken," she hissed at herself. She bent the paper, the wax seal snapping, and bits of red crumbled to the surface of the desk. Very carefully, she unfolded the note that had never made it to her father.

It appeared to be a verse, written in a neat, precise hand. Her eyes started at the first line:

> The cuckoo then, on every tree,
> mocks married men for thus sings he:
> Cuckoo! Cuckoo! Cuckoo! O word of fear,
> Unpleasing to a married ear.

Angelique could feel herself frowning fiercely. It was a Shakespearean passage, and she couldn't begin to guess why someone had sent it to her father. Beneath the passage, there was a single line. This one read:

£1500 Threadneedle St. A small price to keep her memory pure and your fledglings safely in their nest.

Angelique stared at the paper, perplexed and not a little frustrated. She wasn't sure what she had been hoping for, but it wasn't this riddle that had once been wrapped in two shillings. It was an extortion note of some sort, that seemed obvious. But for what? Was this some sort of accusation that her father had been unfaithful to her mother? That he had had an affair of some sort with a married woman? That perhaps he had had children with another woman?

It was the only thing that made sense on the surface. But underneath, Angelique was having a hard time believing it. She laid the letter on the desk and rubbed her face with her hands.

"Angelique?"

She lifted her face from her hands to find Alex standing near the desk. He had indeed changed, and he was clad now in dark evening clothes that graced his lithe body. His hair was slightly damp at the edges where it brushed his collar, and he'd shaven; she could smell the scent of his soap. It made her want to go to him, to run her fingers through the dampness of his hair, to taste that smooth skin with her lips. To pretend nothing existed save for the two of them, if only for a moment. It made her want wicked, wicked things.

"Do you wish to share what it says?" he asked gently, glancing down at the letter that lay on the surface of his desk. He made no move to pick it up.

Angelique felt her chest squeeze, her heart thumping painfully. His kindness suddenly made her want to cry.

"Go ahead." She tried to collect her thoughts and her composure.

Alex held her eyes for the briefest of seconds before he lifted the letter from the desk. He read it twice, his eyes moving slowly and carefully over each line.

"The passage," he murmured. "Do you know where that is from?"

"It's from Shakespeare's *Love's Labour's Lost*. I read it with my mother. It was one of her favorites."

Alex was still gazing at the note thoughtfully. "What was it about? The play, that is?"

"It's a comedy about a king and his companions who try to foreswear the company of women. My mother said she liked that the final message reminded lovers of the seriousness of marriage."

"Mmmm." He was reading the letter again.

"It's an extortion note," she said. "Though I have no idea what my father was being extorted for."

"Yes," he agreed, not sounding surprised at all. "And I

think, at the very least, we can now safely conclude that your missing family fortune was not dropped into the alms box at St. Peter's."

"No. At least fifteen hundred pounds of it was meant to be dropped into something entirely different somewhere on Threadneedle Street."

"Perhaps." He put the letter back on his desk and glanced up at her. "The repeated reference to the cuckoo is somewhat curious, coupled with the last referral to his fledglings. Was it possible your father was having an affair outside his marriage? That he had children outside of his marriage?"

Angelique shook her head miserably. "I don't think so. My parents could barely stand to be apart from each other."

"What about before his marriage? He wasn't young when he married your mother. Is it possible that he had a...relationship—perhaps children—before he married that you are not aware of?"

"Maybe?" Angelique didn't know what to think anymore. "But half the peerage have children born on the wrong side of the blanket. It's not exactly uncommon, and certainly not something that one can generally use to leverage an entire fortune from them."

"Perhaps he was trying to protect your mother? The part about 'keeping her memory pure.' Perhaps he didn't wish her to suffer the humiliation and shame."

Angelique threw up her hands. "But to sacrifice the bulk of our fortune?" She was having a hard time believing that. "And honestly, I think if my mother had been aware of the existence of prior children that my father might have had, she would have insisted that they be raised alongside us. She was not the sort to punish children for the sins of their parents." She stalked over to the hearth and stared into the glowing coals. "Neither was my father, for that matter."

She didn't hear him move but rather became aware of his presence behind her. What she wanted to do was turn around and throw herself into his arms. Which would solve nothing. This man who had already risked so much for her, who had gone above and beyond what any sort of business partner could rightfully be expected to do, did not need a sniveling, hysterical female on his hands. She had never been that woman. She would not start now.

She took a deep, steadying breath. "I suppose I should be pleased that, at the very least, I know that my father's fortune is gone. That I no longer need to waste time with solicitors and courts trying to figure out where it all went."

"Mmmm."

She could feel her nails biting into her palms. "The other good news is that, should you wish it, I will be available for an indeterminate amount of time to deal vingt-et-un on your gaming floor. It would seem I will be requiring a job for the foreseeable future."

"Angelique—"

"The bad news is that this revelation of my father's past does not seem to have anything to do with the situation that my brother has found himself in." She took another calming breath, trying to keep her voice even. Whatever her father may or may not have done didn't, in reality, change anything. He was still dead. Her mother was still dead. The money was still missing. And her brother was still in prison.

She felt his hands on her shoulders, and her vow not to turn into his strength faltered. "I think I've changed my mind," she said, not looking away from the coals. "I can't take the chance that my brother will be found guilty. I can't watch Gerald die too. Can you still help him escape?"

His hands tightened on her shoulders, but he remained silent.

"Whatever it costs, I'll work it off."

"Angelique."

She closed her eyes, knowing that if she turned, if she faced him now, she would not be able to resist whatever it was that kept pulling her toward this man. She would beg him to kiss her, beg him to finish what she had started in that carriage, beg him to make her forget. Take her into his rooms and make her feel loved and safe and protected for as long as it would last.

Which would never be long enough, because one could not run from time.

She opened her eyes and slid out from beneath his touch, putting the bulk of the wide leather chair between them before she turned to face him. He was watching her, an unreadable expression on his face.

A knock sounded at his office door.

"Come in," he called without looking away from her.

The door clicked open and swung silently inward. The behemoth of a man she had come to know as Jenkins stood just inside the entrance, his hands clasped behind his back. From beyond his bulk, a raucous buzz of voices could be heard over the music and made her frown. She'd become familiar with the ebb and flow of the club's traffic, and this was far too early an hour to have such a crowd.

Alex apparently was having the same thoughts because he turned away from her and approached Jenkins. "What is going on out there?" he asked, not looking happy.

"It's an early crowd, Mr. Lavoie," Jenkins said, wincing. He approached Alex and held out a small sheet of printed paper that Angelique instantly recognized as the sort that had been distributed this afternoon in front of her townhome. "I suspect the scent of a good scandal has brought them out in droves." He sent an apologetic look in Angelique's direction. "Beggin' your pardon, my lady."

Alex snatched the paper from Jenkins's hand and glanced down at it, his lips curling angrily. He crumpled it in his fist and tossed it in the hearth. "I'll be out straightaway," Alex told the man. "And destroy any of these that you find in the club."

Jenkins looked relieved. "Very good, Mr. Lavoie." He nodded once more to Angelique and then vanished, closing the door behind him.

The noise was abruptly muffled. If she'd been paying more attention, she might have noticed it, but she'd been too wrapped up in everything else.

Without a word, she turned and went into Alex's rooms. He'd moved her trunk in there earlier, and she'd taken the time to lay out both her turquoise and silver gowns over the top as best she could, not wanting the satin to be crushed for any longer than necessary. She bent, trying to determine which had better survived the journey from Bedford Square to the club.

The turquoise, she decided, pulling the dress from the top of the trunk.

"What the hell do you think you're doing?" Alex demanded from right behind her. She jumped, not having heard him move as usual.

"Getting changed." She straightened and turned.

"Like hell you are." He reached for the dress, but she was faster and evaded. He was scowling. "You don't need that. Not tonight. You are not working."

"I most certainly am."

"You most certainly are not. I want you to stay here." This time he managed to yank the dress from her hands.

She felt her spine stiffen. "You want me to hide in your rooms?"

"Your word, not mine."

"And what, exactly, shall I do?" she inquired, hearing the edge to her voice.

Alex stared at her. He stepped closer to her, and there was barely a handbreadth of space between them now. Her breath hitched slightly but she held her ground.

"Rest. Read. Audit my damn books. Whatever the hell you want. But I don't want you out on that floor."

"Why?"

"Because I don't want to take any chance that you may be recognized," he said after a pause.

"Lying doesn't become you, Alex. Especially when it's not even a good lie."

His face tightened.

"You don't want me out there because you don't want me to hear what people will be saying about my brother. About me, even." The look in his eyes confirmed it. "I am not a child. Whatever they say, I want to hear."

He was shaking his head. "Angelique—"

"If my brother really was set up, then someone, somewhere, knows something. And I understand that it's unlikely that I might hear anything even remotely helpful. But I do know what sort of effect good French brandy and clever suggestion has on one's tongue."

Alex looked away, his expression one of frustration.

"You know I'm right."

"It's going to be awful," he said, looking back at her.

"More awful than the speculation in ballrooms was about why the Marble Maiden is unsuitable for marriage? Or even a waltz?" she asked with a faint mocking tone.

"Probably." She could almost hear his teeth grinding.

"They're words, Alex. Nothing more. Uttered by individuals who understand nothing, but like to think they know it all."

He stared at her.

"Besides, just think what such a captive crowd could do for your coffers. Your balance sheets will certainly suffer if I'm not out there." She tried to make it sound light.

"I don't care about my damn coffers," he growled.

"And I am not going to cower in a corner while someone else fights my battles," she said. "I never have, and I'm not starting now."

"I never expected you to."

"Then give me my damn dress."

It had been awful.

There was a certain macabre glee that seemed to have infected the entire crowd, each recounting of the Marquess of Hutton's sins more ghoulish and chilling than the last. Nothing that Angelique had heard had been anything less than fabricated, and by the end of the night, one would be convinced that Gerald Archer had done nothing short of running through London, indiscriminately slaughtering women and children as he went.

The murderer's peculiar sister was discussed with equal verve. It was recalled Angelique Archer had only had a single season before she'd disappeared into thin air, but not before demonstrating just what an odd creature she was. A number of people speculated about the twins and their ability to assume the title and responsibilities once their brother was hanged. Or was it possible that they were touched in the head as well? Perhaps they might even be committed to Bedlam for examination?

But it had been the last that had almost broken Angelique. Hopes of hearing anything useful had died early. No one was

interested in the truth. No one seemed to know anything beyond what they read in the scandal sheets. And as the night
progressed, the stories had become more wild and the tone
more cruel. Alex had sent Angelique off the floor an hour
before the club closed, and for once, she didn't argue with
him. She simply nodded and finished the hand amid protests
from those few players who had actually come to gamble
and not gossip.

He'd sent one of his serving girls to his office to help her
change out of the elaborate gown, the same girl he'd sent
earlier in the evening to help her dress. Angelique had no
idea if the girl had any clue who she really was. She, like the
rest of Alex's staff, asked no questions, which, as Angelique
understood it, was how all of Alex's employees preferred it.

The girl left and returned to her regular duties as soon
as she'd unlaced the gown, and Angelique was left alone in
Alex's inner sanctum. Part of her wished she'd listened to
Alex and never gone out there. It had been hard to listen to
her brother being tried and convicted in the court of public
ignorance. Just as it had been hard to listen to her nineteen-
year-old self be judged and condemned by people she had
never even met.

The words did not hold the power they once had, though
it didn't make them easier to hear. The gossip had reminded
her of the feelings of inadequacy she had struggled with in
the past. Her inability to become what had been expected
of her. Her mother had loved her and wanted so much for
her, she knew. But the things her mother had wanted for
her daughter had been the things that had made her mother
happy. Things that she had firmly believed would make Angelique happy too. It wasn't until Angelique had embraced
who she was that she had found a measure of happiness and
peace.

She laid the turquoise gown over the foot of Alex's bed, smoothing out any creases. The diamonds she left at her throat, a small piece of armor to remind herself who she truly was. And to remind herself that there were those in this world who admired and respected her for it. One who even desired her for it.

She picked up Alex's robe where it lay over the back of the chair near the cheval mirror. She told herself that she was wrapping herself in it because Matthews and Jenkins had not packed hers when they'd brought her things from Bedford Square. But she was lying.

She climbed up on the bed and lay down, her head on the pillows, her hand smoothing the luxurious cover beneath her. For just a few stolen moments, she wanted to have Alex around her. Wanted to close her eyes and imagine just what it would feel like to belong to him.

What it would feel like to belong body and soul to a man who knew both.

Angelique had fallen asleep, though she'd never intended to. Her eyes opened and instinctively she knew she wasn't alone. She scrambled to a sitting position to find Alex leaning casually against one of the bedposts. He was dressed only in his trousers and shirtsleeves. His back was to her, and Angelique couldn't see his expression.

"What time is it?" she mumbled, looking around. The entire room was still in shadows, the only light coming from the hearth in the corner and a single candle.

"Late. Or early, depending how one might wish to view it." He didn't make any effort to move.

She slipped out of his bed and retreated toward the

washstand as if she had been caught stealing something that wasn't hers, pulling the robe around her more tightly. *His* robe. She felt her face heat, though there was no help for it now. She certainly wasn't going to stand naked in front of him.

"How long were you watching me sleep?" It made her feel uncomfortable and flushed all at the same time.

"You make me sound like a peeping Tom. I wasn't watching you sleep. I was just...thinking."

"You could have woken me sooner."

"Mmmm."

"I didn't mean to fall asleep. I'm sorry."

"I'm not." He took a sip from the glass in his hand that she hadn't noticed earlier. "I'm sorry for what you endured out there. What was said about your brother. About you."

"Don't apologize for something that was my choice. I understood what I would face."

"Angelique, the things that were being said—"

"Truly, I've endured worse and survived," she hastened to assure him.

"Yes. You survived." It sounded flat. "You shouldn't have to just *survive*." Now his words had an edge to them.

"But survival has made me who I am. I learned to rely on myself because there was no one else. To understand that my strengths were not failures. There are many things that I regret in my life, but I cannot regret that."

Alex came around the bed, closing the distance between them. He placed his glass on the washstand. "No," he said slowly. "You should not regret that."

Angelique bit her lip. Just beyond him, she could see her shadowed reflection in the cheval mirror, and instantly she was reminded of the last time they had stood together here. His eyes followed hers, and it was like he was peering into her very soul.

"Do you regret what happened between you and me? Here, that first night. Later, in my carriage."

She shook her head, unsurprised that he had asked. Unable to answer him with anything but the truth.

She couldn't tell what he was thinking now. His eyes were dark gold in the muted light, his face a collection of hard angles. He reached out with his hand and touched the side of her face, a butterfly-soft touch. "Good," he said in a low voice.

Angelique shivered, her entire body suddenly hot. That single word sounded like a promise. Arousal snaked through her hard and fast. Need was humming through her, twining quickly with anticipation, and her body responded in a way that was becoming all too familiar when she was around this man. A throb had settled itself deep within her womb, and her breasts ached.

His hand had dropped to the braid that hung over her shoulder and he pulled the ribbon from the end. He let it fall to the floor, his fingers dragging gently through the weight of her hair, spilling it over her shoulders and back. "I want you," he whispered, his fingers drifting to the exposed skin at her throat where the diamond chain still glittered. "I've wanted you since the moment I saw you."

She recognized his words for what they were. An invitation to finish what had been started the moment he'd stood behind her in the cheval mirror. He'd given her the control and the power to choose. If only she had the courage to do it.

He bent and kissed her softly, his lips warm and gentle. "Don't be afraid." He was reading her mind again. "Never be afraid."

"This isn't my first time," she blurted.

"Mmmm."

"But it was a long time ago." She had no idea why she said that or why it would even matter to him.

"Did you like it?" he asked. His voice was like black velvet, smooth and seamless and devoid of inflection.

"I wanted to."

His amber eyes were completely focused on her. "Tell me about it."

She wasn't sure if she had heard him right. "Tell you about it?"

"Yes. Tell me what you felt. What you liked. What you didn't."

Her face was suddenly on fire. She swallowed, unsure of what to say. Unsure of what he wanted to hear. She was suddenly aware of how completely out of her depth she was. "I..." she trailed off.

He waited silently.

"It wasn't what I thought it would be like," she finally said, trying to keep her voice steady.

He gazed at her, something shifting in his expression. "It was your first time."

"My only time."

"Mmmm." He pushed her hair away from her forehead and tucked it behind her ear. "You found no pleasure in it." There was an intensity to his expression, something that simmered just below the surface that made her quiver.

Angelique shook her head. "No. It...hurt," she whispered. "He...pushed up my skirts and..." she trailed off. "It was over in a minute. I thought it was what I wanted. I was wrong."

She saw his expression darken, saw a muscle along his temple jump. She'd not intended that...disclosure. Something that had held so much regret and shame and disappointment for so long. Except he'd asked. And she'd answered. Because she was standing on the very edge of something that required unembellished honesty.

"That's not what it's supposed to be like," he said.

"I know." She didn't look away. "You make me feel things that... you make me feel beautiful. Perfect." That wasn't quite right, but she was struggling for words.

"What is it you want now, Angel?" Alex asked. He wasn't touching her, but his eyes were hot, an air of barely restrained control surrounding him.

"I want what you do to me. I want how you make me feel. I want... you."

He went still before he reached out and slid a finger along the belt of her robe. With a flick of his wrist, he loosened the tie, and the silk of her robe unwound, the edges barely touching now where they lay against her body. But he didn't push it open. Instead, he moved, circling around to her back. She could feel the heat of his body through the silk.

"It won't be over in a minute, Angel," he whispered in her ear, his breath hot against her skin. His eyes met hers in the mirror, and she shivered, gooseflesh rising.

Now his hands went to the edges of her robe, and he drew it over her shoulders. "I will never hurt you," he continued, the robe sliding down over her upper arms. "But pleasure and pain are sometimes one and the same." He paused, the robe caught at the top of her breasts by his fingers. "You need to be sure this is what you want."

Very deliberately, she reached up and drew his hand away from where it rested against her chest. Silk slipped from her body and pooled at her feet, leaving her completely naked. She watched in the mirror as his eyes followed the robe, felt the exhalation of his breath against her neck, heard the small moan he made in the back of his throat.

She gazed at their reflection, more aroused than she had

ever been in her life. This was what she had always imagined it might be like. To lay bare not only herself but her body to a man and know that both were venerated simply as they were.

His hands went to her hips, and over her abdomen, pulling her against him. They moved up, cupping her breasts, and he dropped his head, his lips grazing the column of her neck. The sight of his darker skin against the paleness of her breasts was captivating, and she arched into his touch, her nipples dragging against his palms.

His head came up, and his eyes were hot, his face set in desire. Without looking away from her, his hands moved, his thumbs circling her nipples that were peaked and hard and excruciatingly sensitive. She felt the muscles in her thighs tighten, felt a dampness gather between her legs. It was utterly indecent, she thought dimly, watching while he touched her body. Indecent and exciting, and she could not look away because the pleasure that was coursing through her was making it hard to think about anything except him. Anything except the way one of his hands was now sliding down over the gentle swell of her abdomen, his fingers caressing the curls at the top of her thighs and then stroking through the folds of her sex.

She closed her eyes, a little afraid that her legs were shaking.

"You're wet," he whispered harshly. His palm pressed hard against the top of her pubic bone while one of his fingers slid deep into her heat.

She gasped, feeling her inner walls clench around the intrusion.

"Jesus," Alex groaned, withdrawing his hand, and Angelique almost whimpered at the loss. "Not like this," he said. "Not this time."

He moved around her, coming to stand in front of her. She opened her eyes to find him watching her.

"Undress me," he said.

Angelique took a deep breath, her body on fire, her skin feeling heated and feverish against the cooler air of the room. And suddenly it wasn't good enough to have just his hands on her skin. She gathered the hem and drew his shirt over his head, letting it fall to the floor. Her eyes roamed over the expanse of his chest. His body was one of long lines and lean muscle and the ridges and valleys that had been denied to her by clothing now flexed under her touch. There were hard edges and planes beneath smooth skin, a scattering of dark hair that gathered in the center of his chest and trailed down to the waistband of his trousers. His nipples were dark and pebbled, and without considering what she was doing, she ran her thumbs over them the same way he had done to her.

He closed his eyes and sucked in a breath. Emboldened, she smoothed her hands over the sides of his ribs and replaced her thumbs with her mouth, her tongue circling and exploring. She felt him tense, felt his hands settle on her waist, his fingers tight.

"My trousers," he rasped.

She withdrew slightly, her fingers dropping to the fall of his trousers. The bulge straining beneath it was unmistakable, and Angelique stroked the hard length. His hips jerked, the muscles in his buttocks and thighs flexing under her touch. She undid the buttons, pushing the waistband down, and his trousers bunched around his calves. He stepped out of them and shoved them aside with his foot.

She let her hands fall to the outside of his thighs, exploring the steel that lay under heated skin. She brought her fingers higher, over his buttocks and the slight hollow at the sides, and forward over the rigid V of muscle at his hips. His erection jutted against the curve of her abdomen, and she closed her hand over his length, stroking him from the base to the tip. It was an erotic exploration, and the small sound of pleasure that escaped him banished any timidity. She let her hand slide back down, all the way to the base and farther, cupping his testicles in the same way he had cupped her breasts. He groaned and pulled her hand away, bending to kiss her deeply.

"So perfect," he murmured against her mouth. "But this is about you." He buried his hands in her hair, tipping her head back and grazing the side of her neck first with his teeth and then his tongue. "You will tell me if I do something you don't like," he said softly. "Do you understand?"

She nodded, but it was hard to think when he was doing things like that with his mouth.

"You will also tell me what you like. What brings you the most pleasure." He was backing her up now, his body pressing into hers.

She nodded again, feeling drunk on the decadent wickedness of his words.

"Good. Now get on the bed."

She obeyed, feeling the coolness of the cloth as she reclined against the pillows and sheets. He stood there for a moment, unmoving, simply devouring her with his eyes. In another life, it would have made her feel uncomfortable. Self-conscious. Today it only made her feel powerful.

"I've fantasized about you like this too many times." He lowered himself to the bed, bracing himself beside her on his hands and knees. "Wearing nothing but these." He reached out, and his fingers played with the diamonds at her throat. His hand slid from the necklace to trace a path from her throat, between her breasts.

His mouth followed. Unhurriedly, he took a nipple in his mouth, teasing, tasting, making her arch off the bed in blinding pleasure before he moved on to the other. His hands splayed over her abdomen and around her hips, slipping along the inside of one of her thighs and pushing it open. "So beautiful," he murmured. He withdrew his hand, but as he did so, he dragged his thumb through the folds of her sex, massaging the bud at the very apex.

Angelique made a muffled sound and closed her eyes. "Yes," she whispered.

"Mmmm." He bent then, and Angelique gasped as she felt his mouth where his hand had just been. His tongue licked, and he sucked gently, and white-hot streaks of pleasure tore through her. She felt her leg fall open farther, giving him greater access, and he took full advantage. It was building again, the need that twisted and writhed deep within her, demanding release. But she needed more than this. This wasn't going to be enough. This time when she came, she wanted all of him.

"Alex." Her fingers tangled in his hair.

He lifted his head and met her gaze. His hair fell over his eyes, casting them even further in shadow, and she wasn't sure if he understood. *She* wasn't sure if she understood.

"I want you," she said raggedly, searching for words to explain. "I want—"

She never got to finish because he'd moved and his mouth was on hers, hard and possessive. He'd shifted, and she could feel the hard muscle of his thighs along the insides of hers, pushing them wider. He was still braced on his hands above her, but now his chest rubbed against hers, sending new sparks of need spiraling through her. And at the entrance to her body that had become so sensitive and wet, she could feel the head of his erection.

For the briefest of seconds, despite her best intentions, despite all of his care, she hesitated.

He must have felt her tense because his lips slid from her mouth to her ear. "Trust me, Angel," he whispered.

She nodded because she had no words, and then he was kissing her again, a long, hot kiss that had her melting beneath him. There was no concession to time. No concession that a world even existed beyond this room, beyond this bed.

He moved his hips gently, and she felt his erection nudge against her folds again. He slipped a hand between them, stroking her clit and making her whimper and her hips rock. And as she did, he thrust, pushing deep. They both stilled.

"Tell me," he whispered. "Tell me what you feel."

He was stretching her, filling her more than she could have imagined. But there was no pain, just a tightness that seemed to throb in time with her pounding heart. She moved her pelvis ever so slightly, feeling that small movement send ripples of pleasure flooding through her. She did it again, gasping at the exquisite friction.

He bent his head and kissed her, letting her adjust. She could feel her body reaching for release, but what she was doing was not enough. Not nearly enough. "Alex," she begged.

He withdrew, nearly all the way out before he thrust again. "Yes," she hissed, her eyes closing at the overwhelming sensations that were battering her.

"Tell me what you feel," he demanded again, and she could see a sheen of sweat on his brow, see the fierce intensity of his eyes, see him wrestling with control.

There were no words for what was coursing through her. No words existed that would ever be adequate. She wrapped her legs around him, slid her hands over his ass, and rocked her hips hard against his, drawing him even deeper. He dropped his head and moaned, her name torn from his lips.

"That," she said breathlessly. "I feel that."

He withdrew and thrust harder, stroking deep into her heat.

"Yes," she whispered. "Don't stop." Her hands slid up to the small of his back.

He surged against her, his muscles flexing beneath her touch, every thrust sending her body spiraling higher. She was panting, uttering small sounds she didn't recognize. She was past the point where she could speak, past the point where she could think. There were emotions crowding her throat and her head and her heart now, but she couldn't begin to sort them through the haze of pleasure that was this man. The only thing she could do was hold on to him. All that existed now was him.

He claimed her mouth again, possessing her, owning her, filling her, giving her what no man ever had. Demanding her complete surrender.

And then she felt that pressure break suddenly, deep inside of her, and she bore down on it. Every muscle within her seized, powerful convulsions radiating outward and sending devastating shockwaves of pleasure crashing through her as she shattered, whispering his name.

⁓

At the sound of his name, Alex's head fell against her shoulder, his breath coming in harsh gasps as his hips thrust once more before he withdrew, spending himself against the soft curve of her abdomen. The shuddering crest of his climax slammed through him, breaking over and over, sending eddies humming through every nerve ending. Alex collapsed against her, and it was a while before he could catch his breath.

The slow seduction he'd promised himself, the perfect reeducation he'd had planned, had almost folded beneath her inexperienced yet instinctive touch. No one had ever undone him the way this woman did.

He collected himself and rolled to the side, sliding out of bed and returning with the cloth from the washstand. He wiped her gently and set the cloth aside, aware that she was watching him. She hadn't moved, only lay back against the richly colored coverlet, her lips swollen, her hair tumbled over the pillow, her skin looking like honeyed gold in the soft candlelight. She looked sated and not a little dazed, and he wasn't ashamed to admit it soothed his battered pride and ego.

He swung his legs back onto the bed and stretched out beside her. They lay there for a long time, simply gazing at each other, before she rolled over on her side so that her face was close to his.

"Thank you," she said. "For that."

He grinned, feeling like he was on more secure footing than he had been in a while. "Was it everything you expected?"

"More. So much more."

"Good. You deserve no less." His hand traced a line over her shoulder and across the slope of her breast. "Thank you for trusting me."

"You're not just an adventure," she whispered.

He froze. "I beg your pardon?"

"You said once that women use you. That you are the scandalous, wicked adventure that they crave in their ordinary, boring lives." She was watching him, her eyes a stormy blue in the low light.

He stared at her for a moment before rolling onto his back and staring up at the ceiling. He had said that. And then she had asked if it made him happy.

"No matter what happens—today, tomorrow, ten years from now—I want you to understand that you were not an adventure. Not to me. Not ever. You are the finest man I have ever met." Her voice was urgent, as if she needed to say this all before she lost her courage.

Alex waited for the right comment to pop into his head, something casual and careless that would reduce the weight of her words. Except nothing came to him. Nothing at all except the need to believe her and a strange emotion that seemed to have thickened his throat and set an ache into his chest. "I am not a good man," he tried, though his words were not nearly as cavalier as he would like. "I am an assassin. And maybe a spy. With a harem and a gaming hell—"

"Stop." Angelique smoothed his hair back from his forehead with light fingers. "Before you insult my intelligence." He couldn't tell if she was teasing him or not.

He fell silent.

"Tell me what happened," she said, running the pad of her finger over the scar that crossed his cheek.

"What sort of story do you wish to hear?" It slipped out before he realized what he had done.

Beside him, Angelique was quiet. Letting him evade if he chose to.

"I was trying to save my brother." He continued to stare up at the ceiling, wondering why he had told her that. "We were sent to drive the landing Americans back to their ships." Now that he had started, he couldn't seem to stop. "Our regiment had scattered. We were outnumbered and outgunned. I tried to convince Jonathon that we needed to flank, use the edge of the trees for cover, come at them from behind, but he ignored me. He was reckless, caught up in the bloodlust of battle. Certain that nothing could touch him. Until a six-pounder took his arm at the shoulder. I was trying to get him off the field when an American infantryman caught us, thinking to finish what the artillery had started. We fought. It took me too long to kill him. By the time I made it back to Jonathon, he was dead, the ground soaked with his blood. I was too late to save him."

He could feel her eyes on him, but she remained silent.

"I don't blame myself for his death," he said, and it was the first time he'd spoken that aloud. "We were at war. But yet I can't escape the constant feeling that..." He trailed off, searching for words that she would understand.

"That you failed," she said quietly. "That somewhere along the way, there was some small thing you might have done differently that would have changed the outcome. Altered his path."

"Yes." Of course she would understand. Her brother hadn't died, but he might yet, and her words made it obvious that she too was questioning everything she had done. "It's always there. That doubt. That regret."

"Yet you can't go back. You can't change anything."

"I know that." It came out more sharply than he'd intended but she didn't flinch. She simply laid her head on his shoulder, her hand resting on his chest over his heart.

"And you can't control everything in the future either."

"I know that too."

"Do you?"

He opened his mouth to argue but found he couldn't.

"It's a lonely endeavor, that," she said.

"What?"

"Trying to control the future." Her fingers were drawing

small patterns over his skin, a simple yet intensely intimate gesture.

"I like being alone," he said, hearing the same words Angelique had once said to him standing in a darkened hall.

Her fingers stopped before they resumed their caress over his heart.

"Liar," she whispered with the same gentleness he had.

Chapter 14

He'd woken before Angelique and simply lay still for long, silent minutes.

He'd never brought a woman into his bed. Into his space, into his privacy, into his very being. But now, gazing down at the one who lay sleeping beside him, her hair a wild mess, her parted lips still swollen from his kisses, her lashes fanning over her beautifully freckled cheeks, he couldn't imagine her anywhere else. She was right where she belonged.

He knew whatever pathetic attempts he'd made to deny that this was anything but business, that she was anything except an asset to his club, were meaningless. The moment he had gazed into her intelligent blue eyes, he'd been smitten. The moment she'd stepped between him and two warders' blades, he'd been lost. And the moment she'd trusted him with her body, gifted him with her raw vulnerability and demanded the same from him, he'd fallen in love.

He'd revealed more about himself to her than to anyone. Which seemed natural and right, because she had done the same. And instead of the regret and disquiet that he had expected with such exposure, he felt...content. It was a strange sensation, this. Nothing that he had ever experienced before. A little like he had run a great distance and couldn't quite catch his breath, all the while his heart thundered on and the joy of it coursed through his veins. All he knew was that he wanted nothing more than to keep her right where she was, where she could be his.

If he knew anything about this woman, it was that she was plenty capable of taking care of herself. What had happened last night certainly didn't change that. But she still needed his help. And not the sort that involved satin sheets and soft whispers in the dark, but the sort that would give her the answers she needed—the answers she deserved—to help her move forward. And right now, there was nothing but an alarming collection of muddy questions and coincidences.

Had he not discovered that Angelique's father had been blackmailed for years, coupled with the suspicious circumstances surrounding his death, Alex might have been more likely to accept the fact that Gerald Archer had simply been in the wrong place at the wrong time, albeit as a result of his own sheer stupidity. But his instincts were sounding an alarm, and Alex had long ago learned never to ignore his instincts.

He didn't know who had been extorting the old marquess. He didn't know who had sent the anonymous note to Hutton about the necklace. But the one name that continued to be linked to Hutton's was Viscount Seaton. George Fitzherbert bothered him. Not only did the man appear to have suspicious ties to the darker side of London, he had been at the Trevane house the night Hutton was arrested.

And then there were Seaton's motivations toward Angelique, both in the past as well as the present. It was possible that Seaton hoped to take advantage of Angelique's perceived vulnerability or isolate her further. In his tenure at Chegarre, Alex had seen individuals so fixated on another that they lost touch with reality. They became so fixated on their desires and fantasies that they would do anything to achieve their ends. Even kill.

Yet if Seaton wanted to be rid of Hutton, for whatever reason, why not simply kill him? God knew no one would even raise a brow if the body of a young buck known for his reckless, irresponsible lifestyle was found in Smithfield, reeking of gin and stripped of everything of value. Why go to all the effort of setting up a complicated plan?

Alex slid silently out of bed and dressed, irritated that his thoughts were simply chasing themselves in circles. As much as he wanted to simply peel back the covers and kiss Angelique awake, and then kiss her some more, she needed to sleep. And he needed some answers. Facts, not suppositions. And he wasn't going to get them here.

~

Angelique was woken by a knock on the door though, when she opened her eyes, she wasn't sure if she had imagined it. What she did know was that she felt more rested than she had in days. Weeks, maybe. Hell, probably years. She stretched, feeling her muscles protest in places she hadn't known existed until last night, and for a moment, simply reveled in all the delicious sensations. She rolled over, already sensing that Alex was gone, but she wasn't concerned. She could see a sliver of light between the curtains that covered the single window of the bedroom. It must be midmorning at least.

There was another soft knock on the door, and this time, it swung open. Light spilled into the room from the office beyond, and Alex came in, closing the door behind him. He was dressed flawlessly, from the complicated knot of his cravat to the polished tips of his boots. He could have passed for a duke. He could have passed for a bloody prince.

"Good afternoon." His lips curled up.

"Afternoon?"

"I was going to say good evening, but that seemed to be pushing it. It's not quite four yet."

"What?" She had slept the entire day? She started to lunge out of bed, stopping suddenly when she realized that she was still completely naked. And that she had no idea where her clothes were. The covers started to slide down her chest before she snatched them back up.

"Please, don't let me stop you," Alex said.

"I'm naked," Angelique said, feeling her cheeks heat, both at the inanity of her statement and the fact.

"Nothing gets by you, does it?" Alex advanced toward the bed. "Though for the record, I approve."

She made a face to cover the fact that a million butterflies were suddenly swarming through her insides. She watched him draw closer, her fingers curling into the sheets. He sat down on the bed beside her, and the mattress dipped under his weight. His hands rested on his thighs, and in an instant, she remembered quite clearly what he had done with those hands.

Her skin prickled, and arousal twisted through her.

"Your brother is well," he said. "Or, as well as can be expected, I imagine."

Desire was abruptly extinguished with guilt. She hadn't even given Gerald a thought since she had woken. "Did you see him?"

"I did not. He is still denied visitors. Nor did I think it wise to press our luck and chance a repeat of yesterday. No, today I simply presented myself as an exalted member of the peerage verifying young Hutton's welfare. Hervey was quite amenable."

Angelique looked down. While she had been sleeping, Alex had been doing what she should have done.

"Don't do that," he said, catching her chin and tipping her head up, forcing her eyes back to his.

"What?"

"Punish yourself. There is nothing you can do for him right now that you haven't already done."

"I could have come with you."

"And done what?"

She shrugged unhappily. "Just...been there."

"You were exhausted."

She pulled away from his touch.

"You're not alone anymore, Angel." He leaned forward and kissed her, a slow, sweet kiss.

She wanted to believe him so badly. That no matter what happened, they could remain like this. Confidantes, lovers, partners.

He pulled back, searching her eyes. "Wait for me here."

"I beg your pardon?" Confusion distracted her. "Where are you going?"

"To have a conversation with Viscount Seaton. I'd like to clear up a few outstanding items with him and inquire just what or who might have drawn him to a tavern in Pillory Lane."

"And he's there now? At the tavern?"

"No."

She felt her forehead crease in puzzlement. "Then where are you meeting him?"

"My neighbor's. And I'm not so sure he's expecting me."

"Your neighbor's?"

"More like the Duchess's neighbors. Miss Winslow runs a very popular, profitable...establishment."

"A brothel."

"Something like that."

"I'm coming with you."

"Absolutely not."

"Odd. Because I'm sure you're not asking me to hide in your rooms again." She could hear the razor edge of steel in her voice. "What does one wear to a popular, profitable establishment?" she asked.

"Clothes," he said darkly.

"Ah. You think that I will be shocked by what I see."

"You're a lady," he growled.

"Sometimes." She was being contrary, but he knew better than this. He knew better than to treat her like a shrinking violet. "And sometimes I deal cards at a gaming hell. For a man who might just be an assassin and a spy. And sometimes"—she let the sheet drop from her chest—"when it suits him, that man doesn't wish me to be a lady at all."

She saw the way he went perfectly still, saw the way every muscle in his body seemed to have tensed. His expression was almost feral, and she knew that she was playing with fire. Yet she didn't care.

She shoved the sheet away from her and crawled forward until she was next to him, her mouth inches from his. "But he doesn't always get to choose when being a lady suits me. I do." She kissed him, her tongue sliding along his bottom lip. "And right now, I am not a lady."

She was going to kill him.

She couldn't possibly have any idea just what sort of erotic torment her words had wrought. The sight of that beautifully rounded ass, the sway of her generous breasts, the feel of her tongue sliding over his mouth sent all sorts of unholy thoughts through his brain and straight to his cock. Alex was so hard it hurt.

"Angelique." He might have been warning her. He might have been begging her.

She deepened her kiss, nipping and teasing with more skill than any woman should ever possess. She had no idea what she was asking for. No idea what—

Her tongue slid into his mouth as her hand cupped his cock. He gasped, jerking to his feet. With a desperation that should have been mortifying, he yanked at the fall of his trousers. She had moved closer, and now she was on her knees on the edge of the bed in front of him, her hands pushing his away. She undid the last button, pushing the waistband down, freeing his throbbing erection.

He grasped the bedpost to steady himself, desire blurring the edges of his vision. He had never wanted a woman as badly as this. He had never lost so much control so fast. He felt the cool air touch the back of his legs, but in the next second, her hand was on him, stroking him to the tip and back down to the base. He shuddered and closed his eyes, feeling his cock jump in her grip. She did it again, adjusting the pressure and the tempo, reading his body and its responses as easily as she did her cards. And then he felt her hands slide around his buttocks and the cool silk of her hair sliding against his thighs as she took him in her mouth. Her lips dragged along his length, her tongue swirling over the tip, and Alex felt his balls tighten and the first pulses of pressure deep at the base of his spine.

His eyes flew open, and he moved away, though only long enough to climb onto the bed behind her. She was still on her knees, and she made to turn, but he grasped her hips with his hands and hauled her back toward him.

"Don't move," he rasped.

He set himself between her legs, his cock sliding against the cleft of her buttocks. His hands slid up the smooth expanse of her back and returned, once again caressing the curves of her hips. He rose on his knees slightly and drew back, and now the tip of his cock teased the folds of her sex. Bloody hell, but she was wet. He was never going to be able to get enough of her.

"Angel," he said, pushing in a little farther, battling against the urge to simply bury himself to the hilt.

He heard Angelique's breath catch, and in the next second, she spread her knees wider, her head dropping, and he nearly lost that battle.

"Yes," she whispered.

Gritting his teeth for control, he pushed deep inside her, feeling her walls close tightly around him. He pulled out slightly and then thrust back in, that tiny friction sending sparks of unbearable pleasure shooting through him. He withdrew again, slowly, and she whimpered, a sound that was almost one of pain.

He stopped.

"What are you doing?" she gasped.

He was trying to think, but it was difficult. "I don't want to hurt you."

She groaned. "You're not."

He swallowed, his entire body trembling.

"Move," she panted. Her hands were fisted in the sheets. "Just...move." She tilted her hips back and up, and he slid deeper.

Alex's vision blurred slightly, and he thrust hard into her heat. Again. And again. Whatever control he might have had was gone, abandoned at her words. His hips pistoned, and he leaned forward, covering her, his hands finding the weight of her breasts, his fingers rolling her nipples. He heard her cry out, felt her tense and shudder beneath him, felt her heat ripple around him. He uttered a guttural sound, driving deep before he yanked himself out, coming harder than he ever had. His mind blanked, his entire world reduced to the powerful riptide of pleasure that tore through him.

He came back to himself presently to find himself slumped over her. She was still on her hands and knees, her head resting on the sheet, her eyes closed and her lips slightly parted as her breathing slowed. He straightened, wiping his semen from the small of her back with the corner of the sheet, realizing with horror that he was still fully dressed. He hadn't even managed to take his coat off, so desperate had he been for her.

He, who had wanted to give this woman every incredible pleasure that bed-sport could bring, had been reduced to rutting like an animal. Reduced to a desperate, needy, selfish lover.

"Let's do that again," she murmured, her words somewhat muffled by the pillow.

He had retreated from the bed, trying to right his clothes, but he stopped suddenly, unsure if he had heard her right. "I beg your pardon?"

"You told me to tell you what I liked. What I wanted." She rolled to her side and sat up. Her face was flushed, and she met his eyes, unflinching. "That. I liked that."

Jesus. He was going to be hard again before they finished this conversation. He fumbled for words, but his brain seemed to have ceased to function altogether.

"I've made you uncomfortable." She had turned his own words back on him, and he thought she might be laughing at him now.

He took a step closer to the bed, gazing down at her. "No.

Never uncomfortable. But determined that next time, that will take longer."

"I didn't want longer. I wanted that. You. Hard. Fast."

He shuddered, wondering just how he had managed to live before this woman. He knelt on the bed, leaning down to kiss her, ravaging her mouth and extinguishing her amusement. He pulled away to find her breathless.

He shrugged out of his coat and went to work at the knot of his cravat. He watched her expression change, saw the same hunger he felt mount.

"You'll have all of that," he said, tossing his cravat aside. "But trust me when I say it's going to take longer. Much longer."

Chapter 15

The brothel was just down from the offices of Chegarre & Associates.

It too had a run-down façade and a heavy, worn door at the top of a set of cracked stone steps. Like the offices of Chegarre, the brothel had tightly closed windows that stared blankly out onto the square and the crowds that had come for the market. And like Chegarre, it gave no clue as to the business that lay within. There were no windows flung open, no gaudily dressed women leaning from the sills trying to entice business. Despite the address, Miss Winslow's was exclusive and private, and there was no shortage of business that came to them.

Alex started up the stone steps, Angelique at his side. The door of the brothel was painted a brilliant scarlet, and as they approached, it swung open. Two men emerged, though they swayed alarmingly and seemed to be working hard to remain upright. They staggered down the stairs, and Alex saw Angelique step back and turn slightly, the hood of her cloak concealing her hair and her face.

A woman was standing in the open door, leaning on the frame, watching the men go with shrewd appraisal, but when she caught sight of Alex, she smiled.

"Mr. Lavoie," she said, stepping to the side and holding the door open a little farther. "Welcome." Penny Winslow was almost as tall as he was, her body made up of sharp angles and long limbs that were evident even under the well-tailored dress she wore. Even her face was angular—from her long, narrow nose to her slanted eyes.

"Good afternoon," he replied as he entered. He was aware that Angelique was right behind him, and he turned. "Miss Winslow, this is my friend Angel." He did not use Angelique's full name because he had no idea how many ears might be listening just beyond. "Angel, Miss Winslow."

Angelique smiled, and to her credit, it reflected only polite regard. She could have been entering a teahouse or an assembly room for all that her expression gave away. "Good afternoon," she said.

"Good afternoon to you." From over Angelique's shoulder, Penny threw him a questioning look. In all the times he had been here to collect information, he had only ever come alone. He still wasn't entirely sure that this was a good idea.

Penny closed the door, and Alex wandered into the entrance of the brothel. Somewhere, off the hall, someone was playing a pianoforte, a haunting, melodic tune. The scent of incense and something stronger was cloying, and as if Penny could read his mind, she pushed the long window at the front of the hall open a crack, wrinkling her nose.

"Never did like the smell of poppy," she grumbled. "But one cannot argue with profits."

"Mmmm." He glanced around the sumptuous décor that hadn't changed in years. He was guessing that the intended theme had been drawn from Arabian Nights, but the effect had a decidedly incongruous French flair. Dark, patterned curtains were pulled over the long windows, and ornate, Louis XVI settees were placed on red and black Persian rugs. Brocaded pillows, many with a fleur-de-lis pattern, were strewn over the settees. Wall sconces flickered with candles, and some-one had hung long strings of glass beads from each to catch the light. There was a collection of painted canvases on one wall—mostly naked, cherubic figures shooting arrows toward more naked, less cherubic figures.

"What do I owe the pleasure?" Penny asked, leading them through the hall. Two hulking men stepped into their path as they approached.

"Thank you, boys," Penny said easily, and the two men fell back.

"They're working out well, then?" Alex inquired. They'd come to his club looking for work with excellent references. Alex hadn't needed additional security but, instead, had di-rected them here.

"Yes, splendidly, thank you. Even the worst of the clien-tele are generally inclined to keep their testicles intact and can easily be persuaded to adjust their behavior to ensure it. Neither my girls nor I appreciate abuse."

"Nor should you."

Penny turned and entered a small room, lit by a cande-labra. This room, in contrast, was almost stark in appear-ance. The floors were bare wood, gouged and scraped, and the walls and ceiling were plain plaster, peeling in places. A desk, chair, and a bookcase were the only furniture. It was clear where the money was being spent. She closed the door behind them.

"You have a customer here that we need to speak to," Alex said bluntly.

From over their heads there came a crash, followed by

a great deal of what sounded like drunken laughter. Penny winced. "I have a lot of customers here this afternoon," she said, going to stand behind her desk.

"Viscount Seaton."

"Ah. One of my best customers." Her eyes narrowed. "The kind that pays for what he buys up front."

"I'm sure."

"What do you want with him?"

"A word."

Penny crossed her arms. "You heard me say he was one of my best customers, yes?"

"I did."

"Hmph. My customers expect a certain amount of privacy, Lavoie." Her eyes flickered to Angelique. "Why is she here?"

It was a good question, one he had been asking himself since they had left. And suddenly, in a blinding flash of inspiration, he said, "To do your books. The Duchess mentioned you were unhappy with how far you'd fallen behind. Profits slip through the cracks like that."

Penny's eyes snapped to Angelique. "Ah. I didn't make the connection. You are Mr. Lavoie's vingt-et-un dealer?"

Angelique was staring at Penny. So was Alex, for that matter.

She caught their expressions. "I ran into Gil late last night." She eyed Angelique. "You must have impressed her. Which is a hard thing to do."

Angelique glanced at Alex and shrugged. "I lent a hand where I could."

Penny narrowed her eyes at him in suspicion. "So this is why you brought her? To update my books?"

"Yes."

"No," said Angelique at the same time.

"Angel is indeed brilliant at numbers. She can do in minutes

what would take me hours. She'll have you up to date, and if
there are any discrepancies in your accounting, she'll correct it.
And it will be done in the time it will take me to have a brief dis-
cussion with Seaton. A fair trade, wouldn't you say?"

"Hmph." Penny was looking at Angelique now in grudg-
ing interest.

He could see Angelique shaking her head. "I did not—"

"Do we have a deal?" Alex asked, cutting her off.

"Yes." Penny came out from behind her desk. "But if you
get blood on anything upstairs, Lavoie—"

"You know me better than that."

She made a face. "I have new linens on the beds. Keep
that in mind. And don't break anything."

"You have my word."

She sighed and then strode to the door. "I'll find out
where he's at and come and fetch you. And then I'll get her
started on my books."

"Thank you, Penny."

The madam gave him a long last look and then disappeared. He could hear the steady rap of her boots as she
headed down the hall to the wide staircase that led up to the
second floor.

"Just what the hell are you doing, Alex?" Angelique
hissed the second they could no longer hear her footsteps.

"What is necessary to get us what we want."

"I doubt Seaton is going to have much to say to you. I
should be the one to talk to him."

"Not a chance."

"I could beg him to protect me in exchange for his stories."

He closed the distance between them. "That's not funny,
Angel."

"So instead, I'll be locked down here doing the books for
a damn opium den—"

"Brothel. The opium rooms are simply something new she's trying in order to maximize profits outside of peak business hours. Don't let any of this fool you. This brothel is exclusive and half the peers of the realm don't have the kind of income that this business does."

Angelique rolled her eyes. "—doing the books for this damn *brothel* while you interrogate Seaton?"

"God, you're beautiful when you curse."

"Don't change the subject. I should be with you."

"I have limits, Lady Angelique, and I have reached them. I brought you here against my better judgment, but I will not drag you into the same room that your former affianced is using to pass time with a pipe. And possibly a prostitute."

"He wasn't officially my affianced. And I'm not—"

"This is not a negotiation. I don't want you anywhere near that man. Not after... not after everything." He wasn't sure if he was talking about Seaton's involvement in her brother's debacle or the way Seaton had once broken her heart.

Her lips compressed.

"You have a rare skill with numbers. I suggest you use it. Not only does it get us what we want, it helps out a neighbor and a friend."

Angelique made a noise of irritation. "And how do you know Seaton will even talk to you? How do you know he will tell you anything?"

Alex heard the quick steps of Penny returning. "Don't worry, Angel. I have my ways."

⌒

Silently, Alex climbed the staircase and made his way down the second floor hallway. He'd never actually been up on Penny's second floor, but the layout was the same as the second floor of Chegarre & Associates. Up here, the scent of opium was much stronger. From behind the closed doors, the occasional giggle or moan filtered through, audible over the sound of the pianoforte that still drifted up through the floorboards.

Alex stopped in front of the door painted with the number four. He listened intently, but he could only hear a slight murmur of voices, the words indecipherable from where he stood. Alex knocked quietly, and the door swung open, a woman with light brown hair wrapped in a simple robe of the same color standing in front of him. She was probably pretty, but the flatness in her eyes and the hard edges to her face had taken away any warmth.

"You Mr. Lavoie?" she asked, her eyes traveling the length of him and lingering on his face where his scar pulled at his lip.

"Yes."

"Penny said you'd be up." She glanced at the crotch of his trousers, her voice laced with innuendo.

Alex only smiled. "I need but a moment of this gentleman's time," he said. "He and I have something we need to discuss."

Her eyebrows rose. "Should have done that before he got a hold of his pipe," the brunette said, pulling the tie of her robe tighter and stepping into the hall. "Though he didn't take much."

"Mmmm." That might be either good or bad, depending how far gone he was. "Is he a regular? With the opium, I mean?" he asked.

The woman rolled her eyes. "Does a hobby horse have a wooden dick?"

"Mmmm."

"Good luck," she said, heading down the hall without a backward glance.

Alex watched her go for a second before stepping into the room, closing the door quietly behind him and locking it. The room was small and square, and the single window on the far wall was covered with a faded curtain. The only light seeped in around the edges. To his right, a large bed dominated the space, a collection of covers shoved to the end and onto the floor. In the center of the bed, Seaton lay sprawled, completely naked. His eyes were closed, and he was muttering something under his breath, his head lolling back and forth.

Near his feet lay a tray with an opium pipe and bowl, and the air in here was already giving Alex a headache. He crossed to the window and pulled the curtain aside, opening it as far as it would go on its tired hinges.

"That's cold," Seaton whined. "Close the window, Missy."

Alex plucked the viscount's coat from the back of the washstand chair where it had been discarded and let it drop to the floor near the side of the bed. He picked up the chair and retreated to the end of the bed, settling himself in and crossing a booted foot over his knee.

"I said close the damn window," Seaton said, louder this time. "I'm not payin' to freeze my bollocks off. I'm payin' to have you do whatever I tell y'to do—"

"At my request, Missy stepped out for a moment, my lord," Alex said smoothly.

Seaton lurched into a sitting position. "Who th' hell are you?" He said it with the care that a drunk uses when trying to convince someone else he isn't drunk.

"A lesser man than I might be insulted that he's been forgotten so quickly," Alex said mockingly, leaning forward into the light.

It took Seaton a moment before he was able to focus on

Alex's face. "Lavoie." His pupils were mere pinpoints, and his face was slack.

"Very good, my lord."

"Get out." He was trying to scramble off the bed, but his movements were slow and uncoordinated.

"Mmmm."

Seaton had managed to stand, and he looked like he was trying to find his clothing. He located his coat on the floor and snatched it up, trying to pull it on. He managed to get one arm all the way in, but the second arm got caught at the elbow, and as Seaton struggled, he lost his balance and toppled face-first back onto the bed.

The viscount lay there for a moment, breathing like a winded racehorse, before he managed to roll on his back, his arms still caught up behind him in the sleeves of his coat. He was making an odd snuffling sound, and Alex couldn't quite tell if he was laughing or coughing.

"Whad'ya want, Lavoie?" the man asked presently.

"A conversation." Alex considered him. Opium was a strange creature. In some, it loosened their tongues. In others, it rendered them witless. "How long this takes is up to you, my lord," he continued. From his belt, he withdrew his knife, fingering the bone hilt. "But I feel obligated to warn you that I am not a man of great patience."

Seaton was staring at Alex's knife, his eyes glassy.

Alex leaned forward. "How did you find out about the necklace the Earl of Trevane had made for his mistress?"

"Jesus," Seaton groaned.

"I find that unlikely," Alex replied. "Try again."

"What th' hell are you askin' these questions for?" he slurred.

"Someone needs to ask them, don't you think?" He tapped the blade on his knee. "Humor me."

"His sister put you up t'this?"

Alex didn't answer.

"She already begged me for help, y'know," he said, apparently taking Alex's silence as an affirmative answer. "But even I, with all my power, cannot save him. It's a lost cause."

"Mmmm."

"Dunno what she thinks you can do that I can't," he muttered.

Alex examined the edge of his blade.

Seaton suddenly laughed, a slightly deranged, incoherent sound. "Y'think she's going t'let you unner her skirts for doing this, don't you?" he wheezed. "Well, take it from me, she's a terrible fu—"

Alex didn't remember moving, but his knife was now pressed against the soft flesh of Seaton's neck. "Be very, very careful, my lord, what you say next."

The viscount swallowed, the movement drawing a tiny bead of blood from under the blade. It would seem his sense of self-preservation wasn't entirely obliterated. "Y'can't kill me. Y'won't." He sounded like he was trying to convince himself.

"I haven't quite decided. Do you know how much surgeons are paying for cadavers right now? And they never ask awkward questions, at least the ones I do business with. Bodies simply…disappear. In little bits and pieces, at any rate. Killing you would not only make me feel better, but make this night profitable. Even after I pay for the ruined sheets."

Seaton was sweating profusely, despite the cool air in the room. "You're insane."

"On occasion." Alex smiled. "But how you answer my next questions will determine if this is one of those occasions. Understand?"

The viscount nodded, his eyes swinging about the room, as if he were trying to focus on something.

"Now where were we? Ah yes. The Earl of Trevane. Did you send Hutton into his house to retrieve the necklace while you cowered in the bushes?"

"What? No!" Seaton gasped. "I never even knew 'bout that. I thought Hutton was there to swive the maid."

"Mmmm." Alex remained unconvinced. "And you never thought to go into the house yourself? Perhaps get in on the action?"

"I 'ave standards, Lavoie, even if Hutton don't. I don't shag the help."

"Standards." Alex glanced around him. "Of course."

"Hutton couldn't afford anything better," he mumbled.

"And why is that?"

The viscount's throat worked again. "He doesn't have any money. Well, he does, but all the damn solicitors still 'ave it up their asses."

Alex stared down at the viscount, stymied. If Seaton was lying, he was a master at it, and Alex did not think he was that good. Especially not while he was naked, inebriated, and with a knife to his throat. "So when Hutton told you he needed money last week, you did what?"

Seaton's forehead wrinkled as if he were trying to remember. "Nothin'," he slurred. "I didn't 'ave what he was asking for."

"Which is why you used your friends in Smithfield." Alex threw that out to see what kind of reaction he'd get.

Seaton's eyes bulged, and his mouth opened and closed twice.

Alex shifted his weight and took the knife away from Seaton's neck, letting the tip of the blade rest at the hollow of his throat. "Your...friends are not as loyal as you might think. Everyone has a price." Alex would let Seaton do with that what he would because he was fishing blindly here.

"Greedy bastards," the viscount grunted. "I pay 'em plenty to look the other way."

"Not enough."

Seaton groaned. "What do y'want?"

"What you have," Alex answered vaguely.

"What did Hutton tell you?" Seaton was looking around the room angrily as though he might find the man in question.

"What makes you think it was Hutton who told me anything? Did you not think others might notice just how wealthy your family has gotten over the last five years? I know your father likes to pretend that it is simply good estate management, but I think we both know better."

Seaton thumped his head back on the mattress. "My father will kill me if this gets out. Maybe he'll sell me t'a surgeon." He suddenly giggled, as though the idea was amusing.

"The duke doesn't have to find out." Alex still had no idea what they were talking about. "I can make sure of it."

Seaton lifted his head, and his eyes seemed to focus on Alex's face. "Give ye five percent of the next shipment."

"Twenty."

The viscount's legs twitched. "It's not bleedin' pepper we're tradin' to the Chinese; it's raw product. D'ye know how many people take a cut? Yer not so special that you get to swallow that much of our profit." He was blinking rapidly. "Ten percent of the next single shipment of trade goods for you t'keep your damn mouth shut."

Alex suddenly understood. The illustrious Duke of Rossburn and his son were covert players in the opium trade. They would be financing the ships and their crews—a high-risk investment to be sure, but one that offered extravagant spoils if it was done right. It explained the sudden, secretive wealth that the duke and his family had come to possess. It explained the mysterious investment opportunity that Seaton had offered to Hutton. And it explained what Hutton and Seaton had been doing in Smithfield talking to corrupt customs agents who were being paid to look the other way when one of their ships came in.

But most of all, it convinced Alex that George Fitzherbert had nothing to do with whatever had happened at the Earl of Trevane's house.

Alex pretended to consider his offer. He was quite certain that a man such as the Duke of Rossburn would rather be drawn and quartered than admit his wealth came from trade.

"Very well," he said slowly. "Ten percent." He let his lips draw into a smile. "I'll send someone up before I leave here with the appropriate paperwork for you to sign. I do like to have something in writing whenever possible, don't you?"

"Now ye sound like Burleigh," Seaton sighed. "He writes everythin' down. *Everythin'*. Prob'ly find a receipt for ev'ry whore he's ever had if ye wanted it." He giggled again before he frowned. "Maybe he should start dealin' with the damn agents, 'stead o' me all the time."

That caught Alex's attention. Had the middling baron also invested with Seaton and his father? Alex considered his next words carefully. "Only a fool does not ensure his fortunes are accounted for."

"Tha's what he's been sayin' for five years. Ev'ry time he loans us capital. Ev'ry time he buys a goddamn ship," Seaton garbled. "But *shhhh*. Don' tell anyone."

Alex made sure his face remained blank, not that the viscount would notice anyway. Angelique had told him that

Burleigh's family was not wealthy. Certainly not wealthy enough to buy a ship. Or ships, as Seaton implied.

He knew nothing about Burleigh, other than what Angelique had told him, and he was cursing himself for it now. He knew nothing about his finances, knew nothing about the man himself. His favorite color, his favorite food, his favorite whore. Knew nothing about the things that motivated him, knew nothing about his ambitions or dislikes.

It was possible that there was a completely reasonable explanation. It was possible that Angelique simply wasn't aware of Burleigh's wealth. She herself had said that she didn't know him well. It was possible that Burleigh had simply scraped enough capital together and invested early and through good fortune had ended up richly rewarded. And that he had reinvested with even more good fortune.

Or it was possible that there was something else entirely going on here.

But what any of it had to do with Gerald Archer, or any of the Huttons for that matter, was still beyond him. Except...

Five years. Alex did not for one second believe that the timing was a coincidence.

"Saved you from getting married." It was a guess. But a good one.

The viscount had closed his eyes, and Alex thought he might have fallen asleep, but at the sound of his voice, Seaton's eyes popped back open.

"What?" He was blinking in confusion.

"Whatever money Burleigh gave you to fund your initial investment. Replaced what you would have gotten from Hutton as dowry money to prop up the sagging Rossburn fortunes."

"Burleigh has a big mouth."

"I'm a smart man, Seaton. No one had to tell me anything."

"That betrothal was never off—official," Seaton sneered sloppily. "I's never wanted to marry her. Never gonna marry 'er. But gave 'er what she wanted 'fore she could figure that out."

Rage shot through Alex with a force that nearly caused him to stagger. A red haze danced at the edge of his vision, and he recognized that his judgment was slipping, giving way to base emotion. Very carefully he sheathed his knife, afraid that he might geld the bastard where he lay. But while that would make him feel better, it would accomplish nothing practical.

And it would definitely ruin the sheets.

Chapter 16

Alex had asked Angelique to wait in the pretty blue drawing room of Chegarre's offices. He'd had a black expression on his face when he'd returned from the second floor of that brothel, and his explanation of what Seaton had told him had been bitten off in short, abrupt sentences. Alex had muttered something about needing more information from the Duchess, and they'd come here directly.

Miss Moore was in Woolwich for the day, the young boy called Roddy had informed them, and wasn't expected back until later this evening. Alex had frowned and then disappeared, but now she could hear him in the hallway giving the boy muffled instructions. She wondered if Alex would have her do Chegarre & Associates' books next. After straightening out Penny's, she was fairly certain that there wasn't anything left that would surprise her. She'd handed the madam back her books with the suggestion that she dismiss the expensive physician that was charging her far too much to regularly examine her girls. God knew Angelique had dealt with enough physicians during her mother's illness, and none of them had ever been able to offer more than a sad shake of their head and a lancet. But there were plenty of retired army surgeons available who were both more practically skilled and knowledgeable. And cheaper. Angelique knew that too.

She wandered around the room, once again taking in the expensive décor. Fit for a duchess, indeed, she reflected idly, thinking of Miss Moore's nickname used not only by Alex but those people who seemed to know the woman best. Angelique stopped by the small table by the settee. On the surface was a piece of sheet music—something someone must have set down at one point and forgotten about. It was Handel's *Giulio Cesare*, and Angelique recognized it instantly. When she was younger, she'd heard the aria sung by an opera singer with a voice like an angel— Her hand froze over the music. The earlier sense of déjà vu she had experienced when first meeting Miss Moore returned, only the explanation now presented itself with startling clarity.

She had once seen the woman who now called herself Miss Moore on one of the grandest opera stages in London. The woman who had scandalously gone on to become the Duchess of Knightley and then disappeared after the duke's death. Though it was now vastly obvious that she hadn't disappeared at all.

Angelique let her fingers trail over the edge of the sheet music to the pretty porcelain dish that sat beside. In it, a handful of engraved cards rested. "Chegarre & Associates" was printed across the smooth, creamy surface, the Covent Square address on the opposite side. They looked similar to the cards her parents had once used to announce their arrival when they went out on social calls. When she was younger, she had always wanted a card of her own. Always thought that she would have one, her name written in an elegant script beneath that of her husband.

Angelique picked one up, frowning. Her eyes skipped over the word *Chegarre* and then back again, picking out individual letters, rearranging them in her mind. For a moment, all she could do was stare, something that felt like admiration and awe unfurling. And she couldn't help the grin that suddenly crept across her face.

She became aware of a movement in the doorway, and she turned to find a tall, broad man standing just inside, his hands clasped behind his back, his ice-grey eyes perusing her with shrewd interest. He was dressed entirely in black, with sun-bleached blond hair tied back in a careless queue. A sword rested in a battered sheath at his waist, and the overall effect made her think that he might just be a pirate.

"Good afternoon." She said it first.

"Good afternoon, Lady Angelique."

"I'm afraid you have me at a disadvantage, sir," she said.

"Ah. Of course, my apologies. Captain Maximus Harcourt at your service." He gave her a slight bow.

Which was ridiculous because Captain Maximus Harcourt was the tenth Duke of Alderidge. Angelique may not take part in society, but nor did she live under a rock. She still read the papers, and if she believed everything she read, then this man was wealthy beyond imagining, if not unconventional. "I should be calling you Your Grace, then," she said.

Alderidge sighed. "If you must. I'd prefer Captain."

"Very well."

"Ah. Splendid. My favorite corsair got my message." Alex strode into the room with a leather-bound book in his hands that didn't look that different from the ledgers she had just perused at a brothel down the street. He frowned slightly. "Did you fly here on a magic ship?"

"Good afternoon to you too, Lavoie," the duke replied. "And I hadn't yet left for the docks. I was here."

"Mmmm. How fortuitous. I assume the Duchess has kept you informed of the current situation?"

"Of course."

With the same clarity that had struck her earlier, Angelique had a very good idea exactly why the Duke of Alderidge had been here long before they had arrived. She gazed at the duke thoughtfully before turning her attention back to Alex.

"Are you going to request I do the books here next?" she asked Alex, staring pointedly at the volume in his hands.

"No. That wasn't what I was going to ask at all."

"Because you were worried that I'd realize that Miss Moore is actually a duchess?"

Alex blinked at her.

"This is lovely," Angelique said, turning over the engraved card she still held in her hand. "And I assumed, when I first came here, that Chegarre was the name of a man. I suspect that generally makes everything so much easier at the outset."

"Mmmm." Alex was watching her closely. The duke simply stared.

"Chegarre is nothing except a clever anagram." She placed the card back gently in the porcelain dish. "Her Grace and Miss Moore are the same person."

"Yes." It was the duke who finally answered, slanting Alex a sideways look.

"I didn't tell her that. Though she figured that out a hell of a lot faster than you, Alderidge." Alex sounded delighted.

The duke scowled. "I didn't realize it was a competition."

"Everything with you is a competition."

"Is your wife here right now?" Angelique asked Alderidge.

"No, she—" Alderidge stopped. He sent another scathing look toward Alex.

Alex held up his hands. "Didn't tell her that either. But you just did."

The duke shook his head, exasperation stamped across his features. "Why am I here, Lavoie? What, exactly, is it that you need?"

"Ships," Alex said. "Indiamen. Specifically those trading opium with the Chinese."

"My ships don't run opium."

"I know that. But you spent a great deal of time pottering about in India. Surely there can't be so many Englishmen with fleets of ships making the run between India and China and then on to England's bonny shores?"

Alderidge frowned. "You'd be surprised. The East India Company licenses many private traders for opium. Though not so many with more than one ship."

"Burleigh," Alex said.

Angelique held her breath. Alex had told her that Seaton, in his drugged state, believed that Burleigh surreptitiously owned the ships that he, and later, Angelique's brother, had invested in. Which couldn't possibly be right. Burleigh had never mentioned that to anyone. And he didn't have the wealth to—

"I can't recall hearing that name." The duke's forehead was creased.

Angelique wasn't sure if she was relieved or disappointed. Of course Burleigh didn't own ships.

"What about the name Cullen?" Alex asked suddenly.

"Yes." Alderidge nodded slowly. "That name is familiar. Owns at least two ships, I think, but I can't be sure. Could be more. Though it wouldn't be that hard to find out."

What? Angelique felt her insides pitch.

"And could you also discover when he bought those ships?" Alex asked.

Alderidge shrugged. "Of course. Though," he added, "he owned ships at least four years ago. I was in Calcutta when I first came across that name."

"Calcutta? Planning another holiday so soon, Captain?" The smooth voice came from behind them. Angelique started and whirled.

A man stood casually just inside the room, and for a brief moment, Angelique wondered if he might be a long-lost descendent of the Tudor kings. He possessed patrician features, pale eyes, and red-gold hair. He was dressed subtly, yet immaculately. A large ruby ring glinted from his hand where it rested on the top of a silver-handled ebony walking stick. A striking man, Angelique thought—almost beautiful—except there was a cold remoteness to him that made her shiver. No matter how civilized he might look, this was a dangerous man. She knew that instinctively, without having witnessed the way both Alex and Alderidge had tensed like drawn bows.

"The museum is just down the road if you're looking for a painting to steal, King," Alex said. "I understand there's a new canvas on display that no doubt appeals to you—a raft full of dead and dying sailors."

"Ah, but there can be beauty in death, Mr. Lavoie. Especially when captured so exquisitely by a skilled young artist."

"What do you want, King?" It was Alderidge who spoke, and his eyes were glacial.

The man called King stroked the top of his walking stick. "Nothing that concerns you, Captain," he replied. "I'm here to see Mr. Lavoie." His pale eyes came to rest on Angelique. "My lady," he greeted cordially. "A pleasure. Gilda speaks quite highly of you."

Alex blew out a breath. "I think everything that has happened in the last five years is connected. I think someone has been trying to destroy your family for a long time."

"But why?"

"That is what I can't seem to determine. But I have a very good idea where to start." He sat down beside her. "Ships, as I understand, are very expensive. Yet at least four years ago, Vincent Cullen somehow found enough money to buy two."

She felt her heart stop for a moment as she understood what he was suggesting. "You think *Burleigh* was extorting my father?" She was trying to picture the nervous, frail man as a cunning criminal and failing badly.

"The coincidence is rather disturbing. And I hate coincidences." He opened the book in his hands. "I can find nothing on record that suggests that Vincent Cullen is anything other than what he purports to be. A middling baron living with his mother in a modest home in the south of London." He scanned the page and snapped the book shut. "And nothing to suggest that his father was anything beyond that either."

"He was my father's best friend," Angelique said, trying to understand the why or how of what Alex was suggesting.

"Yes," Alex said with a sigh. "He was that."

"But if Vincent needed money, my father would have given it to him," Angelique said unhappily. "If only because he was his best friend's son. My father paid for Vincent to attend Harrow, for God's sake, because he knew his family couldn't afford it. I can't believe he would turn around and extort my father. And for what?"

From a folder, Alex pulled out a stack of paper, and Angelique recognized the anonymous notes that had been sent both to her father and her brother. "I brought the extortion note," he said, unfolding the first. "The good captain here has some experience with these. Perhaps he has some ideas." As he unfolded it, another paper fluttered to the floor. Angelique bent to pick it up. It was the letter from Burleigh's mother, obviously caught in between. She started to set it aside before she froze, the hairs on the back of her neck standing straight up. With shaking hands, she put her glass of whiskey on the floor, afraid she might drop it.

Alex noticed. "What's wrong?"

Wordlessly, she placed the letter on Alex's knee, beside the note that had never been delivered to her father.

"Jesus Christ," Alex whispered, looking between the two.

"It was from her. From Lady Burleigh. The Shakespearean passage. The demand for money."

"The writing is the same."

"I never noticed." Angelique pressed a hand to her mouth. "But I can't believe that. She was my mother's friend. She came to sit with my mother when she was dying. Held her hand." She stopped abruptly. "Vincent knows."

Alderidge cleared his throat. "Unless Burleigh is stupid enough to believe that his mother planted a tree in their kitchen garden that grew money, he is aware." The duke crossed his arms. "It would seem that he owns ships that were very likely paid for with your father's fortune."

"Vincent was the only other person who knew my brother needed money," Angelique whispered. "He knew how desperate he was. And he was with him that night. He sent him that note." It was becoming too hard to ignore the pieces that were fitting together in a horrible puzzle. "Was it him? Who had that girl killed?" Another thought struck her, worse than the last. "Who had my father killed?"

Alex stared down at the evidence before him, his face furrowed in concentration.

"But why?" she asked into the silence. "Why would he—they—do this? What did our family ever do to make them hate us so much?"

Alex finally looked up. "I think it's past time we found out."

Chapter 17

The Burleigh home wasn't grand by any stretch of the imagination, nor could it be considered a cottage. It sat on a pretty little plot of land, surrounded by newer homes that had cropped up in the last decade—mostly the dwellings of wealthy merchants. It was two stories tall, the walls made of brick, the roof slate. Roses climbed up a trellis along the south side, and around the back, a garden could be seen bordering the edge of an outbuilding that might have once been used for horses. In the setting sun, it looked a little like something out of a bucolic country painting.

Angelique had only ever been here once when she was a child, and she vaguely remembered it. Most of the time her father and the late Baron Burleigh had spent together had been in one of her father's clubs or, most often, in their own home. Lady Burleigh had joined him frequently, usually when an outing to the theater or a musicale or a ball was planned, and along with her mother, they went as a happy foursome.

Angelique couldn't even begin to guess what had gone wrong from there to here.

At their knock, a housekeeper opened the door, suspiciously squinting at the visitors.

"Is Lord Burleigh in?" Alderidge sounded curt and businesslike. He had insisted on coming.

The housekeeper eyed both Alex and Alderidge, her eyes lingering on their blatantly expensive attire. "He is not," she said a little uncertainly. "You just missed him. Left not even an hour ago."

"Where did he go?"

"Don't know, sir. Said he wouldn't be back for a few days. Would you care to leave a message?"

Angelique felt a strange sensation of dread creep up her spine. It was if the air temperature had suddenly dropped, so palpable was her sense of foreboding. She heard Alex curse softly under his breath.

"I am the Duke of Alderidge, not a sir," Alderidge said coldly. "And no, I would not care to leave a message. This is a matter of grave importance."

The housekeeper's face went pale. "Of course, Your Grace. Whatever you need."

"Is Lady Burleigh in?"

"She's at the church," the housekeeper stammered. "There was a tea. For the orphans."

"Fetch her. Immediately." The duke sounded like a proper ass, but it had the desired effect. The housekeeper's eyes went round.

"Is she in some sort of danger?" she gasped.

"Quite possibly," he replied tonelessly.

"Oh, dear heavens. Yes, of course, Your Grace. Right away." She stepped past them, hurrying in the direction of the spire just visible beyond the neighboring rooftops.

"This is why one brings a duke along," Alex muttered, jamming his foot in the door before it swung closed.

Alderidge made a derisive sound. "I think I terrified her."

"You do have a way with words." Alex waited until the housekeeper was out of sight before pushing through the door. Angelique and Alderidge followed him in, stopping just inside the small but well-appointed hall. Angelique strained for any other sounds that would indicate the house wasn't empty, but there was only silence.

"The study?" Alex suggested.

"The most likely place for a calendar that may indicate where Burleigh went," the duke agreed. He jerked his chin in the direction of a wide door, just off the hall, tightly shut.

Angelique stared at Alex. "Shouldn't we wait for Lady Burleigh? We need to hear what she has to say."

"I want to know what she isn't going to say," Alex said, already moving in the direction of the door. "People are just so secretive when it comes to admitting things like extortion." He tried the knob, but it was locked tight.

Alex pulled a tiny leather bag from the inside pocket of his coat and withdrew a series of what looked like hairpins. Very gently, he inserted them into the lock. In less than a minute, he had the door open.

"And this is why one brings a spy along," Alderidge commented succinctly.

Alex made a face and shoved the door wide. The room was dim, the scent of musty paper and books filling the air. Angelique hurried over to the window and yanked open the curtains, letting the late afternoon light flood in.

And stared.

Save for the wall in which the door was located, the entire room was lined with bookshelves. The shelves were filled, not with tomes or reference books or novels, but with what appeared to be journals of some sort. The empty wall had a collection of paintings, various compositions of flowers and fruit, and a large portrait of a ship of some sort in the middle. In the center of the room sat a large, masculine-looking desk, and Alex was already shuffling through the papers that sat on top of it.

"Do you suppose Burleigh fled?" Angelique asked.

"No. If he had become suspicious or paranoid enough to run, I don't think he would have left his mother here. She is just as involved in whatever this is as he. More, possibly." Alex was opening desk drawers and examining their contents. He straightened, scowling. "There's nothing here that indicates where he might have gone. Or any sort of proof that he's done anything we think."

Angelique felt a pang of frustrated despair. "He'll never admit anything."

"Of course he won't. No one just admits anything," Alex muttered.

"That's what Lavoie's dungeon is for," the duke said, pulling a journal from one of the shelves.

He was trying to make her feel better, she knew. It wasn't working.

"What happened?" Angelique asked, not expecting an answer. "What did my father do?"

"These are the old baron's journals," Alderidge said, turning the pages of the book he held in his hand. "Starting, as far as I can tell, forty years ago. Perhaps there is a clue in one of them." He shoved the book back into its space and went farther down the wall, stopping and selecting another one. He opened it and consulted the date on the inside page. "November 1812." He flipped through the pages, scanning quickly. He made an incredulous face. "The man wrote everything down. From how much the pie he ate for lunch cost to the temperature during the evening."

Alex had moved from the desk to the shelves. "They are all in chronological order. The last one is dated February 1813. The month the old baron died."

Angelique joined them, examining the rows of earlier volumes. She was counting, her fingers drifting along the spines. She stopped suddenly and reversed direction, pulling out a number of volumes and examining the dates before finding what she was looking for. "There are three missing," she said. "April of 1794, September of 1795, and December of 1806."

Alex was watching her. "Do those dates mean anything to you?"

Angelique shook her head in frustration.

"Something odd that might have happened between your father and the baron?" Alex was clearly grasping. "Or travel? Maybe a purchase of some sort?"

"I wasn't even born until January of '95," Angelique grumbled, just as frustrated as he. "And—" She stopped abruptly, a horrid feeling crawling through her.

"Angelique?"

"January 1795. June 1796. And September 1807. Our birthdays. Mine, my brother's, the twins. Do the math, Alex."

Alex stared at her. "The journals nine months before your births. They're missing."

Angelique felt suddenly cold.

Alex pushed away from the bookcase suddenly. "Don't jump to conclusions," he ordered her, stalking back to the desk. "Not yet." He stood in front of it, his hands on his hips, his face carved in concentration.

"Conclusions?" Her voice sounded shaky. No, she wouldn't jump to conclusions because, if she did, she might retch.

"Where would a pirate hide his treasure, Alderidge?" Alex demanded, his eyes on the duke who was still standing by the bookcase. "Where would he hide something that he didn't want anyone to find? But somewhere he could admire it whenever the mood struck him."

Alderidge came around to stand next to Alex and dropped into the wooden desk chair. He leaned back, his gaze settling straight ahead. "Such a fine painting of a ship battling the elements, is it not?" the duke asked. "The artist didn't get the rigging quite right, but a moving portrait, nonetheless. Especially surrounded as it is by a garden full of insipid renditions of flowers."

Alex stalked over to the painting and carefully lifted it away from the wall, setting it down. "And this is why one brings a pirate along," he muttered.

Set into the wall was a hollow, a wooden box inlaid with ebony resting within. Alex reached in and pulled it out, coming to place it on the desk. Without hesitation, he opened it.

On the top rested what Angelique imagined were the three missing journals. Whatever was in them had made them valuable enough to be hidden, but it would take time to read through the pages. Alex passed them to her, but she set them aside for now.

Beneath that was a thin stack of ornate documents—official-looking deeds to ships that listed one Vincent Cullen as sole owner. A thick ledger was just beneath, and a quick glance showed that it was a record of the cargoes and crews, along with tallies of the expenses and profits for each ship and each voyage. Alderidge leaned forward and took those from Alex, examining them closely.

Beneath that, a smaller book lay, this one more like a woman's journal. It was bound with scarlet leather, a ribbon of the same color wrapped around the pages. Alex took that out and laid it on the surface of the desk. He glanced at Angelique, and for once in her life, she let someone else take charge, terrified at what they would find. Terrified at what they wouldn't. He opened it.

The pages were divided into columns, a date and sum of money neatly written into each. The first entry was two months after the death of the old baron. The entries on the first few pages were written in what Angelique now instantly recognized as Lady Burleigh's script. On later pages, some of the entries were written in a differing, heavier hand— the same one that had recorded the ledgers of the ships. Burleigh's writing.

"How much would you like to wager that these amounts match the money missing from your family's coffers?" Alex murmured.

Angelique was biting the inside of her lip so hard that she tasted blood.

At the end of the scarlet journal were three folded papers wedged in between the back cover and the pages. Alex took them out and unfolded the first.

The top sheet was a receipt. The name Trevane stood out, along with a date, a time, and a sum of money. The ugly collection of words continued with detailed expectations. At the bottom, someone had scrawled a sloppy *X*. But beside that was Burleigh's signature. Vincent Cullen had hired someone to kill a young maid.

"Who does this?" Angelique whispered, feeling cold all over. It was as King suggested. A trophy, kept in a concealed place.

"Someone who believes he will never be caught. Someone who believes he is smarter than everyone else," Alex murmured.

There was another receipt under that, something that looked

remarkably similar to the one Alex held in his hand. Except it was dated last June, and the sum and the location were different. Alex turned it over. "You don't need to read that."

It didn't matter. She already knew what it would say. A peculiar numbness had settled into her limbs.

"I'm sorry, Angelique."

She shook her head, unable to speak.

"This is proof that your brother is innocent," Alex said.

"Yes." It was the only tiny light. Why would Burleigh do any of this? What had her family ever done to deserve so much hatred?

From somewhere outside, there was the sound of voices and the frantic barking of a dog. She saw Alderidge set the deeds aside and exchange a glance with Alex.

"The lady returning?" Alex asked in a low voice.

"Maybe. I'll find out. Stall her if necessary." She did not miss the casual way in which his hand came to rest on the hilt of his sword.

"Matthews is still out front," Alex said, "in case you need assistance. Try not to kill her until she has a chance to share her insights on this sordid little mess, hmmm? And perhaps direct us to the location of her son?"

The duke slipped from the room, moving with an unsettling speed and stealth for such a large man.

There was a single paper left in the bottom of the polished box, folded square, and Angelique reached for it. This one was visibly older and worn at the edges and written in a different hand altogether. Angelique's eyes skipped down to the bottom of the page, and she froze.

"My father's signature is on this," she breathed.

"What is it?" Alex reached for the paper, but she pulled away from him. She had to read this. No one, not even Alex, could protect her from whatever was in this document.

Beside her father's signature was the old baron's signature. Her eyes raced back up to the top and she started reading.

"What does it say?" Alex asked. "Is it proof of another murder?"

Angelique reached the end, her breaths coming in heaving gulps.

"Worse," she gasped. "So much worse."

⁓

Angelique was the color of snow, her freckles standing out in sharp contrast to her pallor, her eyes haunted and shadowed. Alex snatched the page from her, reading quickly. What the hell could possibly be worse than discovering that the arrest of your brother and the death of your father had been orchestrated by someone you thought was a friend?

Discovering that your father wasn't your father at all.

Alex read it a second time, as though he expected the words to have changed. And then very slowly and very deliberately, he folded the paper back into its neat square and slid it deep into his coat pocket, out of sight. But not out of mind. It could never be out of mind. The contents of that document could never be unseen.

"You didn't know." It was a stupid thing to say, but he didn't know where to start.

Angelique shook her head, her eyes looking a little wild. Alex pulled her to him, and she went without hesitation, her hands curling into the linen of his shirt, her forehead pressed into the hollow at his throat. They stood like that for a long minute.

"My father loved my mother more than life itself. There wasn't anything that he didn't give her," she whispered presently into his neck. "Jewels. Gowns. Horses. Homes. But he couldn't give her the one thing she wanted most in life."

"No. He couldn't have children."

She shook her head. "But he found a way to do it anyway. Found a way to give her everything. Her happiness was worth more than his pride."

Alex stared sightlessly at the bookcases along the wall. Could he do what the Marquess of Hutton had done? If he had had a wife that he loved more than life itself, could he have allowed his best friend to lie with her so that she might have everything that she ever wanted? So that she might find happiness and he might find a family?

Could he give Angelique to another man?

He tightened his arms around her, the force of that thought nearly overwhelming. The idea of her with someone else was unbearable.

"Why would they ever have written it down?" she whispered raggedly into his coat. "What were they *thinking*?"

Alex pressed his cheek into her hair. He couldn't answer for two men long in their graves. The trust that Hutton had placed in his best friend was, in truth, unthinkable. Perhaps it existed as how it read—a pledge from one man to another— one friend to another. That what would happen was something that would never be used against the other. And each man had signed it. "I can only guess this was supposed to have been destroyed at some point in time," Alex said. "Though I can't imagine why it wasn't."

She pulled back to look up at him. "Lady Burleigh knew. She must have discovered the truth. And this is what my father was trying to protect us from. To protect my mother from." Her voice was toneless. "Heaven has no rage like love to hatred turned, nor hell a fury like a woman scorned."

"Is that more Shakespeare?"

"No. William Congreve. Another one of my mother's favorites." The anguish in her eyes was intense. "I'm a bastard, Alex. And so is my brother. And Phillip and Gregory. And my father beggared us so that no one would find out."

"Yes. A bastard." The voice was low and smooth. "That's exactly what you are."

Alex spun away from Angelique to find a woman standing in the study. Her greying hair was pulled back severely, and hard, cold eyes were set into a lined face. She was dressed at the height of fashion, her walking dress clearly costly. As was the engraved muff pistol she held in her hand.

"Lady Burleigh, I presume." Alex kept his eye on the pistol. It was small, but no less deadly for it. He listened, but there was only silence from the house, while outside the same dog was still barking. Where the hell was Alderidge? Or Matthews, for that matter?

Lady Burleigh's eyes flickered over Alex as if he was of no consequence, coming to rest on Angelique. "Lady Angelique," she said. "Well, not a lady at all, really." She laughed, a faintly unbalanced sound. "All these years you've lived with the superior knowledge that you were better than anyone else, and yet you are nothing more than a gutter rat born to a whore of a mother."

"You knew all along?"

"Of course I didn't. I only found out when my husband died. Found all his dirty little secrets hidden away." She waved the pistol at Angelique. "Did you know he wrote about it in his journals? The times he bedded her? And because his friend asked him to. He was more loyal to him and his whore than he was to his own wife!" Her voice had risen, and her face had flushed with color. "What kind of man does that?"

"So why not just let the world know then?"

"Because that wasn't good enough!" she shrieked, spittle flying from her lips. "I might have killed the whore, but I wanted her children and your father to suffer for their lies and treachery. I wanted the Hutton name destroyed!"

"You killed my mother?" Angelique's voice was small.

Lady Burleigh sneered. "All of you, hovering around her bed, believing her to be a saint. Watching her suffer." Her mouth twisted. "What did you really think she died of?"

"You poisoned her."

"Of course I did."

"And then you blackmailed my father."

"I got what my son and I were owed. He used us, your father. Took from us what was never his. So I took back what was owed me. So long as he kept depositing money into that little bank on Threadneedle and asked no questions, his secret was safe. He was so anxious to protect his family. So anxious to protect his darling wife's reputation."

"And then you had him killed," Angelique said dully. "Beggaring him wasn't enough for you?"

"He'd outlived his usefulness. There wasn't any more money to be had."

"And my brother? What did he ever do to you?"

"He *existed*," Lady Burleigh hissed. "I wanted him destroyed before he died. Wanted him to feel the same humiliation and betrayal that your family brought onto me." She waved her pistol. "Don't worry, my sweet, you'll all die. One by one. Vincent will make sure of it."

"Where is Vincent now?" Angelique asked.

Lady Burleigh smiled, an awful expression that pulled her features into a chilling mask. "To take the rest of the cuckoos out of their nest for good."

Alex felt Angelique recoil against him. "The twins. He's gone to Harrow. He's going to kill them."

Lady Burleigh laughed. "You'll never catch him in time."

Alex edged forward, considering his options. A knife was of little use until that pistol was discharged. Right now, Lady Burleigh had the upper hand. "Put the pistol down," he said.

Lady Burleigh ignored him like he hadn't even spoken and gazed at the papers that lay across the desk. "Your father treated Vincent like a charity case, but now he is one of the richest men in London. His power will grow as his wealth does. And I can't have that ruined now, can I? I had hoped for something better for you, little Angelique, but it would seem you've forced my hand. I suppose I'll just shoot you here."

"Lady Burleigh, you have one pistol. There are two of us." Alex spoke loudly, trying to penetrate whatever fog she was in.

The woman finally looked at Alex, but it was too late. "Doesn't matter," she said with a fatalistic grin. "There's really only one of you I want to see die." She aimed her pistol at Angelique.

Alex threw himself against Angelique, hearing the roar of the shot in his ears. They hit the ground hard, his body covering Angelique's, and he lay for a moment, waiting for the inevitable pain that would come. Except it didn't. He hadn't been shot. How was that possible, given the close range? Oh God, had Angelique been hit? He scrambled off her, and she sat up, pale but breathing hard. He frantically looked for blood but there was none.

"It wasn't her pistol that went off, Lavoie," the Duke of Alderidge said from somewhere above him. "It was mine. Or one of Matthews's, in truth."

Alex's eyes flew to where the duke was standing to find him holding a familiar pistol, the faint remnants of smoke drifting around his hand and the stench of gunpowder hanging in the air.

Lady Burleigh lay in a lifeless heap on the floor.

"What took you so long?" Alex demanded, hauling himself upright. "Where is Matthews?"

"He went around back, looking for her. It would seem that Lady Burleigh returned much earlier from her tea than expected."

"And the housekeeper?"

"Sent her to post an urgent message to London on my behalf."

Angelique was on her feet now, terror stamped across her features. "The twins," she said raggedly. "We have to leave."

"Go," the duke said. "I heard what she said about Harrow. I'll take care of things here."

"There is enough here to get Hutton out of prison," Alex told him. "But the journals can't be found. And the body can't be—"

"I met my wife redressing a corpse, Lavoie. You think I don't know how to make this look exactly how we need? I've got this handled. Now *go*."

Alex was heading toward the door, Angelique on his heels. "Would the boys go with Burleigh? If he shows up at the school?" he asked her.

She nodded, her expression stricken. "Yes," she whispered. "They've known him since they were children."

Chapter 18

The ride toward Harrow was an excruciating one, a silent, tense, anxiety-filled interval that seemed to go on forever. Although Matthews pushed the horses hard, he had no choice but to slow the horses or risk both them and the carriage as darkness fell. Burleigh had an hour on them. He wouldn't have been traveling as fast, but that was a lot of time to make up. Alex could only hope that they would catch him on the road. Before he got to the school. Before anything could happen to two boys who deserved none of this.

He'd loaded and primed the two spare pistols Matthews kept and fetched his rapier from the rear of the carriage, leaving the weapons resting on the floor at their feet. It was all he could do though. He hated this, this feeling of helplessness. He'd been here before. Chasing, hoping, praying that he wasn't too late. It sat like a greasy weight in his gut, compressing his chest and making it hard to breathe.

He couldn't even imagine how Angelique was feeling right now.

He glanced at her. She was still sitting beside him, unmoving and silent. Her entire world had come crashing down around her in shards of secrets. Nothing was as it seemed.

"They'll be all right." He wanted to say something. Anything to reassure her.

"They're twelve," she said starkly. "None of this is their fault."

"None of this is your fault."

She looked up at him, though he could barely make out her features in the darkness. "I can't lose the rest of my family."

He stroked her hair back from where it had escaped its pins. "You won't," he said. "I promise." He had no right to make such promises. He was smarter than this. He did not make promises he wasn't sure he could keep. Though he was certain that he was prepared to die trying.

"I'm not sorry she's dead," she said into the silence, and her voice had lost some of its desperation and gained an edge he hadn't heard before. "And I'll kill Burleigh before I let him hurt my brothers."

The carriage suddenly jolted, and he heard Matthews swear loudly, shouting at his horses to slow. Alex lunged across the squabs to the window and peered out, but he could see nothing. The carriage came to a shuddering halt, and now he could hear the steady drum of more hooves and the snort of a horse fighting its bit.

"Stay in the carriage," he told Angelique.

She nodded.

"I mean it." He handed her a pistol. "You know how to use this?"

"Yes."

"Good." He picked up the second for himself, along with his rapier, and shoved the door open. The temperature had dropped, and the air was heavy with the promise of rain.

"What the hell is going on?" he demanded, his boots hitting the dusty road.

"Highwaymen," Matthews answered in a clipped tone. "At least eight of 'em. An' they got some other toff's carriage off the road just ahead." He was reaching for his own pistols.

Alex swore loudly. They did not have time for this. On the road ahead, a lantern was hanging at a strange angle from the side of a carriage that was tilted in the ditch. In the pool of light, Alex could see at least one man with a scarf wrapped over his face busy at the front of the equipage, unharnessing the horses with a speed that suggested he'd done it a thousand times.

The man Alex presumed to be the other carriage driver was lying in a heap on the side of the road. Alex wondered if he was dead until he heard him groan faintly. Alive then, but of no help. The occupants of the carriage must still be inside, he guessed.

Six men were approaching them warily, their horses drawn up tight and their pistols leveled in their direction. No doubt they were mindful of the weapons that were aimed in return and were approaching with due caution.

Alex evaluated the odds, aware of the clock ticking. Fighting was not a good option. They were outnumbered, and there was a good chance that he or Matthews would end up shot. Six highwaymen on fast horses weren't bound to miss six times.

Running was out of the question. Matthews could send the carriage crashing through the road, though the tired carriage horses would never outrun them. Escaping on foot was equally as impossible—they'd be cut down before they'd gone ten steps.

"What do you want?" Alex demanded when the men were less than a dozen feet from them.

"Just collecting taxes," one of the highwaymen said.

"You have us at a disadvantage," Alex said. "And a gun fight right now is in no one's best interests. How much will it take for you to ride away?"

"A man of business," the highwayman said with some surprise.

"How much?" Alex demanded again.

"How much do you have? I've got nine mouths to feed at home. And this chap here has six." He jerked his head in the direction of the man on his left. "We're all family men, you understand."

"A number then—"

"Harold?" It was Matthews who spoke incredulously from his perch. "Is that you?"

The highwayman jerked in surprise and then squinted at Alex's driver. "Who's asking?"

"Who's it sound like?" Matthews demanded.

"Mother Mary and all the saints, it's Matthews," the man exclaimed. He lowered his pistol and uncocked it, shoving it in his waist. He yanked his scarf down from his face. "This man saved my life in a stinking hole outside of Badajoz." He waved his hand, and the rest of his men's pistols lowered.

"It was more of a ditch," Matthews said.

"I didn't recognize you all the way up there on a fancy cart. I thought you sat on the beasts, not behind them."

"Yes, well, it seems they've managed to teach an old dog a few new tricks."

"I'm impressed."

"How is Marjorie? And the kids?" Matthews asked.

"Doing well. Growing like weeds, the lot of them. Just had a new baby. A son."

"Congratulations."

"Thank you." The man named Harold was beaming with obvious pride.

"I thought you were still in London."

The highwayman made a face. "Nah. Too cramped. Too much competition for the scraps, you know? You can make in a single night out here what you can make in a month in the city, and you can be home in time to tuck your kids into bed. And you don't have to kill anyone too often. Out here, these fancy carriages pass with rich people in them all the time, loaded to the roof with all sorts of baubles."

"Like that one?" Matthews asked.

"Yes. Driver tried to outrun us, but all he ended up doing was busting an axle and knocking himself out when he fell. Too bad about the axle. Carriage would have been worth something if we could have taken it, though Charlie there is fetching the horses. Had to settle for them, a nice pair of boots, and a turquoise cravat pin, but that's about it. The toff was traveling light. Meek little bugger, that one."

Alex had been listening to this exchange first with a sense of relief and then with a growing sense of impatience. But at the highwayman's last description, he froze.

"What does he look like?" he demanded.

"Who? The toff?"

"Yes."

Harold was looking at him askance. "Dunno. Thin, blondish hair, not real tall."

"He still in there?" Angelique's question came from behind him.

Alex had no idea how long she'd been standing there. But long enough. "Angelique—"

"Is he still in there?" she asked the highwayman again, as if she hadn't even heard him.

"Yes," Harold answered slowly, looking between

Angelique and Alex and Matthews. "Hard to run far with no boots."

"Did he give you a name?" Angelique was already walking forward. "The occupant of the carriage?"

"Never asked for one." Harold shot a questioning look at Matthews. "Why?"

Angelique didn't answer, only slipped between the horses, heading toward the broken and tilted carriage. She still held the pistol in her hand, and Alex wasn't sure what she intended. He bolted forward, hearing Matthews speaking in low tones.

He got in front of her, forcing her to stop.

"It's Burleigh in that carriage," she said. "Run off the road by highwaymen."

"Yes." Alex would have laughed at the unbelievable irony of it all had Angelique's expression not been so chilling. "What are you going to do?"

"I don't know."

"Are you going to kill him?"

"No. Yes. I don't know." It sounded unsteady.

"Will you let me handle this?"

She stared at him, shadows of emotion playing across her face. "Yes," she said finally.

"Good."

The highwayman who had been unharnessing the horses had left the animals and moved into the road when he'd seen Angelique coming. He was watching the pair of them warily.

"I'd like a word with the gentleman in the carriage," Alex said pleasantly. "If you might be so kind."

The highwayman glanced past them back at Harold, and he seemed to get some sort of direction, because he turned and picked his way down the slope of the ditch, wrenching open the carriage door. There was a flurry of muffled voices, and then Burleigh was dragged out by the collar of his coat and, stumbling in his stocking feet, was shoved against the side of the carriage.

Alex made his way down the bank and into the pool of lantern light.

Burleigh caught sight of Alex and blanched before his expression dissolved into one of relief. "Mr. Lavoie!" he said. "I'm so happy to see you! You must help me. These men have murdered my driver and accosted me most foully."

Alex stood and stared at him, aware his own driver had joined him. He passed his pistol to Matthews, who took it with a grim expression. "You want me just to shoot him, Mr. Lavoie?" Matthews suggested hopefully.

"Not yet."

Burleigh watched this exchange with wide eyes. "What are you doing?" he sputtered.

Alex hefted his rapier in his hand, testing its weight and balance. "Debating whether I should kill you right here."

"What? Why?" Burleigh's voice was pitched high.

"Because it would make me feel better." Angelique stepped out from behind Alex. "I know everything."

Burleigh's eyes widened before his expression shuttered. "You know nothing."

"You're right," she hissed. "I don't know everything. Were you going to slit their throats, Vincent? Or just shoot them?" she asked, and there was steel in her words. "Or perhaps you were simply going to pay to have it done. How does one go about executing children these days?"

The baron's narrow face had changed, the guilelessness that he had displayed only seconds earlier replaced with a mask of hatred and spite. "I don't know what you're talking about."

"Did your mother send you to do this or was it your idea?"

"You have no right to speak of my mother!" he shouted. "Your existence is a blight on her very life. On this earth. A daughter of a whore has no right to anything." The significance of her words seemed to penetrate then. "What did you do to my mother?"

"I did nothing," she said with complete honesty.

"Where is she?"

"What do you want me to tell you, Vincent?"

"Did you hurt her?"

"She's dead."

"I don't believe you!" Burleigh's eyes were wild, and he lunged toward her but was brought up short by the tip of Alex's rapier. He fell back against the carriage, his hands behind his back to steady himself.

"You sure I can't shoot him?" Matthews asked again.

"What do you want to do, Angelique?" Alex asked gently. "This is your decision."

"Don't kill him," she said quietly. "That makes me no better than him. Or his mother."

"Do you want to take him back to London?"

"Yes. I imagine that they have an opening in the White Tower by now. He can face the justice he deserves there."

"He'll make claims," Alex warned.

"But he no longer has proof." She looked up at him. "Right?"

"No. He no longer has proof. His claims will be nothing more than the ravings of a lunatic. The Duchess and her pirate will make sure of that. Trust me."

She was watching Alex, suddenly looking utterly exhausted and spent. "I trust you."

Angelique turned away, and Alex moved to grab

Burleigh. Too late, he saw Burleigh's hand come out from under the back of his coat. Too late, he saw the small pistol he held in his hands. Too late, he lunged toward the weapon.

His rapier caught Burleigh's arm as the gun went off. A searing pain streaked through Alex's hip and down his leg. Alex stumbled back, the steep bank of the ditch making it hard to keep his balance, and he went down, his ears ringing. He tried to get his feet under him and get a better grip on the hilt of his rapier, but his hand seemed to be slipping and his leg didn't seem to be working quite right.

The baron's face was twisted with rage, and he staggered toward Alex. His mouth was moving as though he was screaming, but Alex couldn't hear over the muffled ringing still in his ears. Time seemed to have slowed, and Alex became vaguely aware of hands under his arms, pulling him farther away from the carriage.

The baron took one more step and then pitched forward. Alex blinked, making out the form of Matthews standing in the wavering lantern light, both his pistols smoking. Time resumed, and along with it, the sounds of the night.

"Should have let me shoot him sooner, Mr. Lavoie," his driver said.

"Alex." There were hands lifting up his shirt now, and he pushed them away. The vegetation beneath his back was cold and scratchy.

"What are you doing? I'm fine." He tried to turn over.

"For God's sake, make yourself useful and hold him down." It was Angelique, and she was ordering someone about in a tone of voice he'd never heard her use. Now there were more hands. There was also a ring of concerned faces floating above him.

"You're not fine," Angelique snapped. "You're bleeding like a stuck pig. Stop moving."

"Never saw no pistol when we stopped him." Harold was fretting from somewhere beyond his view.

"Jesus, but that's a lot of blood," another voice said.

In the next breath, Alex felt a cold blade against the skin at his waist and then there was the sound of tearing fabric. The leg of his trousers was suddenly peeled away, and the night air chilled his exposed skin. "What the hell are you doing?" he grumbled, trying to sit up. Someone shoved him back down.

"You said you have a wife?" Angelique was asking. Who? Harold?

"Yes," the highwayman answered.

"Close by?"

"Not too far."

"How good is she with a needle? Specifically how good is she with a needle and flesh?"

"Did you forget what I do for a living? You don't think she hasn't had to patch up a few of our hides from time to time? And for the record, that's goin' to need more than a needle."

"I'm fine," Alex tried again, except no one seemed to be paying any attention to him.

"We'll take him there. That shot must have nicked a vessel. He's losing too much blood."

Now his leg was being lifted and squeezed and something coiled around his limb with enough force to send bolts of pain through him. Bloody hell, but the pressure was insufferable.

"Let's get him into the carriage," Angelique ordered.

"Right away, my lady." Alex was pretty sure that was Matthews.

He shook his head. No, he didn't want to go to Harold's. He needed to get back to London. But everything seemed to be slipping from his control, and he was suddenly too tired to figure out what to do about it.

"Can you make that body disappear?" Angelique was asking someone else now. "Don't want you blamed for something that wasn't your fault and don't want anyone to come looking for something they don't need to find. Ever."

"'Course," said Harold. "All sorts of good hidey-holes around here."

"Do it. And make sure the hole you find is deep," she instructed.

"Understood. What about the carriage?"

"The carriage as it is just looks like it broke down. Is the driver still insensible?"

"Yes."

"Good. Take him to the nearest inn and get him a room. Tell the innkeeper the truth—that he took a tumble when his carriage axle broke and that he simply needs rest. Put the horses and harness in the stables. I'll replace the value of what you would have gotten for them plus the cost of his accommodation."

"And what happens when he wakes up?" the highwayman asked.

"Best case, his memory is blurry. Worst case, he remembers you and your men. Though if there's a message left from the baron that he's traveled on by coach, and his horses are accounted for and his carriage just needs to be fetched for repairs, you can't possibly be called anything more than good Samaritans."

Harold was issuing rapid orders to his men now. From somewhere on the horizon, a rumble of thunder sounded, and a few fat drops of rain fell.

"Thank God," Angelique muttered under her breath. "I was wondering how I was going to explain the blood."

Strong hands were lifting Alex up now and carrying him to his carriage. This was even more intolerable than the throbbing that gripped his leg. He didn't need to be carted about like a swooning debutante. "Put me down," he managed to demand.

"Put him in," Angelique countered, ignoring him. "And hurry."

He was manhandled into the interior of his carriage, coming down to rest on what felt suspiciously like burlap. The carriage door snapped shut, and the interior was plunged into darkness. The equipage jolted into motion almost instantly.

"Alex." Angelique was beside him, smoothing the hair back from his forehead.

"Let me sit up," he mumbled.

"Please don't. The damn bullet cut a trough down the length of your thigh. You're going to need a hell of a lot of stitches. Your upholstery will never recover if you move."

"Mmmm. Have I ever told you how beautiful you are when you curse?" He was fighting a strange dizziness, and his leg was burning like a thousand stinging wasps had descended upon it.

He heard her make a muffled noise. "Yes."

"Did you order a highwayman to hide a body a moment ago?" he asked.

"Of course I did." It was unapologetic. "What kind of idiot leaves a body in the middle of the road?"

"Oh God." He was gasping, and he thought it might be with laughter.

"Alex." Her voice was worried. "Stop. Stop moving. Stop talking. Stop *thinking*. You're going to be all right. I've got you."

"I'm supposed to say that," he said.

"What?"

"I've got you. I'm supposed to say that. I'm supposed to save you."

She was quiet for a long time, and he was beginning to doubt that he had even said the words, as light-headed as he felt. Darkness was starting to crowd in on the edges of his mind. God, he was tired.

"You did," she said suddenly. "You did save me. In every way that counts."

He felt the brush of her hair, of her breath, and her lips grazed his in the darkness. "I love you, Alex," she whispered against his skin.

Something exploded in his chest, filling every space and corner with a warmth that was almost suffocating. This, this was what happiness and joy felt like, washing through his mind and his body like a summer storm. He wanted to throw himself into this feeling, wanted to drown in it. He would remember this moment, this feeling forever, for as long as he lived. Because he loved her too.

And then he remembered no more.

Chapter 19

Alex had been sent to hell.

His leg had been cauterized and stitched from his hip to his knee, and he'd battled a fever for almost ten days before both it and the puffy redness in his thigh had receded. Angelique had stayed until his fever had broken, or at least that was what the battle-ax named Marjorie had told him. But then Angelique had left for London, leaving him weak as a kitten and at the mercy of a highwayman, his wife, and their nine children.

He had been given his own pallet in the two-bedroom cottage that was his prison, and since he'd regained his senses, he'd been bombarded with little sticky fingers, offering bowls of gruel, bits of bread, and favorite toys that were no more than sticks and pieces of ragged fabric tied together. Marjorie had regularly poked and prodded at her handiwork along his leg, grumbling and threatening to hogtie him if he didn't stop moving so much. He endured it all, knowing he owed her a great debt. He was fortunate that he would leave this cottage outside of Harrow in possession of a long scar and his life.

But a week after he'd regained his senses, Alex had been ready to climb the walls. After a fortnight, he'd considered throwing himself down the nearest well.

Matthews had visited once after that first week, but Alex's pleas to whisk him back to London had fallen on deaf ears. His driver was properly terrified of Marjorie, and Alex wasn't sure if he'd ever be able to forgive him. Matthews had, however, brought him a copy of the *Times*, the story of the heroic actions of one Gerald Archer, Marquess of Hutton, splashed across the front page. In covert cooperation with Bow Street, Alex read, the young marquess had risked his own safety in a ruse meant to catch an innocent girl's killer. Vincent Cullen, Baron Burleigh, was now wanted for murder. Unfortunately, it seemed that both the baron and his mother had fled the country. Not a trace of them could be found anywhere.

That entire story had Ivory Moore written all over it, though it was clear that the Duke of Alderidge had become as skilled at managing scandal as his wife. There was not a whisper of the late Marquess of Hutton. No mention of extortion, no mention of a fortune lost, no mention of anything that linked the Cullen and Archer families save the efforts of the marquess to bring a killer to justice.

And there was no mention of Angelique. And Alex's inability to speak with her, to touch her, to be near her, was killing him more surely than a bullet wound might have.

I love you.

She had said that to him in the carriage. When she had probably believed him to be dying. People said strange things when faced with the possibility of death, and Alex wasn't at all sure that this wasn't one of them. Because now that she knew he was recovered, there had been no word from her, as if she was deliberately putting space and distance between them. There had been messages from Jenkins about his club along with a handful of forwarded documents requiring his signature. There had been a loving, if scathing, message from his sister, accusing him of bringing a knife to a gunfight and promising that she'd never forgive him if he did it again. But there had been nothing but silence from Angelique.

He'd attempted to write to her, but each attempt had ended in agonizing failure. How did a soldier turned gaming hell owner ask the daughter of a marquess to stay with him forever?

She didn't need him anymore, he knew. Her brother was no longer a criminal, but a hero, and the ton would be falling all over themselves to reassure him that they never once believed that he could have done what he'd been accused of. Knowing the Duchess, it was even possible that some of the Hutton fortune might be quietly recovered. Angelique could return to whatever life she wished.

And so he'd signed Jenkins's documents, replied to his sister, left Matthews with a handful of instructions, and watched him disappear for another week, aching for something he wasn't sure was attainable. Aching for something he hadn't ever believed he'd wanted until it had slipped away from him.

⌒

Angelique was sitting at her desk, a stack of ledgers in front of her, frowning in concentration. This was trickier than her usual cases in that she wasn't searching for anomalies and inefficiencies, but rather, she was searching for a way to make these numbers appear to be something that they were not.

Smugglers were a complicated lot, she muttered under her breath, though she couldn't deny that she enjoyed the challenge.

There was a knock on the door, and Jenkins stuck his head in. "Did you want the vingt-et-un tables prepared now, my lady?"

Angelique glanced over at the clock on the mantel, startled by how late the hour was. She should be getting ready. The ledgers would have to wait until tomorrow.

"Yes." Beyond the door, she could hear the sounds of music competing with a sizable crowd. Attendance had been up as of late, and it pleased Angelique to no end. "Could you please send in Esther to help me dress?" she asked.

"Right away, my lady." Jenkins nodded and closed the door.

She glanced in the direction of the bedroom and the turquoise silk she could see laid out over the end of the bed. Angelique sighed, her thoughts drifting as they always did to the man whose presence she missed more with every breath she took. At least another week, Matthews had said when he'd last returned from Harrow. Marjorie wasn't going to let Alex undo everything she had done just because he was in a hurry to get back to a club in London. It had been hard leaving him, but Angelique knew he was in good hands. She could do more for Alex here than sitting next to him in a cramped cottage. And if she wanted to be brutally honest with herself, she had retreated if only to stay reality for a small window of time.

She had told Alex she'd loved him because that was the truth. Ironic, really, because it was probably the only truth she had never uttered to him amid the raw candor that had been characteristic of so many of their conversations. She had no idea if he'd even heard her from that carriage floor, half-insensible from blood loss. Which was probably just as well. Alex had never promised her his love.

He had never promised her more than he could give.

She stood, tidying up the stacks of paper and putting her inkpot and quills safely aside. She heard the door open and close.

"Thanks for coming, Esther," she said, without looking up.

"Esther isn't coming."

Angelique whirled, a startled gasp escaping her.

Alex was leaning against the door, looking like sin. He was dressed impeccably in black evening clothes, his complexion rich against the snow-white of his shirt, a faint shadow of stubble over his jaw. His eyes were the same color as the amber liquid he was swirling in the crystal glass he held in his hand. He looked dangerous and divine, and in a heartbeat, an unbearable and familiar longing rose.

Her pulse stumbled, her breathing accelerated, and desire pooled low in her belly. It had been like this from the beginning. No matter how much time and space that might be put between them, it would be like this until the day she died.

"Alex." She stood awkwardly beside the desk. "I didn't know you were here." Her thoughts had scattered.

"Mmmm. I instructed Matthews to bring me some civilized clothes when he came to fetch me so that I might come through the front. See for myself how my club had fared in my absence." He made no move toward her.

"Ah." She bit her lip, waiting for him to continue. When he didn't, she asked, "How are you feeling?" She winced, hating the utter inadequacy of the question.

"No longer dying, thank you." He took a slow sip of

his whiskey, considering the bottom of his glass. "Did you know," he said looking up from his drink, "that I witnessed a young man serving liquor in my club on my way in?"

"Ah."

"Since when does Lavoie's have men serving drinks?"

"Since over a third of your clientele are women."

He blinked at her.

"Your female customers are three times more likely to purchase liquor if they have a very handsome, very...attentive young man serving them. The experience is positively decadent. Or so I've heard."

"Three times?"

"Yes. I kept track over the course of five evenings. You don't think I hired two male servers on a permanent basis without having the numbers to back it up?"

"I see." She couldn't read his expression. "I was also informed that my club now serves *rum*." Now his lip curled slightly.

"It does."

"Did Alderidge get into my cellars? Because that seems like something a pirate would suggest."

"No, that was my suggestion. It's mixed with a variety of fruit juices and a splash of absinthe, given an exotic name, and sold for twice that of a glass of French brandy."

"But rum is cheap."

"Nothing gets by you, does it?" she said wryly.

"And it *sells*?"

"People like exotic, even if it's only an illusion. I'm fairly certain it was you who taught me that."

"Mmmm." Now his expression changed, and he pushed himself away from the door and came toward her. "You've been busy."

Angelique forced herself to keep her ground. "You're

welcome to reverse any changes I've made now that you're back." She was pleased with how evenly that had come out. Because right now, her heart was hammering so hard against her ribs that she thought her chest might simply explode.

"Mmmm." He stopped in front of the desk. "Tell me, how is your brother?"

"Sober."

"Good." He was quiet for a moment. "Matthews told me he has decided to do a bit of traveling? See the sights of the Continent? Expand his horizons, as it were?"

She nodded. "Miss Moore thought it best if he was removed from the entire situation. Just until things . . . settled."

"You mean until a new scandal arises that makes the Marquess of Hutton wholly forgettable."

"Something like that. My brother has, however, left the overseeing of the Hutton fortune in the hands of one Duke of Alderidge, who has generously offered his significant experience and guidance in the area of shipping, specifically import and export with India."

"The Hutton fortune?"

"Did you know that purveyors of fine art are also purveyors of fine forgeries?"

She saw comprehension dawn across Alex's face, and his eyes hardened. "King." His fingers were white around his glass.

"Yes. A fascinating collection of books he keeps," she said. "Took me almost a whole day to get through them, which is saying something. He's very particular. And precise. But then, so was his forger. You can't imagine how relieved the Hutton solicitors were to recover the deeds of ownership and income, as well as the supporting documentation from the bank. They, like me, truly had no idea my father had invested so heavily in shipping. Almost everything was recovered and accounted for. Life can now resume as normal."

Alex's face was like granite. "As normal. Of course. And what, exactly, does that mean to you?"

For the briefest of moments, Angelique felt like she was nineteen again and was standing on the edge of a dance floor, trying to work up the courage to step out.

She picked up a card from a stack on the desk and handed it to Alex.

"What's this?" He held it up to the light.

In the center of the card was the silhouette of an angel, the form unmistakably female, wings spread gracefully up and out. Underneath, in bold letters, was written *Book Keeping and Accounting Services*, and under that, the address of the club.

"It's my card. I've always wanted one," Angelique said carefully.

Alex's eyes flickered to her and then to the pile of ledgers on the corner of the desk. "Those aren't mine."

"No."

"Whose are they?"

"A client's."

He gazed at her, his thoughts infuriatingly hidden. "You've gone into business?"

"Yes. I used your address. I hope that is all right. I—well, Gerald, sold the Bedford Square house. It seemed silly to have it if no one was there."

He put his glass on the edge of the desk. "What are you still doing here, Angelique?"

"The club wasn't going to run itself," she said, raising her chin.

"The club could have been closed. Or Jenkins could have managed well enough to insure the doors opened and the place didn't burn down." He came around the desk to stand in front of her. "Why are you here?"

Angelique felt her pulse roaring in her ears, felt the breath slowly being squeezed from her lungs. She had come this far. She would not hide anymore. She needed to step out onto the floor.

"Because this is me." She gazed around the office. "This is what I'm good at. Numbers. Books. Cards."

He smiled at that, a smile that set her insides on fire and made every fiber of her body spark. He lifted a hand and ran his fingers down the side of her face. "Yes."

"And because I think you and I could be very good together."

She heard his breath catch, saw something shift in his eyes. "Yes." His fingers trailed lower along the column of her neck and down to the edge of her bodice.

"Because I love you."

His hand stilled, his eyes closing briefly before they opened again. "I'm not dying."

"What?" She stared at him.

"I thought maybe you said that because you thought I was dying." His voice was hoarse.

She laughed, a slightly desperate, ragged sound, because she was terrified of the emotion that was playing over his face now. Terrified to hope. "Bloody hell, Alex, if I thought you were dying, I would have asked you where you kept the key to your desk drawer."

He made a muffled noise, and Angelique suddenly felt herself yanked up against him, his mouth on hers, his arms around her. "I love you, Angel. So much. Please stay. Stay with me." They were mumbled words, rough and urgent against her lips.

She pulled back from him, an overwhelming surfeit of

joy and love making her entire body shake. "There is nowhere else I want to be," she whispered. "There is nowhere else I belong."

He let out a shuddering breath and rested his forehead against hers. "Nowhere else you will ever belong." After a moment, he straightened and reached into the inside pocket of his coat. Very carefully, he withdrew a worn, folded square of paper that had once lain in the bottom of a wood and ebony box. A corner of it was now stained dark with dried blood. He held it out to her.

"Perhaps I should have destroyed this earlier," he said. "But I wanted to put that power in your hands. Where it belongs."

She took it from him, the secret that had cost so much already. Without unfolding it, she simply moved to the hearth and threw it on the glowing coals. The edges smoked and curled before the paper burst into flame. It was oddly anticlimactic, she realized, as she stared down at the tiny wisps of ash crumbling through the coals. While she recognized the need to bury this secret forever, to secure and protect the futures of her brothers, Angelique herself felt strangely removed.

Because she already knew who she was. And it had nothing to do with who her parents had been.

"Nothing in the past can make you any less than a lady," Alex said, as if reading her mind.

She looked up, a fierce happiness flooding through her. "Nothing from the past can make me anything less than whoever it is I wish to be."

She started moving toward him, desire coming hard on the heels of happiness. She saw him shift, saw his own arousal flare in his eyes. She stopped in front of him, aware that she was breathing too fast.

"Tell me who it is that you want to be," he said. He was leaning back on the edge of his desk, his hands braced on the edges.

"I want to be the partner of an assassin and a spy," she said, coming to stand a whisper away from him, his legs on either side of hers. "I want to be his lover and his friend. His forever." Her hands went to the ties of her dress, and she loosened the bodice, letting it fall to her waist. She heard him suck in his breath, saw his fingers tighten on the edges of his desk. She turned her attention next to her stays and her skirts, and they too fell away, leaving her standing only in her chemise.

She leaned forward, brushing her lips over his, savoring the taste of him. Her hands ran down the lapels of his coat, over the buttons of his waistcoat, stopping at the fall of his trousers.

"Angel," he whispered thickly, his own hands reaching for her and sliding up the length of her back, over her shoulders, and along the tops of her breasts. She felt his fingers pull at the ribbon at the neck of her chemise, felt the soft fabric loosen and slip over her shoulders. His hands were resting over her heart, and she raised hers to encircle them.

"Sometimes, when it suits me, I will wish to be a fine lady," she said. She met his beautiful eyes that were shining with love and not a little wickedness. "And sometimes, when it suits me," she whispered with a smile, pulling his hands away and feeling her chemise drift to the floor, "I don't wish to be a lady at all."

Did you miss Kelly Bowen's Lords of Worth series?

To save an innocent girl, Gisele Whitby needs a daring man to help her with her cunning scheme. But when she meets Jamie Montcrief, the rogue in question may foil her plan—and ignite her deepest desires . . .

Please see the next page for an excerpt from the first book,
I've Got My Duke to Keep Me Warm.

Chapter 1

Somewhere south of Nottingham, England, May 1816

Being dead was not without its drawbacks.

The tavern was one of them. More hovel than hostelry, it was plunked capriciously in a tiny hamlet, somewhere near nowhere. Her mere presence in this dismal place proved time was running out and desperation was beginning to eclipse good sense.

Gisele shuffled along the filthy wall of the taproom, wrinkling her nose against the overripe scent of unwashed bodies and spilled ale. She sidestepped neatly, avoiding the leering gaze and groping fingers of more than one man, and slipped into the gathering darkness outside. She took a deep breath, trying to maintain a sense of purpose and hope. The carefully crafted demise of Gisele Whitby four years earlier had granted her the freedom and the safety to reclaim her life.

True, it had also driven her to the fringes of society, but until very recently, forced anonymity had been a benediction. Now it was proving to be an unwanted complication.

"What are you doing out here?" The voice came from beside her, and she sighed, not turning toward her friend.

"This is impossible. We'll not find him here."

Sebastien gazed at the sparrows quarreling along the edge of the thatch in the evening air. "I agree. We need a male without feathers. And they are all inside."

Gisele rolled her eyes. "Have you been inside? There is not a single one in there who would stand a chance at passing for a gentleman."

Sebastien brushed nonexistent dust off his sleeve. "Perhaps we haven't seen everyone who—"

"Please," she grumbled. "Half of those drunkards have a dubious command of the English language. And the other half have no command over any type of language at all." She stalked toward the stables in agitation.

Sebastien hurried across the yard after her.

"The man we need has to be clever and witty and charming and courageous and...convincingly noble." She spit the last word as if it were refuse.

"He does not exactly need to replace—"

"Yes, he does," Gisele argued, suddenly feeling very tired. "He has to be all of those things. Or at least some of those and willing to learn the rest. Or very, very desperate and willing to learn them all." She stopped, defeated, eyeing a ragged heap of humanity leaning against the front of the stable, asleep or stewed or both. "And we will not find all that here, in the middle of God knows where."

"We'll find someone," Sebastien repeated stubbornly, his dark brows knit.

"And if we can't?"

"Then we'll find a way. We'll find another way. There will—"

Whatever the slight man was going to say next was drowned out by the sound of an approaching carriage. Gisele sighed loudly and stepped back into the shadows of the stable wall out of habit.

The vehicle stopped, and the driver and groom jumped down. The driver immediately went to unharness the sweat-soaked horses, though the groom disappeared inside the tavern without a backward glance, earning a muttered curse from the driver. Inside the carriage Gisele could hear the muffled tones of an argument. Presently the carriage door snapped open and a rotund man disembarked, stepping just to the side and lighting a cheroot. A well-dressed woman leaned out of the carriage door behind him to continue their squabble, shouting to be heard over the driver, who was leading the first horse away and calling for a fresh team.

Gisele watched the scene with growing impatience. She was preoccupied with her own problems and annoyed to be trapped out by the stables where there was no chance of finding any solution. Still, the carriage was expensive and it bore a coat of arms, and she would take no chances of being recognized, no matter how remote this tavern might be.

She was still plotting when the driver returned to fetch the second horse from its traces. As he reached for the bridle, the door to the tavern exploded outward with enough force to knock the wood clear off its hinges and send a report echoing through the yard like a gunshot. The gelding spooked and bolted forward, and the carriage lurched precariously behind it. The man standing with his cheroot was knocked sideways, his expensive hat landing somewhere in the dust. From the open carriage doorway, the woman began screaming hysterically, spurring the frightened horse on.

"Good heavens," gasped Sebastien, observing the unfolding drama with interest.

Gisele stood frozen as the unidentifiable lump she had previously spied leaning against the stable morphed into the form of a man. In three quick strides, the man launched himself onto the back of the panicked horse. With long arms he reached down the length of the horse's neck and easily grabbed the side of the bridle, pulling the animal's head to its shoulder with firm authority. The horse and carriage immediately slowed and then stopped, though the lady's screaming continued.

Sliding down from the blowing horse, the man gave the animal a careful once-over that Gisele didn't miss and handed the reins back to the horrified driver. The ragged-looking man then approached the woman still shrieking in the carriage and stood before her, waiting patiently for her to stop the wailing that was beginning to sound forced. He reached up a hand to help her down, and she abandoned her howling only to recoil in disgust.

"My lady?" he queried politely. "Are you all right? May I offer you my assistance?"

"Don't touch me!" the woman screeched, her chins jiggling. "You filthy creature. You could have killed me!"

By this time a number of people had caught up to the carriage, and Gisele pressed a little farther back into the shadows of the stable wall. The woman's husband, out of breath and red-faced, elbowed past the stranger and demanded a step be brought for his wife. Her rescuer simply inclined his head and retreated in the direction of the tavern, shoving his hands into the pockets of what passed for a coat. He ducked around the broken door and disappeared inside. He didn't look back.

Gisele held up a hand in warning.

"He's perfect," Sebastien breathed anyway, ignoring her.

Gisele crossed her arms across her chest, unwilling to let the seed of hope blossom.

"You saw what just happened. He just saved that wretched woman's life. You said courageous, clever, and charming. That was the epitome of all three." Sebastien was looking at her earnestly.

"Or alternatively, stupid, lucky, and drunk."

It was Sebastien's turn to roll his eyes.

"Fine." Gisele gave in, allowing hope a tiny foothold. "Do what you do best. Find out who he is and why he is here."

"What are you going to do?"

Gisele grimaced. "I will return to yonder establishment and observe your newfound hero in his cups. If he doesn't rape and pillage anything in the next half hour and can demonstrate at least a tenth the intellect of an average hunting hound, we'll go from there."

Sebastien grinned in triumph. "I've got a good feeling about him, Gisele. I promise you won't regret this." Then he turned and disappeared.

~

I am already regretting it, Gisele thought dourly twenty minutes later, though the lack of a front door had improved the quality of the air in the taproom, if not the quality of its ale. She managed a convincing swallow and replaced her drink on the uneven tabletop with distaste. Fingering the hilt of the knife she was displaying as a warning on the surface before her, she idly considered what manner of filth kept the bottom of her shoes stuck so firmly to the tavern floor. Sebastien had yet to reappear, and Gisele wondered how much longer she would be forced to wait. Her eyes drifted back to the stranger she'd been studying, who was still hunched over his drink at the far end of the room.

She thought he might be quite handsome if one could see past the disheveled beard and the appalling tatters currently passing for clothes. Broad shoulders, thick arms—he was very likely a former soldier, one of many who had found themselves out of work and out of sorts with the surrender of the little French madman. She narrowed her eyes. Strength in a man was always an asset, so she supposed she must count that in his favor. And from the way his knees rammed the underside of the table, he must be decently tall. Also an advantage, as nothing caught a woman's attention in a crowded room like a tall, confident man. Beyond that, however, his brown hair, brown eyes, and penchant for ale were the only qualities easily determined from a distance.

It was the latter—the utter state of intoxication he was rapidly working toward—that most piqued Gisele's interest. It suggested hopelessness. Defeat. Dejection. Desperation. All of which might make him the ideal candidate.

Or they might just mark him as a common drunkard.

And she'd had plenty of unpleasant experience with those. Unfortunately, this man was by far the best prospect she and Sebastien had seen in weeks, and she was well aware of the time slipping past. She watched as the stranger dribbled ale down his beard as he tried to drain his pot. Her lip curled in disgust.

"What do you think?" Her thoughts were interrupted by Sebastien as he slid next to her on the bench. He jerked his chin in the direction of their quarry.

She scowled. "The man's been sitting in a corner drinking himself into a stupor since I sat down. He hasn't passed out yet, so I guess that's promising." She caught sight of her friend's glare and sighed. "Please, tell me what I *should* think. What did you find out?"

Sebastien sniffed and adjusted his collar. "James Montcrief. Son of a duke—"

"What?" Gisele gasped in alarm. She involuntarily shrank against the table.

Sebastien gave her a long-suffering look. "Do you think we'd still be here if I thought you might be recognized?"

Gisele bit her lip guiltily and straightened. "No. Sorry."

"May I go on?"

"Please."

"The duchy is…Reddyck, I believe? I've never heard of it, but I am assured it is real, and the bulk of its lands lie somewhere near the northern border. Small, but supports itself adequately."

Gisele let her eyes slide down the disheveled stranger. "Tell me he isn't the heir apparent."

"Even better. A bastard, so no chance of ever turning into anything quite as odious."

Giselle frowned. "Acknowledged?"

"The late duke was happy to claim him. Unfortunately, the current duke—a brother of some fashion—is not nearly so benevolent. According to current family history, James Montcrief doesn't exist."

Giselle studied the man uncertainly, considering the benefits and risks of that information. Someone with knowledge of the peerage and its habits and idiosyncrasies could be helpful. *If* he could remain sober enough to keep his wits.

"He hasn't groped the serving wenches yet," Sebastien offered.

"Says who?"

"The serving wenches."

"*Hmphh*." That might bode well. Or not. "Married? Children?"

"No and no. At least no children anyone is aware of."

"Good." They would have been a difficult complication. "Money?"

"Spent the morning cleaning stalls and repairing the roof to pay for his drink last night. Did the same the night before and the night before and—"

"In other words, none." Now that was promising. "Army?"

"Cavalry." Sebastien turned his attention from his sleeve to his carefully groomed moustache. "And supposedly quite the hero."

She snorted. "Aren't they all. Who says he's a hero?"

"The stableboys."

"They probably had him confused with his horse."

"His horse was shot out from under him at Waterloo."

"Exactly."

Her friend *tsk*ed. "The man survived, Gisele. He must know how to fight."

"Or run."

Sebastien's eyes rolled in exasperation. "That's what I love most about you. Your brimming optimism."

Giselle shrugged. "Heroes shouldn't drink themselves into oblivion. Multiple nights in a row."

Sebastien leaned close to her ear. "Listen carefully. In the past twenty minutes, I have applied my abundant charm to the chambermaids and the barmaids and the milkmaids and one very enchanting footman, and thanks to my masterful skill and caution, we now possess a wealth of information about our new friend here. The very least *you* can do is spend half that amount of time discovering if this man is really as decent as I believe him to be." He paused for breath. "He's the best option we've got."

She pressed her lips together as she pushed herself up off the bench. "Very well. As we discussed?"

"Do you have a better idea?"

"No," she replied unhappily.

"Then let's not waste any more time. We need help from some quarter, and that man is the best chance we have of getting it." Without missing a beat, he reached over and deftly plucked at the laces to Gisele's simple bodice. The top fell open to reveal an alarming amount of cleavage. "Nice. Almost makes me wish I were so inclined."

"Do shut up." Gisele tried to pull the laces back together but had her hand swatted away. "I look like a whore," she protested.

Sebastien tipped his head, then leaned forward again and pulled the tattered ribbon from her braid. Her hair slithered out of its confines to tumble over her shoulders. "But a very pretty one. It's perfect." He stood up, straightening his own jacket. "Trust me. He's going to surprise you."

She heaved one last sigh. "How drunk do you suppose he is?"

"Slurring his *s*'s. But sentence structure is still good. I'll see you in ten minutes."

"Better make it twenty," Gisele said slowly. "It will reduce the chances of you ending up on the wrong end of a cavalryman's fists."

Sebastien's dark eyes slid back to the man in the corner in speculation. "You think?"

Giselle stood to join the shorter man. "You're the one who told me he's a hero. Let's find out."

~

Jamie Montcrief, known in another life as James Edward Anthony Montcrief, cavalry captain in the King's Dragoon

Guards of the British army and bastard son to the ninth Duke of Reddyck, stared deeply into the bottom of his ale pot and wondered fuzzily how it had come to be empty so quickly. He was sure he had just ordered a fresh drink. Perhaps the girl had spilled it on the way over and he hadn't noticed. That happened a lot these days. Not noticing things. Which was fine. In fact, it was better than fine.

"You look thirsty." As if by magic, a full cup of liquid sloshed to the table in front of him.

Startled, he looked up, only to be presented with a view of stunning breasts. They were full and firm, straining against the fabric of a poorly laced bodice, and despite the fact that they were not entirely in focus, his body reacted with reprehensible speed. He reached out, intending to caress the luscious perfection before him, only to snatch his hand back a moment later when sluggish honor demanded retreat. Mortified, he dragged his eyes up from the woman's chest to her face, hoping against hope she might not have noticed.

He should have kept his eyes on her breasts.

For shimmering before him was a fantasy. His fantasy. The one he had carefully created in his imagination to chase away the reality of miserable marches, insufferable nights, unspeakable hunger, and bone-numbing dread. Everything he had hoped to possess in a woman was sliding onto the bench opposite him, a shy smile on her face. And it was a face that could start a war. High cheekbones, a full mouth, eyes almost exotic in their shape. Pale hair that fell in thick sheets carelessly around her head and over her shoulders.

He opened his mouth to say something clever, yet all his words seemed to have drowned themselves in the depths of his drink. He cursed inwardly, wishing for the first time in many months he weren't drunk. She seemed not to notice.

Instead she cheerfully raised her own full pot of ale in a silent toast and proceeded to drain it. At a loss for anything better to do, he followed suit.

"Thank you," he finally managed, though he wasn't sure she heard, as she had somehow procured two more pots of ale and slid another in front of him.

"What shall we toast to now?" she asked him, her brilliant gray-green eyes probing his own.

Frantically Jamie searched his liquor-soaked brain for an intelligent answer. "To beauty," he croaked, cringing at such an amateurish and predictable reply.

She gave him a dazzling smile anyway, and he could feel his own mouth curling up in response. "To beauty then," she said. "And those who are wise enough to realize what it may cost." She drained her second pot.

Jamie allowed his mind to slog wearily through her cryptic words for a moment or two before he gave up trying to understand. Who cared, really? He had a magnificent woman sitting across the table from him, and another pot of ale had already replaced the second one he had drained. This was by far the best thing that had happened to him in a very long time.

"What's your name?" Her voice was gentle.

"James. James Montcrief." Thank the gods. At least he could remember that. Though maybe he should have made an effort at formality? Did one do that in such a setting?

"James." His name was like honey on her tongue, and her own dismissal of formality was encouraging. Something stirred inside him. "I like it." She gave him another blinding smile. "Why are you drinking all alone, James?" she asked.

He stared at her, unable, and more truthfully, unwilling to give her any sort of an answer. Instead he just shrugged.

"Never mind." She tipped her head back, and another pot

of ale disappeared. Idly he wondered how she still remained sober while the room he was sitting in was beginning to spin. She tilted her head, and her beautiful blond hair swung away from her neck, dizzying in its movement. "You have kind eyes."

Her comment caught him off guard. He did not have kind eyes. He had eyes that had seen too much to ever allow any kindness in. "I am not kind." He wasn't sure if he mumbled it or just thought it. Inexplicably, a wave of sadness and loneliness washed over him.

"What brings you here?" she asked, waving a hand in the general direction of the tavern.

Jamie blinked, trying to remember where *here* was, then snorted at the futility of the question.

"Nowhere else to go," he mumbled. The accuracy of his statement echoed in his mind. Nowhere to go, nowhere to be. No one who cared. Least of all him.

"Would you like to go somewhere else, James? With me?" Her words seemed to come from a distance, and with a frantic suddenness, he needed to get out. Out from the tavern walls that were pressing down on him, away from the smells of grease and bodies and smoke and alcohol that were suffocating.

"Yes." He shoved away from the table, swaying on his feet. In an instant she was there, at his side, her arm tucked into his elbow as though he really were a duke escorting her across the ballroom of a royal palace. He could feel the warmth of her body as it pressed against his and the cool silk of her hair as it slid across his bicep. Again he wished desperately he weren't so drunk. His body was dragging him in one direction while his mind flailed helplessly against the haze.

"Come," she whispered, guiding him out into the cool night breeze.

He went willingly with his beautiful vision into the darkness, dragging in huge lungfuls of air in an attempt to clear his head. He pressed a hand against his temple.

"Are you unwell?" She was still right beside him, and he was horrified to realize he was leaning on her as he might a crutch. He straightened abruptly.

"No." He concentrated hard on his next words. "I don't even know your name."

She stared at him a long moment as if debating something within her mind. "Gisele," she finally said.

He was regretting those last pots of ale. Thinking was becoming almost impossible. "And why were *you* drinkin' alone, Gisele?" he asked slowly.

The sparkle dimmed abruptly in her face, and she turned away. "Will you take me away from here, James?" she asked.

"I beg your pardon?" His mind was struggling to keep up with his ears.

She turned back. "Take me somewhere. Anywhere. Just not here."

"I don't understand." Blade-sharp instincts long suppressed fought to make themselves heard through the fog in his brain. Something was all wrong with this situation, though he was damned if he could determine what it might be. "I can't just—"

Jamie was suddenly knocked back, tripping over his feet and falling gracelessly, unable to overcome gravity and the last three pots of ale. Gisele was yanked from his side, and she gave a slight yelp as a man slammed her back up against the tavern wall.

"Where the hell have you been, whore?" the man snarled. "Like a damn bitch in heat, aren't you?"

Jamie struggled to his feet, fighting the dizziness that was making his surroundings swim. He reached for the weapon at his side before realizing he couldn't recall where he'd left it. He turned just in time to see the man pull back his arm to slug Gisele. With a roar of rage, Jamie launched himself at her attacker, hitting him square in the back. The man was barely half his size, and the force of Jamie's weight knocked both men into the mud. A fist caught the side of his head in a series of short, sharp jabs, only increasing the din resonating through his brain. Jamie tried to stagger to his feet again, but the ground shifted underneath him and he fell heavily on his side.

"Don't touch her," he managed, wrestling with the darkness crowding the edge of his vision. Usually he welcomed this part of the night, when reality ceased to exist. But not now. This couldn't happen now. He had to fight it. Fight for her. Fight for something again. He pushed himself up on his hands and knees. He looked up at the figures looming over him. Strangely, Gisele and her attacker were standing side by side as if nothing had happened. The buzzing was getting louder as Gisele crouched down beside him, and he felt her cool hand on his forehead.

"So sorry," he mumbled, his arms collapsing beneath him. "I couldn't do—"

"You did just fine, James," she said. And then he heard no more.

Fall in Love with Forever Romance

WICKED COWBOY CHARM
By Carolyn Brown

The newest novel in Carolyn Brown's *USA Today* bestselling Lucky Penny Ranch series! Josie Dawson is new in town, but it doesn't take long to know that Deke Sullivan has charmed just about every woman in Dry Creek, Texas. Just as Deke is wondering how to convince Josie he only has eyes for her, they get stranded in a tiny cabin during a blizzard. If Deke can melt her heart before they dig out of the snow, he'll be the luckiest cowboy in Texas...

THE COTTAGE AT FIREFLY LAKE
By Jen Gilroy

In the tradition of Susan Wiggs and RaeAnne Thayne comes the first in a new series by debut author Jen Gilroy. Eighteen years ago, Charlotte Gibbs left Firefly Lake—and Sean Carmichael—behind to become a globetrotting journalist. But now she's back. Will the two have a second chance at first love? Or will the secret Charlie's hiding be their undoing?

Fall in Love with Forever Romance

TOO WILD TO TAME
By Tessa Bailey

Aaron knows that if he wants to work for the country's most powerful senator, he'll have to keep his eye on the prize. That's easier said than done when he meets the senator's daughter, who's wild, gorgeous, and 100 percent trouble. The second book in *New York Times* bestselling author Tessa Bailey's Romancing the Clarksons series!

THE BACHELOR AUCTION
By Rachel Van Dyken

The first book in a brand-new series from #1 *New York Times* bestselling author Rachel Van Dyken! Brock Wellington isn't anyone's dream guy. So now as he waits to be auctioned off in marriage to the highest bidder, he figures it's karmic retribution that he's tempted by a sexy, sassy woman he can't have...

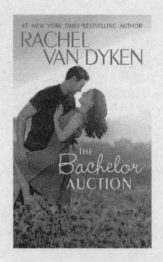